The single word sent [...] *wear to ya, Leon, I didn't know w* [...] *kill 'er. I thought—"*

"You thought what, [...] *d wife? My family? To do what ex* [...] *the hell are you to take part in such a—" This time when he shook her, the tears fled their prison and leapt across her cheeks. "That's what you are—you're Amaskan," he whispered. She winced when his fingers squeezed what little flesh clung to her bones, but she didn't look away. The quiet anger within left him breathless, yet he lifted her off her feet before he flung her to the floor with a snarl. "Who are you? What are you to crawl into my bed, into my heart. For ten years—"*

The knock at the door startled them both. "Your Majesty?"

"Send the captain away," she hissed from where she'd fallen, her robe torn where she'd tripped over it.

"Why should I do anything you ask?"

"Because I'm the only one who knows where your daughter is."

Praise for EPIC Awards 2016 Finalist
AMASKAN'S BLOOD

OTHER TITLES BY RAVEN OAK

The Boahim Trilogy
Amaskan's Blood (Book I)
Amaskan's War (Book II)*

The Xersian Struggle
The Eldest Silence (Book I)*

Class-M Exile
Joy to the Worlds: Mysterious Speculative Fiction for the Holidays
Untethered: A Magic iPhone Anthology
Magic Unveiled: An Anthology

* forthcoming from Grey Sun Press

AMASKAN'S BLOOD

The Boahim Trilogy Book One

Raven Oak

Grey Sun Press
Seattle, WA

AMASKAN'S BLOOD
Book One of the Boahim Trilogy

Raven Oak

This book is a work of fiction. All characters and events in this book are fictitious. All resemblance to persons living or dead is coincidental.

Copyright © 2014 by Raven Oak

First printing: January 2015

Cover art by Jamie Noble
Map by Raven Oak

ISBN: 9780990815709

Library of Congress Control Number: 2014960295

Grey Sun Press
PO Box 99412
Seattle, WA 98139
www.greysunpress.com

Books by Grey Sun Press may be obtained for educational, business, or promotional purposes. For more information, please contact: Grey Sun Press, PO Box 99412, Seattle, WA 98139, info@greysunpress.com

This book is dedicated to my husband.

My biggest cheerleader, supporter, beta-reader extraordinaire,
and most of all, my best friend.

You are *still* everything.

THE
Little Dozen
Kingdoms OF
Boahim

Aruna

SADAI

∞

Harren Sea

Baudwin Bay

NARIBOR

Legend

 United
Council

∞ Order of
the Amoskans

 Capital City

 Major Town

 Tribor Clan

 Holy Temple
of Adlain

PROLOGUE

The Forest of Alesta, in the Year of Boahim 235

She was thirsty.

Thirsty was an understatement. Her tongue felt thick beneath the sour cloth jammed in her mouth, and Iliana swallowed hard. Tree branches thick with leaves whipped her shoulders as they passed. She did her best to make herself small, invisible, if only so the big one would stop looking at her.

His eyes—pale blue moons set in skin so dark Iliana couldn't tell what was skin and what was fabric. All three Amaskans wore solid black from head to foot. No ornamentation or lacings. Just tight, black silk, bound at the waist and wrists.

The same black fabric that bound her wrists together.

The big one glanced over his shoulder as the horses galloped through the forest. They traveled as fast as the muddy terrain allowed, which wasn't fast enough as the big one shouted a lot and gestured—all stabbing fingers and waving hands. They spoke to one another in a strange language—but Iliana knew when they talked about her. They called her *moquesh*.

Bait.

Most of the words were foreign, but that one bore enough similarity to Alexandrian that she could guess the meaning.

Another tree branch slapped her, this time across the cheek, and she closed her eyes against more tears.

Why had her father sent her away? The big one peered over his shoulder again, and she shuddered. It didn't help that rain poured down overhead—hard enough that not even the trees' thick canopy could block it out.

Had she been allowed to talk, she would've asked for a cloak. Either way she'd probably still be wet. The gag left Iliana able to do little more than groan as they traveled. And to think. And cry. Iliana stuck her bottom lip out, which trembled as she sobbed against the black rag.

She hadn't *really* thought her father would send her away. Tears rolled down her cheeks to mix with thick raindrops. *Papa, why did you send me away?*

Something had been off.

First, there had been her father's unusual appearance in the playroom. When Iliana and Margaret had raced for him not even the nanny's lurch forward and stern remarks had protected him from the onslaught of childish arms and legs.

Second, he'd allowed it. They had clambered up his six-foot frame until he balanced one sister on each shoulder.

But the final clue had been his smile. Lines had gathered around his mouth and eyes—lines that multiplied every time another rock hit the side of the castle walls. But as her father had smiled at his twin daughters, his eyes had remained muted and distant.

One moment she was on her father's shoulder and the next, he had rushed through the castle passageways until he'd reached the stables. Uncle Goefrin had been waiting with the three Amaskans, one of which he had told Papa was his brother. That was the first Amaskan, who led their horses at the front of the line.

They didn't look like brothers. His nose wasn't big enough.

Iliana had screamed until they gagged her. Then she'd kicked with her booted feet, but she'd been tossed astride a monster of a horse so ugly and large, she'd clamped her mouth shut out of fear it would buck her. Hands bound to the pommel, they'd left her feet free in the stirrups. A swift kick had done nothing.

The horse had ignored her until one of the Amaskans, a female, had spoken to the gelding. Then the horse had moved forward at a canter. Her father had cried out to her, and Iliana had craned her head and seen Goefrin restraining her father by the shoulders as he shouted her name. Her father's face had crumbled, and he had hidden it behind his hands as the Amaskans took her away.

He had said it wasn't safe.

At first, she'd cried too hard to notice much more than a blur as they passed through the city, but as the small group reached the outer walls, blood painted the ground crimson and the cries of the dying left her mute astride her horse. Arrows and rocks flew overhead as they pelted the Alexandrian guards and bounced off stone walls. The clash of steel nearby frightened her, and when the female Amaskan slit the throat of a nearby enemy, Iliana huddled as close as she could to the saddle and shut her eyes tight.

They were already halfway through the forest when she gained the courage to open them, and that was only because her horse stopped. "If ya want to live, don't run. Understand?" the female asked. When Iliana nodded, the woman unbound her hands and lifted her from the horse. When the woman set Iliana down on the leaves below, she slid in the mud and fought for balance. The Amaskan—Shendra, her father had called her— pulled a black tunic and boy's breeches out of a bag and shoved them at Iliana. "Change into these."

Iliana tried to ask where, but the gag muffled the question. The woman must have figured it out as she only shrugged. "There's no one here but the four of us. Change now, or I'll do it for ya."

While the two men stood guard, Iliana tugged at the laces of her dress and tried not to cry. *Always be brave* were her mother's words earlier that morning, and Iliana bit her lip. The knots came loose, but she struggled to get the thick, layered fabric over her head. The hem, caked with mud, clung to her face and tangled in her arms. In a panic, she shouted into the gag. When the sound of ripping fabric reached her, she twisted and screamed louder.

"Stop it—hush," Shendra hissed as she hacked away at the dress's fabric. The ruffles of blue fell to the forest floor, and Iliana's green ribbon floated into a muddy puddle, more earth-colored now than moss. Iliana's cheeks flushed while goose pimples pricked her bare skin. She tugged the tunic over her head and the Amaskan helped her buckle the breeches. Before Iliana could grab the ribbon from the mud, Shendra plopped her back on the horse and bound her hands to the pommel.

The trail of horses continued their gallop until darkness made it impossible to see, and by then, Iliana's teeth chattered and her stomach rumbled. The big one watched her until Shendra stepped between them. The woman removed Iliana's gag and unbound her hands. Iliana tried to swallow, but her mouth was too parched. "Here," the woman said, and she held up her canister of water.

Iliana coughed on the first swallow. The water only reminded her of her hunger, but she dared not speak. The look in the man's eyes kept her silent as they set up a campfire. Only a droplet or three from an overhead leaf remained of the earlier rain, but Iliana huddled against her horse for warmth as her clothes were soaked through.

"Here, make yourself useful." Shendra tossed a brush at Iliana, and its coarse bristles poked her hands when she caught it. Iliana stared at the horse in front of her.

She couldn't brush all of him. She couldn't even reach his forearms. Shendra whispered something in Sadain, and the horse lay down. Iliana touched the brush to his back and giggled as he squirmed beneath it with a whinny. The brush caught on specks of mud and blood; the latter Iliana tried not to think about. A good ten minutes left the horse much cleaner and drier than before. When the beast stood, mud and leaves from the forest floor stuck to his underside and legs.

The big one spoke, the sound just behind her, and Iliana spun around to find him looming over her. He held a dagger in his hands, and she screamed before falling to her knees. The shadow over her shifted, and Shendra knocked the dagger from the big one's hands. "What's this now?" asked Shendra.

His grin left Iliana shuddering. "We have our orders."

"Yes, to bring her to Bredych."

The man shifted on his feet, and Shendra matched his movements. "Someone hasn't been given the full plan," he murmured. "No matter, I'll see my part of the job done."

A leaf crackled behind Shendra as the second man approached, but the woman didn't move. Fear drove Iliana to the other side of her horse where she peeked through the gelding's legs. "What in Thirteen Hells are you blatherin' about? The job was to get the girl, take her back to Bredych for ransom."

"Not quite. Bredych's orders are to kill her."

"I don't believe ya—I know you're fairly new to the Order— Sayus, is it?—but Amaskans don't kill children. We aren't Tribor."

Iliana cried as she clung to the horse's leg. Her tears distracted the man, and in one heartbeat, Shendra moved. One moment she stood several lengths away and the next, she hovered over the man with her blade against his neck. He chuckled as he held out a piece of parchment, which she seized with her empty hand. "Damn," she whispered.

"Looks like you don't know Bredych as well as you thought," muttered the second man from behind Shendra. He held his blade against her neck, though his arm shook and a whisper of blood appeared.

"That's my brother you're talking about. He wouldn't order this. He couldn't," shouted Shendra, and the birds in the trees overhead cawed in protest.

Iliana crouched down and slapped her hands over her ears. She didn't see when the body dropped, but heard the thud as it landed in the soft soil.

One of the men uttered a groan and then a pop as his lungs filled with blood. The second man fell after a scrape of blades and a few grunts. The squelching sound of boots in the mud approached, and Iliana clamped her eyes shut harder.

When Shendra touched Iliana's shoulder, she screamed. Iliana didn't stop screaming until Shendra shook her. "Hush," the woman whispered. "I won't hurt ya."

Iliana pointed at the dead bodies. "I don't b-believe you."

The woman pointed at the mark on her jaw. "Do ya see this mark? Do ya know what it means?"

"It means you're Amaskan."

"Yes, it does. Amaskans serve Anur, God of Justice. Have ya done evil?"

Iliana wrapped her arms around her shoulders. "I took my sister's ribbon." Her favorite. The green one.

"That's not evil. Would it serve Anur to kill ya?"

"N-no, I guess not. But you killed—"

"Amaskans don't kill children." Shendra picked up the forgotten brush and set about picking the mud out of the horse's hair. Iliana backed far away from the killer and leaned against a hollowed out tree trunk. The wet wood seeped into her already wet clothes. When a beetle climbed across her arm, she jumped.

She wanted to go home.

A howl from the trees sent her stumbling back toward the woman with the sword, killer or no, and Iliana watched the woman finish removing the mud from her horse before moving to the next. "Go sit at the fire if you're wet."

Iliana's jaw ached, but she stood by the woman's side. "I-I'm fine."

Shendra paused mid-stroke. "You're cold. Go warm up." When Iliana refused, Shendra asked, "What? Why won't ya go sit by the fire?"

"If that–that Bredych wants me dead, who cares if I'm cold?"

The hug was unexpected, and Iliana flinched at the contact. "No one's gonna kill ya. I promise. On my life to Anur, I swear," Shendra whispered.

Iliana touched a grubby finger to the tattoo across Shendra's jaw. She'd expected it to feel rough somehow, scratchy, but the black circle was smooth to the touch.

"As long as you promise..." she whispered. Iliana peered out into the night made darker by the forest trees and shivered.

PART I

CHAPTER ONE

Aruna, Sadai; 255 Agaen 20th

Murder was a crime against the Thirteen, punishable by death. *What I do, I do for the Little Dozen and all its people. Anur's blessing upon my hand.* The invocation wasn't required before a job, but Adelei felt better having said it and swung first one leg and then the other over the ledge of the windowsill. She stiffened as her feet touched the wood floor. Sweat trickled down her face and neck but left no trail in the dark ebony grease smeared across all visible skin.

Don't get caught, her master had warned her—not that she ever had—but as she waited in the darkness, she remembered.

Her roommate. Her friend. Sent outside of Sadai to the Kingdom of Alexander. A bitter taste tinged her tongue at the image.

Limbs cut from her friend's body and tossed across the border, where they had lain rotting in the Sadain Desert sun until a merchant's guard had found them. He had uncovered the head a mile later and had recognized the tattoo at her stubborn jaw line.

They'd said she'd be safe in Alexander. Adelei squeezed her eyes shut a moment; outside the open window, someone kicked a stray stone. It clattered across the cobble in the darkness, and she leaned against the wall, using the flapping curtains to hide her.

Not that the child below could see her in the dark room, and he didn't look up as he hummed his way across the alley.

I am honored, Luthia, for your blessing of silence. The child rounded the corner, moving out of view. *This Amaskan needs all the help she can get tonight.*

Amaskan—in the old tongue it meant assassin, though Adelei doubted many knew more than a smattering of the old language. Besides, the term wasn't exactly accurate. A closed-mouth grin crossed her greased face.

She waited ten heartbeats after the child had passed, alert and ready as she stood one shadow among many. Tonight her orders had come from the King of Sadai himself, though evidence to the fact would never be found since the Order protected its clients. If caught, no one would come to her defense. Or her rescue.

Tonight of all nights, she had to be careful. To be sure. To be safe.

Adelei listened again for signs of an awakening house, and her eyes scanned for a shift in the shadows. A fine layer of dust coated the silk bed sheets, and a heavy iron candelabra hung from the unusually high ceiling.

Rich enough to have smooth wood floors but not wealthy enough to invest in enough servants to clean unneeded rooms until necessary. The knowledge matched what the Order had told her about the Magistrate. With hope, the map was just as accurate.

Adelei pictured the map of the house's interior. Two rooms to the left and through a sitting room. Across the hallway and through the fourth door on the right. That room would be the library. She'd take the back exit and go down the hall. He would be in the first room on the right.

The hallway outside the door remained silent. Some grease from her pouch applied to the door's hinges helped prevent any noise as she squeezed it open enough to slither through. In the corridor's darkness, her black silk clothing clung to her body and hid her lithe frame, but even with the disguise, she trod carefully—each step placed with great care. Adelei counted the doors as she made her way through the house fifty times the size of her room at the Order.

The pig lived there alone, except when he had "visitors." Her lips curled in a grimace at the thought. It wasn't his solitude that made him a mark, but his enjoyment of children—particularly young, defenseless children.

Most criminal activity in the Little Dozen Kingdoms of Boahim fell under the jurisdiction of local constables. If necessary, a kingdom's guards might bring the crime before the King. But a crime against the Thirteen meant the involvement of the Boahim Senate. Not even royalty could escape punishment.

If caught, that was where she'd end up, assuming they had the balls to do it. The hinges of another door bore the hint of rust, and she rubbed more grease across them before testing it. A small squeak echoed through the library, but the only response was from the mouse that scurried across the woven rug near the entrance.

The Order of Amaska had escaped their wrath thus far, though how, Master Bredych wouldn't say. Her hand touched the wooden door of the library's exit, and she flinched as another mouse squeaked in protest at her sudden appearance. Such a creature shouldn't have startled her. Focus on the job. Politics later.

The job is the life. The life is the job. Taumen.

A single candle burned toward the hall's end, its wick drowning in melted wax, and her footsteps carried her to it. She didn't have to pinch the candle as the wick dipped under the weight of the flame. Black covered her as she paused outside his door to listen.

The Boahim Senate couldn't touch the Magistrate. Something about his uncle. The fools. Not-so-delicate snorts and grunts from one sleeping with a head cold issued forth. Probably from taking too much Vrint. While the herb would certainly help him with his particular proclivities, it often led to congestion if used too often. Adelei smirked but allowed no laugh to escape her thin lips.

His door opened readily enough, and once inside, she casually observed him and the room for a moment. A doll collection rested in the corner, which he claimed had been passed down through the family.

Only if his particular avocation was a family hobby as well. Adelei slid a small dagger from its sheath at her waist. Three more blades adorned her body—two throwing knives hidden in the bound sleeves of her tunic and another dagger tucked into the top of her boot. She easily could have used the throwing knives—

quick and efficient in their entrance through his more than ample body—but her orders were to make it slow.

"*Make sure he knows he's dying.*" Her orders from the King himself. "*What he did to my niece—make him hurt, Master Adelei.*"

She shouldn't relish his fear, but he was a monster. This deserved justice. She gripped the plain dagger's hilt, sliding his bed sheet away from his face to expose a chest of curly red hair. From the small pouch at her waist, Adelei removed a pinch of Ysbane and sprinkled it on his naked flesh. Boiled, the drug released a potent toxin that caused the body's muscles to relax.

Adelei swallowed against the bile in her throat. It wasn't the job—she'd outgrown that phase long ago—but the vile concoction she'd swallowed to counteract any Ysbane was pitching her stomach about. Standing over him, she sent a silent prayer that the man was stupid enough not to have taken the same measures. His frame sank a touch more heavily into the feather stuffed mattress, and she leaned over him, one hand holding the dagger while the other clamped strong fingers over his fat-lipped mouth. His sea-blue eyes popped open, and he twitched. Many of his muscles were unresponsive to his brain's commands. With a huff, the Magistrate tried screaming, but her hand muffled it.

He spotted the simple circle tattoo that marked where her jaw met her ear, and the muffled screams multiplied. "Shhhhh..." she whispered, and she tightened her grip as he tried in vain to turn his head. "Moving won't help you now."

Magistrate Meserre's gaze moved across her body—a solid sheet of black from head to toe. Her tanned skin was revealed only on her fingertips, which were still pressed against his mouth. The whites of his eyes stood out against the rosy tinge of his cheeks. He tried to roll his body away from her, the veins across his neck and forehead bulging with the effort. Sweat beads peppered his forehead as he caught sight of her dagger, and an acrid odor hit the air as he wet his own bed.

"I hear you like little girls." Her voice scratched the air like gravel beneath her horse's hooves as she spoke. What few muscles worked twitched in response, and his eyes blinked in a rush. The Magistrate slid his gaze across the flat chest and narrow hips before him. When he tried to smile, the Ysbane twisted his lips into a half-snarl, and she forced a laugh at the grotesque expression. He gargled something incoherent before his body shook, the movement more of a convulsion.

Adelei's stomach churned at his reaction, but she played her part as she studied him. "Or maybe you only like little girls of the blood. Like Ereina Lhordei."

Despite the Ysbane, a slight bulge rose beneath the sheet for a moment before it, too, relaxed. His reaction was enough. His jerky twitches stilled as the realization swept across him. Adelei leaned closer, her skin inches from his. "By the Order of His Hand, King Monsine of Sadai, you are hereby sentenced to death for crimes of...oh hell, being a sick, perverted bastard who likes to break little girls like Ereina."

Magistrate Meserre floundered in his sheets as the drug reached his internal organs. His breaths came in muffled gasps as he struggled like a fish buried in sand, and Adelei leaned away from the sight of his efforts. No sign of guilt crossed his bloated features, just fear. Not that it mattered. He was a monster. He deserved it. If he were repentant, he'd get on with it already and die.

"I am Justice: Amaskan judge in the face of your crimes. I seek justice for all those harmed by your sins," she whispered the words from the Book of Ja'ahr. He smiled at her, though how he managed through the drugs, she didn't know, and she placed a hand on his hardening stomach. "You laugh, Magistrate, but today is special. Today, I am also Vengeance. Did you know it was the King's own niece you broke?"

A gargle and then a hiss issued forth from his throat. "Yes, His Majesty sent me personally to ensure that your death is slow. Painful. Well, not *that* slow by the look of things. Maybe I used too much." She laughed at him, but inside she wanted to flee.

It wasn't right. Amaskans weren't murderers; they weren't common assassins seeking vengeance. Watching him fight for each gasp of air was difficult, and her stomach heaved, leaving behind the putrid smell of bile to tickle her nostrils. Magistrate Meserre watched helplessly as her knife moved across his skin, marking his body with the sigils of the Thirteen. Whoever found him would know his crimes and know justice had prevailed. The release of blood heralded the release of his bowels, and after too short a time, the release of his soul.

If the bastard even had one. Adelei wiped the blood clean from her dagger with the Magistrate's own white silk sheets. Bastard had died too quickly.

She'd been ordered to make it last, but it seemed he'd been a coward to the end. Adelei closed her eyes a moment and whispered, "Anur, forgive me my vengeance."

Risky to take the time to pray, but her conscience required it. She crossed the room and listened again for sounds though she expected none. Several minutes' walk had her free of the house and down the back alley, the sight of his body burning fresh in her mind.

At the street corner, she ducked behind a bush and pulled a moist, white rag from the bag she'd tossed beneath the bush earlier in the evening. She clinched her eyes shut as she scrubbed her face and ground her teeth from the burning sting. Odorless though not painless, the oil on the rag removed the grease from her face and hands.

She continued scrubbing until the white fabric's corner came away clean, although she left a smudge or two on her forehead and cheek. Too clean a face and she'd stand out in the dirty cloak she had retrieved from the now empty bag. Goat piss stained the cloak's bottom corner. Adelei's nose twitched as she drew it closer to her body and raised the hood to cover her bald head.

Adelei didn't hide as she made her way across town toward the inn, but she didn't advertise her presence either. She took notice of the boot heels scraping on the cobble or a cough from an ambling night guardsman. Anything that meant someone other than her was out and about in the predawn hours. As she passed through another dark alley, her footsteps echoed, and she slowed her pace. The echoes slowed, but a moment too late, and Adelei ducked around the corner of the bakery, dropping to her heels in one swift motion. The crates out front masked her shadow, but the second shadow didn't join her. Instead, whoever followed her stopped just out of sight around the building's brick edge.

A black pebble skittered across the road and came to rest three inches from her feet. A second one and then a third joined it moments later. Adelei leaned against the crate beside her.

"You heading to the inn?" a voice hissed. The Amaskan stepped around the corner, his hood casting deep shadows across his face. He angled his pointed chin to expose the circle tattoo at the jaw joint. Neither his voice nor the marking told her his identity, only that he *could* be Amaskan.

He studied her as much as she did him: both stood with more unease than their relaxed shoulders conveyed as they stood feet apart with their weight resting on their toes. Their dark-colored outfits appeared identical, though his sleeve bore a slight tear near his wrist, and his hand, curled up within the layers of his breeches, surely must have rested on knives of his own. When their gazes met, neither smiled.

"Anur's blessing this night," she said. The hand on his blade twitched, but he said nothing, and she repeated the question, this time with the correct deity. "Asti's blessing this night."

"May blades find evil in its height."

Three tests passed. Adelei removed her hand from her pocket and suppressed a chuckle as he mimicked her action. Across the street, a dog barked. Someone shouted, and the sound was silenced. "Why are you here?" she asked.

"There's been a change in plans." Adelei frowned, and he continued, "Is the job done?"

"It is."

She dug the heel of her soft shoe into the dirt at her feet. Great. The King must have sent him to ensure the Magistrate had died slowly. A bead of sweat on her forehead trickled down the side of her face, but she made no move to wipe it away. Instead she ignored it completely and cast a bored look down the street toward the inn.

He caught the motion and nodded in the inn's direction. "You're to return to the Order at once."

"Too risky to travel at night. Leaving town now will draw only unwanted attention."

When his hand reached for his belt pouch, she tensed. Adelei ignored the piece of parchment he retrieved, and her gaze moved directly to the gold coin between two of his fingers. Not merely gilded as some Sadain coins were, but solid gold and bearing only circles in the markings. When he held it up, she swallowed hard.

He was an apprentice to the Masters. Why was he sent way out here? Why was he sent after her?

"Your orders are to return at any risk," he said and palmed the coin. Adelei took the parchment and unrolled it with unsteady hands.

Return with all haste. -B.

One simple line in handwriting she recognized. Master Bredych. She nodded to the man and muttered, "Anur's blessing."

Her nerves itched to shoot down the road at a dead run, but that would bring more attention than her exit already would. Instead she snatched one of the discarded broken bottles from the bakery's porch and tucked herself back behind the stack of crates.

Why risk two Amaskans in town just to get her home a day earlier? Out of sight, she unwound the wrapped fabric from her waist and arranged it as a veil, wrapping it around her head and chin. The corners were tucked into the top of her skin-tight tunic, and she dragged her fingers across her jaw to make sure her tattoo was well-hidden from view. She gave her head a good shake and adjusted the veil until convinced it wouldn't come loose.

Swift fingers removed a crimson sash tucked into one of her boots, which she wrapped around her waist to give her outfit some color. She couldn't do anything about the tunic's tightness—she'd have to hope nobody paid it much mind with the noise she was making. She would have changed clothes anyway as the streets grew too wide to hide in, even at this hour, but she hated the next part. Drawing attention to herself was not her strong point.

She'd arrived in town a regular sword-for-hire. It was how she had intended to leave as well. Adelei stepped out from behind the crates and mimed taking a swig from the bottle. There were eyes on her, but she didn't know if it was the Amaskan or someone else.

For all she knew, the apprentice was off checking her handiwork. She swallowed hard and wished the second swig of air she took from the bottle was something real, something potent to drown the confusion she felt.

Adelei stumbled further down the open road until she neared the inn's stables, where she faked another drink of the "potent liquid" and tripped on a jagged piece of cobble with a loud belch. She allowed herself to stumble over her own feet before stopping in plain sight of the stable hands inside. "'Scuse me," she muttered and followed it with a forced hiccup.

A stable hand no older than ten poked a bucktoothed head around the archway. His grin lacked intelligence, but one look at her demeanor and he returned to brushing a sable-colored mare. "Just a drunkard," he called out to someone she couldn't see, and she grinned beneath the façade.

Her fingers fumbled at the heavy wooden door, which she allowed to slam into her backside, and Adelei pitched forward. The few face down in their own ale paid her little mind. The barkeep glanced once at her and returned to pouring another glass for a bushy-haired man with cheeks as red as Adelei's sash. Another mimed drink and another stumble as she reached the lip of the stairs. She continued her charade until she was safely in her own room and the door bolted shut behind her.

The window was closed and locked, just as she'd left it, and her saddlebags stowed under the crooked wooden-frame that served as a sad excuse for a bed. She shucked off her soft shoes in trade for her travel boots. Nothing else was unpacked— everything ready to go at a moment's notice.

Adelei retrieved an extra throw blanket from the mouse-infested chair in the corner and stuffed it under the bed's lone covering. It wouldn't fool anyone at close glance, but it might slow someone down from a distance. She removed the bright sash and tossed it into her bag. If she had to, she'd leave it behind. Nothing in the travel bag would give away her identity, and everything inside could be replaced, though she winced at the thought of parting with her bracelet. It was a simple thing, woven of simple grasses in square patterns, but it was the only token that remained from her childhood, from her time before the Order.

The window opened easily and without sound, and she leaned out with a deep breath of air. She hiccupped again and allowed herself to drop the already broken bottle. It rolled down the sloped roof and shattered when it hit the cobbled street. "Oops," she muttered and cast a glance at the streets below. If anyone noticed her "accident," they didn't give evidence to the fact, and she ducked back inside the window.

Her foot twitched. What could possibly be so wrong as to risk detection? *Dammit, Bredych.* Someone might have seen her leave and put two and two together.

Adelei leaned out the window again. Nothing moved. In the bar room downstairs, two men argued before falling into a raucous laughter. She held her bag out first and eased it down until it rested against the rooftop. When still nothing outside moved, she swung her legs over the window's sill and lowered herself just as carefully until her rear rested against the wooden shingles. One foot at a time, she inched her way forward until she and her bag sat at the roof's edge.

When a patron banged his way out of the inn, she clenched her hands into fists and held her breath until he'd moved a few buildings down. There were no doors on this side of the building. Only one lone window lay below, shuttered in preparation for the storm that loomed in the clouds overhead.

She had picked this night for the darkness. *Because* of the storm. She hadn't thought she'd be traveling in it. Traveling now meant abandoning her horse, or she risked losing the drunkard pretense, but someone would retrieve the mare later when it was safe to do so. Another Amaskan. Possibly one of the merchants the Order dealt with regularly.

A gust of wind whipped a tree limb against the building, and she used the sound to cover the ones made when she dropped to the ground below. The bag landed before her, and she rolled when her feet hit the cobble. A stone dug into her shoulder, and she winced when she rose to her feet.

This better be important, Master. That's going to bruise.

She traveled on foot until she reached the last farmhouse at the edge of town where she "borrowed" a horse and saddle from the sleeping family. Ten silver left behind in the stall would more than replace the old gelding, though she'd shorted them on the saddle. It was all she had, so it would have to be enough.

The spotted horse bore the muscles of a working farm horse, and she scratched him between the ears. *You're not exactly built for a fast run through a forest, but you'll have to do.*

Once saddled, she secured her bag and led him from his stall and out into the night air. He didn't buck when she mounted him, though his gate shifted here and there, unsure of his new rider. Both Adelei and the horse eyed the forest. The clouds overhead didn't rumble, not yet anyway, and she urged the horse forward and into the night.

Here's hoping we aren't seen, old boy. I don't relish a run through the woods this evening.

CHAPTER TWO

The City of Alesta, Alexander; 255 Agaen 21st

Princess Margaret's hand shook a moment before completing its movement toward the apple slice resting on the solid oak table in front of her. She stared at her father a moment longer before taking a bite of the fruit.

"You have said nothing of the news, my sweet," King Leon said, his fingers twirling his apple core, its leftover juices leaving small trails of liquid on the table. His brows furrowed in concern, which Margaret dismissed with a shake of her head. Instead she pictured Prince Gamun Bajit of Shad and smiled.

"The news is welcome to my ears, Father. I was lost in thought of my future and ask forgiveness for my silence and the concern it caused you." His face relaxed as he tossed the apple core into the bowl. He stood and stretched his arms above his head. Her father's six-foot frame and muscular bulk had provided a protective shelter since her earliest memories.

Except when she'd been sent away.

She blinked the memory from her mind, returning to the prince. At age twenty, she rarely sought her father's embrace but knew it was there should she need it. *I hope Prince Bajit is as safe. And as tall.* A grin decorated her graceful face, and she smoothed away the smile-lines. The face of a princess. *Our children might resemble the handsomeness of my father. It would please him, I think, to see that.*

"Lost in thought again, little lamb?" King Leon patted her hand.

Margaret nodded and took another careful bite of her apple. "Father, tell me again about Prince Bajit."

He returned to his seat and gestured to a servant with a flick of his thick wrist. The boy filled his cup with watered-down ale, which he sipped slowly before speaking. Margaret caught the sour look before her father schooled his expression.

There is nothing wrong. Father's only worried over the wedding preparations. Despite the thought, the worry creases at the corners of his eyes set her stomach turning. Margaret set the apple on the plate in front of her, unfinished.

"When I first met him, he was nothing more than a young man of sixteen. His Highness smiled and talked and assured all who would notice that he was confident and worth their trouble, but I knew he bore the typical doubts of a second son—unsure of his future, what lands he would hold, and whom he would marry. He knew, of course, of the treaty between our kingdoms. A promise made long ago at the end of the Little War of Three."

"But he didn't know of me."

More tension in the lines of his face, and the apple's once sweet smell soured. Margaret pushed the plate across the table and nodded for its removal. "He knew he would marry, yes, but not whom. That meeting was when his father and I told him of his future. Of you. The treaty guaranteed the joining of our families through this marriage that would bring peace to an age long feud."

She'd only been ten. A less mature and less graceful princess, her head full of horses and flowers. Margaret had rushed into the audience chamber to tell Papa how far she'd ridden her pony, only to find two adult faces staring at her: her father, with slight humor, and his guest, with a coldness that still made her shudder. She was set to turn tail and run when she spotted the prince.

She recognized him, even if he didn't find her familiar.

Prince Gamun Bajit of Shad wiped the scowl from his face and smiled, his grin sending a blush from the roots of her dark hair to her bare toes. When his eyes had stopped on her feet, she'd fled the room with a hasty bow. It had taken her three days to finally tell her father what had been so important.

Listening to her father recall it now, she drummed her fingers on the table until she thought she would burst. "I know how you met, Papa. Tell me more about *him*."

"All right, all right." Her father's chuckle was hesitant, forced. "Prince Bajit still has black hair and brown eyes. Resembles his father more than his older brother does, though I suspect the elder of being the bastard of another woman—"

When Margaret gasped, her father patted her hand. "My apologies, my lady. I spend too much time among men that I forget myself." King Leon winked, and Margaret relaxed shoulders held too tight. "The women say he has a good frame. Good for fighting and protecting a kingdom, I suppose. When he visited, he was strong and quick at the hunt. Took out three buck with the bow from several pole lengths…"

While her father rattled on, Margaret forgot the knots in her stomach and allowed her mind to drift. At twenty-six, he was probably more handsome and broader in the shoulder. More refined and intelligent. All her life she'd waited for this. The vision had changed as she had aged, as she had gained maturity, but it never had disappeared. She would marry the perfect prince, and together they would rule. They would lead Alexander in continued peace and happiness.

So maybe the vision was a bit…naïve. Maybe even *too* perfect.

The alternative gave her nightmares as the wedding approached, so she pushed it from her thoughts as often as possible. *Focus on the future, the hope he brings to the kingdom.* Margaret glanced up from her trembling hands to find her father had stopped speaking.

"I think I lost you there," he said, his steady voice calm despite the expression he wore.

"Papa—" She took a drink of the water to cool the flush from her cheeks. "Is it wrong to be…scared?"

"Depends on what you're scared of, poppet."

Margaret continued drumming her fingers on the table, a nervous fidget she was forever trying to quit. If for no other reason than to please her tutors. "What if he doesn't like me? Prince Bajit—" Margaret blushed when his name crossed her lips. "He's never met me."

King Leon reached out to pat her hand and stopped when he caught her frown. When the twinkle in his eyes reached his lips, her face grew hot. He was laughing at her.

Margaret tucked a stray hair behind her ear and used the motion as an excuse to brush aside the tear that carved an unwilling path down her cheek.

The motion was not hidden, and her father's joy lost its zeal. "Poppet, everyone gets nervous before their wedding day. It's perfectly natural. Your own mother fainted four times before our wedding—in fact, she had fainting spells throughout the ceremony itself. All the fuss will be over soon enough. You'll be Alexander's queen, ready to rule our lands once I'm long gone from this world."

She gasped. "But I'm not ready to be queen. Besides, you're well and healthy, Father."

"Life is flighty, poppet. And no one is ready to rule."

He cleared his throat to cover a cough and then drank deeply from his cup. "Is your cough still bothering you?" she asked. He busied himself by summoning a servant for more ale. "I thought the healers had given you something."

"They have, but you know how Echain is—one moment the trees are blooming and the next, they are tempered with frost and the bite in the air sends one's lungs to the dungeon."

He spoke of the season as if this cough visited every Echain, and Margaret wracked her brain. How many seasons had passed since the cough had arrived? How many more would he carry it? What if... She halted the thought. Her father, the King, was strong. He would live a long while before Margaret would rule.

"I wish Mother were here."

His face froze, all humor in his eyes dissolving. Margaret wished she could erase the words, take them back into her mouth to stay politely in her head where they belonged. Once again she'd caused him pain. As her own did, she was sure his mind rushed back to that memory, her younger self sitting in front of her mother while they both clung to the saddle.

Their horse climbed a hill during the heavy rains of Echain, mud splashing them both in their escape from Alexander. The memories were hazy, but even in the warmth of the dining hall, Margaret shivered. Bone cold had pierced right through her woolen cloak, and rain had pelted her hood. This time, closing her eyes didn't rid her of what came next.

> *The snap of a twig sounded up ahead, and the guards in front of them stopped. They shouted orders several times, all of which was muffled by Margaret's hood. Her mother's hand clamped over Margaret's mouth, and she whispered, "Shhhh..."*
>
> *They sat astride the horse, unmoving as they waited for something, some action to dictate fight or flight. Margaret leaned closer to her mother, and Catherine wrapped one arm around her. "It will be all right, Margaret," she whispered in Margaret's ear.*
>
> *A cry from the trees sent most of the guardsmen running toward the source. Margaret clamped her eyes shut, and when a nearby guard uttered a short gurgle, she opened them as he slid to the forest floor. Margaret and her mother were alone, and the sound of fighting in the distance diminished.*
>
> *Her mother lurched forward, pressing Margaret against the saddle. The pommel dug into her shoulder, and she twisted in an attempt to free herself from her mother's weight.*
>
> *"Momma?" she called out, but her mother didn't move. Margaret waited for a guard to free her, but no one came.*
>
> *It wasn't until the horse moved on its own to reach the nearby grass that Margaret realized just how silent her mother had become.*

"Your mother would have been a nervous wreck about this wedding."

Her father's words jerked her back to the present, and a frightened squeak escaped her dry lips. "I'm sorry, I didn't mean to startle you," said King Leon and he leaned over the table corner to pat her hand. "You must have been long lost in thought."

Margaret didn't trust herself to speak. She stared at the table to hide her tears. King Leon cleared his throat and resumed cutting another apple into thin slices. When her courage returned, she said, "I was thinking about Mother. About the day she died…"

"I'm still amazed you remember. You were only five."

"It's like a plague I can't cure. I remember it too well."

Nodding, he said, "For me, too. Well, a change of topic is in order—think on your prince instead. Surely that can cure you of your blues."

Despite the melancholy that threatened to swallow her good mood, her prince gave her partial reason to smile. "Maybe there will be a son in my future. Surely a child can cure what ails me." Even her arms flushed at the audacity of such a bold thought, and King Leon bellowed a laugh that bounced around the empty hall; tonight was a private dinner, held at a late hour.

"Once again my daughter thinks ahead to the kingdom's health. A grandson. My girl, that would be wonderful." He gave her hair a slight tussle, an action left over from childhood, and she lowered her gaze to the table. "I wish the two of you all the world's happiness. May your days be warm and full of laughter, and your nights full of love."

If she could just survive until the wedding, all would be well. *It has to.* Margaret stood and rounded the table. When her father rose, she embraced him and pressed her head gently to his chest.

His heart beat in her ears, and for a moment, a fainter heartbeat, lighter and slower pulsed. The smell of rain surrounded her until she could feel the forest's stillness. Margaret could sense the horse beneath her, feel the pommel digging into her shoulder, and then the extra heartbeat faded away. It left her beside her father as she sought the strength of knowing he would always be there, that he would never, ever leave her.

Then he coughed.

A great shudder ran through him, and she thrust his cup into his waiting hand. Another hack shook his frame before it settled, leaving him pale and shaking. "Father, are...are you sure you're well? Maybe we should delay the wedding until you're better?"

His energy waned too much to give more than a half-hearted smile as he sank into his chair. "I appreciate your concern, but the treaty must be upheld. Too much is riding on it to delay things now. I'll be fine, pet. I promise."

The hand that held his cup trembled, and the liquid sloshed over the rim. Her grandfather's carved face swam beneath the ale now pooled on the wooden table.

"Father—" Margaret began, and then she paused.

"What is it, poppet?"

"I've heard something, and I would know if it were truth or just the wagging of tongues."

A page entered the dining room and paused at King Leon's side. Her father nodded at Margaret without looking up from the note the page held. "Go on, ask your question."

"Well, it's about—"

"Damn the Dozen."

Margaret flinched.

"She returned alone?" he asked the page.

"I-I don't know, Your Majesty. I mean, I think so. That's what the captain said."

King Leon's chair scraped against the stone floor and tumbled over as he stood. "I'm sorry, poppet. We'll have to talk later. This needs my immediate attention." Her father still held the knife in his hand, his apple forgotten, and he tossed it on the table. The blade skittered through the ale, painting a macabre scene across her grandfather's face.

"But—"

He passed through the archway before she could finish her sentence and left Margaret alone with a single servant. Margaret sent the girl away with the wave of a hand.

"Damn," she muttered and felt her cheeks grow hot with the utterance of such a word. She didn't feel any better having said it either. Instead Margaret seized the knife from the table and stabbed the leftover apple slices.

There are rumors, Father. I know better than to listen to gossip, but the things they say… Instead of her prince's perfect face, the features in her mind twisted until his mouth snarled and his eyes flashed his anger. She could imagine it: those hands around her neck, those eyes watching as life fled her body, and his voice speaking her father's words.

"The treaty must be upheld. Too much is riding on it."

Margaret pulled her knees to her chest and wrapped her arms around her them as the candlelight on the table wavered. She hardly noticed it flicker and sputter before going out, leaving her alone in the dark with the rumors.

King Leon stood for a moment outside the door to his audience chamber. His sepier had returned from her mission alone. She understood the consequences of returning empty handed, yet here she was awaiting him alone.

I can't see her right now. If I do, I just might kill her. Former captain of his royal guard, Captain Warhammer held the unique position in his kingdom of being the one person he could trust with special tasks, delicate tasks he trusted no one else to complete. Leon sighed and resumed his walk down the hallway. Away from the captain. Away from her failure.

Damn her.

Of course, the moment his brain pictured her, his heart lurched in his chest while his brain cursed her existence. And another part of him wanted to turn right around and burst through the door, to grab her by her scarred shoulders and kiss lips he'd kissed for over a decade. He cursed again, and a page flinched before ducking through a nearby door. King Leon shifted his thoughts to his daughter, but she was no more pleasant to think on than Ida Warhammer.

He did her a disservice. He sighed and held his breath to prevent the cough that fought to erupt from his chest. It was hardly her fault for thinking of her mother at a time like this. Memories that haunted him plagued her as well, and he paced the castle's hallways, a lost visitor to its walls rather than its ruler.

The horse had wandered with Margaret trapped beneath her mother's corpse for a long enough time to send Margaret into shock.

One member of the guard, his arm burned and bloody, had stumbled back to the castle. King Leon's heart had shriveled up in his chest. He had believed the worst. He wanted nothing more than to ride his own horse until the poor beast collapsed in search of his wife and daughter, but as bad luck would have it, Shadian troops attacked at midday. The attack left him at the beginning of the Little War of Three, a war that lasted a full three years and ended only when the Boahim Senate stepped in.

If the Shadians hadn't attacked, I would have done it. I would have ridden out to find them and probably gotten myself killed in the process. Thank the Thirteen for little favors.

He tried not to think on it too often, but nights like tonight, as his lungs ached and his daughter worried, the memory grabbed hold. Only more ale relinquished its hold on him. It didn't help that he feared this wedding. King Leon leaned against the chilly stone wall. Could he give his only daughter to a Shadian?

A lifetime of hatred gripped his heart. The generational feud between the two kingdoms didn't die with the peace treaty, no matter what the Senate thought. *Will this marriage even bring us true peace?*

He slammed his fist into the stone, and weathered knuckles came away bloody. King Leon ignored the red, his mind reaching back to his father's time. *Never trust a Shadian. Their blood runs black.*

"How I miss the old man…"

"Sire?" A servant approached, eyes widening when he spotted the drying blood across his knuckles; King Leon waved him off.

"Leave me."

As much as the Boahim Senate had wanted the end of the war, the peace treaty wasn't one he would have signed had he been the man and king he was now. The arranged marriage…the things he'd heard about Prince Bajit.

Rumors reached Leon's ears, rumors of a psychopathic monster that haunted the Shadian country, preying on young girls and leaving destruction in its wake. A few of the darkest rumors hinted that someone in the royal family was behind the trail of broken girls, that maybe even Prince Bajit himself was this monster, but no proof existed. Many of the sources that propagated these rumors disappeared overnight, leaving Leon's own spies confused and lacking anything substantial.

As a king, it worried him but only to a degree. It wasn't his kingdom being attacked by this monster. If there were any truth to the rumors, surely the Boahim Senate would step in since the aforementioned crimes broke the Thirteen. As a father, he worried. Worried that his last remaining daughter was marrying a monster made of nightmares.

A cough rose and shook his massive frame, bitterness coating his tongue. Useless healers. They gave him tonics aplenty, but nothing ceased the shredding of his lungs. How long could he hide whatever it was that turned him inside out? *My days are numbered, but please, Delorcini, bless me and keep me here with Margaret until—*

His ankles shook and King Leon gripped the wall for strength as another coughing fit washed over him. "Your Majesty. Are you well?" A nearby page dashed toward him, tripping over his own feet in his rush, but King Leon stopped the boy with the out-turned palm of his hand. The page slid across the smooth, polished stone and halted just before the King.

"I'm—fine." King Leon tried to push the page away, but weak, he fell back against the wall hard enough to rattle the door behind him. Eyes wide, the boy turned tail and took off down the hallway. Probably fetching a healer. As if there were anything they could do for him now. *Not even I can command what I cannot control.*

This next cough rendered him breathless, and Leon wondered if this was it—the cough that would burst his lungs and orphan his child. *Not yet. Please, Itova, don't come for me yet.*

The page returned, dragging a healer by the arm. "Another fit, Your Majesty?"

At his nod, the healer pulled a packet of powder from his robe and offered a pinch to the King. Whatever herb it was couldn't heal him, but King Leon seized it with shaking fingers, his mouth puckering up with the bitter taste that parched his mouth.

"My thanks." The effort to catch his breath left beads of sweat upon his brow. To the page, he said, "Don't worry, lad. It's just a cough. Now hurry along to bed."

At first the boy paused, but when the healer nodded, he scampered off. "You should be in bed yourself," said the healer, and his eyes narrowed as they lingered on Leon's face.

Leon self-consciously wiped the spittle still at his mouth and came away bloodier than before. "I'm heading there now. No need to lecture."

"Take the rest of this with you." The healer handed King Leon the small packet. "Remember, one pinch at mealtimes. And rest."

It was the same old lecture the healers had been dictating for several seasons now. More rest, less stress. The kingdom wouldn't run itself. The marriage couldn't come fast enough. And with that thought, the worry returned. What if she were marrying a monster? His kingdom needed him now more than ever. He couldn't die now. Not yet.

The room spun slightly, a side effect of the herb, and the healer took his arm to steady him. "Let me help you to bed, Your Majesty. Time for you to rest."

No, not yet. Not until I know Margaret is safe. King Leon allowed himself to be put to bed like a child, but inside, his brain spun plans. It was time to make sure of Prince Bajit. To make sure King Leon's bloodline would continue to thrive.

Soon enough I'll rest. For now, I must be King.

CHAPTER THREE

The Order of Amaska, Sadai

The council room's polished stone floor reflected the painted blues and greens of the carved walls, and Adelei drew in a breath at the sight. It wasn't just that powdered gold mixed with colors had been brushed along the walls, though that was impressive, but the carvings of the Thirteen deities—those that had created her world—held her enthralled with their detail.

Someone cleared his throat, and Adelei found herself face to face with a room full of people. It wasn't Grand Master Bredych she was reporting to, nor any of a dozen individual Masters. It was all of them. Every Master who sat aboard the Amaskan Council and held voting rights waited for her.

The hair on her arms stood up despite the tightness of her tunic's fabric. *Oh, damn. Double damn.* The thoughts whirled and bounced around inside her head as she studied their grim faces, stretched long with weariness. She stepped up to the dais and bowed her head until Grand Master Bredych acknowledged her. When she met her mentor's eyes, he didn't speak. He beckoned for her to follow him through the blue arch that led to the Order's great chamber. As she passed beneath the arch, the familiar tingle ran through her body, relaxing stiff muscles and calming her mind. For once she minded the intrusion.

If I messed up, I don't want complacency. Just tell it to me straight. She stepped left, toward the common seating area, but one of the

Masters cleared his throat, and she followed to the right, their steps taking them into a room reserved only for Masters.

Damn. Either she had just gotten promoted, or something was very wrong. Adelei forced her own steps to a slow, calm stroll, but her fingers twitched and danced in her pockets.

No words were spoken as the Masters took their seats in the sacred chamber. Adelei remained standing, awaiting Bredych's nod indicating she was permitted to sit, but his head held firm. To keep the quaking of her legs to a minimum, she studied the chamber's smooth walls, its sigils carved in a language so ancient that Adelei felt less than a babe in its presence. She'd been in the room once—when she had stood before the Masters to ask admittance into the Order.

I think I'm more intimidated now. Why am I here?

It was in this room that the Masters decided which jobs they would accept and which they turned away. The room where they deliberated and discussed the secrets of an Order stretching back many centuries, back before Boahim was torn asunder by war and back before it stood united. This was a room of Justice.

Not every job calls for an Amaskan—words repeated to her at an early age. "We pick our jobs carefully, for truth and justice for the people," Master Bredych said to her six-year-old self. "Murder is against the Thirteen, but we accept this sin for the lives of others. Ours is a heavy burden, but we walk in the path of Justice, in the light of Anur."

Looking at Master Bredych now, his raised shoulders and tense jaw betrayed his nervousness. He was not the relaxed man who had taught her of justice. Not today. Even at seventy he could whip her in a fight, yet he refused to meet her gaze.

"Master Bredych—" Speaking was a mistake, and she clamped her mouth shut when he rapped his knuckles on the table.

Do not engage unless invited to do so. His words rang in her ears, and she winced that she'd forgotten instructions ingrained since she was ten.

All around her sat men and women double and triple her age, Amaskans with long reach. While she could give their Amaskan names, their birth names remained hidden. Secrets upon secrets. Every one of them wore a mask, their pasts hidden beneath layers of lies she couldn't begin to unravel. And yet she trusted them completely.

They knew her birth name and had held it safe for fifteen years. She had nothing to fear from the council. Adelei risked a slight smile. When she glanced at her mentor and adopted father, Bredych held no lopsided grin for her. He turned his tanned face to another member beside him.

A bird let loose in her stomach, twisting and turning while pecking holes in her confidence, and she frowned. Still she remained standing, all eyes on her. Was this about the job? Or something else?

"Iliana Poncett."

She flinched at the name from his lips. "That name is dead, like the body that carried it," she spoke, and the corner of his eye twitched. Despite her words, her mind reached back without bidding, and horses' hoof beats trampled across her memory. Fuzzy and darkened, the images scattered in the confusion of people shouting and then silence.

Her life before the Amaskans. Before Master Bredych had adopted her and given her a new life. And along with it, a new name.

She kept her eyes forward until finally, the nod came. The chair scraped against the stone floor as she pulled it away from the end of the table. Bredych tapped a gnarled knuckle on the table. "Report."

Adelei wiped her greasy hands on her pants. No windows gave light to the room, and while its sole door gave them protection and privacy, the dimness reminded her of her heavy limbs and eyelids. What she wouldn't give for a bed. Outside the walls, the sun splashed hints of light across the horizon, and she stifled a yawn.

"The mark has been cleared."

A rush of relief shot through the room. Whereas the others whispered their excitement and thanked her, Bredych remained still. A few wrinkle lines scattered unfamiliarly across his face. The corners of his mouth sagged a hint as he cleared his throat. "We are proud that this task has been dealt with." The statement was an unusual compliment, and she froze, waiting for the stir of dark clouds. "Iliana—"

She shook her head, eyes widened as the bird in her stomach fought to escape. He never made mistakes like that. To use her birth name...again. A quick glance held the others still smiling. Either they hadn't heard him, or they had ignored it. Neither of which was good.

He turned a blind eye to her concern. "You've been given a new job. One outKingdom."

Jobs outside of Sadai weren't unknown, though they were uncommon. *He must be worried about the risks. Still, I haven't met a challenge yet that I couldn't tackle as easily as wading through a calm river.*

"Your job calls you to the Kingdom of Alexander."

Adelei broke protocol and stood, palms flat against the white table. "Alexander? What possible reason could this Order have for sending me there? It's a death—"

Master Bredych silenced her with a raised hand. "You are ordered to guard her Royal Highness, Princess Margaret. You will work as a body double until your services are no longer needed."

Her left temple throbbed. When she curled her fingers into fists, grease smudged the table. Adelei took one breath and then another before speaking. "Grand Master, the Order does not...usually accept positions such as this—any guardsman could complete such a task," she said and ignored the gasps at her impertinence. "Body doubles are a lifelong task. You ordered me back at high risk and for what? This? Why would the Order accept this job? In Alexander no less?"

"There have been assassination attempts," he said before he took a swallow from his cup of water. "Possibly Tribor. You will eliminate the problem."

"Tribor are nothing new. That's not the reason. Grand Master, Amaskans are not tolerated in Alexander. To enter that kingdom is a death sentence. Why would you send me there?" Her voice cracked, and she winced.

When the Bredych's fist struck the table, fourteen sets of shoulders jumped. "Do you question the ability of the Masters?"

"No, Grand Master."

"Do you doubt your own abilities?"

"No, Grand Master."

"Then you will do the job before you as you are told." His fingers were pale in the candlelight and a trickle of sweat beaded upon his brow. The bird in her stomach plummeted to its death in the bottom of the cage. She returned to her seat but wrapped her ankles around the chair's legs in a defensive position. "You recall the Little War of Threes?" he asked.

"The Kingdoms of Alexander and Shad battled for three years over borderlines, wiping out chunks of their population until the Boahim Senate stepped in with the compromise. It took a decade for their countries to recover."

But what does this have to do with me?

"The compromise reestablished the kingdom boundaries. Both sides swore not to *adjust* their borders. King Leon's daughter, Margaret, will marry Prince Gamun Bajit of Shad, uniting the two families and ending the brutal feud between the two kingdoms."

"I knew that was part of the compromise, but I didn't think the wedding would proceed. I mean, to allow your daughter to marry the son of your enemy...not exactly demonstrating good parenting." But then, King Leon had never been a good parent. "Master, if the Tribor are suspected, any one of a dozen freelancers could take them out. To endanger the life of an Amaskan by sending them into Alexander, much less into the heart of the capital—" Her tongue wouldn't lie still as it gave voice to her doubts. "I'm sorry, Master. Forgive my tongue its injury."

"King Leon III has asked this as a...personal favor. You will be sent."

Adelei bowed her head, but inside her brain flew like a hurricane. The Masters watched her, their masks carefully in place. They were withholding something from her. Information? The truth? She opened her mouth and shut it again.

"You have a question to ask?" he asked.

"You said this job would last until I was no longer needed. What do you mean by that?"

"Until either you are dead, or the King no longer sees a need for your services."

A lifetime job. She was right. The air before her ceased its movement, and her lungs burned as she held her breath. He was sending her away, probably forever. *That's one hell of a favor.* Terror gripped her, familiar in its feeling, and she failed to shake it off.

Fear has no place in the mind or heart of an Amaskan. Not even these ancient words could smooth the dagger's edge.

"Grand Master, maybe it would be best if you brief her...alone," said a Master on her left.

The whites of Bredych's eyes matched the paleness of his skin. *He's afraid.* While the knowledge sank in, the other Masters stood and one by one, they retreated. When she was alone with her father, only then did the mask fall, tears unstoppable as he awaited the questions. Ignoring them all, though her mind screamed for answers, she went to him, falling into his arms for probably the very last time.

Alesta; In the Year of Boahim 235

"What do you mean she's gone?" King Leon's voice rose and with a quick peek toward the door to his bedchamber where Margaret slept, he reined in his voice to a whisper. "She was sent there to be protected, damn you."

Goefrin flinched and stepped back a pace or two as he raised his hands in protest. "My contacts say she never made it. The party was ambushed—much like the ambush that attacked your—"

His glass shattered on the stone floor, missing his wife's favorite rug by inches. The wine spread. Running like Catherine's blood, leaving a splash of red pooling on the back of Margaret's small hood. The red was too bright, too jarring, and Leon shook his head. Out of the corner of his eye, Goefrin stepped out from behind a tree and bowed before the fuzzy horse.

But he wasn't there. He was here in the castle with me. Is in the castle here with me. How did we get here? Leon rubbed his eyes, and the fuzzy image faded. Goefrin busied himself with picking up the remnants of broken glass.

"I'm sorry, Your Majesty. I'm sorry for your loss."

Leon narrowed his eyes to focus on the advisor, but the man was more jagged edges of color than solid form. "My wife is dead," he mumbled. Goefrin handed him another cup, and Leon ground his teeth in frustration. Here he was going through normal motions like drinking while his wife, his daughter—

"My wife is dead. Margaret nearly so, and you come to tell me that Iliana is dead as well? That all of these plans to send them to safety have not only failed but have resulted in the death of most of my family? Please, tell me more about how this is my fault."

"Daddy?"

The tiny voice behind him drained him of his anger, and he spun around to face Margaret, whose frail, five-year-old body slumped in the doorway. Sleepy eyes blinked up at him in the dimness of the drawing room. "You should be asleep, poppet." And the drugs the healers have given her should have had her sleeping through two wars. *Damned healers. Can't get anything right.*

"I heard shouting. I thought—" She didn't finish her sentence. Instead she screamed. Her wide eyes darted about the small room as her scratched hands slapped the air, battling nothing.

Leon grabbed her by the shoulders and wrapped his strong arms about her shivering body. "Shhhh... It's okay, I'm here. No one can hurt you."

"Should I go get the healers?" Goefrin asked, and Leon nodded against the top of his daughter's head.

My only daughter now.

"Daddy?" Her voice was tiny. Thin and distant. When he tilted his chin down to look at her, she stared off, the whites of her eyes clearly visible.

She pointed at nothing, and he blinked hard. The lump in his throat grew, and he held her close. Whatever she had seen during the attack had scarred her. *I will find who did this, and they will die. Slowly.*

Margaret relaxed in his grasp. "I thought those men were back," she whispered.

Behind him, the healers arrived. It was the first time she'd spoken about the attack since she'd been found, a bloody, muddy mess clinging to a wandering horse in the northern woods. He held up a hand to stop the healers at the door. "What men, poppet?" A small sob escaped her lips, and he squeezed her tighter. "You're safe. They can't get you. I'm here."

Her face fell, and his heart tightened in his chest. "These men came out of the forest. Th-the guards. They went to find them. And then, then M-momma, she cried out and...and then my horse was moving, and I couldn't get out. Momma was too heavy, and I couldn't move. I tried, Daddy. I tried. But she was too heavy, too—" Sobs ripped across her frame, pierced only by little hiccups.

This time when the healers approached, he allowed it, and one of them held out a glass. "Here, make her drink this."

"I take it this concoction will work better than the last?" He held the glass up to Margaret's mouth. At first, she twisted away from the bitter smell, but he pressed it to her lips, tipping it back until she swallowed a large gulp.

He expected her to spit it out, healing tonics being vile and whatnot, but she took another swallow and another until the blueish liquid was gone. By then, her eyelids drooped, and her sobs lessened. Margaret passed quickly into a deep sleep, and King Leon passed her to her nursemaid.

"How in all the Thirteen Hells did she wake?"

"I don't know, Your Majesty. She should have slept through a siege with the drugs we gave her," said the healer.

King Leon sighed. His own muscles struggled to bear his six foot frame, and he stumbled before falling ungracefully into the chair beside him. Its wooden legs scraped across the floor, and the healer winced. Leon held his breath a moment, straining his ears for the cries of his daughter. When silence was the only reply, he released the air in his lungs and centered his sights on the healer who was trying to exit unceremoniously through the open door.

"A moment if you will, healer." The woman paused, her hand resting on the door handle. "When she wakes and is better, will she recall more about the—the attack that killed my wife?"

"Probably not. She spent two days on a wandering horse in the cold rain. We're lucky she didn't catch a chill or worse. She'll probably block out the event completely. It would be better that way. To forget."

"My wife's death."

"Yes, Your Majesty. My apologies, Your Majesty."

"You may leave."

Not that he would want her to remember this. *Poor child. Poor Catherine.* Three days since, and only now did he think on her. The loss hurt, but less than he'd expected. A miracle he didn't deserve. Their last days together weren't those of the ballads. She had hated him. King Leon paced and glanced at the door. The least he could do was grieve her loss.

He glanced at the door for a fourth time. Goefrin hadn't returned. Not that he blamed the poor man. *First he has to inform me of my wife's death, and Margaret little more than breathing, and then Iliana—* King Leon gripped the chair until his fingers were chalky white.

"Oh, Iliana, child." he cried out and was glad for the drugs the healers had given Margaret.

Alesta; Present

King Leon bolted upright, soaked bed sheets clinging to him in a mad tangle. The colors and emotions of the fifteen-year-old memory warred with the vision of the present—his bedchamber draped in darkness and silence as the castle slept.

Goosebumps spread across his damp skin, and he gasped for air. Like a hunter, his heart pounded in his chest and echoed between his ears. He lay back against the frame of his empty bed. Funny that he would dream of her death now, or maybe not. Even Margaret thought on her often with the approaching wedding.

Unable to sleep, he rose and stuck his arms through the sleeves of his robe while crossing to one of the few windows in his bedchamber: a tiny square that afforded him a view of the capital city of Alesta and beyond it to the forest in the North.

It used to be said that good tidings came from the North. Now they came from the West. He laughed aloud at the thought.

He retreated to his dresser where he fingered the letter from his sepier. The paper still smelled of sweat and leather, of *her*, and its corners bore her dirty fingerprints. He thrust a fist in the air, the grin stretching his cheeks too wide. Iliana was coming home. Leon's fingers shook as he unfolded the letter.

To His Majesty, King Leon Poncett III,

At your request, I delivered your letter. It was several days before I heard back from my contact, who told me this morning that the master has agreed to your terms.

Though he warns that should I ever set foot in Sadai again (or you for that matter), he can't be responsible for what may or may not happen. She's to meet me in Brieghton, assuming I make it out of Sadai alive.

Your Servant,

-I

The closing of the sitting room door alerted him to the presence of someone outside his bedchamber. "His Majesty is still asleep," said one of the guards.

"Not anymore," Leon muttered. He opened the door to Goefrin's hunched frame and stepped out into the sitting room. The old man tried to appear relaxed, a sleepy smile on his weathered face, but his tight grip on his walking stick gave him away. "What is it, old friend? Why such a tense visit this early in the new day?"

"Odd news reaches these ears; news that I didn't quite believe."

"Leave us," said King Leon to the guards who retreated to the outer hallway. He gestured for the advisor to continue and took a seat to a chorus of creaks and pops.

Both of us are getting old, neither of us moving with ease anymore. Goefrin was old when I became King, but now he's ancient. I have to wonder if he sleeps at all these days. Heavy bags dragged under Goefrin's green eyes, bags that took up more room than the sallow sunken cheeks did. Was it all an act?

"You look at me as if I'm dying, boy. It's just age."

King Leon forced a laugh. "You just remind me of my own mortality."

"Another coughing fit, I hear. You should rest more," Goefrin replied. "Which is why the news I've heard is so concerning."

Blood rushed to Leon's face, and he took a slow, steady breath. "Well, what news? I assume you've come to tell me."

"My connections sent word that an Amaskan agent is heading for our border."

Now they got to the point at hand. "An Amaskan?" Leon feigned ignorance.

"I am curious to know if any of this is true, Your Majesty. You swore never to have dealings with the Amaskans again after—after the death of your daughter, Iliana."

Ah. So Goefrin lies. Impossible that he doesn't know what happened to my daughter.

"Oh. I know of whom you speak. Your connections aren't as good as they used to be. Know you not who comes to our borders?" said Leon.

At his shoulder shrug, Leon continued, "Six months ago, my connections brought me word that there was one among the Amaskans that bore a striking resemblance to Princess Margaret, one who, for all that she is a killer, moved with the grace of my late wife."

Goefrin's eyes bulged. "Surely not—"

"Yes, Goefrin. The agent in question is my daughter, Princess Iliana. She's been alive all these years, hidden away and raised by the Grand Master himself."

"Impossible. Are you sure?"

Leon tilted his head and stared at the old man. "Very sure. I've no idea how, but my daughter is alive."

"Your Majesty, this is great news. How ever did you manage this information?"

The false glee in Goefrin's voice didn't reach his eyes, which widened to their whites. It was the confirmation Leon needed. "Of all the things you taught me over the years, the most important was having good contacts and sepiers."

"I'm glad I c-could help."

"Let's just say that I called in a favor, and now, the Princess is on her way home where she belongs."

"Amazing." His tone was flat like his eyes, and King Leon hid a grin behind his hand as he feigned a cough.

Goefrin poured a glass of water and offered it to the King. After a few sips, Leon said, "It's more than amazing. My contacts are scouring the Little Dozen for the truth. I mean, someone has kept her from me. And they've made you look quite the fool, too, by passing word to your own kin that my daughter was dead."

"S-so they have, Your Majesty. I will have to find out who has betrayed us all."

"My people are on it, old friend." His grimace must have been quite fierce as Goefrin jerked back. "We will find who is responsible, and they will pay. Starting with the Grand Master himself."

This time Goefrin's gasp was genuine. "Your Majesty. No one goes up against the Order of Amaska. No one. Not even the Senate. No one even knows the Grand Master's identity, let alone how to find him—"

"I do."

Goefrin's elbow bumped the pitcher of water on the table beside him. Water sloshed over the side and wet the dark blue tablecloth.

"Also, if I recall your kin found him. Remember? They arranged for Iliana to be taken to safety."

"Y-yes, Your Majesty. But that was many years ago. Those sources are long gone to me."

"But not to me. Not to a King."

Leon studied his "old friend" and watched him squirm under his gaze. "Trust me when I tell you, Goefrin, that these Amaskans will pay, and all those who work for them. Even if it takes me to the end of my days, I will make them suffer."

The Order of Amaska; 255 Agaen 21st

Bredych told her to rest. Get a few hours' shuteye before meeting him for the job's details. Not that she could sleep. Even after a night's ride through the rain, Adelei's limbs were pins and needles after the Masters' revelation.

Her body refused to relax, and Adelei spent the time alone in her room. Tiny though it was, the room was home and had been since being named a full member of the Order. Just enough room for a cot, the room made use of its vertical space. The only bookshelf was built into the cot's headboard. Several shelves lined the walls, though Adelei owned few knickknacks. A storage chest for clothes and weapons rested at the foot of the bed, and beyond that, the door itself.

One entrance and exit. No windows.

Every room in the complex was built this way. No one could pinch her between two enemies, and they'd be lucky to surprise her with the bells hanging from the door's knob. Adelei brushed her fingers over her books. She supposed they would be sent to her in Alexander. She doubted she'd be given pack mules enough to take it all.

Weapons would go with her, as would clothes. Not that she had many. Four years in Amaskan black left little need for much else. Though she supposed she would need a disguise or two. *I can't imagine entering the Kingdom of Alexander in these clothes—I'd be riddled with arrows before I'd even touched the border.*

She kicked the chest, and it rattled, the metal latch clinking against the lock. "This is ridiculous." No one affirmed or denied her statement, and she stared at the door. When Grand Master Bredych didn't stride through it, she sighed and thumbed through her books for the familiar green spine of *The Book of Ja'ahr*. Adelei flipped through pages at random. A few minutes later, she tossed the book to the foot of the bed where it lay, pages splayed like her emotions.

I don't want comfort. I don't want some holy words to reaffirm the Masters' decision. What I want is for my father to explain himself.

The flush spread over her face and arms, and she leaned back, knocking her head against the wooden frame. "Damn, that hurt." Adelei rubbed her fingers across the nape of her neck. The stubble on her scalp tickled her fingers as she massaged the smarting spot, and the door remained stubbornly closed.

Her foot tapped on the blanket and when she noticed her fingers drumming across her knees, she stood and stretched her arms over her head before bringing them down to the stone floor. Adelei balanced her weight on her arms and lifted her feet slowly until she stood in a handstand. The blood rushed to her head, and her pulse throbbed in her ears.

Blood is life. Life is blood. I am alive in all things, and in all things do I live. The words came unbidden, and when she pushed them aside, her arm wobbled. Adelei's elbow gave and as she tumbled to the ground, the bells on the door chimed.

She rolled upright on her toes to find Grand Master Bredych standing in the doorway. "You look like you've energy to burn. Let's go to the field."

His pace left her little time to do more than slam shut her door before sprinting after him. Neither spoke as they traversed the main building's hallways. Other Amaskans greeted them as they passed—a word here, a nod there—but most recognized the seriousness of their posture and allowed them quick passage toward the rear exit.

Sparring generally took place in the training hall, but if the training called for mounts, Amaskans went to the field. A hundred acres of land: some of it housed mares and their foals, but the majority of it held riding trails with a variety of obstacles. Simple jumps and lightly roughened trail for the greenest of riders lay nearest their path, though the paths would eventually lead to over a dozen trails to challenge even the hardiest of riders.

Both horsemanship and weapon work could be trained out in the field. Adelei didn't stop when they reached the path leading to a building used for scaling and acrobatics. She continued around the hoof-scuff trail that led to the stables. "Don't use Midnight," he ordered, and she veered left instead of right. "Midnight will need all his strength for the trip through the desert. Just use one of the training horses."

When she approached a sturdy mare of fifteen hands, she spoke not in Sadain but Ja'aran—the old tongue of the Order dating back tens of generations. At her word, the mare relaxed and allowed herself to be handled. Adelei rubbed the mare's neck. "Good girl."

Once saddled, Adelei met Bredych outside and followed him as he led his horse to one of the gentler courses. His hand rubbed his right knee, but when he caught her watching him, he turned his attention to the horse's reins. She hadn't thought that crossbow bolt to the joint bothered him anymore. *He got it trying to escape Alexandrian guards, damned fool. Amaskans don't cross that border.* The corners of her lips slipped down into a grimace.

"There are things you must know about this job, Adelei. I know you have questions, but let me tell you what I can first. Can you do that?"

"Yes, Master."

Bredych turned sharp flint on her and squinted. "Come now, daughter. Surely we can speak candidly." He kicked his horse into a healthy trot.

Her response was to stand up in the stirrups and release the reins, her balance held by the grip of her thigh muscles. The showy move was a risk with her muscles sore and body lacking sleep, but she held a twisted enjoyment in taking such a risk. When he uttered a single word, her horse shifted into a canter, and she wobbled. Youth held her in place until they passed a clearing, and Adelei returned to the saddle. Her thighs ached, heavy with sleep toxins. But the feeling meant she was alive.

But for how long? If she was sent to Alexander—

"I regret sending you to Alexander." He interrupted her thoughts with a whisper. "I don't do this by choice, Adelei, but necessity makes fools of us all. How much do you remember of your childhood?"

"You mean my time before the Order." He nodded, and she closed her eyes a moment. Brief snatches of memories: a forest, being cold, her mother's voice, a doll. Adelei shook her head. "Not a lot. Just brief bits and pieces really."

His hands played with the black threaded circles along the reins. "I've never kept it a secret from you, how you got here."

"You mean how *that* man—my *birth father*—" The word was poison on her lips. "—sold me into slavery to keep his kingdom from war?" Bredych shifted his weight in the saddle, and she sucked in a swift intake of air. "Is *he* why I'm going back?"

Her father didn't answer, but she'd wait him out. They passed several Amaskans on the trail as they rounded the corner. "Your father has ordered you home."

"What right does he have—he's not even my father—"

"Adelei, he knows our location, the Order—" Adelei caught her breath. "— If I don't send you home, he'll disclose it to the Boahim Senate. The entire Order would be at risk."

"King or not, he's a client, nothing more. He can't possibly know our location. Why entertain his desires?"

Master Bredych shook his bald head. "He sent...someone directly into the Order. Someone I'd not seen in a long time. When he says he knows our location, he knows." When her mount danced, she found her fingers wrapped in a death grip around the reins. She relaxed stiff fingers and stretched them until they regained a healthier pink color.

"There's another reason why I'm agreeing to this charade," said her master. "There are rumors. People believe that your fa—" she scowled, and he corrected himself, "—King Leon is adjusting his borders. It's not something the Order gets involved in, but there are some who believe he may be gearing up for another war with the Shadians. True or not, if his military is accumulating land by way of dead farmers, that would be something worth knowing."

Bredych faced her. "Go ahead. I can see the question on the tip of your tongue."

"Father, I-I understand the need to investigate this, but sending me across the border is a death sentence. Even if the King ordered me there, I'd never make it across the border. The people of Alexander would kill me before I was allowed to reach the capital city. I can't go back there, certainly not to a man who sold me. I want nothing to do with this man."

"The Order requires you to complete this job."

"Is there even a job to take? Is the Princess under attack, or is that a guise to force your hand? Did you even think of that, Father?"

His sigh was one of reflex, an action so engrained in her memories she could picture it without trying: the slump of his shoulders, one of which bore a spider-webbed scar from an arrow; the way he closed his eyes right before the exhale; and the slight tick near his mouth as he prepared his argument. His fingers held too tight to his reins until she apologized. "As far as we know, there have been attempts on her life. Possibly by Tribor. Before you ask, yes, we investigated it. And at high cost, too."

The rolling hills gave way to rockier terrain as they approached the coastline. The Harren Sea stretched out before them, a hazy blue-gray with white tipped peaks scattered here and there. Instead of turning with the trail, Adelei pulled the mare to a stop to watch the smaller waves break across the rocks up ahead.

How could she leave this? The spray filled the air with the smell of salt and seaweed.

"Every time I look across this ocean, I think of you, Father. When I first came here, I was so young. My mind was confused, like the waves. I thought the ocean was ugly. Grey and gloomy. Depressing." Adelei dismounted and gave the mare lead enough to munch on the tall grass nearby. When he stepped up beside her, she lifted a hand to his face and stared into his blue-grey eyes. "I've grown to love the grey."

Tears welled up and threatened to spill over his wrinkled lids. "I have no choice, Adelei. If I could undo this, I would."

"This is my home. My family. I'd be leaving this forever." She'd be leaving *him* forever. A lump rose in her throat then, and she inhaled deeply of the sea air to cover it.

"You're the best Amaskan I've ever trained, daughter, and I need you to be the best. Return home to your birth father. Protect the Princess from these assassination attempts. Find out what beast swims within the murk."

"I wouldn't be who I am without you." He dabbed at the corner of his eyes, which she ignored. Adelei tossed a stone into the ocean where it sank beneath the waves. "How did King Leon find out our location?"

Bredych lowered his frame to the ground, his knees popping as he crossed his legs. "I don't know."

His fingers traced patterns in the ground. He was lying. He always doodled when he was hiding something. "Father, the Boahim Senate has come after the Amaskans before. What's changed? Let them come."

"I'm too old to start a war against the Senate. We kill because Anur says we must, for Justice—not even the Senate can change that—but if we compromise the location of the Order, we put at risk not just Amaskans, but anyone who has ever hired us, anyone who has ever cried out for our help. Even the Gods themselves may not be safe."

The air cast a chill about Adelei, and she pulled her black cloak tighter about her shoulders. *How can Gods not be safe?* Something about the way his jaw pulsed kept her from asking, though she itched to do so. She gazed at the ocean and waited. Maybe time would loosen his tongue if words would not.

The tide rolled in while their horses grazed until the sun's passage and their growling stomachs reminded them that life continued. As they gathered up their mounts, Bredych said, "You wanted to know how you're going to get into the Kingdom of Alexander."

"Yes."

She saw the knife too late, its metal glinting in the setting sun. By then his hand had already moved between the distance, and the blade peeled across her jaw. Adelei didn't shout, didn't scream though she ground her teeth and clenched her fingers into fists. Grand Master Bredych held the knife before him, a piece of her skin dangling from it. Blood ran down her jaw to land, hidden on her cloak.

Her tattoo was gone.

CHAPTER FOUR

The Order of Sadai

"You can't enter Alexander as an Amaskan."

Adelei held the absorbent cloth to her jaw and glared at her master. The astringent stung as she huddled near the ledge, but that wasn't what brought tears to her eyes. *Damn him. How dare he?* She closed her eyes and breathed deep of the ocean air. The trickle of blood slowed and she tossed the rag to land a few inches from his feet, where he stared at it.

"Adelei?"

When she didn't answer, he strode toward her. Adelei wiped sweaty hands across her breeches and held one palm up. "Don't. Don't come near me."

"I had no choice," he whispered. One of the horses pawed at the ground and nickered. "If you aren't Amaskan, you can pass easily into the kingdom and do the job required of you."

"The job?" She sprang to her toes and closed the distance between them. "Is that all you care about? The job? What about me? If I'm not Amaskan, what am I?

Bredych placed a gentle hand on her shoulder. Adelei blinked back the tears, and her father wrapped his arms around her shoulders. "Even with the tattoo gone, you are still Amaskan. No one can take that from you. The Order is a way of life—you know that—and even if you leave here, you take a piece of it, of me, with you."

He misjudged her tears. *He would, selfish bastard.* "They've struck me from the histories, haven't they?"

Her father nodded. "The truth has to stand up to scrutiny. If any spies look, it has to appear that you are not Amaskan."

Adelei pulled away from his embrace and kicked a pine cone over the ledge. It tumbled down and bounced off a rock before landing in the sand. Salt water collided with it, then tossed it over the crest of a wave.

Sitting for hours before this ocean had brought calm. Focus. But now, as she watched the waves crash along the rocky shore, the ocean was the enemy. Waves upon waves of emotions that she didn't want. Didn't need.

"If I'm not Amaskan, why should I care about the Kingdom of Alexander? Why should I do this job? Or even take orders from you?"

She didn't wait for his response. Her feet left the ground, and she was astride the borrowed horse before he'd done more than blink. The mare set off at a fast gallop, and she left her father alone in the twilight.

A thick giggle rose in her chest. "My father? Which one? The one that sold me or the one that sold me out?" she shouted to no one at all. The mare beneath her shifted her gait in response, and Adelei tightened her grip on the reins.

By the time she reached her room, night had fallen and most members of the Order sat in the dining hall or relaxed in one of several entertainment rooms. She avoided all of them, hand held to her throbbing jaw.

Adelei kicked open her chest with a booted toe and snatched her travel bags from their pegs on the wall. In went clothes, travel gear, her extra daggers, and two books she wouldn't travel without. When everything she could take was packed, she tumbled into her bed, her muscles screaming for sleep. At first she fought it, determined to leave that night and flee the family that had betrayed her, but when her body sank into the wool-stuffed mattress, her eyelids drooped until she woke in the pitch black.

The candle had burned out hours ago, but she didn't relight it. Something had moved on the other side of her door. *That or I'm having some vivid dreams.* Adelei swung her feet to the floor in one move and crept forward, one step at a time. *Four. Five. Six.* She touched a hand to the door itself, but nothing moved on the other side. *Not now anyway.*

The bells on the knob didn't sound, and after another minute had passed, she returned to light the candle. When she turned its lit wick to the door, a piece of parchment lay on the floor, her master's mark upon it. With trembling hands she broke the official wax seal.

Lady Adelei,

> *You have twelve hours to vacate your room at the Order. You will be given enough food and supplies to get you to the border, and your horse has been readied.*
>
> *Tell no one of your visit and burn this.*

Signed and sealed
by the Order of Amaska
this 21ˢᵗ of Agaen.

Below the date was the signature of every master in the Order, including her own father's, and she snapped her eyes closed. Something shifted in the envelope, and her finger felt around until it rested on a tiny note tucked inside. The same handwriting that had brought her rushing home from the last job had scripted her name across the front.

Dearest Daughter,

> *You probably hate me. I hope one day you'll understand that I had no choice in this. This was not my decision alone, nor was it my idea to evict you from your home, but the council felt I saw this through the eyes of a father. They are right.*
>
> *No matter what they have done, you are Amaskan. You were Amaskan the moment you came to me and dedicated yourself to our cause. Travel safely to Alexander, my daughter, and serve Justice for the people. When you find your truth, I hope you can find it in your heart to forgive me in my weakness.*
>
> *You still are my daughter. You're the best thing that ever happened to me. Always remember that.*

Find your Way home, back to us. To me.

-B

Adelei crumpled the paper into a ball and tossed it into the empty washing basin. She dipped the candle's flame into the bowl until it lit the note, then tossed in the council's letter. Both burned as she stood, waiting. *Waiting for what? For the council to change their minds? For Master Bredych to—* The candle flickered when she tossed it into the bowl.

"Damn them all," she whispered, and she strapped her dirk to her thigh. Her throwing knives she slid into their sheaths before slipping her dagger in place at her waist. The knots of her cloak were thick to her trembling fingers as she struggled with it at her neck. Adelei slung a travel bag over each shoulder and stood in the middle of her mostly empty room.

Ashes were all that remained of her life, her home here. When she shut the door behind her, she used her foot to soften the jingling of the bells that chimed softly in the night. No one remained in the halls, marking the hour later than she thought. The kitchens stood silent while Adelei stuffed travel rations and canteens of water into her bag.

Her next stop was a room of clothing—chests and chests of shirts, skirts, breeches, and even corsets. Anything an Amaskan might need to operate anonymously. She went for generic hired sword gear and ignored the rest. If she needed upper class clothing, there would be plenty in a city like Alesta.

A dozen feet from the stables, Bredych stepped out from the shadows and into her path. "You're leaving in the cover of night?" he asked.

Adelei tried to step around him, but he grabbed her wrist as she passed. "Let me go."

"An Amaskan to the bone. Only an Amaskan would move in the shadows like this."

His words stopped her forward momentum. "I've little choice in the matter. I've been given twelve hours to leave the property, remember?"

"I do, but surely you could rest until the morning. Please." He clasped his hands together. "I know you think this horribly cruel. What can I do to help?"

"Let me go."

Ancient shoulders that had carried her as a child trembled beneath her stare, and he stepped aside. As she passed, he might have mumbled "I love you," but she couldn't be sure.

When she spun around to answer, he was already gone.

Sadain Desert; 255 Agaen 27th

Blowing sand whipped at Adelei's face and left a thin layer of dust behind in the process. Even her desert bred horse nickered in protest at the sand spinning around them in varying shades of tan. Night brought neither of them relief as she spent several hours shaking sand out of her bedrolls, her hair, and her ears as it burrowed into the tiniest of crevices.

Not even the Order's desert tents could block out the sand, so she slept with her scarf around her face. Even then, she awoke the past four mornings with a dried-out nose. Why couldn't the country be across a body of water? Or a forest? Anything had to be better than crossing the damned desert.

It would have been easier to take the simple trade route through the mountains, but too many questions would be asked. Too many people to notice the cut across her jaw and her bald head. She supposed she'd have to let her hair grow out now.

Pulling her hood closer to her face, she slowed her horse and glanced at the map through the grit. Two days at the most would put her at the border. As Adelei urged her caravan of horse and camel forward, her horse exhaled a muffled sigh. A battle steed like hers was built for rough terrain: muscles all over and a lack of fear required in battle. But his hooves struggled in the shifting sand.

Days of travel wore on the body. Though they had sworn the sandstorms were done for the season, they persisted, and Adelei was grateful for the protective gear. She leaned over the pommel and patted Midnight between the ears.

The wind picked up, and her tunic shifted, chafing the skin beneath. Each night Adelei treated her horse's skin and hers with a thickened aloe paste in hopes of staving off infection in any wind burned areas, and so far they'd made it through with only a few wounds from the grit.

"Can't have you lamed, now can we? Who knows if we'll get back home again," she whispered to Midnight. But between the scarf's thickness across her face, the ear nets Midnight wore, and the blowing wind, her words were lost, snatched from her mouth before she'd done much more than inhale. The direct sun bore down on her hooded neck, and her flesh burned beneath the white fabric.

Boredom had set in two days before, and Adelei sighed. No need to practice her Alexandrian. Now she knew why Bredych had encouraged her to keep fluent. He knew all along he'd be sending her back, back to a family she didn't even remember. Still, it passed the time.

By midday, she'd run through a variety of grammar rules and verb conjugations before dozing in the saddle, weary of the sand and thoughts of her master. She wondered if he'd burned the plaque, too. When he'd formally adopted her, she'd carved a plaque out of a piece of driftwood as long as her arm. The wood bore the shape of a sword, and she'd used hot pokers to carve the words *Motzecha Amaskan* into its flesh. *One in the Blood.*

She'd never thought he'd adopt her. King Adir of Sadai had declared it in writing while Master Bredych had declared it in blood. The flesh of his palm cut, he'd allowed the droplets of his blood and then hers to mix across the soil of the Order. He told her she was gaining more than a Way of life—she was gaining a family.

Another gust of wind scattered sand across her vision, and she blinked until the stinging of her eyes ceased. And now she'd lost another family. The hollowness in her chest ripped the air from her lungs. Tears stung the micro cuts sprinkled across her face where sand had crept around the head scarf, chafing on its journey through the wind whipped desert.

The sun almost dipped below the horizon. She'd been in the saddle longer than she'd wanted and scanned the skyline for any hills suitable for an evening campsite. Trees, a cave, a hill, somewhere protected from the wind, and yet nothing presented itself but sand and more sand.

With a weary sigh, she nudged Midnight and the camel up a sand dune. "This will have to do. Nothing else around, but at least the bank should protect us from getting buried in this sandstorm that's brewing," she said, and Midnight's ears flicked beneath their hoods.

Adelei eased herself from the saddle and stripped Midnight of the thickly woven tent. The camel could wait. Sweat clung to her brow as she drove wooden stakes deep into the desert sand with a horizontal slant. She removed several rolled up bags and scooped the warm sand inside until they were full, then she pushed their heavy bulk over the tent stakes to weigh them down. Once secured, she crawled inside the opaque tent, using the flexible bamboo rods to expand it as she moved. Soon she and Midnight would fit inside its interior.

"The wind is too wicked for you to be out in," she said to her horse as she retrieved a bowl from one of her bags on the camel. She'd left any trace of easily obtainable water behind this morning. According to the map, it would be noon tomorrow at the earliest before she reached another major source.

Water could be retrieved from the desert's small and stark plants, but certainly not enough to thoroughly water her horse. As it was, Adelei used the last of her own water canteens on Midnight, dumping all four into the bowl for him to drink. Adelei's mouth watered at the sight of it, but her thirst would have to wait as she checked Midnight's hide for any signs of wear or burns. Nothing appeared on the skin itself, but when she touched his hind flank with light hands, Midnight's skin twitched in response.

Another saddlebag held the sealed pot of aloe paste, which she coated across the irritated skin. Next Adelei retrieved several small, dried hay cubes which she broke apart and offered to Midnight. At first, he turned up his nose at such an offering, but after sniffing the bottom of the tent and finding no grass, he dug in without complaint.

The camel outside leaned close to the tent, casting shadows across it. He stepped away to the length of his tether and munched on what little brush sprouted. Animals' needs met, she dug through one pack and pulled out the treated wood cubes for her fire. Adelei grimaced at the foul odor. "At least they'll burn," she muttered before venturing out into the wind.

She leaned several hides and sticks together on the ground where she laid the firewood. Coated with flammable oils, the fire squares would burn long enough to get some food into her growling stomach.

The night before, she'd choked down dried jerky and a chunk of hardened bread before collapsing into her layer of blankets. *Tonight I need something with a bit more substance. The air's got a kick to it.*

Adelei carried Midnight's now empty water bowl toward a yellow-flowered cactus whose roots reached deep into the cool underground. She dug with the bowl until she exposed half of the plant's roots and pulled, ripping loose ten inches of root.

She trudged back to the fire pit where she warmed several roots until she could crush them and release precious water from inside. Her tongue stuck to the roof of her mouth as she watched the root. A few greens and jerky from her saddlebags and she had quite a stew cooking.

As the sun set, the temperature dropped. The hides protected her fire, but by the time the stew was done, the flames were little more than glowing embers. A crunching of twigs sounded nearby, and she flinched. Nothing smelled unusual other than her slightly burned dinner. The only creatures moving nearby were Midnight and the camel.

Slowly she stretched her muscles as she approached the tent. Her ears strained above the hiss of sand blowing, albeit lighter now that night had truly fallen. The crunch from earlier reached her again from beneath her own feet, and she peered down. Blue-green beetles the size of a fingernail scurried across the sand.

Adelei stepped inside the tent. Midnight lifted his hoof, which was smeared with the innards of a beetle. Another beetle lay crushed nearby.

"I don't see anything else out here but the three of us. Could you crunch beetles quieter next time?" she asked Midnight. After standing stock still for five minutes and having nothing jump out at her, she settled back down near the fire outside.

Despite the slightly burned taste, Adelei devoured the entire bowl. Stomach full and thoroughly exhausted from over a day in the saddle, she crawled into her sleeping roll on hands and knees and slumped down with her eyes already shut. Midnight would have to defend her from any stray beetles that might crawl into the tent.

After another day in the desert, Adelei sighed in relief at the lack of wind. Gritty sand gave way to larger swaths of grass with a few hardy trees here and there, and from her seat in the saddle, she squinted into the distance. Somewhere out there was the border.

Two tan towers rose up from the sand about a half mile apart, and several guard stations sprinkled the distance between the two. They could see her by now, or at least the trail of dust she was kicking up. Her hand shadowed her eyes from the sun's brightness.

There was no need to spur Midnight into a faster pace as he kicked up his step with a small hop. *I wonder if he can smell the food and rest from here.* The wry grin cracked her chapped lips, and she rubbed them beneath her hood. She laughed in spite of it, if for no reason but to hear a sound other than the hiss of sand.

Her humor was short-lived as she eyed the border, drawing closer with each of Midnight's steps. Before, traveling alone bothered her little. She always had known she'd travel home. But now—now she was never going home.

Adelei's stomach rolled, and her hands clenched the reins. Midnight slowed and bounced in place a moment or two before neighing his concern. She inhaled as deeply as she dared in the sandy air and forced her muscles to relax.

She could turn back, leave now and just travel...somewhere. Anywhere. She'd be an outcast, but at least she wouldn't be crossing into enemy territory, into a death trap. At least she'd be alive.

Midnight sensed her hesitation and turned, which Adelei corrected with a tightened thigh. *No, I'm stronger than this. King Leon may be the man who sold me over land rights, but he's not my father. My father is Amaskan.*

And he betrayed me, too.

She spurred Midnight forward at a gallop, the ground sturdy enough for the increased speed. Another hour of ignoring her introspective worry, and the border loomed before her. A stone wall ran along both sides of the towers as far as she could see, with well-armed guards at each gate. Simple math had her impressed as she counted the troops along the walls.

They looked ready for war.

It wasn't every kingdom that could afford that many garrisoned outside the tower itself, let alone however many were inside the walls. At least not the countries she was used to visiting. It was what made slipping in and out so easy for the Order.

Except for Alexander. As long as she'd been alive, that kingdom had been off limits. Outlawed even. Maybe the Order reminded dear King Leon of some sin or other too much. *Don't know and don't care. I just want to get this job done and get back to normal.*

The guards allowed her to approach unhindered. Even with the scarf around her head and white clothes disguising her, they followed her movements closely. She slowed Midnight to a stop just before the gate but did not dismount. Instead Adelei allowed them to approach.

A young man stumbled his way toward her, beads of sweat popping up across his brow as he took in her massive horse. Midnight remained still, yet the sergeant stopped a good ten feet from her. His face betrayed his youth, and she reexamined her impression of the Alexandrian guard. Even if a full garrison was housed at each tower, if they were all this green, that wasn't a great sign.

Luckily for him, the young man kept himself in full view at all times. "Master Adelei, you are expected. If you'd lead your horse through those gates on the left, there's a stable where you can take care of his needs and leave him while you rest. Lieutenant Thomas will be with you shortly." With a nod of thanks, Adelei led Midnight through the gate and across the border into the Kingdom of Alexander.

Crossing over didn't magically change the appearance of the land around her, but her muscles tensed in response to her unease. A group of people stood on the other side of the gate, and their mannerisms and postures changed upon sight of her. One person in particular, whose uniform held much more embellishment than the others, glared at her, and she studied the various insignias stitched into the rugged blue cloth.

Must be our Lieutenant Thomas.

For him, she dismounted, doing so slowly and deliberately to give them all a full view of her weapons and relaxed posture. No one offered to take her horse. *Good—with me this tense, Midnight would rip the hand off anyone who approached me in this state.*

A nearby soldier pointed a shaking hand toward the stable to her left, which was enclosed on all sides with grey stone instead of the sandstone she was used to seeing. A whistle escaped her mouth and behind her, the well-decorated man said, "Impressive, isn't it?"

"So much stone."

"Have to keep the sand out or it will rub our mounts bare. Wood would only wear away."

"Why not sandstone?" she asked. A small turn of her head showed that he followed her at an acceptable distance while he watched Midnight.

"This is Alexander, Master Adelei. We have no intention of resembling your home country."

"Lieutenant Thomas, is it?" He nodded, and she continued, "There's no need for the title. I am no Master."

He tapped a finger against his thin lips. "Our orders from the King stated that a Master Adelei of Amaskan would be traveling from Sadai to Alesta. Are you not her?"

"I-I am. I hadn't expected your king's acknowledgement of my status. I'll have to thank him upon my arrival." He didn't catch the sarcasm in her voice, or if he did, he hid it well. She rubbed her finger across the puffy scar forming at her jawline.

She was no Master. She never would be. She wasn't even Amaskan anymore.

He followed her into the building, which was divided into small stalls, and by the smells and sounds, she noted cows and goats in addition to the horses. She led Midnight into the empty stall and removed her gear, starting first with the saddlebags. Her escort shifted from side to side as he waited, and when Midnight drank thirstily of the provided water, he cleared his throat in reminder.

"Now that Midnight's been cared for, I suppose formal introductions are in order. Adelei," she said, and when she extended a hand in greeting, he ignored it.

"Lieutenant Thomas," he said, and Adelei passed through the stall's gate. "I'm in charge of the garrison at this stop of the border. I'm to provide you any supplies you may need for your trip to the capital city of Alesta, along with your escort."

"I appreciate the supplies. Desert is brutal this time of year." He turned, expecting her to follow him, but she rifled through one of the saddlebags until she found the small jar of aloe.

His thinning hair betrayed the sweat underneath as he ran well-groomed hands through the black and gray strands of what hair remained. Wonderful Gods—a newly promoted lieutenant. She didn't let it bother her that he feared her; that reaction came with the job, but his lack of experience made her question the military strength of Alexander.

Their troops wouldn't know the first thing about protection detail if the Tribor were involved. Adelei rubbed salve across the few sore spots on Midnight's skin while she kept a watchful eye on the Lieutenant.

He'd returned, along with his scowl. "Is this...necessary? We have stablehands who could treat your horse."

She schooled her face to a complete mask of neutrality; ten years of training had cured her of giving away more than she wanted, and yet today she found herself at odds with her training. Vulnerable. Exposed. That's how this country made her feel— either that or she was more tired than she suspected.

Master Bredych's voice whispered in her ear—*vulnerability leads to death*—and she clenched her teeth as she rubbed the aloe into another sore spot. Midnight shifted his weight and harrumphed, much to the Lieutenant's dismay.

Adelei dove into the task before her, and the massage coupled with the salve's relaxing odor let her own body relax. Once it was obvious that she had no intention of leaving until her horse was taken care of, Lieutenant Thomas blathered on at length about the kingdom, the capital city, and anything at all. His own nervousness kept him blissfully unaware of hers as he babbled. She pulled out of her partial trance when he mentioned the princess, Margaret Poncett.

Let's see what the greenie will tell me. She asked in Alexandrian, "What can you tell me about her?"

He opened his mouth and closed it quickly. Thomas schooled his own features, mostly failing though she applauded the attempt. "Princess Margaret is marrying Prince Gamun of Shad, as was arranged in the peace treaty signed at the end of the Little War of Three. More than that, I wouldn't know—being so far out here at the border."

"Among my people, travel is encouraged," she said as she took a brush to Midnight. "You've been stationed here at the border, as you said. Have your people not seen a Sadain citizen before?"

His hands tensed along the stall's gate. "We have, Master Adelei. What gives you the impression that we have not?"

Adelei faced him. "Since the moment I set foot in this garrison, you and everyone stationed here have been nervous, if not borderline rude. I have to wonder why that is? Surely your orders from His Majesty stressed the importance of my visit."

"My apologies, Master. My soldiers...well, they think you're Amaskan, and honestly, I understand their assumption." His eyes stopped on the corner of her jaw just below her ear and then continued on to her bald head, which peeked out beneath her scarf.

"I assure you that I am not, despite my appearances. There are sects in Sadai, holy orders that share the belief of removing hair from the body, the vessel, in order to remain closer to the Gods."

"And the scratch?"

"I cut myself shaving." For a moment, she worried he might push the issue, but after a heartbeat, he nodded ever so slowly. "I appreciate your concern for the safety of your people, I do. It's the sign of a good, strong commander. I think perhaps I would like to find somewhere to rest, if I might."

"Certainly."

She followed him from the stables where soldiers busied themselves at their tasks as if not a one of them had been eavesdropping on the conversation between their lieutenant and the supposed killer in their midst.

A tavern easily ten times her own in height stood nearby. Another stable, what looked to be barracks by the number of people entering and leaving, and several smaller buildings stood to her right. To the left, a rectangular stone structure that smelled of a dinner hall set her stomach rumbling.

A young woman exited, her hands full with a plate of food. When she caught sight of Adelei and the lieutenant, the woman stumbled back a few steps, and the tray tumbled from her fingers. Adelei sighed at the reaction, but followed as the Lieutenant led her toward the smallest of three buildings. The door slid open to her guest quarters, complete with a private bathing area.

These were quarters reserved for dignitaries for sure. People with more money than her. A few rugs and paintings decorated the larger living area, which gave the place a roomier feel than the garrison's exterior. On the occasion that she could afford to stay at an inn, she'd enjoyed the ability to bathe regularly without the need of a creek or lake but always in a common bath house. Never in private. *Not like this.*

Being dirty was dangerous as sweat grew into smells that even the stuffiest of noses could detect. Despite this, not even the Order had the wealth or the room to give every member a private bath. Alexander must have been rich indeed to afford guest rooms this elaborate at the border.

"Just about everything you need should be here. If you should get hungry, the larger building north of here is the dining hall. If you need anything else, all you need to do is ask Sergeant Fenton. He'll be just outside your room—for your protection."

So she was to be guarded. *Good.* For all they knew, she was a ruthless killer. To the lieutenant, she nodded her thanks. He took his leave, and with sore feet she scampered to the bathing chamber where she found water pipes, a small metal tub, and plenty of lye. Lye soap wasn't the most comfortable way to bathe, but the small metal tub was a vast improvement over no bath at all. One turn of the knob and hot water poured from the pipes to fill the tub.

Using her own bristled brush, she scrubbed her skin near raw and removed a week's worth of dust and grime. Only after she'd repeated the scrub three times over, did her body feel clean. Adelei left the mud-colored water behind. Without a thought for anything else, she crawled, eyes drooping and stomach forgotten, into the available bed and was asleep before midnight for the first time in a week.

CHAPTER FIVE

Brieghton Border Garrison; 255 Cercian 2nd

Adelei woke, muscles stiff and blankets twisted around her legs and feet from a night of dreaming. Something about fleeing on horseback, only she had been thrown over the saddle. The same old dream. The muddled memory puzzled her, and she pushed it aside. When she stood, her thigh cramped, and she stretched up on tiptoes to release the strain.

Last evening, she'd lacked the time and energy to examine the room, but now that the sun shone through the single window, she found it less impressive than the day before. Sleep gave her fresh eyes that noticed the hole in the colorful rug and the burn mark on the window covering.

With sunrise, heat enveloped the room like a roaring fireplace. Adelei chose another tunic and breeches of thin, white silk to wear and winced at the sight of it. White. Why did it have to be white? It was too easy to stain and made her a moving target. Her fingers lingered on the black clothing in her travel bag.

She pulled the tunic over her head and tucked the ends into the waist of her breeches. A cloth belt wrapped around her waist, and two more around the sleeves of her tunic. Adelei kicked at the air, testing the tight fabric's movement. Not as flexible as the Order's gear, but it would have to do.

Her black riding boots marred the outfit's appearance, but she didn't have the room in her travel bags for color coordination. Outside her door was the promised guard, awake and alert. He twitched when he saw her, but Adelei ignored him as she stepped foot outside. She stifled a laugh when he scrambled to catch up to her.

"Is there something you need?" he asked. He leapt in front of her, his boot kicking hers. "Food," she answered, sidestepping him to continue on her path. He accepted her comment for the moment and trotted along behind her. Like a giant puppy. A giant, annoying puppy. She grimaced as he tripped over a rock in the path. It was necessary, but there was nothing she hated more than being babysat.

The dining hall itself was larger on the inside than it looked and filled with dozens of benches and tables, each squeezed close together to maximize the available space. The sun having risen hours before, the dining hall lay mostly empty.

Adelei was used to small spaces, but she didn't relish the idea of being packed in among so many who hated or feared her and was thankful most were already gone. She'd have to get used to it if she would be in the capital city for this job, especially if she were dining with the royal family.

She would rather move around unnoticed, but that would be difficult in such crowds. Still, it wouldn't be the first time. A few people lounged, plates mostly empty as they chatted while savoring what few crumbs remained.

A table as long as the wall lay in front of her. No servers stood near the table, not that she'd expected any. Most garrisons were of the self-serve variety. Closer inspection showed typical military grade food—good tasting only if one didn't pay serious attention to what one was eating. And safe enough not to give a soldier the trots.

Her stomach rumbled audibly, and she picked a few pieces of rabbit out at random before adding some dried fruit and bread to her plate. It would all taste the damned same anyhow. Her mouth watered just the same. While not picky on the food, she did choose her seat carefully—far enough away from those who remained to be left alone, yet close enough to invite conversation if one were so inclined.

Their conversation ceased as she took her seat, and two left the dining hall before her backside hit the wooden stool beneath her. Of the two remaining, the woman flicked a crumb across the table. Her history and familiarity with combat was written across her body by way of scars and old wounds, while the man seemed as green as the rest of the soldiers she'd seen.

After a moment, he, too, found reason to flee the hall, leaving the two women alone. The Alexandrian was old enough to be Adelei's mother, and her hair held more grey than black. *Amazing that she's survived this long. Don't see many her age still in this line of work.*

Adelei tore off a hunk of bread. The silence was now covered by the sounds of chewing and interrupted only by the occasional clank of a cutting knife. When the sound ceased, a shadow moved across the floor and then across her food. Without looking up, she nodded at the table. "Have a seat," she said between bites.

Several minutes passed before a choked, bitter voice broke the silence. "So you're a member of the Order."

It was a statement rather than a question. "No," she said, and at the woman's raised brow, she added, "Former." *I don't know why I'm being honest with her—maybe because she's not running away scared.*

"Former? No such thing. Like a guard. Once a guard, always a guard."

Adelei waited for the warrior to continue and chewed a hunk of rabbit with the purposeful slowness of a slug. The warrior wore the same standard blue tunic and pants as the men in the garrison and the same leather mail over the top, but the insignia at her collarbone was unlike any Adelei knew from her studies. The two horizontal circles overlapped to create a sideways eight. *Some kind of dignitary? Special service to the King maybe?*

The words interrupted Adelei's thoughts and were achingly slow, as if the act of speech caused the warrior pain. "Killed a lot of people in my time."

Adelei leaned closer to her meal, and thus closer to the warrior woman. A thin scar ran horizontally across the warrior's throat, from ear to ear. How she had survived a wound like that, only the Gods knew.

"Never seen an assassin as young as you. The name's Ida. Captain Ida Warhammer, Sepier to the King." Strong fingers stretched out to shake Adelei's own, the first genuine greeting she'd received.

Sepier? Nothing popped in her Alexandrian vocabulary or Sadain. "Ili—Adelei of Sadai." The moment the beginning of the name spilled out, she cursed under her breath. It'd slipped out of her mouth like it was natural to call herself such. *Damned country.* One day inside the border, and she was already making every rookie mistake she had made at twelve.

Ida rose to fetch herself another drink, and Adelei suppressed a whistle. The woman was tall enough to stare at the top of Master Bredych's bald head, and he was quite imposing with his six-foot lithe frame. When Ida returned, she claimed a seat much closer to Adelei with a thump. "How'd ya get into the Order so young? Kill someone in the cradle?" Ida let loose a hearty laugh and sloshed her watered down ale when she slapped the table.

"Not quite. I was raised by a member of the Order."

Ida nodded. "Ah, that explains it. Makes sense, I say. Get 'em young and train 'em is the best way to ensure they're good at their job, eh? Unlike here, where I'm surrounded by the greenest grass."

It was Adelei's turn to laugh. "What's the story with that? I'd figure a kingdom like Alexander would've secured better troops in the years since the war."

"Know about that, do ya?" Ida took a sip of her drink, her fingers subconsciously rubbing her throat.

"If you don't mind my asking, what's the story behind that old wound?"

The veteran's eyes grew moist, something contrary to her rugged exterior. "How much do ya know about the Little War of Three, youngin'?"

"Just the basics. The Kingdom of Shad wished to renegotiate borders with Alexander. King Leon of Alexander refused, and Shad set out to engulf the land and claim it by force. The war lasted three years, nearly destroying both countries in the process, until the Boahim Senate forced a peace treaty upon both lands. At the cost of Princess Margaret's hand in marriage, I assume."

The last sentence left a sour taste in Adelei's mouth. Any father who'd sell out his daughter like that deserved to be king of nothing. At least Master Bredych was honest in his killing. *My father*—she frowned at the words—*kills through treaties, slavery, and human sales.*

Ida laughed again and slapped a hand on the wooden table. "Good. I'm glad ya know what you're getting into then. Playin' this body double's going to be tricky work."

Adelei stared at the woman. The soldiers would be told she was heading for the capital. It was a matter of security for them to know, and all in all, not a huge surprise. But to know the details of the job was different.

She stood, her feet halfway to the door before she registered the bulk of Ida's square shoulders blocking her path. Not many people could move with the speed and silence of an Amaskan. That Ida had done just that and had done so without Adelei's knowledge was not only impressive, it was dangerous. "Let me pass," Adelei hissed.

"I can't do that. We need to talk." Ida braced her arms against the door frame's sides.

She's expecting a fight and rightfully so after this little incident. How could the Order send me into such a trap? She charged—not at the woman but the window, hoping to escape the building without harming anyone.

As she reached the window, something hit Adelei in the back of the head. Before she blacked out, Ida faintly mumbled, "Damn, didn't mean to hit ya that hard."

The dirt floor confused her, though the room itself reminded Adelei of her old room at the Order. Touching her head with shaking fingers left her muttering curses as her hand came away from the knot bloody. She winced and flexed her muscles slowly. Nothing else hurt, nothing else complained.

"Gonna kill whoever did this," she muttered, and a chuckle reached her. She leapt to her feet, and the world tilted in a blend of color. Sharp pain in her skull sent her back to the bed.

"You're not the first one to wish me dead, though I do wish you'd waited for me to finish what I'd been sayin' before trying to bolt. I'm sorry I hit ya so hard, but ya left me little choice."

Now I remember. The warrior woman. I'm in Brieghton. Adelei leaned her head gently against the pillow behind her, but the contact sent dizzying waves through her.

"You could've let me go. What gives you the right to hold me?" Adelei snarled. *This job's getting off to a great start.*

Ida approached—she didn't tiptoe or mince her steps, which would have raised suspicion. Her boots tromped along the dirt floor with a slight scuffle. Adelei opened a bleary eye to glare at the woman. Her vision swam, and she blinked several times in the dim light.

"Relax, child. If I'd wanted ya dead, I would've killed ya while you were out." The woman pulled up a chair and fumbled with several items on the table beside the bed. The "torture instruments" Ida held weren't the expected but instead were crushed herbs floating in bowl of water and a rag.

The warrior's hands weren't gentle as she cleaned the knot on Adelei's head; jagged fingernails occasionally scraped across her scalp, and the herbs stung. She sent a brief prayer to Sharmus, God of healing. Whether it was the herbs or Sharmus himself, the pain subsided from a rampaging bear to a dull throb in a few minutes.

"Now," said Ida as she wrapped Adelei's head in a worn cloth, "Before we had the hammer to the head, I was sayin' that I'm here to escort ya to the King. My job's to fill ya in on the details as we travel, provided you don't flee to the hills."

Ida didn't have to give the look, though she did, and a flush crept across Adelei's face, warming her cheeks and neck. Not only had she allowed herself to be trapped, but she hadn't gotten the lay of the land before tumbling into said trap. Master Bredych would have had her hide if he had known.

She composed a mask of neutrality and merely shrugged. "You could've said as much when you introduced yourself rather than baiting me and leaving me to think I was being cowed into a corner. Hard to break the habits of...mine. You're lucky you survived the attempt."

"If I'd have known you'd be so easily trapped, I wouldn't've bothered. I was, after all, expectin' an Amaskan, and not some green trainee."

Ida rinsed the rag in the basin, her back to Adelei. She couldn't tell if it was bravery, stupidity, or just the knowledge that she wasn't a threat. *Dammit.* It was the crux of it. She was no threat to anyone. She wasn't even Amaskan. The warrior left the room, and the sound of running water reached Adelei's ears. She was like a female version of Master Bredych with a harsher bark.

Ida reappeared in the doorway with a pitcher of ale and two glasses, one of which she offered to Adelei.

"I'm not," said Adelei.

"Not what?"

"Amaskan. Not anymore."

"So ya said before." Ida's finger touched the healing scar at Adelei's jaw. "Good, clean cut."

The Captain nodded at the cup in Adelei's hands, and Adelei swallowed the watered down liquid in several long draws. The second glass went down slower, and her taut muscles relaxed. "There, now that you're more balanced, we can have a proper chat," said the woman.

Adelei ground her teeth, and Ida's barking laugh could have split her skull in two. *Dammit, what's wrong with me?* It were as if every meditation she had ever learned had abandoned her, leaving a knot of tension and doubt in their place. She closed her eyes and pictured the blue sphere in her mind.

Smooth. No flaws. Like an empty vessel, it fills me. Instead of silence and calm, Ida's continued laughter echoed in her ears, and Adelei shook her head.

A mistake. Pain from the wound lanced her slow breathing, and she gave up. "How do you know so much about the Order? You're reading me too well, which points to good training. Better training than I like."

Ida settled down in her chair and poured herself another glass. "It's a long story, young one. Starts back durin' the Little War of Three, when I'd just been promoted to captain of the royal guard. Back when I was much younger and a lot less wise."

The word popped into Adelei's head, and she blurted out, "What's a *sepier*?"

"To put it bluntly, I'm a spy. I do odd tasks for the royal family—whatever's needed of me."

"Is the word Alexandrian?"

"No."

Adelei bit the inside of her cheek. *A spy, huh? Makes sense that my escort is in service to the King. She's certainly old enough to have battled in the Little War of Three. But that doesn't explain her knowledge of the Order. She could be a threat.*

"Seein's how your head's probably throbbin', I'll give ya the condensed version if ya don't mind." When Adelei nodded, the warrior continued. "The King and his late wife had no male heir—just two twin girls. His Majesty sent them away to protect them, but it wasn't enough. We were losin' the war when news came of the Queen's death. Assassins from Shad. Probably Tribor."

The warrior brought two fingers to the top of her brow and closed her eyes for a minute. *That's a sign to ward off evil, to keep Itova at bay. Lots of people know it—but only those in Sadai who follow Anur's chosen path.* Ida's hand caressed the hilt of her sword as an afterthought. *Still, she was a warrior. Amaskans weren't the only ones to follow that particular path. It warranted watching.*

Despite the drink, Adelei's parched tongue sat in too dry a mouth, and she swallowed hard as the woman continued. "The poor princess under her own mother's body for three days, trapped under a rottin' corpse."

Ida shuddered and refilled both their glasses. "Even worse was the news that the other princess died tryin' to reach safety. The king had no choice but to agree to the terms of the peace treaty if he wanted his survivin' daughter to live."

Adelei lifted her chin and said, "He sold her for a peace treaty."

"Ya don't understand. He'd only the one choice: his child's hand in marriage or the death of the entire royal family. The death of them all. Right down to the serving staff. Our country would've died, leaving an empty shell full of corpses. What would ya have done?"

"I would have fought, and if I'd gone down fighting, at least I would have known it was a good death."

"There's no such thing as a *good* death." Ida cast haunted eyes about the room.

With three years' service, Adelei's own ghosts haunted her. Ghosts she tried to ignore. At least she was serving justice, saving lives. The sharp bitterness spilled across her tongue, and the words tumbled out before she could capture them. "How convenient that his other daughter died. Left Princess Margaret quite the nice package—marriage to a prince, treaties with their sworn enemies. What more could one ask for?"

Ida's mouth hung open. "Convenient? Is that what those bastards at the Order told ya? He mourned her. He mourns her still." The warrior slammed her fist on the table beside the bed. The bowl and pitcher clattered together. "One could hardly call marriage to a sworn enemy a 'nice package.' Use your brain, child."

"Fine, fine." Adelei waved a hand in the captain's direction. "We'll save the philosophical debates for another day. Could you at least tell me where in the Thirteen Hells I am? I assume we're still in Brieghton?"

"We're in my guest quarters. I thought it best to bring ya here."

Adelei's head throbbed. *What a job.* She got to play bodyguard to a spoiled princess, probably without one thought between her ears. And her escort was convinced dear old "dad" had done the best he could. *Like hell he did.*

If she focused hard enough, she could almost remember him. The fuzzy face that appeared in odd dreams. But thinking on it brought the rest of the visions: herself on horseback, thrown over the saddle at times as the rain poured overhead; crashing thunder and the endless shivering in the cold; and several figures in black, one of which glared at her from beneath his hood. The faces faded over time, and their voices ran together like wine.

There was a woman. She remembered that. The itch reached out, and then it was gone.

"Ya look far away," Ida whispered.

"I was...remembering the past. Being here, it's odd. I'm not myself, and the pictures in my head clash together. Makes my head hurt." Adelei shot Ida a hard smile. "Old dreams can haunt a person."

"Dreams are but visions of truth and place holders of what our mind calls justice."

Adelei held her breath a moment. "How do you know the *Book of Ja'ahr*?"

"Is that what it's from? I've wondered." Ida stood and gathered up the empty pitcher and bowl from the table. When she left the room, Adelei tried to sit up. The room no longer spun in wild circles, but her headache increased. Just as Adelei swung her feet over the edge of the bed, Ida returned.

"Just where do ya think you're goin'?"

"I need to empty my bladder if that's all right with you."

Ida retrieved a chamber pot from beneath the table. "Here."

"I'll wait." The woman shrugged and returned to her seat next to Adelei. She had no intention of being there long enough to need it. Adelei lay back against the pillow and sighed. "I would appreciate help getting back to my own rooms."

"It would be safer for you to remain here."

"Safer? Am I in danger?"

"Ya have to ask?"

"Yes, I do. I—I thought I'd walked into a job I've been trained for, and yet here I am in a country whose army looks wholly unprepared for what everyone tells me is coming. I'm being escorted by someone who quotes from the Order and isn't Amaskan. I'm not sure of anything at this point." Adelei's stomach chose that moment to growl audibly, reminding her that she had no clue what time it was. "How long was I out?"

"Approaching midday. I'll admit, you've walked into a nasty situation, that's for sure. I'd hoped to be on the road today, but it looks like we'll have to wait for the morrow. In the meantime, I'll grab us some lunch."

The woman crossed the room again and ducked through the arch. The sounds of her talking with a guard drifted to Adelei. There was a guard there as well. *Great.* She'd have to leave through the window.

Ida returned quickly and smirked when Adelei remained in the bed. "Glad to see you restin'. You've got quite the concussion there. Dangerous to go about with that. At least today. And since ya need to be awake for a while still, I'll do my best to tell ya what I can."

Adelei sat up in the bed. Information from a spy could be useful indeed.

"At the time of the war, His Majesty, King Leon, worried that the peace treaty was a trap. In the event the castle should fall and his family be taken prisoner or killed, he needed to know that at least one of the royal family would survive."

At least he was smart enough to know a trap when he saw one. To the warrior, she said, "Makes sense. If a battle's coming, family is in the way if you're lucky and a casualty if you're not."

"That's a fairly callous outlook," Ida said, surprising Adelei. "Warrior and veteran I am, but blood is important. Family makes us who we are, would ya not agree?"

"Family does have a hand in shaping us, yes, but when it comes to the job, everyone is expendable."

"Even family?"

"Especially family."

Ida didn't laugh. Instead she buried her nose in her mug as if communing with it. "I can see why you're the best," she whispered. "To be so hardened so young though."

The quiet settled between them. Like the sea back home. Calm until a good squall whipped it into a fury of choppy waves and tides. Ida would never understand the necessity of Adelei's words. Soldier and warrior Ida might be, but she was no Amaskan. *She can never understand what it means to follow our code or to sacrifice everything for justice.*

As if she heard Adelei's thoughts, Ida spoke again, "Ya think I don't understand the path ya walk, but I say ya don't either. Ya don't know what you've walked into, nor where it'll take ya. The King believed he was doin' the best to protect his family. It was a tough decision and one ya could learn from."

Adelei itched to add that the bastard then sold his daughters, each to their own prisons, but she held her tongue. Her jaw popped with a yawn that near split her head in half.

"Your horse's being well-looked after, and your belongin's have been moved here at my order. I think ya could safely get some rest now, if ya like." Ida plopped a stool in front of her chair and stretched out with her feet propped up. The warrior pulled a book off the table. Whether she read it or not, Adelei couldn't tell. The woman's eyes didn't move much, but she turned the pages at steady intervals.

Looks like she doesn't trust me to stay put. Adelei stifled another yawn. *Dammit, I got plenty of sleep last night. Damned head wounds.*

She tried closing her eyes, but behind them her mind raced. The King was told Adelei was dead, but that was a lie. Maybe he had told people that. Guilty conscience and all. Besides, what would this Ida know? Sepier or not, she was hardly the King's ear.

While the thoughts plagued her, the wound on her scalp pounded. Like hoof beats on that dark night.

CHAPTER SIX

Brieghton Border Garrison; 255 Cercian 3ʳᵈ

No matter how tolerable sleep had made the concussion, there were some things sleep couldn't fix. Her temper for one. Especially if Ida didn't stop staring at her.

The warrior woman sat on a stool, her legs crossed and propped up as she waited for Adelei to finish breakfast. When Adelei had entered the small living area of the guest house, Ida's plate had already been empty, as well as her ale mug—though she showed little sign of drinking to excess. Adelei's own plate held a mix of bread, fruits, and a few dried pieces of meat.

She straddled the small bench and grabbed for the hunk of bread, which she wrapped around the dried meat. Even then, her mouth twisted in disgust at the taste. Ten days of tough, dried-out jerky had left her wishing for time to hunt a proper meal. As she chewed, Ida Warhammer stared.

Adelei chased down the old venison with a bite of a juicy pompaello fruit whose seeds she spit onto her plate. The fist-sized, green fruit didn't last long, and she licked her fingers clean. Still Ida stared.

As she tore off another hunk of bread, she ignored Ida's furrowed brow, but the fifth frown stopped her mid-bite. "Is there something about me that you find displeasing?"

A flush spread across Ida's face. "You're all Amaskan, all right."

"I already told you—former Amaskan. Besides, what's that got to do with anything?"

"I can't help but wonder if you're capable of playin' body double to Her Highness. Your manners leave a lot to be desired."

This time when Adelei grabbed a piece of fruit, she let the juice run down her fingers to her wrist as she squeezed it. "This is excellent fruit," she said, and she slurped loudly as she cleaned up the juice by way of her tongue. Ida sighed but didn't comment further.

"I'm trained well enough to know how to act when need calls for it. Right now, I need to eat breakfast so we can get on the road already, a task that would go much faster without you staring at me as if you're waiting for me to wipe my arse on the table."

The warrior's chuckle was half growl, and she massaged her throat. "Point taken."

When Adelei had woken up that morning, her jaw had still ached from the knowledge that she'd fallen asleep and missed her opportunity to flee her escort, but once she'd seen the abundance of food, she'd decided to stick around. Besides, she wasn't sure she could get into Alesta on her own without being accosted.

"What did the Order tell ya about Her Highness?" asked Ida.

"Mostly idle gossip from the few towns I crossed through on the way here. She's flighty and fanciful and possesses a cow's brains. Pretty enough on the eyes but nothing betwixt them. Completely in love with life but never having experienced it." Adelei aimed for a bored monotone but failed, the last of her words spoken with more bite than she'd anticipated.

"And I take it ya don't approve?"

Adelei shrugged. "Who am I to tell a princess how to live? If she wishes to choose stupidity over intellect, so be it. It's no skin off my back."

"But it is," said Ida, who leaned across the table. Her rancid breath tickled Adelei's nose. "If you're to guard her, how she lives *is* your concern and could mean 'the skin off your back' as ya put it."

Her ears burned, but Adelei merely shrugged. Most people didn't live long enough to intrude on the personal space of an Amaskan. Most people didn't even try. Her gut told her to pin the warrior to the stone floor and find out her angle. Something was afoot. Patience would gain her better access, even if she did want to add another scar-line across Ida's throat.

"If you're to guard the Princess, to serve as a body double, you'll need to act like a princess. So far, what I've seen is a youngling with too short a temper. Does Master Bredych no longer teach meditation?"

When Adelei stood, her chair fell and landed with a loud crack on the floor behind her. "How do you know that name?"" she whispered, fruit forgotten.

"*Augh*, we don't have time to get into this. We've delayed too long already." Ida dropped several bags at Adelei's feet. "Grab your things—we need ta go."

"We will make time. Now." The words were a command, sharp as the knives Adelei carried.

"Not now. Not here."

Adelei hesitated. Ida knew too many things she shouldn't. She was more than she let on. A danger to the Order. If Master Bredych had been here, he'd have killed Ida. Adelei retrieved her bags but kept her gaze on the woman in front of her. If Adelei returned to the Order, she'd be an outcast. Ostracized for dishonoring them and worse, labeled an oathbreaker. She might have been stricken from the records, but at least she wasn't marring them.

As she closed the door behind her, she paused a moment. "I will go with you, Sepier Warhammer, because this job has been given to me, but you will explain yourself once we reach the privacy of the road. If I feel you've been dishonest with me or have endangered my mission, you'll find out how dangerous the Amaskans are, as I will kill you where you stand without hesitation or mercy. For the good of the people."

The warrior smiled then, a half-smile that came with knowledge and a sense of power. "I would expect nothing less of a...former Amaskan."

Ida mounted her horse: a large, dappled grey and black beast that stood a full two hands taller than Midnight. *No way she could get a horse of that breed, much less handle mine, without access to the Order. She wears no tattoo that I can see, but somehow she's had Amaskan training.*

While Sadai's main export was horses, the kingdom's specialty was trained war horses. Expensive and smart, the beasts were well-built for combat and easily trainable. Mounts were taught simple commands like *enemy* and *guard,* making them invaluable to anyone in the battlefield. *I'd never be able to afford one— lucky for me that Midnight was a gift from King Adir. Even on a captain's pay, she'd not be able to afford such a mount. Just how close is she to this King Leon? A relative perhaps?*

More questions than answers set a worry knot between Adelei's shoulders, adding to the throb at the base of her skull where her head wound lay. No pack beasts, just the two horses stood outside the building. Forest lay between here and Alesta, capital city of Alexander. Plenty of small towns between, and thankfully, no desert.

Ida spun her horse around to face Adelei as she tied her saddlebags in place. "I'll answer, but only because His Majesty's ordered me to do so. Ya don't intimidate me, and ya aren't the first Amaskan I've encountered." And with those words, Ida's grey mare trotted off toward the eastern road and left Adelei hustling to catch up.

And you're not the first pompous captain I've dealt with either. I've coped with women like you before—known a few in the Order in fact. It wouldn't surprise me if you've tried to gain membership to the Order and failed out or quit. I wonder which it is?

Adelei urged Midnight into a canter. She was in no particular hurry to catch up to the woman. She reminded Adelei of Min—what a bully she was. Adelei smiled at the memory, her mind falling into it with the steady lull of hoof falls.

One brutal day found Adelei skipping her way out of the stables after a riding lesson, her mind still buzzing with the joy of it. She'd been allowed to jump her horse in the Field. Not the training course, but the honest-to-Gods challenge jumps.

Snow on the ground left parts of the path slick, so she'd chosen her jumps carefully. Given the rare compliment by her teacher, the words rang in her ears as she skipped toward the bridge and tossed up snow with a booted toe. It wasn't until she'd crossed the wooden planks over the river that the thump hit her square in the back.

She shed her winter cloak without much rush. A gift from her adopted father, the rare-white cloak was lined with fluffed rabbit fur. Snow would do little to harm it, assuming that's what smacked her between the shoulder blades.

When she flipped the cloak around, the remains of a snowball stuck to the deer hide. Adelei brushed the snow away. Below the cold snow lay a scrap of parchment, balled up and soaked in ink. The moisture of the snow sent the ink cascading across the hide, marring the beautiful white cloak, and Adelei scanned the snowy field for the perpetrator.

Min. The girl rested comfortably on a tree branch a few feet away, her long legs dangling down from the branch. Her laughter rang across the snow. Young enough for tears to win out, Adelei trod over to the tree and brushed at the tears that dampened her cheeks.

"White. Yet another reminder that you aren't Amaskan and never will be. No matter who your daddy is," Min called out.

He said to work it out on my own, and so I will. She balled up her fingers into fists. *Forget the words.*

When she reached the trunk of the tree, Min's long legs hung down just low enough for Adelei to reach. But only if she jumped. Adelei wrapped her arms around Min's legs and went limp. The seventeen-year-old came tumbling down to land butt-first in the snow.

She didn't give Min time to react. Adelei flew at the trainee, fists waving and feet flying. Most never found their target, but a few found purchase on Min—one or two across her beaky nose.

One heel to the face was all it took for Adelei to realize her mistake. Min retaliated, her heel knocking Adelei in the jaw. While she sprawled in the snow, Min punched her in the nose. Pain multiplied her tears, and blood cut through the snow. By the time the pain subsided and the blood stopped, Min was long gone and Adelei's cloak with her.

The sun dipped well below the horizon when Adelei dragged herself home. Head down and shoulders slumped, she made an arrow-line straight for the wash room. Her nose throbbed, and her head spun. She touched a wet rag to her nostril and sucked in air through clenched teeth. The swelling sent stars before her vision, and the room swam.

The front door's bell-chimes caught her off guard, and she dropped the rag into the water basin. His shadow crossed the wall first, and then his elegant frame filled the doorway.

"Where were you? Your lesson ended hours ago—" He stopped to take in the bloody rags and shirt, then he plucked a clean cloth from the shelf. Without speaking, he nursed her wounds with gentle hands. His silence scared Adelei more than Min, and finally, she opened her mouth to accuse her attacker.

Master Bredych pressed a finger to her lips. "Your nose is not broken. You're lucky this time. I would not advise that you attack an Amaskan again—be it one in training or not. You may not live to regret it."

"But she's a trainee and—" The cry sounded childish even to her ears, and she winced.

"A trainee who's had years of practice and learning that you have not. You'd best remember that the next time you see Trainee Min."

"She took my cloak." Adelei couldn't stop the tears this time.

Her father waited for her to cry herself out, his embrace aware of her throbbing nose. Once her tears transitioned into the occasional hiccup, he released her. He captured her attention with all the seriousness and practice of one of her teachers, and she noticed the difference immediately. "Trainee Min has returned your cloak—" His upright hand silenced her before she could take more than a swift intake of air. "But it will not be returned to you until you are more deserving of such a gift. She's apologized for her poor conduct and is serving her own punishment for her actions. Dealing with a problem does not always mean that one should resort to violence, a fact that you should know by now. You have seen us train, yes? What is the number one lesson we teach?"

"Violence is only one way to a resolution. Death is a permanent end, only needed for a permanent cause," she whispered, eyes downcast. "I'm sorry, Father."

"I would not have wished this so soon, but it seems you have adopted more of my traits than I thought possible, including a disregard for the rules and a certain stubbornness. My intention has always been for you to learn as much as you could about the world and to choose your own path, but it seems you are destined to learn...other ways as well. Tomorrow, if you wish, you may petition for entrance into the Academy as a trainee."

For a moment, she forgot to breathe. "B-but I'm ten. Will they even allow it?"

"The earlier one learns, the better. Not everyone has an opportunity such as this. Are you willing?"

"Yes."

Her father grinned. "Remember though," he cautioned, "you won't learn everything overnight. You still have many, many years of training and study to do before taking up the arts of a Journeyman or even thinking of petitioning for full Guild membership."

Master Bredych ruffled her hair with his hand, familiar lines decorating the corner of his mouth. "Besides, you could use some discipline. Someone's got to teach you that fighting is more than random fists and feet."

While both horrible and life changing, the event wasn't one Adelei would forget. As time passed and wisdom engrained itself into her mind, she and Min became good friends and remained so until the woman's death two years prior. Justice had been swift and carried out by Adelei herself. Taking out the traitor who killed her friend exposed a weakness in the Order itself. Though the weakness was quickly covered up. No need for their enemies to find out.

This task and the knowledge that had come with it had earned Adelei's promotion from Journeyman to full member of the Order. Captain Warhammer was made from the same cloth. Patience would help work this out, as it had with Min.

The reminder of home settled like a calm across Adelei's shoulders, and it shifted the unease she'd felt since crossing the border into the background. Several hours travel passed, and Ida allowed her to trail behind at a steady distance until Adelei urged her horse forward. Midnight matched Ida's mare in pacing until they were nose to nose.

The landscape, thick with trees now, held privacy for them and left a fragrance of life through the woods. Once or twice the wind kicked up, and dark and light greens rustled and whispered around them.

After the desert's heat, Adelei welcomed the shady canopy's drop in temperature. "This is nice." Adelei tried engaging the warrior in small talk as their horses crossed a trickle of a stream. "In most of Sadai, there are two seasons: hot and less hot. Some places along the coast are lucky enough to see all four seasons, but it depends upon which mountainside one lives."

"I remember." Adelei tilted her head and gave the warrior a knowing look. Ida said, "I've visited the capital several times. Been a long time now, but I remember the heat. And the beauty. We should come up on the town of Tarmsworth in a few hours. How's the head?"

The muted ache in her head had faded, and Adelei nodded. "I've given some thought to our earlier conversation. We both have our orders, which may differ or even conflict." Adelei pulled the stopper from her water bag and took a long swallow. Ida's mare slowed to keep them even paced. "If I'm to do my job and protect the Princess, I must know the entire truth, even if it's something you don't wish to discuss. If anything is kept from me, no matter how seemingly insignificant, it may cost your princess her life." *And me, mine.*

Ida's silence was a good sign that she was thinking, and Adelei allowed her the quiet. *Probably weighing her options against the orders she's been given. I know that's what I'd be doing about now.*

When the warrior spoke, her voice was calmer than Adelei expected. "I told ya yesterday that news spread quickly about the second princess's death. King Leon only wished to hide his family away, to protect them. I would know what ya think of this."

"His Majesty had the right idea in trying to hide his family, a better move, I think, than what did happen. Still, he should have sent his family away sooner or not at all. Waiting until the city was under attack was foolhardy."

"While it was probable that Alesta would be attacked, His Majesty couldn't have known the city would come so close to fallin' into enemy hands. It never has before. He was hopeful that a peaceful resolution would make the issue moot."

"Then he was a fool."

The mare halted, and Ida faced Adelei. "Why? Because he wished peace? Or because he believed peace possible? Or maybe ya think because he loved his family and didn't want to send them away?"

"All of it but mostly the latter. Families are a liability one cannot afford in battle. When war is on your doorstep, you can't hope the enemy won't notice your family tucked away in the bower. Peace means running in the opposite direction."

Sensing Ida's frustration, Adelei held a hand up to stop the woman's retort. "Look, Gods know I would love to believe peace possible—then I could grow old somewhere in a nice cottage, tucked in a forest like this. Maybe even grow fat. I wouldn't have a need to live by these," she said, sliding one of her throwing knives partially from its sheath at her wrist. "But men don't live by peace. They live by passion, and passion leads to war."

"'Passion is of the heart. War is of the soul.' Ya truly believe that?" Ida took a light heel to her mare as they moved forward again.

Now I know she's trained or lived with the Order. She's studied the works of Yesler Finn, and those works are only obtainable in the Grand Library of Amaska.

"Would ya agree that 'there are many little ways to peace, none of which can be found at the end of a sword'?" Ida asked.

This time it was Adelei who stopped her horse. "You walk the Way of the Warrior, yet you quote Master Bredych as if you know him—how do you know teachings not meant for stray ears?"

Ida's horse whinnied, shying away from a stray stick breaking nearby, and Ida patted her mare's neck absently. "'Tis only a deer, silly girl."

Midnight sidestepped and gave Ida's mare wide berth. The deer ahead stood erect, waiting for their next course of action. Adelei remained silent and listened to the trees for signs of more than a simple deer. Hearing nothing, they moved on, Ida one hoof fall ahead of her.

"A long time before ya were birthed, I lived another life, followed another path. More than that, I won't tell ya yet. And some of it, I won't tell ya at all, as it's not my story to tell. You'll have to ask your father about that."

Which one?

The nagging uncertainty returned by way of a knot in her stomach and dull ache behind her eyes. The next riverbed they encountered was no trickle. Its currents chopped the water in areas, and Adelei dismounted to test its depth with a few tossed rocks. "The saddlebags will need to be raised, but the horses should cross easily enough. We'll get wet though," she said and found Ida stripping off her leather mail.

They hoisted the saddlebags into the saddles and tossed their clothing above that. Both women took their time crossing, neither speaking as all their concentration focused on the movement of their horses and the river's flow as they swam across.

After both women sat safely astride their horses, Ida said, "This isn't somethin' King Leon wished me to tell ya, as he wished to discuss this particular topic with ya himself. But seeing as how this information could prove a liability for ya, I'll tell ya what ya need to know. As much as I can at any rate."

Good to know she'd commit treason when reason called for it. Midnight whinnied and Adelei tried to relax her thighs and her grip on the reins.

"You're worried."

It wasn't a question but a statement of fact, and Adelei nodded. "Most people aren't so willing to commit treason. I know that I asked for answers, but—"

"What if I were to tell ya that those rumors ya heard were wrong? That the second princess had been hidden away all this time from even her own father?"

"Hidden? Or sold?"

"Sold?"

Adelei smirked. "The other princess was sold in secret to buy the peace treaty, and her sister sold by way of this...marriage."

The mare danced in place as Ida stared at Adelei. "I-I don't know why they'd perpetuate that tale. Actually, I do. That sounds just like the bullshit Master Bredych would tell to ya. I hate to break it to ya, but he was lying. Princess Iliana Poncett was kidnapped while being sent to safety."

She ignored the jibe at Master Bredych and asked, "And who kidnapped her?"

"We think the Shadians were behind it."

She was lying. She knew a liar when she saw one. The frown had crossed Ida's face after the fact, and the warrior had shifted her weight forward a few inches in the stirrups. *Patience.* Adelei listened to the internal voice and filed away the questions.

As the trees grew denser, both women gave their horses free rein to find their own footing. Adelei leaned across the pommel to duck under a low hanging branch as thick as her waist. The familiar movement sent a tremor through her. *These trees. There was darkness, just like this. Hanging over the saddle.*

"...Was kidnapped." Adelei shook off Ida's words.

"How much travel will be through thick forest like this?"

"Quite a lot. Alexander is heavily treed land—certainly not sparse like Sadai."

Adelei's eyes scanned the thick brush ahead, and she caught the captain doing the same. It would be the perfect place for an ambush. They'd left the junipers and sagebrush of Sadai far behind as thick evergreens stretched far up into the sky. The occasional deciduous tree helped populate the forest, and between the two, little sunlight reached them at the forest floor. The transition had been gradual enough that Adelei only noticed now that afternoon brought a shift in the sun's placement. Even in the summer's day warmth, Adelei shivered.

"I know ya were raised by Amaskans," Ida said, her eyes never leaving the forest. "But what do ya remember of your life before the Order?"

"Not much. I was very young when I was taken in. Five, I think, but obviously you knew since you asked."

"Do ya remember your birth parents?" At the shake of Adelei's head, the woman continued. "It's funny that ya almost gave me your birth name when we met rather than your Amaskan name, as is customary."

Adelei flushed. "Leaving was...difficult. This job. Coming back here. I don't think I was thinking all that clearly."

"I guess it makes sense that you've forgotten your time before the Order. Bein' so young."

She tugged on the reins, and Midnight danced in place. "Can we stop playing this game now? We both know who I am."

Ida dismounted, her back to Adelei. "Ya know?" she whispered. "Ya know, and yet ya left your father thinking ya were dead? What type of person does that?"

"What kind of person sells their child to the Amaskans?" Adelei retorted, her skin hot with anger. "I'm what he wanted. He sold me to keep his kingdom and his peace, and I don't owe him a damned thing. The Order took me in, and Master Bredych adopted me. Not just in thought, but on paper. He saved me and loved me and brought me a family that your king never could."

Adelei urged Midnight forward until he stood before the captain, and Adelei lowered her chin to look down on the woman. "I am Amaskan, tattoo or no, with a family who loves me. I'm not some damned princess. Certainly not Iliana P-Poncett."

Ida gave Adelei a long, pained look before her gaze found the forest floor. She tucked a stray hair behind her ear. "I knew Master Bredych could convince a snail it was a race horse," Ida whispered, "but I never thought 'im capable of such deceit. Whether ya believe me or not is your choice, but your father never 'sold you.' He didn't give ya up willingly. In fact, it was only at the persuasion of those he trusted that he sent his family away at all."

"You expect me to believe all this? Not just that my father is a kidnapper and liar, but that my birth father is somehow a *victim*?" Adelei laughed, a panicked sound made of half wounded-animal and half-incredulity that shook her voice and her shoulders. "He bargained with the Shadians over...my sister's hand. If he sold her away to his enemies, what makes me believe he wouldn't do the same to me?"

Adelei kneed her horse forward, leaving Ida standing alone in the dark forest. *Oh Master, what have you done?*

CHAPTER SEVEN

Alesta, Capital City of Alexander; 255 Cercian 1ˢᵗ

Waiting was something King Leon excelled in, a task of which he was a master; after all, he'd waited many long years to seek revenge upon the Amaskans for the "death" of his daughter. But waiting for Iliana's return was like waiting for the winter snows when the heat of summer was just creeping over spring flowers.

Over the years, the sitting room had remained constant, its blue and gold decor reminding Leon of his late wife.

Leave it to Catherine to want to redecorate as armed men marched toward our kingdom. His eyes rested on the empty blue chair beside him. It wasn't her chair anymore, not for over a decade, but every time someone sat in it, the memories of her washed over him like good ale: it both burned and soothed going down.

The moment his sepier had reported that Iliana was alive, his search was both more and less frantic. On one hand, he wanted her home. Immediately. Whatever the cost. But on the other hand, having her home didn't bring him the head of one Master Bredych.

His heart twitched when he thought of Ida, and his mind immediately jumped to Goefrin. *Imagine my surprise to learn that dear old Goefrin has been playing me all along. While waiting for Iliana is torture, waiting to deal with that worm is even harder.*

As if his thought had summoned the old man, Goefrin entered the sitting room by way of a low bow. "Your Majesty called for me?"

"I did. Join me for a moment if you will."

Goefrin's eyes fluttered with a speed his old body lacked, nervousness that had not left since hearing of Iliana's inevitable trip home. "Might I inquire—might I ask what I may do for Your Majesty?"

Leon's grin was genuine and bordered on a smirk as the advisor squirmed. "Surely you know. As my most trusted advisor, your job is to anticipate my needs, is it not?" *Come on, you worm, confess so that I might stretch your neck over a chopping block and be done with your rotten self.*

"Yes, Your Majesty." When Leon didn't elaborate, Goefrin added, "I'm sorry for not knowing what I should, Sire."

Two emeralds squinted back at Leon from a pasty, wrinkled face, and a trickle of sweat rolled down the leathery folds of Goefrin's neck. *I should just choke the man and be done with it.* Instead, Leon waited.

Still, it would be interesting to find out how the weasel had gained his father's trust enough to sit upon his council. Leon gestured for the man to sit in the chair to his left and winced as the man's joints popped from the effort required to lower his frame into the chair.

King Leon clenched his jaw. *Catherine's chair, you worm. If I didn't know any better, I'd think you had chosen that chair on purpose.*

"My daughter should be home soon," King Leon said, a forced smile on his ample lips. "Of course, she's not the daughter I remember. For one, she's not five anymore."

"No, Sire." Goefrin's laugh sounded forced.

"She's one of them now, an Amaskan. Did you know she's the best, Goefrin? They say she's the best they've ever trained."

"That's wonderful, Your Majesty."

"Wonderful? You think so?" Goefrin's jowls jiggled when he nodded too fast. "You think it wonderful that my little girl is returning home after all these years a murderer? A killer?"

"No, Your Majesty, I mean—"

King Leon slammed his fist onto the arm of his chair. He dug his fingers into the mahogany wood until his knuckles turned a pinkish-white. It wasn't the King who wanted to lunge across the small space separating the two, it was the father. And the father lacked the King's patience.

"Cease the pretenses. You know damned well why you're here. You're the reason my daughter returns to me a killer."

"I don't understand—"

"Enough." The word escaped in a roar of fury and for a moment, King Leon saw stars before him. The last thing he needed was the healers interrupting again. He took a deep breath to calm himself, which only half worked. "It was your idea to send Iliana to the Amaskans."

The words should have inspired terror in the old man, but instead Goefrin laughed, a tight, thin little laugh that erupted shrilly. "Surely you don't blame me for a plan gone wrong, Sire. How could I possibly know the Shadian army would intercept and kill your daughter? They were everywhere. 'Tis folly to think I could do more than I did."

When King Leon remained silent, Goefrin's smile faltered, and his eyes narrowed as they lost their sparkle. "Your Majesty?"

"I know who you are."

Five simple words. Goefrin stood, all pretense of a feeble body gone as he hurtled toward the door and threw it open in a wild panic. Armed guards stood between him and escape.

"Come, Goefrin. Have a seat, please. Let's discuss treachery and Shad."

When Goefrin didn't move, King Leon nodded and a guard placed his hands on Goefrin's shoulders and pushed him back through the doorway. "Sit. I insist."

Goefrin's entrance into the plush blue chair was much less controlled this time as he fell into its cushions, his eyes set intently on his king. "It seems you've been quite busy, Your Majesty."

"Indeed I have."

"I've been meaning to ask, how did you discover Iliana was alive?" His gaze flicked to the fireplace mantel, which still bore a painting of the child. "Was it perhaps your obsession with the Order? Your never-ending watch of their members?"

"It was," he answered honestly. "My turn. Why Shad?"

"They have deeper pockets."

"So this was about money?"

Goefrin shrugged. "I suppose."

"And now you confess so easily?" Geofrin merely grinned. King Leon knelt before the man, his eyes searching the man's face. "You were my father's most trusted advisor and friend. You were mine. What madness could lead you into dealings with those devils? Surely if money was all you sought, you could have remedied that easily enough in my coffers."

"You've always been a spoiled child, not worthy of the throne your father left you," the man hissed as he leaned in close. Behind him, the scraping of steel sounded as guards stepped forward.

Leon ignored them all. *That smell. Sour ale and something else, something bitter or tart.*

His face must have changed as Goefrin leaned back in a rush, but King Leon seized the front of his shirt and pulled the man closer. "Your breath smells familiar...foul. What sorcery is this? What play are you running, traitor?"

The ear-splitting grin of heavily yellowed teeth caught Leon off guard, and he released the man in too much of a hurry. Goefrin's chair fell back and toppled the old man to the hard floor. "Recognize it, do you? You should. You're intimately acquainted with it, Your Majesty."

Leon's eyes widened further as the memory crept over him, his father's body still warm as it lay in the massive bed he'd called home for the six months prior to his death.

"I'm sorry, Your Majesty," the healer had said, and Leon had flinched at the use of the title. "Your father, the King, is dead. Gods be with him."

Beside the bed laid scattered brews and bowls of poultices meant to ease the King's suffering, too late as he no longer had need of such things.

Leon had expected the room to smell different—sour with the smells of death and illness, but instead the odors had been surprisingly clean and fresh as if summer stood outside and not the harsh chill of winter. Leon had glanced to the window, expecting it to be open, ushering in the scent of the pine trees outside. But the glass had stood shuttered.

Like his father's eyes.

"Did someone clean this room?" he had asked the healer.

"Yes, Your Majesty. Advisor Goefrin ordered it at your father's passing. He thought it better that the family receive the King's body in proper peace."

At the time, the words had made sense. In fact, Leon had been grateful for the idea, not wishing to subject his new bride to such a sight as his father's death filled bedchamber. Especially not the mess it had become in his final days.

Despite the cleanliness of the fresh sheets and fragrant room, it had been Catherine who'd first noticed the odd smell lingering about His Majesty's body—a bitter smell that soured it prematurely. The healers had not known what it was and had chalked it up to mere humors of the body. As they had prepared the former King to be received by sacred ground, Leon had pushed it from his mind. He had believed them.

But now sitting before Goefrin, the pieces slid into place. "You killed my father."

The advisor's only answer was a smile, which faltered as the man's eyes rolled back into his head. King Leon lunged forward to catch him, and his nose caught the smell again. "What have you taken? What have you done?" he shouted and shook the man who lay limp in his arms.

Goefrin's eyes fluttered open a moment and that hideous grin returned briefly. "I came...prepared."

The body convulsed in Leon's arms. "Fetch the healers. Be quick." Leon shouted.

They'll never reach us in time. Goefrin's body ceased convulsing, and his chest stopped rising with the air of life.

Alone with the body, King Leon ran his trembling hands through the man's pockets. In the smallest pocket sewn inside his overshirt, Leon discovered a vial of deep brown liquid with a few drops remaining.

Leon opened it carefully. The strength of the bitter odor sent the room spinning, and King Leon's hands faltered. He dropped the vial as he rolled back. His head missed the chair's corner, and the soft rug on the floor pushed up against his cheek.

Feet moved. He could hear them in the distance, but his vision swam so that all that appeared before his eyes was a whirl of color and then blackness.

Hoof beats announced Ida before she spoke. "This is difficult for us both. It wasn't my place to make this revelation to ya, but ya insisted on knowing everythin'. Your father, King Leon, used my connections to the Order to bring ya home."

"Why? And why now? What connection could you possibly have that would result in this?" asked Adelei as they continued through the trees. The sun dipped lower in the sky, and the forest grew darker with each minute. Soon they would need torches to see at all.

"Your father used a friend, someone he trusted with his life...and yours, to arrange your escape from Alexander. To keep ya safe, he sent ya to the Amaskans. What better place to hide ya, to protect ya, than with those whom everyone feared? Not even the Boahim Senate's brave enough to come after the famed Order of Amaska. Ya were to be hidden there 'til it was safe. But somethin' went wrong. Your father was betrayed, and you—ya were gone."

"The Amaskans aren't kidnappers." The moment she said it, she winced. She, too, was lying. Her brain tried to flee the deluge of memories and failed.

How many times had the Order kidnapped someone, to make the killing easier? Longer? Or just to gain the information needed to trap someone? For justice. Her mind sifted through the histories stored in her brain. It was done often enough—she had played a part in several.

"Ya weren't supposed to stay there. It was meant to be temporary. They were to instruct ya in subjects...more appropriate to one of your station."

A rich, bubbling laugh escaped Adelei in her panic. It sang among the trees like a dying songbird. "I was sent there until it was 'safe'—but never to become an assassin." Her laughter tensed her thigh and shoulder muscles. "That's rich. The princess returns home a killer. Welcome home and hello, Papa. Need someone killed today?"

Ida sighed. "Ya weren't supposed to be gone forever. King Leon was told ya were captured and killed on the way to Sadai. Until recently, he'd no idea ya were even alive."

"Who told him I was dead?"

"The friend who suggested ya be sent to the Amaskans in the first place. He came back with the word of your death. He's the one who betrayed your father." Ida shifted in her saddle, and Adelei's eyes narrowed.

"How did the King discover otherwise? Did this traitor confess?"

Ida laughed. "Hardly. Since your 'death,' King Leon has watched the Amaskans. Probably closer than the Boahim Senate, I'll wager. One of the reasons Amaskans aren't allowed in Alexander. Part of my job—as His Majesty's sepier—is to watch the Order. I've been in and out of Sadain borders two or three dozen times in the past fifteen years."

"Why?"

"To find those responsible. Almost a year ago, I passed ya on the streets. The moment I saw ya, I knew who ya were."

"How?"

"Ya truly are twin to your sister."

Adelei pursed her lips together. "You're lying. You're not telling me everything, and without Master Bredych here to defend himself—well, let's just say that I doubt he played the role you think he did. Someone else has their fingers in this yarn. Either way, I'm no princess now. Nor have I any interest in becoming one."

"Of course not. Your father's no fool, child. He didn't bring ya home as a princess. Do ya see any royal guard or a procession proclaimin' ya alive? You're better off dead."

"Nice to know he cares."

"By Echana, must ya act like a child? I just meant that hidin' in plain sight will make your job easier."

"He left me dead until I was needed." The words left her tongue, which she bit. Deep breaths did little to still the turmoil. She needed control of herself before they reached the capital, lest she set loose her tongue in such a way as to be banished from her own kingdom. *My own kingdom. Ha. As if they'd allow a murderer, an*

Amaskan, to take the crown. Even my own sister's death couldn't bring about that *scenario.*

A thought popped into her brain so vile, she pushed it away with a mental hand. Bitter she might be, assassin she might be, but killer she was not. Her kills brought justice, not pure vengeance.

Pictures of her last kill flashed before her. A little voice inside her head whispered, *but weren't you made of vengeance? Didn't you relish the kill, causing the pain to last as you killed me?* It was Magistrate Meserre's voice that echoed in her skull.

Normal to feel something at the loss of another human—but the Order existed to serve justice when others could not. Killing for the Order meant helping people. Or so Adelei had convinced herself. It was a crucial tenet of her belief system—the belief system of all Amaskans.

Leaves crackled under her fingers as she dug her nails into the dirt on the forest floor, its rich, earthy smell mixing with the bile in the back of her throat. She knew not when she tumbled from her horse, but moved clumsily through the dirt, stumbling into the brush to lose all traces of her breakfast. Only when dry heaves remained, her body left shaking, did she rise on unsteady feet. Not even the swish of water could rid her mouth of the taste of vomit and death, joy and bitterness—a vile concoction going down, much less coming up.

"I'm sorry ya had to hear this from me. And this way. This can't sit easy in ya." The kindness in Ida's voice hit all the harder after the disturbing thoughts that had crossed her mind, and she shook her head before returning to the saddle. Midnight sidestepped at her hurry and bumped shoulders with Ida's mare.

"Who are you? You know things...more than mere research. Who are you? Are you the traitor who named me dead?"

Adelei's dagger was in her hands and against Ida's throat swiftly enough, despite her stomach's quivering. "Answer me." she shouted and leaned closer to the woman. The blade pressed against the horizontal, puffy scar.

"No. No, I'm not the traitor who did that—but I did betray ya, and for that, I'm sorry."

"Who are you? I'm not going to ask again."

"I'm the one who kidnapped ya."

"Your Majesty?"

The words were worlds away, but King Leon nodded. Or at least he thought he did. When the words were repeated and his shoulders shaken, he pried open an eye to a fuzzy world, unfocused and very blue in color.

"Stop...shaking...me." The words took an army's effort as his tongue felt thick in his mouth.

"Your Majesty, do you know where you are?"

His vision sharpened some, and he recognized the tapestry on the wall of the field where he and Catherine had first met, her slender frame walking toward him. She'd been a complete stranger. The bravery it must have taken to travel so far, only to marry a complete stranger.

"Catherine?" Leon whispered.

"Your Majesty?"

Leon shook his head and blinked back time. The world snapped into focus. He lay in his bed. The same bed where his father had been murdered. The healer before him sighed and pinched Leon's arm to check the flush.

"What happened?" Leon asked.

"We found you with Sir Goefrin's body. You were near death, Your Majesty."

"Did you find the vial?"

The healer glanced behind him at King Leon's personal physician, Roland, before nodding. "We did, Your Majesty. Foul stuff 'twas."

Roland held the vial between slightly swollen fingers. "How did Your Majesty come by this?"

"Goefrin. He had it." Leon's tongue still felt like a pile of leaves more than a proper tongue, and he tried to roll it around in his mouth. "He...he killed my father...w-with it."

Roland sent the other healers out of the room with a nod. "I suspected as much at the time but couldn't prove it. I didn't want to raise suspicion against such a trusted family friend if I was wrong."

"I understand. He admitted committing several acts of treason, and—"

"Your Majesty, there's something more you must know—"

Roland's concern was touching, and Leon reached up to grab the healer's hand. "I know. I know. He's been poisoning me, too, hasn't he?"

The physician nodded.

"Is it reversible? This cough I have. Can this illness be undone?"

"I'm sorry, Your Majesty. I think your body has taken in too much of the poison. However many days you have left, I can't fathom a guess. But you will eventually die from this poison."

King Leon stared at the tapestry hanging on the wall across from his bed. Tears swirled the picture into a mass of green. How many people would this traitor's actions cost him? First his father, then his wife, fifteen years with Iliana, and now his own life.

"Order his rooms searched. I want to know who hired this weasel to plot against my family," said Leon.

"It is already being done, Your Majesty. When we thought you dying—immediately dying, I mean—I ordered the search in hopes of finding answers." King Leon nodded and closed his eyes again. "Rest, Your Majesty. We will discover the root of this evil."

Ah, my poor Margaret. I hope I live long enough to see you happy. And to see you home, Iliana. His body weighed him down, weary from his thinned hair to the tip of his toes. *Gods help us discover the snake in our home and root it out.*

Gods help me live long enough to see it done.

CHAPTER EIGHT

Forest of Alexander / Town of Tarmsworth

"My name's Shendra Abner, sister of Malaki Abner—but ya know 'im under his Amaskan name. Eli Bredych."

Adelei wobbled in the saddle, and she grabbed hold of the pommel for support. "Sister to Master Bredych?"

"Yes. I was also Amaskan. I was servin' the Order when I—" Adelei's head spun in confusion. "I brought ya to the Amaskans under my brother's orders. I thought...I thought I was bringin' you to safety, but when I discovered that they planned to kill ya, I couldn't do it, child. I asked to be released from the Order."

"But you can't—"

"—Leave. I know. How do ya think I got this?" Ida pointed at the long scar on her neck.

"If you're Amaskan, where's your tattoo?" When Ida tilted her head for Adelei to better see the old scar that ran across her neck, the scar's tip began where the tattoo had been. Underneath the slightly raised and lighter skin, hints of the circle remained. Like random dots that formed a quarter circle. Invisible unless one knew what to look for.

"My own, dear brother, the one ya call Father, slit my throat and left me for dead. Someone found me and healed me. After, I fled east and returned to Alexander with the intention of tellin' your father the truth, but the hands of Amaska are ever reachin'. I feared they would silence me for good. So I hid. Different name. Different person."

Ida's eyes teared up as they pleaded with Adelei. "But once I saw ya, grown up and-and—alive, I returned to His Majesty and confessed. Now I'm ordered to bring ya home safely, as I couldn't do before. I'm so very sorry for my part in this."

"Tell me."

"What?"

"Tell me what you told him. Tell me exactly why you kidnapped me."

"I would ask that it wait 'til we reach Tarmsworth. I feel the need for a good pint and a comfortable chair before I tell it."

Adelei sheathed her dagger. "You don't deserve the reprieve, no matter how temporary, but a drink sounds like an excellent idea for soothing betrayal. We'll wait until Tarmsworth." *And if you don't tell me there, I'll kill you myself and finish the job Bredych started.*

A hard silence lay between them, its sharp edge slicing them both with words unspoken. Their horses continued picking their way across the dense forest toward the town of Tarmsworth. Master Bredych wouldn't have slit her throat unless she'd betrayed the Order. Once an oathbreaker, always an oathbreaker. If King Leon still trusted her, they were going to have a problem.

Ida wisely remained mute through the evening. She lit a torch to guide them and finally broke the quiet. "Troubled as ya are, I thought it might help ya to know that despite your upbringin', your father chose to send for ya once he learned ya were alive. He wished to make the best of the situation."

"Then he should have left me at home."

"Angry as ya may be, he can't just bring ya back from the dead and introduce ya as a princess. Even *you* must see the folly in *that* plan. He's doin' the best he can though, and the least ya could do is live up to the expectations of the Order. I know it's not the ideal situation or the easiest news to hear, but ya must move beyond the wallowin' and prepare to do the job your kingdom has asked of ya."

"Which kingdom?" Adelei retorted. "If I'm to believe you, my father's a liar and a kidnapper. Everything I know about him is false. And I'm supposed to just do my job as if nothing's changed."

Ida rested a gentle hand on Adelei's shoulder, a pained expression on her face. "Forgive me, Adelei. I forgot how young ya are, despite your reputation. I don't expect ya to wall it off, but if ya aren't in some control when we reach Alexander, your emotions may get your sister or ya killed. We don't have much longer before we reach the capital, two days at the most. Deal with the betrayal later. For now be Amaskan."

Even Adelei's slow breaths were jagged and her chest ached. "If ya must," Ida said, "perform the Ro-maá."

Adelei swallowed hard and handed her reins to Ida. Horse secure, she sank into the darkness of closed eyelids and pushed away thoughts until her mind sat empty. The wall was there. Waiting. Brick by brick she built it—between herself and the emotional turmoil. Her mind tapped against it, but Adelei hummed beneath her breath and focused on stillness.

Another memory popped into her mind and dissolved a brick. The first time she'd seen the Ro-maá as a trainee. It was the last job they'd accepted from Alexander. Poor woman had been captured by those who had hired her and tortured her for information. They had wanted the name of who had ordered the hit on some child. *Oh Gods—they were asking about me. I didn't see it then. Damn you, Father.* Adelei ground her teeth and focused on repairing the mental wall.

When Mersi's body had been discovered at the border, her mind was a storm and her body a bloody hurricane. The healers helped Mersi into a trance and helped her build the Ro-maá—the wall. When the woman awoke, much to the shock of Adelei and her classmates, Mersi was calm and alert. Adelei had protested— they couldn't turn emotions on and off like that.

"Mersi will process the situation as slowly as she needs, but for now, she can carry out her duties without endangering herself or others," the healer had said.

Even now, Adelei shivered inside the memory. *I know it can be damned useful, but it still creeps me out. Certainly never thought I'd need it. But then no one ever does.* The meditation technique worked, though Adelei didn't understand why. Only that it did, and she breathed as she built up her wall again and pushed the old memories back.

Empty the vessel. Like water I flow to the sea, nothing between it and me.

She sank deeper until the wall was twice the width of Midnight's shoulders and covered in ivy. Adelei lay down in the water that ran alongside it, reveling in the chill that washed over her. Ice water to her temper, to her flame.

When she opened her eyes, she sat relaxed in the saddle. While she wasn't pleased with Ida, she didn't feel the need to kill the woman either. A calm neutrality.

Turning to Ida, she said, "I apologize for my behavior and immaturity these past few days. It will not happen again."

Ida studied her face, surely critiquing every line and muscle movement. Satisfied, she nodded and returned Midnight's reins. "Good. We approach Tarmsworth."

Adelei unrolled the map from her saddlebag and located Tarmsworth with a steady finger. *A third of the way to Alesta, the capital city. She was right—maybe another day or two in the saddle at the most before we reach Alesta.*

Unbidden, her thoughts turned to her sister, a person she didn't remember and didn't know. Maybe it was better that way. It was another job guarding another stranger.

Several hours after sundown, they reached the town of Tarmsworth which was nestled in the forest like an afterthought. At first, Adelei wasn't sure they hadn't simply stumbled upon some hunter's cabin in the woods.

Two buildings came to view from astride her horse. Beyond them, three dozen more tangled through the torch-lit area. All surrounded an opening in the center which was unusually clear of trees. A man bearing a lantern walked through the clearing and nodded to them, then moved on his way with his bundle of wood. Ida led them toward the small inn tucked into the corner of town.

Only one of four stalls in the stable remained, and Adelei led Midnight and Ida's mare into it. The horses would have little room to move about, but it was better than someone losing a hand or rib trying to 'capture' a wandering horse. Well stocked with feed and water, both women needed only to groom their mounts and remove the saddlebags before retiring themselves to the inn.

"The stable's packed. Will they have room available for us?" Adelei asked as she untied the saddlebags.

Ida pulled a coin out of her pocket and tossed it to Adelei, who flipped it over in her palm. The silver coin bore the face of a serious looking man whom she assumed was her birth father. His crown bore hints of color smelted into the silver. "That coin will get us a room in any town, full or not," said Ida.

Adelei frowned as she tossed it back. "I wouldn't want to kick anyone out of their room. If there's not one available, I'd be just as happy sleeping out here with Midnight. Done it before many a time." While she meant it, after the day's turmoil, she wanted a room. She'd even share one, so long as it was something softer and warmer than hay and a blanket.

Both women entered the inn and conversation paused as the occupants glanced up from drinks. Once the peek was given, talk and drink resumed inside the rather simple inn. The sun's warmth was long gone, and a chill clung to the air. Adelei steered herself closer to the fireplace's warmth as they approached both it and the innkeeper behind the bar.

The gray-haired bar matron cleaned a glass with the sleeve of a yellowed blouse bearing more stains than her full skirt. She flashed equally yellow teeth at Ida, her grin splitting her face into two reddened beets.

"Ida. Good ta see you makin' the rounds agin. What's it this time? Servin' on the border?"

Ida grabbed the woman's outstretched hand with a grip that spoke of the strength and joy of longtime friends. Still smiling, Ida slid a bar stool up to the bar. She wasn't even seated before a mug was in her hands. She drank long of the brew before answering. "Nope. 'Twas visitin' family. Headin' back to the capital now."

The barmaid rested her eyes on Adelei. The rugged voice matched the rugged exterior. "Are ya with Ida here? Somethin' I can help you with?"

Ida rested her hand on Adelei's sleeved arm. "The poor thing was out in the woods, lost and confused. Haven't heard a word outta her yet, but I figure I'll take her with me to the capital. See if maybe someone would have use for 'er. I figure she's tired and all—whattcha have by way of a room for tonight, Mel?"

Adelei pulled her hood closer to her face and widened her eyes, feigning fear. Mel, who certainly looked man enough to bear a man's name, frowned but let it go with another mug for Ida.

The barkeep led them up a rickety flight of stairs to a room in the rear.

"I remembered ya preferred th'room in the back. I'll let ya have it tonight for tha usual." No money exchanged hands, nor any indication as to what the "usual" was, but good to her word, the woman left them alone.

The door closed, and Adelei threw off her hood before falling into one of two small beds in the room. Her feet hung off the bed by a good twelve inches, but her hips sank into the stuffed mattress. Adelei sighed in comfort. Ida, mug still in hand, sank into the only chair, which stood by the fireplace.

Ida warmed her fingers as she drank deep of her ale. "Nice inn for the room to have its own fireplace," Adelei commented from behind drooping eyelids.

"Um-hmmm," was the only reply the warrior gave.

Adelei's mouth watered, her tongue tasting the air for the drink's flavor. Probably watered down or a mild ale, but at this point, she didn't care. Anything besides stream water.

The room's warmth and her exhaustion lost her the battle, and she awoke a good twenty minutes later when a light knock sounded on the door. When it opened, a small boy entered, carrying a tray twice his size. The tray was loaded to the brim with food and drink.

Through slitted eyelids, Adelei winced at the serving boy's reaction when he saw her. Even though she was lying down, he could see her bald head. Ida took the tray from his trembling hands with thanks and a small coin. Fear forgotten, he beamed at the coin as she gently pushed him out the door and locked it behind him.

"Keep the hood on next time," said Ida. The woman scooted the room's tiny table and only chair closer to Adelei's bed—not that it had far to go in so small a room.

Adelei picked up the glass of goat's milk from the tray. "What in all hells is this?"

Ida chortled. "I guess ya looked like someone in need of milk." Two more glasses of ale sat on the tray and before Ida could lay claim to both, Adelei switched out the milk for a glass of ale.

"I've had worse," she said after a sip. "Just strong enough to numb the senses some." She alternated sips with strips of deer meat and potatoes. Ida helped herself to food and even drank down the offending goat's milk before returning to her ale.

"As we approach Alesta and the castle, keep your head covered. Did ya bring any head wraps or scarves besides your hooded cloak?"

"Both."

"Good. No need to announce your presence like we just did with that boy."

"Will it be a problem?" When Ida cocked an eyebrow, Adelei clarified, "The boy?"

"No. If he tells Mel, Mel knows to keep her trap shut."

Adelei finished her mug of ale, but still felt thirsty. Maybe she should have drunk the milk after all. A knock on the door brought an entire pitcher of ale, and Adelei settled cross-legged on the bed. "How does King Leon wish me to appear once on the job?"

"Depends on what ya thinks necessary, I guess." Ida belched and pounded her chest once. "Sometimes, you'll dress as the Princess to be the body double. Though ya might need to use some makeup or somethin'—ya look entirely too much like Princess Margaret. Oh, and you'll need to wear a wig or a head covering of some sort at times. You'll be introduced as a guard in special service to the King—that way the royal guards will listen to your commands."

"Like a sepier."

"Similar enough, I guess."

"How many attempts have been made on Her Highness?" Adelei asked, and Ida held up two greasy fingers. "Any idea who hired the hit?"

"Yes, His Majesty'll give ya the details when ya arrive. The weddin's two months away, and just about everyone will be in the capital for the royal wedding. The various lords and ladies and dignitaries will be at the castle by the time we arrive—at least those travelin' from afar. Considerin' it's unitin' two families who're once sworn enemies, it'll be a big weddin'. Lots'a state dinners, dances, and the like."

Ida scowled, and Adelei asked, "I take it you don't approve?"

"No. I don't believe His Majesty sold Her Highness for the peace treaty, but I know he would've avoided all this if given half the choice. We'll be passin' half of the kingdom on the road tomorrow, so we should get some rest while we can."

"Aren't you forgetting something?"

The warrior sighed and filled her mug with ale. "Let's get this over with…"

Capital City of Alesta—254 Adlain 15th

The sleeping woman in his arms shifted, her heel connecting with his shin. The jagged scar to the right of her eye bunched together with worry lines. One of her hands flitted to the scar tissue along her throat, and she whimpered in rhythm to the twitching of the facial muscles around her eyes.

"Shhhhh," King Leon murmured, running his thumb down her jawline. Through the deep blue bed curtains, tiny hints of light streamed in from one of four windows which left most of the room dark in the early dawn.

Even with the lack of light, the scar running parallel to her jaw stood out in contrast to the others along her body. The puffy and angry line stretched the full width of her neck, from ear to ear. Ten years together, and still she never spoke of it, never talked of the wound that walked in and out of her nightmares.

She thought she'd kept her past from him, but a few paid informants gained a king whatever information he wished. That and the fact that she talked in her sleep. A smile lifted the corners of his thin lips as he stared at the woman wrapped beneath the heavy winter blankets.

He had never set out to find someone else after Catherine, but Ida—she was everything Catherine was not. Strength to a flaw, impertinence in her honesty, and a passion that burned long after the sun set.

His thumb froze at the shift in her breathing, and he peered down to find blue eyes staring up at him. Instead of their usual humor, the deep, blue pools were haunted by shadows, and the smile fell from his lips. "Your sleep was troubled," he whispered.

She sat up, pulling the blanket with her. Her shoulder twitched, and he reached out a wrinkled hand to touch it before he leaned forward where he could see her face. When a few tears decorated her cheeks, his hands tightened on her shoulders.

"What is it, Ida? What's bothering you so? Was it something in Sadai?"

"I begged ya not to send me." The scar across her throat jumped when she spoke, and her voice resembled gravel.

"Since when has my sepier been afraid of anything?" The former captain of the royal guard didn't answer as another tear slid down a cheek more gaunt than it had been a few months before.

Has it only been four months since I sent her to her homeland? There was more bone beneath his fingers than he was accustomed to.

"Ida, love, I know you hate Sadai, but we all must make sacrifices for duty."

Her body stilled while long pale fingers gripped the bed sheets. "You know nothin'."

Leon didn't know what shocked him more, that she was angry with him or that she was afraid. "I know the healers in Sadai saved you—" He ignored her gasp and continued, "—and that you fled your homeland for Alexander. But you worked your way to the top of my army because you were fearless."

Unlike now.

Instead of pushing further, he waited and wrapped the blankets around them both as his arms encircled her waist. She gave in to her emotions, and Leon bit the inside of his cheek. In ten years as his mistress, he hadn't once seen her lose her composure, much less cry, and her weakness left knots in his gut.

"'Twas a mistake to return to Sadai," she whispered.

"I sent a woman I trust into that country, a tenacious spy who feared nothing, and she's returned to me broken. I was going to wait until the sun rose before asking for your report, but considering your tears, I have to ask. What happened? What brought you back early and afraid?"

Ida rose from the bed, her bare feet picking their way across clothing strewn haphazardly on the floor from a few hours before when she'd returned. Near midnight, she'd crept into his chambers, her return from Sadai just shy of a week early.

The look on her face had led him to ask no questions, but as she stood in the sprinkling of sunlight the morning brought, dread seeped into Leon's bones. Her fifty years did little to mar her body, but a decade of leading battles had left scars aplenty across her frame, and Leon frowned to see a fresh mark across her thigh, its scab already sloughing off and healing.

"I've failed ya, Your Majesty." Her shoulders slumped forward before she faced him.

"Were you not successful then in finding the location of the Order of Amaska?"

Her lips trembled. "I—I was successful, Your Majesty."

King Leon sucked air through clenched teeth much too fast, and the ever-present congestion in his lungs leapt forth. Another coughing spasm whipped through him.

Stars danced before his eyes, and Ida's footsteps sounded nearby. Shortly after, she pressed the mug into his waiting hands. Some of the medicine sloshed out of the cup before it found his lips, and several swallows later, the spasm passed, leaving hope in its wake. "Where is the Order located?"

"Sire, there's more—"

"Where are they?"

"They're near the coast, near the town of Haif—"

He was two feet out of bed and halfway to the door before he remembered the need for clothing, and despite his bruised lungs, he quickly dug through his clothes chest. Leon seized the first clothes his fingers touched: an old pair of breeches a touch too loose at the waist, and an undershirt that bore a hole from a moth.

He didn't care what he looked like. After thirteen years, he had finally found the men who had massacred his family. His giddy footsteps carried him across the room where he rang for a page. When the boy appeared, his face flushed at the sight of Ida's nudity as she stood near the window. Leon grabbed the boy's sleeve, pulling his attention into line. "I need Captain Fenton brought to my sitting room immediately."

When the door shut behind the young page, Ida wrapped a robe around her and knelt before Leon, who gestured for her to rise. He haphazardly dug through a box of letters. "Once Michael arrives, you'll tell us both about their location. We have plans to make."

"There's more, and ya must hear it alone."

When he faced her again, she still knelt on the stone floor, and her shoulder length hair spilled limply across her face. "What more is there? After thirteen years, I finally have the location of the bastards. Today is a good day, Ida. Today I will have my revenge."

"Will ya march across Sadai's borders to take it?"

"If necessary."

"You'd bring the wrath of the Boahim Senate down upon us? Would ya rip this land apart again for 'nother pointless war?"

King Leon took her hands into his own as he knelt down beside her. "I thought you would understand this. Those bastards killed my wife. My daughter. What else would you have me do? The Boahim Senate has done nothing to stop the Amaskans. If they won't seek justice, then I will."

The knock at the door interrupted them and as Leon rose from his knees, Ida seized the edge of his shirt. "Ya think you've the whole of it, but ya must hear me out. Please. Send the good captain away 'til you've heard the truth."

King Leon sighed, and when the page knocked on the door a second time, he opened it a crack. "Tell Captain Fenton I'll be with him shortly."

"Speak. Tell me what has kept you tossing in your sleep."

At first, she didn't make a sound, choosing instead to stare at the carved pieces of wood inlaid in stone across his bedchamber floor, and he ground his teeth at the silence. When his lips smacked open, she said, "I never intended to hurt ya. Know that I'd no idea what they planned, I swear to ya, but I found—in Sadai—your daughter's alive. Iliana's alive."

This time when the air left him, he worried it would not return as his lungs froze in place. He sputtered twice before his vocal cords worked again. "You speak madness. She died by Amaskan hands."

"I believed it, too, Your Majesty, but I swear to ya that I saw your daughter alive...and well. You sent me home to find those responsible for her death, but she's alive and traipsin' through the capital city of Aruna. It's her; I'd swear my life on it."

Leon gripped the handle on the door as he squeezed his eyes shut. "I sent her away for protection, and the Amaskans killed her outside the city walls. That's what Goefrin told me."

"Bastard's a traitor."

King Leon heaved her to her feet by her bare shoulders. Rough hands tilted her face to look at his, but even then, her eyes veered sideways as she refused to meet his gaze. "You speak in riddles. You tell me my daughter's alive, you tell me you have the location of my enemies, and that my most trusted advisor's a traitor. You will explain yourself and how you know this to be true."

"G-Goefrin's my uncle. Was sent here to get close to your father, to gain the royal family's trust, and then to give evidence to interested parties of your family's coup to overthrow the Boahim Senate." As the words spilled from her mouth, he could feel the wrinkles in his brow multiply.

Don't do that, Papa. The wrinkle monster will get you. Hearing Iliana's five-year-old voice in his mind left him weak, and he stepped sideways as his balance wavered. Three steps found him alongside the bed he'd shared with Ida minutes before, and he reached out to one of the four bedposts. His aim was true, but he stubbed his big toe on the chest at the foot of the bed. Leon cursed under his breath.

Ida massaged her throat as she spoke. "I grew up in a family that told me...things, things that'd make it easy for me to believe that my own actions were just and true. When the Little War of Three began, it—it was the perfect opportunity. Uncle Goefrin and my brother sent three of us here to Alesta."

King Leon dropped the letter in his hand.

"—Our task was simple. While the King was busy with the enemy at his border, we'd take the child Uncle Goefrin arranged for us to 'protect.'"

"No."

The single word sent her blue eyes to drown in unshed tears. "I swear to ya, Leon, I didn't know what they planned. No one said they were to kill 'er. I thought—"

"You thought what, exactly? You would kidnap my children and wife? My family? To do what exactly? Go for a walk in the woods? Who the hell are you to take part in such a—" This time when he shook her, the tears fled their prison and leapt across her cheeks. "That's what you are—you're Amaskan," he whispered. She winced when his fingers squeezed what little flesh clung to her bones, but she didn't look away. The quiet anger within left him breathless, yet he lifted her off her feet before he flung her to the floor with a snarl. "Who are you? What are you to crawl into my bed, into my heart. For ten years—"

The knock at the door startled them both. "Your Majesty?"

"Send the captain away," she hissed from where she'd fallen, her robe torn where she'd tripped over it.

"Why should I do anything you ask?"

"Because I'm the only one who knows where your daughter is."

He stared at the stranger before him, the jaguar who had slipped into his castle only to shred him with jagged claws as it toyed with his life. "I'll send him away, but only so he doesn't see the mess I've made when I'm done with you."

Her tears only made it worse. If she had acted like a cold-blooded killer, it would have been easier to kill her. *Damn her.* The wooden door shook as Michael resumed pounding on it. King Leon opened it enough to poke his balding head outside.

"Your Majesty, are you well? I heard shouting—"

"I'm fine. Give us a moment." Captain Fenton frowned, but nodded once before Leon shut the door.

"You have my attention for five minutes. Use it well, Ida. And leave nothing out—be truthful...if you're capable of it."

Ida nodded before wiping a few tears from her cheek with the back of her hand. "B-before I was captain of your guard, I was Amaskan. My brother's Malaki Abner, though few know his birth name as he hides in shadows, under many names and many labels. One ya may know is Eli Bredych."

Leon clenched his jaw against the words he would speak. *She's sister to the Amaskan leader. She may have just bought herself more time.*

Her hand moved along her scar, and when she realized the action, Ida clenched her hand into a fist. "Goefrin had a deal with my brother, though not the deal you think. His job was to convince ya that sendin' away your family was the best way to keep 'em safe. The Shadians paid the Amaskans to wipe out your line, and once you'd sent your family outside these walls, they were marked as kill on sight."

She swallowed hard. "I swear I didn't know my brother ordered Iliana killed. Not 'til we'd already seized her and had crossed into Sadai. He...he knew I'd have trouble with killin' a child. We all should've. That isn't justice, and it isn't what we..." Ida swallowed hard and closed her eyes a moment before continuing. "When the others told me what my coward brother couldn't—that we were to kill the child, I refused. The others attacked me. They said I was a traitor to justice."

"Did you kill them?"

"Yes, though I had little choice if either of us was to live, and when I returned to my brother with your daughter alive, he...he punished me for my failure to complete the job."

"He slit your throat."

"Yes, and he took pleasure in the act. No one leaves the Amaskans, not alive anyway. He grabbed your daughter and tossed me dyin' in the woods. My own brother abandoned me. And the last thing I saw was his blade to Iliana's throat. I don't know how the healers found me, or how they managed to heal such a wound, but I knew I couldn't return home. I swear to ya, when I set out for Alexander, I didn't come here with the intent to betray ya, Leon—"

"Then what was your purpose?" He could feel the vein in his temple pulse as his eyes drifted to the four-poster bed in the corner. The sheets were still a jumble of blue fabric, and bile threatened to choke him at the rush of memories that flooded to the forefront of his mind.

She continued talking, her shoulders slumped forward toward her knees. "All I could think about was how my brother killed a child. I fled here to try and make things right, to make up for my role in this. I didn't know I would fall in love with ya."

Despite the quaking in his belly, he held himself still as his fingers tried to carve half-moons into the wood of the bedpost. "Get up," he ordered, and she flinched before rising on trembling legs. "How is Iliana alive?"

"I don't know." Leon slapped her with the back of his hand and his ring left a bleeding scratch across her proud cheekbone. "Y-Your Majesty, I swear to ya—"

"Your oaths mean nothing. You betrayed this kingdom. You betrayed me. Get dressed."

Leon couldn't risk looking at her, couldn't risk seeing her clothe herself—an action he'd indulged in many mornings over the past decade. He forced his eyes to look upon her shadow as she gathered her clothing from the floor. It wasn't as simple as his love for her. His body knew what was before him and urged him forward, but his mind knew better. She was Amaskan—the deadliest of killers. One moment out of his sight, and she could kill him before he'd done more than blink.

While parts of him danced as he listened to her clothing brush against her supple skin, others winced at the thought of her blade in his guts. He caught a glimpse of bare shoulders as she pulled on an undershirt.

Shoulders I kissed in the darkness of night. Breasts I—he halted the thought with the biting of his tongue. His stomach roiled at the thought of touching her now, and her shadow moved to pull leather boots over her feet.

Ida Warhammer knelt before him for a second time. "Why did you return? You had to know doing so would mean your death."

"I-I couldn't let ya continue to think on her as dead. When I saw her in the capital, wearing the Order's garb, I nearly ran my horse to ground to return—"

"Wait. Back up," he said as he waved a hand at her. "Why was my daughter wearing the garb of the Order?"

His sepier's mouth twisted, and she tilted her head back to expose her scar to the light that streamed through the window. "If ya wish to finish the job my brother began, I wouldn't blame ya."

She didn't answer his question, nor did she have to. She was Amaskan. His daughter was Amaskan.

For a moment, he was sorely tempted, but here at last was the brave woman he loved. Awaiting her death by his hand. With legs almost too shaky to bear his weight, he stumbled over to where she knelt and touched the scar along her throat. He couldn't forgive her—not yet. If ever. But use her, he would.

"Does anyone in the Order know you were in Sadai?" he asked.

Ida opened her eyes in confusion. "I'm not sure. It's possible I was spotted, though I don't think they knew who I was. Why?"

"I have one last job for you."

"Ya would trust me enough to—"

Leon shook his head. "No, trust doesn't even begin to enter this picture. Now listen and listen well, Ida...if that's even your name. You're going to return to Sadai for me." He waited a moment for comprehension to sink in and when it did, her reaction was everything he'd hoped it would be.

He laughed as her eyes sought an escape, an honest laugh that shook him from the belly up, and he retrieved her sword from the chest beside him. When he handed it to her, she fumbled the blade. "Please, kill me if that's what ya wish, but don't ask me to go before my brother again—"

King Leon pressed a finger to her lips. "You will go to Sadai and not return until you have my daughter with you. You will return her to me. And if you fail me in this, the Boahim Senate will be the least of your worries, as I will hunt you down like the traitor you are. Don't fail me."

"My brother won't release her. She's his best Amaskan."

Inside his chest, a piece of his heart wilted, and he struggled to remain standing as another coughing fit brewed. "Do whatever it takes."

She handed him another glass of the healer's brew. "I'm sorry, Leon," she whispered before disappearing through his bedroom door. Outside, Michael cleared his throat, but King Leon ignored him as his bravado shriveled up and died.

His daughter was alive.

The mug in his hand shook and sloshed liquid across his knees. He had no knowledge of when he'd found his seat, but he rested on the chest at the foot of his bed which still smelled of the soaps Ida used. Fingers curled around the mug's handle before he sent it skittering across the floor, the remaining tea leaving a trail across the rug.

"Your Majesty?"

His ears heard the words, but his brain ignored them. *My Iliana. Now alive.*

And now a killer.

When the shakes began this time, he didn't stop them. He couldn't.

Alesta, Present Day

Ida. Always Ida. Why must she haunt his thoughts now when there was so much to do?

"Your Majesty?" The servant at his arm peered up at him, the bundle of flowers still in her hands. He motioned for her to withdraw, and the dozen servants left him alone in the audience chamber. For weeks they'd pestered Margaret about the flowers, the seating arrangement, what entertainment would play. The list continued until finally she'd thrown up her hands and stormed off in a bundle of stress and tears.

He thought he could help, but what did he know of such things? They scurried around planning the wedding, and all he could think on was Iliana.

And Ida.

His heart still leapt when he thought of her, and his hands still shook with the urge to strangle something. How could he love and hate someone at the same time? She plagued his thoughts—an irritating distraction when he needed his wits the most.

Word came that she awaited his daughter in Brieghton, and then nothing. Leon's thoughts flickered back and forth between past and present, while he outright ignored the future. Maybe this wedding would do him good. Provided it wasn't a trap.

King Leon stared across the mostly empty room until one of the royal guards cleared his throat. Captain Fenton approached and bent down on one knee before the throne. "Your Majesty."

"What news?"

"Messenger pigeons in from the border. Captain Warhammer returns with a guest." Leon released air he hadn't realized he'd been holding, and Michael continued, "Sire, Lieutenant Thomas says the woman is Amaskan. He asks if he should send anyone to kill her, or if Captain Warhammer will do the task."

Leon gripped the gilded armrests of his throne. "Do nothing. No one will harm her."

"Yes, Your Majesty. May I speak boldly, Your Majesty?" Leon nodded. Captain Fenton's booted toe traced a circle in the blue rug. "If she's Amaskan, as Captain of the Royal Guard, I should know. Or if nothing else, the Grand Marshal should be notified—"

"Captain, I understand your concern, but the woman traveling with Ida isn't Amaskan. She's a Master Guardsman out of Sadai, and I've sent for her to protect Margaret as her sepier."

"Is that wise? It's good for Her Highness to have a sepier, but to be frank, Her Highness isn't the easiest person to protect. If anything, this sepier may need a sepier herself just as a shield from Her Highness's shrieking tongue."

Leon laughed at the picture the young captain painted. "Point taken, Captain," he said once he'd caught his breath.

"Truly though, is this wise, Your Majesty? How much do you know about this Master Guardsman?"

The majority of the audience chamber stood empty, the exception being the royal guards who stood watch over King Leon. As such, most of the candles remained unlit, leaving the throne area a blazing brilliance of gold and blue in a dark and shadowed hall. Even in the dim lighting where Captain Fenton rigidly stood, Leon could see his furrowed brow.

"Put aside your worry," King Leon said with a broad smile.

"But, Sire—"

"I know all I need to, Fenton, all I need."

Or he hoped he did. *Iliana, come back to me a daughter.* He ran his fingers through his thinning hair and used the motion to hide his concern from the captain. *But a daughter isn't what you need.*

You need a killer.

CHAPTER NINE

Margaret stood unmoving, her eyes light slits as fabric moved across her frame before settling into place on girlish curves. A prick at the small of her back made her flinch, and she wobbled on the stool.

A servant latched onto Margaret's arm to steady her, and Margaret jerked her arm away. She scowled before turning her attention to her lady-in-waiting. "If you keep eating like a bird, my lady, this dress will fall off you before the wedding night, if you pardon my saying so," Lady Nisha said as she slid more pins into place.

Margaret's skin flushed, and she patted her cheeks to cool them. Two months. Two months before she would marry Prince Gamun, and yet she still blushed at the thought. She forced her eyes to the mirror. A delicate frame wrapped in a cocoon of pale blue silk, pale yellow threads embroidered the edges along her bosom and feet.

Beautiful dress. Not a beautiful princess. She frowned again, her lips pouting beneath a nose just a hair too large for her slight-jawed face.

"What is it, my lady?"

"Am I beautiful?" Margaret's eyes saw angles instead of smooth flowing fabric.

"Of course, cousin. You're very beautiful," Nisha replied.

Margaret spun away from the mirror to face her lady-in-waiting. Instead of fleeting eyes or fidgeting fingers, she found Nisha waiting with a wide smile that lit up her dark skin like a star. Margaret's frown deepened, and she tugged at the fabric bunched at her bosom. Trembling fingers danced over the flowered embroidery, but only saw the marred flesh at the edge of it.

Hoof beats rang in Margaret's ears.

Cold shadows as the horse moved, and a heavy weight leaning against her back which pressed the sharp edge of the pommel against her chest.

The princess shuddered and blinked back the memory. "I'm not worth the months it took to make this dress. Prince Gamun will take one look at me and declare me an impostor. Look at me—all bones swimming in yards of fabric."

Nisha stuck pins into the soft fabric and pulled it tighter to Margaret's frame. Margaret winced as another pin poked her, and she couldn't help but tug at the dress's waist, her hands smoothing the fabric over hip bones that protruded like rocks along a river bed. She bit one of her nails, then stilled her hands at her sides.

Her lady-in-waiting nodded at the correction and ordered more pins to be brought into the room.

If this dress is sent to the seamstress for adjustments one more time, I think Papa might bust the seams of his own britches. Margaret looked down on the black head of Lady Nisha and said, "I can't help it. I'm just too nervous to eat anything."

Nisha bent over the stitching on the back, clucking her tongue as she slid more pins. "The dress will have to be sent back to the seamstress for adjusting."

The woman rose, and Margaret took her hand in her own. "Thank you, Lady Nisha."

"Whatever for, my lady?"

"You've been like a sister to me, and I know, times like this how you must miss your home and your sister."

Her lady-in-waiting stared into the mirror at nothing and murmured, "Shad is no longer my home, and my family is dead. But you have given me both a new home and a new family, and a status I'd been stripped of in Shad. I am indebted to you, my lady."

With the pins in place, Margaret wiggled and squirmed as Nisha pulled the dress over Margaret's head. It was retired to the chest in the corner until its return to the seamstress. Margaret's shoulders slumped as her handmaidens dressed her. Their deft fingers made quick work of the task, yet Margaret frowned. "What is the matter, my lady?"

"My father. You know what he'll say when the dress goes back for a fourth time." She sucked in a breath as the handmaidens pulled on the laces of her corset.

Nisha chuckled. "Worry not. It's normal for a bride to be so, I swear it."

Margaret settled into her embroidery chair and picked up the stitching from earlier. "Would you recommend a purple or blue for his tunic?" Prince Gamun's embroidered face resembled a blob more than the image in her memory. Not that she recalled all that much. He was handsome, that she remembered. Still, no one would notice with the snow-topped mountains behind him.

Nisha settled next to Margaret. "I would choose the blue of your kingdom."

"I agree. Have you heard anything of interest lately, Lady Nisha? Please, take my mind from my nerves." Her fingers trembled as they pushed the threaded needle through the coarse fabric.

"Nothing."

Her lady-in-waiting stared at her feet, her own embroidery forgotten, and Margaret pushed the matter. "What have you heard? I know a lie when it's before me. Speak."

"There are rumors about the Prince. I don't wish to say, my lady."

Margaret caught the woman's arm, her fingers tightly gripping Nisha's brown skin. "You will say. I would know what things are said of my future husband."

Nisha stared at the stone floor as she whispered, fingers bunched in her russet skirts. "Some call him 'the Monster.' They say he enjoys things he ought not."

"Such as?"

"Young maidens."

Margaret flushed, the heat spreading across her almost gaunt cheeks. She wasn't supposed to know of such things, or at least that's what her father and tutors said behind cracked doors when they thought her not listening. But the books in the royal library held quite an education if one was so inclined. *Not that I read the entire book. Some parts were just too unseemly. As if men and women conducted themselves so.*

She shrugged at Nisha's words. "Most men prefer women to other men." The heat that spread across her arms and chest at this admission was more than embarrassment, and she pretended to study her too-short nails.

"No, my lady. The things they say he does, he hurts them. There are houses in Shad for men such as this, and it is said he frequents such places. The tales from Shad and Nicen—"

When Margaret stood, the embroidery tumbled to the floor and left the Prince a blob against the grey stone. "And where would you hear such unseemly topics? A lady of nobility such as yourself? Or be you the bastard the women say you are?"

Nisha's lip trembled and tears gathered in her eyes. "No, my lady. My sister, before she was killed, she told me of such things."

"Your sister is as unseemly as these tales of hers. I will not listen to such conversation. Now," Margaret said, taking in a deep breath before returning to her chair, "What color for his boots, black or brown?"

"B-black."

Margaret misplaced a stitch and picked at it, trying to remove the thick thread from the fabric's heavy weave. The piece of art was her wedding day gift to her new lord, and it had to be perfect. When Margaret said nothing of her lady-in-waiting's tears, the handmaidens busied themselves with cleaning the bower for a second time that day.

The thread broke, and Margaret bit the inside of her cheek. Rumors reached her ears as well, though she tried to dismiss them as lies. *Who knows the sources of such words? Besides, my father would never give me to some monster—someone like that.*

Nisha sniffed, and Margaret placed the sewing aside. "Nisha, come and talk with me. I am sorry that I chided you so. I haven't eaten. You know how I get when I forget to eat."

Nisha returned to the chair beside Margaret where she sorted the thread colors in the basket beside them. "Your memory of His Highness is perfect," she whispered.

"Is it? Maybe I remember only the perfect prince my mind wishes to see."

"There's little difference between ladies of noble birth and those cleaning the chamber pots." Margaret gasped, and Nisha continued, "Both are capable of speaking in lies to twist the mind. Pay no worry to the words spoken on your new Lord. I'm sure he's both handsome and perfect."

Margaret smiled, her eyes gazing at the stitching of the half-done Prince. "Just wait until he's done, Nisha. Better yet, just wait until he's here." The princess returned to stitching the blues of his tunic.

Two more months. Only two more months, my prince.

She had used him. Ida had used the King to escape the Amaskans and later, to save her own neck.

Adelei didn't remember her birth father, but after the story Ida told, she understood his fury. And his wish to kill Ida with his bare hands. If Adelei had half the brains, she'd do it now and save everyone the trouble. As the story had flowed, so had the ale. Ida's heavy snores punctuated the silent room, and Adelei frowned.

There was no way she was getting to sleep with all that racket. Not to mention the thoughts that bounced around in her brain. She breathed slowly to still her pounding pulse. *Might as well go see what there is to know.*

The dagger, she left behind, as well as most of her throwing knives. She kept the one tucked into her wrist as it was the hardest to detect. She pulled her hood around her bald head and rested her hand against the door.

No change in Ida's snores or any in the hall outside, and Adelei cracked the door. No guards waited outside nor were any people lingering in the hall. By the sounds of the clinking glasses and frothy talk, all the action was downstairs, and Adelei set out for a table near the bar.

When Ida and Adelei had first arrived, the random scattering of people at the inn had ignored the two women, but as Adelei reached the last rickety step, all dozen heads turned toward her. The servant from earlier pointed a shaking finger in her direction and looked up at Mel, the barkeep. "That's her. That's the Amaskan." he said, and Mel pursed her lips together.

"That true? You Amaskan?" asked Mel while she poured a bottle of something red into a glass.

Damn. Adelei slumped her shoulders toward her chest and forced a shudder. Instead of answering, she played the part of simpleton and looked on the crowd with fearful eyes.

"You hear Mel, girl?" The man closest to her stumbled drunkenly into reach, his nose bumping hers, and she held her breath to keep the stench of his breath from making her gag. She backed up a step and let her bottom lip tremble.

No way was she squeezing out tears when she was this angry. Ugh, why had they picked now to be so observant?

"Didn't Ida say she was stupid or somethin'? Mabbe tha boy was wrong," said the man to Mel's right, the owner of the red liquid in a glass.

Mel came out from around the bar and shoved the man with the horrible breath out of the way with one burly arm. "If that's tha case, what's she doin' down here? You hear me, girl? Whatcha doin' downstairs?"

Adelei pitched her voice as high and squeaky as she could. "I was thirsty."

"She can talk." The boy tumbled backward to land on his rear end, and the audience laughed.

"Of course she can, ya fool. See, Mel, I told ya this boy been spinnin' lies again."

The barkeep grabbed Adelei's chin and jerked her head side to side as she studied Adelei. Her white hooded cloak covered her healing scar, though Mel didn't give Adelei's jaw much look at all. Her gaze lay intently on Adelei's cheeks and chin. She must not have known where the tattoo was normally marked.

"I'll bring you somethin' ta drink. Go sit down," said Mel.

In the corner of the room rested a small table with only one chair, and Adelei chose it as her spot. She kept the hood close to her head, and maintained the look of frightened girl as she watched everyone with widened eyes.

When Mel plopped the mug down, it wasn't milk this time, though it didn't look like the ale she'd served Ida. Nor was it the red, foamy liquid the man at the bar savored. Adelei held the cup with shaking hands and sniffed it before turning up her nose in a soured face. "What is it?" she asked.

"Mead. Go ahead and give it a try."

Adelei suppressed the urge to roll her eyes and took a sip from the mug. Watered down raspberry wine more like—not a proper mead at all. She rubbed one hand across her leggings while scrunching up her face for their benefit.

The men in the room guffawed and bellowed. "She's no Amaskan, Mel. Look at that face. That's the face of someone who's never had good mead before," one patron yelled, and Mel grinned as she returned to the bar.

As her customers resumed their drinking, Adelei leaned the chair back against the wall and listened. Most of the chatter involved women—who had one, who was looking, and who was avoiding theirs by sitting at the inn—but none spoke of the upcoming royal wedding or the attacks on the royal family.

"Heard the shepherd boy got himself a new bundle of thatch."

"Oh? Does he look ta be buildin' a house?"

"So it seems. He's rather sweet on the baker's girl."

Adelei ignored the conversation and turned to the table to her left, which fared little better. "My Lady of the House of Hertwig is looking for a good breed mare. Might be seein' if ol' Betsy has a few more in 'er." Laughter followed the statement, and she stilled the tapping of her foot.

I'd say they were avoiding the conversation with me in the room. Even if I'm a harmless dull-wit.

She sat in her corner nursing her "first glass of mead" for an hour with little of use said in the candle lit room. Her jaw-splitting yawn was a warning. Boredom and fatigue were not friends to an Amaskan. Unwilling to arouse more suspicion or fall face first into her mead, Adelei sauntered back up the stairs to the room she shared with Ida. The warrior answered the door's groan with a loud snort.

Adelei stripped off her clothes and pulled on a long tunic for sleep. Between the loud snores and her throbbing head, she ended up staring at the planks of wood overhead and imagining she was home.

In Sadai.
Where I'll never be again.

Sounds of people and animals moving outside the inn's walls announced the morning too early for Ida, who cursed and grumbled her way through dressing. Despite Adelei's late evening, she awoke alert and rested.

By the time both women entered the empty stables, the sun had spread across the small town. It cast shadows in corners and curves and nooks and crannies as people went about their business. Both horses whinnied and stomped their feet, their tails dancing in the sun.

It must have been a rough night in the stable if Midnight wanted to hit the trail again. She wiped down the stallion's back before tossing a riding blanket over his side. Ida's fuzzy-headed fingers made saddling her mare a chore.

Adelei was long finished saddling Midnight as Ida swore, dropped the bridle, and then swore again. "Damn fingers feel like pig guts this mornin'."

"Do you need some help?"

Ida's groggy stare was enough to light all the fires in the inn's hearths at once, yet Adelei continued to grin as she waited. Payback was warranted.

After half a candlemark, they were on their way, and Adelei's fingers traced the outlines on the saddle's pommel. Ida spoke, her voice tired and thick with hangover. "Ya were five when ya were taken from Alexander, but much has improved since the war. No longer are the people comprised of starvin' and poor farmers, them dyin' in the streets. The poor still exist, but rebuildin' brought change to these lands. Alexander's a major trader of many goods across the Little Dozen."

The woman paused to stare across a patch of dense forest. "This forest used to hide our enemy, and pockets of it were destroyed in the fires of war; but now it's home to many. The forest grows thick, as does the kingdom's wealth."

Adelei could taste the burned stench in the air. "I clung to the saddle."

"I'm sorry?"

"I clung to the saddle. The trees whipped past me. I could barely see through the hood you tossed over my head, but I could smell the woods. The land reeked of blood and smoke." When Adelei opened her eyes, the forest was clear of the past.

At some point, Midnight had stopped, digging her hooves into the dirt and leaves below. Adelei swallowed hard. "We passed through here—along this pass, didn't we?"

"Yes. 'Twas the only way to get past the Shadian army. 'Twas the forest or not at all. I'd forgotten we'd come through here." Both horses moved on, a quicker journey as both women sought to escape the ghosts swinging in the trees.

"I'm surprised the King is going through with the marriage." Adelei inhaled the pine fragrance to try and rid herself of the acrid scent burned into her nostrils. "After all these years, surely Alexander could build a strong enough army to defeat Shad if they attacked. Why not refuse the marriage?"

Ida hissed in a swift breath. "And be an oathbreaker? Never."

"Better an oathbreaker than to sell your child to the enemy, I would think. Especially one who may be behind attempts to take out the royal bloodline."

Silence followed both women for a time as they passed a smaller town and crossed yet another creek. As they approached the second town of the day, people ran up to Ida and reached up hands to greet her. Children cried out for her to stop and tell them a tale, while parents offered invitations to stop and quench her thirst.

She refused all offers as they traveled and once away from starving ears, she resumed their conversation. "I know ya view this marriage with serious doubts, but the princess is excited about it. She's found her prince and is ready to become Queen." Ida pitched her voice too high.

She was lying again. Adelei asked Ida, "Has she even met the man she's to marry?"

"Once. 'Twas an arranged meetin', of course, but they got along well enough."

"Has anyone considered that the Prince of Shad or his people could be behind the assassination attempts on Her Highness?"

"Of course," Ida answered. "King Leon for one. But I don't know the details of the event, or the investigation that happened after. His Majesty's keeping those details to himself. I do know that Princess Margaret's not aware an attempt has been made on her life." Another lie, another twitch of the woman's cheek.

Adelei held her tongue as they passed the first travelers on the road: a horse drawn carriage with numerous guards who were wary until they spotted Ida's sigil on her tunic. They glared at Adelei with deep frowns and kept their hands near their weapons.

"How does Her Highness not know? Or more importantly, why doesn't she know?"

"I'm not privy to that information. 'Twas your father's choice not to tell her. The attack was made the very same day she met Prince Gamun, who prevented its success. More than that, you'll have to ask your father. He doesn't trust me enough to tell me anythin' these days."

The crushing of leaves ahead of them caught Adelei's attention, and she pulled her hood tighter before ducking closer to the saddle. It was probably another traveler. Gods knew there would be enough of them between here and Alesta.

Ida sat in the same position, her eyes scanning the trees in front of them. Adelei almost missed it—the slightest hints of emerald green that didn't match the surrounding trees' muted colors. The bright tone rocked back and forth a fraction of space.

Adelei's fingers, hidden from view by Midnight's neck and massive head, pointed in the direction of the color. At Ida's nod, she rolled out of the saddle to drop to the leaves below. At the same time, Ida kicked her mare, which reared up. Midnight sidestepped to avoid the mare, and Adelei used the noise and size of her horse to shield herself from movement until she could lean behind a tree.

Stepping carefully, she made her way around the clearing and used the trees for cover. Adelei cursed her lack of green clothing to camouflage her movements. While the forest held shadows, her white clothes were too bright. As Adelei moved, Ida tried unsuccessfully to regain control of her horse as the beast continued stepping away from her.

The mare reared, stomping around in the underbrush and making quite the racket. Ida gave the mare conflicting signals with the words she spoke, and the chaos provided cover. The distraction worked as Adelei stepped behind the hidden foe crouched behind a bush.

His knocked arrow wavered as it followed Ida's movements, but it ceased its path when Adelei's dagger touched his throat. "Drop the bow and arrow," she whispered.

The foe did both readily enough and stood at her urging. Adelei guided him out into the clearing where Ida's mount instantly settled. Ida approached them both, her hand on her sword's hilt. "Are you alone?" Adelei asked as she peered out into the trees.

When the man didn't answer, a trickle of blood appeared at his throat in warning. "I'm alone."

"Good. Who was your target?"

Beads of sweat popped up across his forehead and rolled down a freshly shaved cheek. Ida's six foot two inch frame leaned over him, her grin harsh and nightmarish on its own, and his throat convulsed as he swallowed hard. "I believe we asked ya a question, son," Ida hissed.

"I was—I was ta look for a companion. A warrior bein' brought in from outKingdom."

So I was the target. But he thought Ida was the warrior. She glanced at Ida who nodded. She, too, caught his mistake.

"Who sent you?" Adelei asked and pushed the knife a smidge closer to his flesh. Instead of answering, the man lunged forward, shoving his neck deeper into her blade. The arterial crimson sprayed out and coated the leaves at his feet. Adelei pulled the knife away and released the man to the forest floor.

It wasn't soon enough. The attacker bled out in the dirt and leaves.

"Damn." As he breathed his last breath, Adelei's hands shuffled through pockets along his body. She was careful and tried to shield probing fingers from poisoned bits that could stick her. Well acquainted with such techniques, Adelei avoided his wrists and waist until she stripped him of his clothes and weapons.

Ida stood guard, her eyes never leaving the forest. On the inside of his right ankle, Adelei found what she'd been both hoping for and praying against—a small triangle burned into the skin. It was red and puffy from recent marking.

"He's Tribor."

The former captain wrenched her gaze away from the trees and at the new tattoo. "Gods be with us," she whispered.

Adelei dragged his body by the arms away from the clearing and into a patch of thick underbrush where she covered it with twigs and leaves. Ida kicked up dirt to cover all traces of his blood. It wasn't the quickest or cleanest way to cover evidence, but it was all they had.

"We dare not stop now. We must reach the city of Menoir before nightfall," said Adelei as she cleaned her knife on some of the leaves from the forest floor.

"That's a day's travel at a steady pace. If we push the horses, we could make it by sunset." Once they were both astride, both forced their mounts forward at a gallop.

They already knew where they were. No need to hide their horses' passage at that point. If they didn't reach the walls of a city by nightfall, one of them might not make it there at all.

"You have more experience with the Tribor than me, being closer to Shad. What do you know of them?" she called out to Ida as they brushed past the trees.

"Assassins. Not Amaskans—no morals, no creed outside their worship of Itova, the Death Goddess. They're hired thugs who'll do any job, no matter how dirty." The warrior spit on the ground. "It's rumored they hail from Shad."

"So nothing the Amaskans didn't already know. Damn, I was hoping you knew something more."

Ida shook her head. "I wish. Might make your job simpler."

"If the Shadians support the Tribor, they may be behind the assassination attempts on the princess. But why not just cancel the wedding and declare war? Why the pretense of a treaty?" A deer up ahead fled from their horses' hooves as they passed, and Adelei ducked beneath a tree branch that came close to smacking her in the face. "Ida, if the princess dies after the wedding, who gets the crown?" Ida cocked an eye brow and tilted her head. "No," Adelei answered the unspoken question, "No, I don't want it. Assuming that, who would get it if the royal line is exterminated?"

"The prince would rule on behalf of any children 'til they were of age. If there are no children, the treaty states the prince would rule, and upon his death, our country would return to the Alexandrian bloodline if he begot no heirs. Some cousin or another would take the crown."

So they need the marriage to put the prince in line for taking over the crown. Once there, he could attempt to change the laws any way he saw fit— after all, with my sister and father out of the picture, who would be left to stop him?

Following Adelei's line of thought, Ida called out, "The people of Alexander would never stand by and allow a Shadian to wrest away control of the crown."

"They may not have a choice if the Shadian army invades. They can't be too obvious about it—so they'll use their pet Tribor to kill off the royal family. Nothing but a bunch of murderers." In this case, the term was accurate. The Tribor didn't take sides; they killed indiscriminately.

They even kill children. We're in trouble. Not that Adelei couldn't take on a Tribor or two, but she was willing to bet she would be outnumbered. And racing for safety with her back to the enemy. The thought sent a shiver through her, and Adelei leaned closer to the saddle to minimize herself as a moving target.

The two women kept their horses at the pace as long as they could. Sweat coated their hides while foam gathered at their mouths. Adelei patted her horse's neck. "I promise you all the water and warm oats you can eat if you can get us to Menoir. Just hang in there," she whispered in Midnight's ear.

As they broke free of the forest, the main road held throngs of travelers headed for the capital. With the joining of two royal families, everyone who was able packed up for an extended stay. It was a chance to visit with family and friends seen rarely enough and an excuse to imbibe to excess at the King's expense. And with the roads thick with travelers, it would take some a good month's walk to reach the city.

The crowd forced them to slow their mounts, lest they trample some child running underfoot. The guards at the gates raised bows as their battle mounts trotted toward the entrance to the city.

Ida held the gold coin in the air. Within a breath, someone called for the gate to be opened just wide enough to allow the women through, single file, before the tall, wooden doors were slammed shut. The guardsmen threw the heavy bars into place to lock it.

The crowds outside whined, and a few demanded entrance. Adelei ignored them as she slid off her horse. Midnight's foamy mouth shuddered as he panted, and she leaned against him for support as she fought to catch her own breath. Her closeness kept him calm as people moved around them, their shoulders bumping her as they carried their travel bags in the direction of whatever inns the town held. She could see why they had closed the gates. The town was overrun with travelers as it was.

A hand reached out to touch Midnight's flank and Adelei spun, dagger in hand. Steel slid from scabbards, but Ida touched Adelei's shoulder and shook her sweaty head. The shadow that had fallen over the horse stood before her, and his hand remained on his sword.

Ida stepped in front of Adelei, placing her muscular frame between the two parties. "Nice to see ya again, Lieutenant Gerald," she said, no trace of a smile on her face.

The officer glared at Ida, his grip on the hilt of his sword relaxing just a hair. He didn't offer a hand or a smile, but instead, turned about face and strode to the stairs of a guard tower.

"What's his deal?" Adelei said.

"The good lieutenant doesn't like managin' a city. Feels his talents would be better suited in a position such as Captain of the Royal Guard or even sepier." Ida chuckled as she unstrapped bags from her horse. "Who knows, he may yet replace me in that regard with everythin' that's happened."

A younger sergeant, blue eyes like the Harren Sea and a bright smile to match, saluted them both. The young man squirmed under Ida's gaze, his face slightly flushed, but he remained in place at attention. Before the sergeant could speak, Ida's thick arms wrapped around his bean-pole frame. When she released him, she stepped back, her eyes traveling his length. "Ya need to eat more."

"Really, Mom? They feed me well enough."

Ida laughed. "This's my son, Sergeant Leolin. Leolin, this's Master Adelei of Sadai."

The young man's grip reminded Adelei of Ida herself, firm but friendly, and just a touch suspicious. His lankier height didn't detract from a face that mirrored Ida's own. Dark complexion led to Ida's blue eyes and a crooked nose that bore her spirit as well. But his chin was wide and strong, not like the tapered chin of his mother, and his long, tailed hair was as dark as night.

"Is there somewhere we can speak? Privately?" asked Ida.

Leolin nodded. A quick whistle brought several stablehands forward, who stopped when Adelei's hand shot up in warning. She patted Midnight's flank and whispered to him, "*Shie-neah*," and the horse relaxed. Midnight followed where the stablehand led him. Leolin, Ida, and Adelei crossed the courtyard and entered a building that looked more like a barn than a proper military building. Though once inside, Adelei admired its efficient use of space as offices; guest rooms were crammed back to back like a large jigsaw puzzle.

What space wasn't allotted for rooms held storage shelves and bins aplenty. Every space served some purpose. Sergeant Leolin ushered the women into a meeting room of sorts, and his frown deepened as he watched his mother rake her fingers through her graying brown hair.

"We're headin' out tomorrow," Ida said as she lowered herself into a chair. "But I'd have ya know that we were attacked on the way here."

Leolin leaned over the table toward his mother, searching for signs of a wound. "Who?"

"Tribor."

"Are you sure?"

"Yes."

His fist struck the wooden table, and a small crack appeared in the polished wood, which widened when he struck the table again. "How do you know?"

Adelei said, "He bore the mark."

"And just who are you? Unknown master of what exactly?" His mother gasped and uttered his name, but he continued. "Who are you to know about the mark of Tribor? Was he after you?"

When Adelei stood, she allowed her hood to fall from her head. Almost two weeks' travel had left sharp, black stubble across her head and even with the scab at her jawline, the boy must have put two and two together as he shook his head while he stood between the two women. "I'm a former member of the Order, like your mother," she whispered. "But this isn't public information, understand?"

In the military's blue uniform, his tall stance aged him. But when he gaped at her, the young man became the boy again. He was younger than he looked. She had thought him her age, but he couldn't be much more than sixteen, maybe seventeen. To Ida, she asked, "I take it you two have a bone to pick with the Tribor?"

"We do. They killed Leolin's father."

Footsteps outside alerted them to someone's approach. Adelei threw her hood over her head, and all tongues stilled as the door opened. A soldier poked his head around the door. "Sergeant, I heard a loud noise from inside here. Sir, I'm sorry to intrude, but is everything all right—"

"We're fine. Leave us." The young man nodded once to Leolin before closing the door with an audible click.

"I thought you said this room was private, Sergeant."

Leolin crossed the room and locked the door. "It normally is, Master Adelei. Whatever your business here, it had better be worth this. The Tribor don't stop until their mark is dead. You put a great many people at risk by being here."

"Son, we understand the risk. But what would ya have us do? Out there, we'd be dead once dark hit the trees." She patted her son's hand gently. "I hate to burden ya further, but we need a room for the night. After that, we'll be gone, and the Tribor hopefully with us." A silent plea passed from mother to son.

Leolin beckoned them to follow him. "I'll get you a room. But you must leave by morning. I cannot risk the people of this town or the travelers outside the gates with your presence. If the Tribor are on your tail, we're all in danger. Security is nightmare enough, especially with an ever changing border. Mother, I'm sorry, but I can't do more."

The woman wrapped her son in a hug. "I'd expect nothin' less from ya my son, nothin' less."

CHAPTER TEN

Leaving Menoir proved uneventful, no further evidence of the Tribor present as both women journeyed the half-day toward Alesta. While Ida relaxed in the saddle, a tension knot ached in Adelei's neck that sang of nerves on edge and too long on the road. The morning proved quiet for both of them, leaving Adelei time to worry about the assassin that was or wasn't on their tail.

She was sure Ida worried about the son she'd left behind, no matter how relaxed her stance appeared. Adelei had never encountered a Tribor assassin in person, but the stories whispered behind closed doors at the Order were enough to give her pause.

"As the saying goes, flee before that which makes Amaskans fear," Adelei muttered.

"What brought that up?"

"I was thinking about the price on my head is all. I feel like I'm walking into a death trap."

"Look at it this way," Ida said as she chewed on a piece of apple, "They're of such small numbers; they probably won't be a huge threat once we reach the city."

"I've heard there's fewer than twenty members, but if they all came here, this could get ugly."

Ida waved her hand in the air. For all her carefree action, her thighs clenched against her mare's side. She was as nervous as Adelei.

They passed by more travelers along the path, and Adelei lost herself in thought. The thoughts, worrisome though they were, held a distraction from their approach to the capital. Alesta's outer walls and smaller dwellings on the outskirts blended in so well with those they'd been passing for a candlemark that she didn't realize they stood before the city until Ida's mare stopped and Adelei took a good look at the city sprawl.

The capital city spread across Adelei's view like a swarm of bees; houses and people scattered across the horizon in their busy lives. *I had no idea the city was this huge.*

While the capital city of Sadai was a large city, Alesta was three times its size, stretching across a spread of land easily five miles in diameter. The castle lay off in the distance, tucked safely behind several sets of city walls.

Each wall must have been built as the city expanded with the populace. Or after each war. She searched the castle for any indication of its size but couldn't see much more than spires and the occasional tower poking above the brick and stone. As they approached the outer ring of walls, Ida removed the royal coin from her bag and held it in her hand.

Their horses pressed up against the throngs of people seeking entrance at the gate. Midnight whinnied and pranced beneath Adelei, and she patted his neck. While trained for the noises and confinement of battle, this group was a different setting all together. So many people. The good news was she'd be difficult to find in such a mess. Of course, if she were hard to identify, so were the Tribor.

The guard at the first gate stopped them without so much as looking up from a piece of parchment. "Names?"

Ida spoke as they'd decided last night in Menoir. "Captain Ida Warhammer, returnin' from duty, and guest."

The guard glanced up from his parchment and tried to peer under Adelei's hood. He studied her a moment longer before giving Ida a pained expression. "Sorry, Captain, but I need her name."

"No, ya don't."

He stared again at Adelei and waved a hand in front of her. "Hey—you have a name, honey?" A slight smirk played across his face. When she didn't respond and instead stared over his head, he laughed. His hand moved to slap her thigh, though it made it only halfway as she caught his wrist in her grip and squeezed his fingers. He winced and tried to wriggle out of her grasp.

"I believe she told you it wasn't necessary."

Adelei released his fingers, which he rubbed before jotting something down on his paper. "My apologies, Captain. My lady," he mumbled and bowed in Adelei's direction.

As they passed through the gate, Adelei whispered to Ida, "Please make note of him. If I was given entrance so easily, who else might ride through the gates with a royal escort?"

"Indeed. You're certainly goin' to chafe a lot a highborns with security changes."

"Just part of the job," Adelei said.

The road, if it could be called such, was dirt covered and littered with yet more dust and grime. What few people were out, bustled quickly about their business, gathering baskets or livestock or both. The business oozed out into the street, and she steered Midnight around many bodies too preoccupied to notice the massive beast alongside them.

She kept her eyes forward and while she studied her new home, she tried not to think about how many people lived in a city *this* large.

Another pass through the second set of city walls saw a shift in both decoration and poverty level. People lined the dirt road, selling anything from food and clothing, to sex and herbs that would send the mind away from the body. Here the people noticed their passage. They had little choice in the narrow, overcrowded streets.

But even here, the people fought over every notch and penny spent on goods. Fierce bargainers crowded near every booth, and Adelei had to fight Midnight's nerves as they passed. It wasn't until after they passed the third and final inner city walls that she relaxed her grip on the reins and allowed herself to take notice of the change in the city.

If going through the second walls had been a change, this was a complete metamorphosis. Two-story homes of brick rather than wood lined the now cobbled street, and the people moved about with upper-class airs, gloved hands pointing as servants manhandled the merchandise sold by street corner vendors.

Handsomely dressed men or mothers escorted young women who carried finely woven baskets or bags as they shopped.

Here among the rich, Ida was noticed and as quickly dismissed. "Could you imagine, Cordelia? Riding such an ugly beast as that and like a man no less." one elderly woman muttered, a scowl marring her face.

The young woman ignored her mother and reached out a hand to touch Adelei's leg. "Look at the white of it, Mother. It's so bright and soft. Like kittens."

The mother guided her charge away by the shoulders, and Adelei chuckled at the woman's chagrin. "Is white so rare in Alexander?"

"The minerals used to lighten the fabric aren't easily available in these parts. 'Course, you'll see it with nobility, but not so much among the commoners. I'm a bit surprised she treated ya as such. To them, ya appear of noble birth so to be rude and risk your displeasure could have dire consequences for them."

The clicking of Midnight's hooves as they trotted through the city bore a certain rhythmic lull, and Adelei relaxed in the saddle. The castle loomed overhead, a quarter of a mile away at the most, and from this distance the castle wore its age with less grace. The six-hundred-year-old bricks bore pocks and nicks from countless battles over the centuries. High up, windows scattered across the grey walls, but no matter how much Adelei searched, no one stood looking down on her. She doubted she'd be able to see anyone anyway from this distance.

The calm held until the castle walls were close enough to touch, and as they rode through the fifteen-foot-high archway that led to the castle grounds proper, Adelei's stomach clenched and churned, making the apple she'd had around noon sour in her belly.

Ida smiled gently at her, but there was little she could do to prepare Adelei for the reunion with her family. Another stop to identify themselves to more guards, and they passed on. "It's good to see the guards asking even you to identify yourself. Most city guards would look at your coin and wave you on through, never mind that you could have stolen it."

"Anyone who snatched this would've had to kill me. If that was the case, I'd say they earned it." The women led their horses across an open courtyard and toward the massive stables to their right. "After the war, security was much greater a concern. We could tighten it up, or open ourselves up for attack all over again."

Over a dozen people ran in some form of mild panic as items and decorations were carried to and from various parts of the castle. Adelei imaged the chaos inside was something to behold, though she'd rather not encounter it. It would only get worse as the wedding approached.

Sweat trickled down the small of her back beneath the white silk. Despite their distance from the desert, the heat outside left Adelei sweltering beneath her cloak. In the forest's cool shade, she'd needed the warmth, but here the direct sun tried to melt the skin from her bones. Adelei tugged at the corner of her hood and wished she could remove it.

A stablehand awaited their approach, eyes wide at the sight of Midnight. Even calm as the boy was with Adelei by his side, the horse towered over him. Ida handed her mare to the lad, but Midnight stayed firmly in Adelei's control as she followed the stablehand into the stables. He indicated with a shaking finger which stall she should take.

While large enough for maybe a small pony, the stall was too small for a horse, and it was dwarfed in comparison to Midnight. He'd spend the entire time bumping his shoulders against the sides. He'd be unable to turn around to drink or eat. Every stall was occupied as wedding guests arrived well in advance of the wedding. One of the larger stalls further down held a pony of only twelve hands. Adelei leaned across the stall's door and spied his saddle slung across a shelf in the stall's rear. A well-polished, clean saddle embellished with purple ribbon. That was a royal horse if ever she saw one.

"Stay," she told Midnight, who settled into a guard-like position. Adelei approached the pony, and he sniffed her outstretched fingers that reached over the gate. His breath tickled her fingertips, and she smiled. When she opened the gate, he nuzzled her shoulder as she hoisted his saddle up with both hands.

She led the pony to the smaller stall next to Ida's own mare, and set his gear down beside him. The stablehand rushed over, his face pale as his words ran in a fountainous rush. "You can't touch Hero. Please, just put—put 'em back."

He stepped too close to Midnight in his rush, and the battle steed aimed a kick backward. It missed the boy's head by inches. Warning delivered, the boy stumbled and fell to his rump in the hay.

"Let her be, lad. It's obvious her mount needs the bigger box." The voice came from her rear-left, and Adelei listened for the man's movements as she patted Midnight's neck. Hero seemed just as happy to be in a new place, and immediately noticed the replacement of his feed. With a *harrough*, he dug into the food and ignored the stable boy's commotion.

When Adelei turned to take Midnight's reins, she found a grown man holding them, and Midnight nibbled at the collar of his brown tunic. The fact that Midnight was friendly with the man was amazing; that the horse wasn't trying to kill him was nothing short of a miracle. A roughened hand was thrust in her direction as the voice from earlier continued. "Horse Master Will."

She held out her own hand to the man and found his grip spoke of hard work and strength. "Master Adelei of Sadai."

"A master of horses?"

"No, weapons work."

"I wondered what with a horse like that. You must be like Captain Warhammer then." At first she thought he meant Amaskan, and her body tensed. But he turned his back to her as he led Midnight to his new stall. "Sepier to the King of Sadai or some such?" he asked.

Adelei didn't answer as he stripped her horse of tack and saddlebags. "Adelei, we're needed elsewhere," Ida said from behind her, and with one last glance at Midnight, she followed the warrior out of the stables.

"Why didn't Midnight take his hand off?" she asked Ida.

"I taught Master Will how to deal with battle steeds out of Sadai."

"Ah, that explains it." As they stepped around the corner, they were met by a page garbed in blue and silver from head to toe.

"Captain, Master, if you'll come with me, please," he stuttered with a quick bow. The page led them to the castle entrance where a welcoming party of one waited, the older man dressed in a similar blue. No crown or marks of royal blood, though his finery probably meant he was ennobled in some fashion or another.

I guess I don't rank a formal welcome. But then, no Amaskan would.

The man stepped forward and inclined his head to them both. "I am to welcome you, Master Adelei, to Alexander. Our King welcomes you as well and regrets that he could not be here himself to greet you as his daughter's wedding soon approaches. I am Lord Dumont Darras, Grand Advisor to the King."

Adelei stepped forward and bent at the waist. "I am Master Adelei of Sadai. I thank you for your welcome, as I thank your King as well."

He nodded before leading them through the gate and into the castle's interior. Adelei couldn't help herself. Her mouth gaped at the splendor of Alexander's wealth, clearly visible from its smooth stone walls to its decor. Hints of silver and sapphire gleamed back at her as the sun bounced off the hallway's corners. "Magnificent, isn't it? Though I would think it nothing compared to the capital city of Sadai."

"No, this far surpasses it," she replied, honest in her evaluation.

Rich tapestries hung across the walls, sewn with thread that could be made of silver and gold itself, and rugs of a similarly fine weave lay across the ground. The pale, grey stone floor gleamed like polished glass. She was tempted to drop to her hands and knees to see how the effect was done. Instead she vowed to discover the secret as soon as time allowed. Assuming she lived long enough.

As they followed several long hallways toward the castle's center, the imagined chaos of Adelei's mind became reality with people of all stations everywhere at once. Maids, servants, pages, and squires all dashed about in a not-quite-so-orderly fashion, every last one of them carrying something taller, wider, or heavier than themselves. Ladies and lords gathered in grand rooms and hallways to gossip, each one trying to outguess the other on whether or not the wedding would even occur.

Would the princess marry a Shadian? Would she order him killed first? Would the bride wear a royal crown from Shad or from Alexander?

The gossip alone could drive Adelei into hiding until the wedding was over. It was stressful enough returning here after fifteen years without finding it full of a bunch of biddies all aflutter over some overly expensive excuse to drink themselves into oblivion. It wasn't even their wedding, yet it was all about them. As it always was with high court.

As much as it bothered her, she took note of each person the best she could in such a massive group of people, searching for weapons or motives and listening for sounds of discontent or anger. It was challenging to do as they moved at Dumont's brisk pace, but she filed away what little she could. *I'll think on it later when I've had the chance to walk the castle, alone and better disguised.*

Up four flights of stairs and down another hall before they reached the royal family's suite. The number of guards and servants in the halls doubled. As they passed one room, a flush-faced handmaiden stumbled through the door, her hands full of lace as someone on the other side shouted. The maid scuttled away, and Adelei silently counted to ten.

The shout was no doubt her royal spoiledness, throwing a royal tantrum over Gods knew what. Only a princess could screech like a banshee. Dumont waited for Adelei at the second door and ushered her inside.

The sitting room was more luxurious than any room she'd ever seen, and she whistled. Blue decorated every item in the room, right down to the rugs and paintings, and yet some blues were so light they neared white and others so dark that they more closely resembled the blacks of the Amaskan silks. The variance in color added such depth to the room that the blue wasn't overwhelming, just richly ornate.

"This is Her Highness's sitting room. Your room is the first door on the right. After that is Her Highness's study and then her own bedchambers. The stairs here," he said, pointing straight ahead, "lead to Her Highness's bower."

Much to Adelei's relief, he led her to her rooms rather than those of her sister. While her new room was lavishly decorated, it paled in comparison to the room she'd just left. *Baby blue.* Why couldn't it have been dark blues? Instead she got the room meant for the royal heir. The shades were the stuff of nightmares.

"Just out of curiosity, what purpose did this room serve before being prepared for me? Something about the color scheme makes me doubt it has always been for a visiting Master."

"Um, yes, it—it used to be the room for the Princess's sister, may the Gods bless her."

Had she really lived in this room? She held no memory of it, and she frowned. Might have been for the best with a color scheme like that. Not that she'd be spending much time there anyway.

The single bed wedged into the corner, and a small desk stood in the opposing corner with a chair missing a leg. A few empty bookcases lined the walls. Instead of anything useful, flowers and decorative art plastered itself along the walls and shelving. It wasn't functional. It was...*pretty.*

My first task is redecorating. I damned well won't live in a flower pot like this. The lack of furniture left the feel of space, but the space was empty. And she alone in it. Another door led to her private bathroom, complete with an actual tub, but even that struggled to conquer her moodiness.

Adelei grimaced as she left her room. "Is something to your disliking, Master Adelei?" Dumont asked.

"I think the blue has made me ill."

Dumont cleared his throat. "Very well. His Majesty has requested that you remain in your room or the sitting area if you wish until you are called for. He will see you at his earliest convenience."

As he left, Adelei touched his arm. "Wait—can you tell me where Captain Warhammer is now? I hadn't realized she didn't follow us in."

"She's standing outside the royal suite. Do you wish to see her?"

"Yes, please."

His clean boots squeaked on the polished floor as he walked. "Captain?" he said as he stuck his head out the door, and Ida followed him into the sitting room. "Captain, you have but a few minutes as His Majesty wishes to see you at once."

The door closed behind him, and Adelei spun once around the room. "Overdone much? I think I might die of a case of the blues."

Ida grinned as her fingers trailed over the back of a blue upholstered couch. "This's goodbye for now, I'm afraid."

Adelei shook Ida's outstretched hand. "Are you stationed in the capital or elsewhere in Alexander? When you aren't playing escort, that is."

"Normally, my job's to guard His Majesty. I watch people. Look for problems that need my handlin'. Sometimes I run errands or go places His Majesty can't. With your bein' here and truth about me bein' out, I don't know what His Majesty will do with me."

While Ida smiled, the corners of her mouth didn't stretch far enough, and the smile's light didn't reach her eyes. "I'm sorry for my part in all this."

Adelei touched the armor bearing shoulder. "I know you were doing your job, as I'm doing now. When the Master sends you to Justice, your blade must carry you through." She swallowed the lump in her throat. "If I had it my way, I'd be home in Sadai right now and not on this job."

"This is your home, Iliana Poncett, whether ya agree or not. I hope ya remember what this place once meant to ya."

"May we meet again soon, Ida."

"May ya find your Way here, and may the Way be home."

Adelei drew her hand to her mouth in surprise at the ancient blessing. It was a blessing given between only the closest of family, the very same blessing Master Bredych whispered in her ear as she left Sadai over a week ago. Tears sprang to her eyes, which she blinked away rapidly. All three saddlebags were dragged into her room.

This isn't home.

She could give into the morose mood that had settled in behind her thoughts, but she decided to redecorate in earnest. All flowers, embroidery, and tapestries were removed and tossed into the chest at the bed's foot. Even the floor rug, a hideous baby blue with cherubs bouncing around on clouds, was stowed away, though she regretted the loss as the stone floor was cold right through her boots.

No fireplace warmed the room, and she vowed to get more appropriate rugs and bedding soon. She needed to secure several blankets if she didn't want to freeze to death at night. No windows was both a blessing and a curse. She was safer than some, but unable to see the enemy coming. It also meant she couldn't leave the room any other way than through the main door.

Unpacking her few belongings kept her from thinking too long and hard about the inevitable meeting with her father. Adelei's stomach knotted. She stashed her reserve weapons around the room in easy reach: one beneath the corner of the bed's mattress and another inside a now empty vase.

Most of her books remained at the Order. She didn't know if they would send them to her or not. What would a former Amaskan need with such texts? Her finger brushed against the three books she had packed, and she set them on one bookshelf where they rested as footnotes to the empty case.

It would do for now. Adelei leaned carefully on the chair to test its strength. It wobbled, and a small creaking confirmed it was as useless as the decorations had been. Nothing else to do, she sat on the bed and studied the furniture. What was a liability? What was a weapon?

The bed's location was a problem. Pushed against the wall with a chest at the foot left her only one direction to flee in a fight, and chances were that would drive her straight into the sword of an attacker. Bookshelves were pushed out of the way and not a concern, but the desk faced the wall, leaving her back exposed to the door and only means of entrance.

There was room to work with, too much in fact. Adelei removed her cloak and left it folded on the bed. Free to work, she spun the desk around to face the door until it rested perpendicular to the wall. The two mostly empty bookshelves could be moved behind the desk and against the rear wall, but their heavy mahogany resisted the stone floor, and they remained in place.

When someone knocked on her door, she stubbed her booted toe on one of the bed legs, and a guard opened the door to find her leaning over the desk cursing. His mouth fell open, and she schooled her expression into one of boredom. Adelei returned his stare and said nothing.

He retreated quickly and shut the door behind him none-too-gently. A few words were spoken outside the room. *No doubt muttering about the crazy person tearing her room apart.*

Continuing the task of liberating herself from a poorly designed room, she dragged the chest closer to the door and pushed the bed until it was centered along the front wall. Only the bed's headboard was against a surface, giving her three means of retreat. Anyone who entered was going to look to the rear wall first, expecting that to be the bed's location and giving her the chance to fight or flee before she was seen.

"There," she said. Sweaty but satisfied, she sat cross-legged on the bed and used her sleeve to wipe the sweat from her face.

The expected knock at the door still startled her, and she rose in a rolling motion. She expected a guard come to escort her to the King, but her heart knocked against her chest at the possibility of Tribor. When the door opened, the guard she'd expected was not the face she met—instead, a face similar to her own, yet older and weathered by pain lay before her, the royal circlet across his brow.

Her father.

He was both what she expected and what she had not—royalty and finery, yet a pallor to his skin that spoke of illness. *Recent illness.*

King Leon filled the doorway with his tall frame and searched her face. The King battled the father in his eyes; she could see it in the twitch of his hand and tenseness of his jaw. The father wished to wrap her in a hug as if that could erase the distance between them. Fifteen years of distance. His arms shook at his side, and he halted the lift that would have led to outstretched arms.

The King, however, knew the moment would wait. A deep baritone filled the space between them. "Master Adelei, I would welcome you formally but would rather do so after the enemy hand has been stopped. I would discuss your purpose here with you."

The guard behind him relaxed and stepped back, giving the King room to close the door. Before it shut, she noted the curiosity in the guard's face. Bodyguards didn't typically sleep in former Princess's bedchambers, and the guardsman knew it. She needed to spread the word around as to her purpose here, maybe even sleep on the floor outside Her Highness's bedchamber.

Keeping this in mind, she angled for light conversation. "I would offer you a chair, Your Majesty, but mine is sorely in need of repair," she said, gesturing toward the three-and-a-half-legged stool. She executed a formal bow and kept her head down until his hand touched her shoulder. While she expected the touch, it surprised her as foggy memories swept over her of his hand doing just that, many times before as she "played" princess at court.

"Iliana—"

The whisper of the name made it all the more powerful. She rose from her bow and held up a hand to silence him. Then Adelei pointed at the door and cupped her hand around her ear to mime listening. King Leon nodded, and she returned to the bed where she folded herself into a seated position with ease. "Your Majesty, Master Bredych sent me here at your request to guard the life of your daughter. I assume I'm to attend the wedding to protect Her Highness from these assassination attempts. I'll check the castle's security and do some of my own investigating, with your permission of course."

"My people and the people of Shad will know their future Queen is well-guarded by the b-best in the Little Dozen." He stumbled over the word as if it were soured. "We are honored to have you here and—and wish to know if you have been to Alexander before? You speak our language very well."

For a moment, she stared at him, unsure. He knew who she was—or did he? Then her father slowly winked one eye. "I was here before, as a child, though I was too little to remember the...visit. But I was taught several languages as part of my training."

His throat bobbed and several tears trickled down his flushed face. He approached her then, touching a gentle hand to her damp cheek, wet despite her own volition not to feel anything for the man before her. The man who abandoned her for dead. But he had believed he'd made the best choice by sending her away. A choice made out of love for his child. Would Bredych have done any different?

Her master's name lanced her heart of compassion, and she couldn't return her father's smile, though she allowed him the touch before she said, "While I have visited here with my father, he sent me away long ago for a peace treaty. I grew up in the Order with my adopted father, Master Bredych, who values your friendship very much to send his own daughter into such a difficult situation. Despite my own misgivings, I will not dishonor him in my service to you, my liege."

His face fell a moment before the professional and kingly mask slipped into place, the moment with the father now gone. What the father couldn't deal with, the King would. "When you leave your room, you must ensure that you are disguised enough that no one knows your background, no one knows who you...are."

She nodded, and he continued, "There may be times when...another role will be required of you, but we will speak of this later with my daughter present. Her Royal Highness marries in just short of two months' time. Tomorrow morning, a servant will see to whatever you will need to be present at the event itself. A servant will be assigned to you as portrays your rank—"

"But I'm not a—"

King Leon silenced her with a look. "—As Master of the Sword. Ask whatever you need of your servant, including a new chair. I would tell you, there is more to these attempts than the good captain knows."

The smell of his sweat reached her, and she gave him a questioning look. "Is she not to be trusted? I thought her your sepier."

"Yes, well, suffice it to say she can't be trusted. But that's not important." Her father closed his eyes and when he opened them, the fierceness of those muddy ovals worried her. "I suspect the Shadians may be behind this."

He said the words like they were some great, all-telling statement, and she frowned. "So Captain Warhammer said." He picked at the corner of a fingernail until she thought she would scream. Instead of terrorizing His Majesty, she merely said, "Whatever's on your mind, please speak it truthfully. If I'm to do my job, I need all the information you have, Your Majesty."

"Even rumors?"

"Especially rumors."

"Why? Gossip serves its purpose well enough at court, but little truth be had from such a creature."

Adelei's smile reflected in his eyes as he watched her. "Ah, but there's where you're wrong, Your Majesty. Usually a kernel of truth can be found at the root. Rumors will often lead to fact."

"There are rumors about my daughter's future husband." Her leg muscles tensed, and the bed groaned as she shifted her weight. "People say he isn't a man but some sort of monster. Some sexual deviant who prowls through cities, leaving broken people in his wake. No evidence is ever found. No one left alive to speak word against him. But if this is true, I cannot uphold the treaty. I must know if this man who's to join my family is what they say he is."

It was Master Meserre all over again. Just the thought of the man's name brought her blood to flush across her skin, and she bit the side of her cheek. "Your Majesty, I will do what I can to protect Her Highness, no matter who the enemy may be—be they Shadian, Tribor, or the captain herself."

He nodded and opened the door to leave. Her father turned back once, the mask slipping. Regret stretched across his frown only to be replaced a second later by a strength she'd never had the chance to know. "We thank you again for coming to us in our time of need, knowing that it cost you greatly to leave your home, as it would cost us greatly to lose a daughter." And with that, his great frame was gone from the doorway, leaving a puzzled guard who only glanced at her once before leaving to renew his post outside the door.

Adelei wanted nothing more than to curl up in her bed and wallow in a good round of self-pity, but the job stretched before her—a mysterious blank canvas. She rose, wearing her own mask as a shield in front of her.

Now was as good a time as any to get the lay of the castle and the people in it. Better now than as they approached the wedding, where there was sure to be an attempt on Her Highness's life. The door to her room closed behind her, shutting off the flow of emotions and all thoughts of her father. For the time being, she was Amaskan.

Nothing more. The job was all that mattered.

CHAPTER ELEVEN

Three guards stood outside. They tried not to stare at Adelei, whose brown dress would have been more at home in the servant's quarters than in the royal suite. The long, black tresses from her wig were braided up into an elaborate twist tied with a satin ribbon. The simple dress, rough spun and bearing little embellishment, washed out her complexion, but to the high court, she would be one random person among many.

A man twice Adelei's age cleared his throat. "Is there something we can do for you, milady? Are you lost?"

"I'm fine, thank you." She didn't blame them for not recognizing her. The "small and lost" disguise worked well. Adelei made it one step before the eldest guard blocked her path. She side-stepped and he stumbled forward, misjudging his grab for her arm. His forward motion gave her the advantage, and she twisted his arm behind him. The other two drew their swords, but neither moved against her.

Useless, like the statues in the tapestry behind them.

As quickly as she gained access to the guardsman, she released him with a gentle shove, and he tumbled into the other men. "Rule number one: don't assume someone is innocent and unarmed because of their attire. Not all assassins dress so obviously—in fact, almost none do. And rule number two: pay attention to who comes and goes from the royal suite. Who has entered these doors in the past hour and not left?"

The shortest of the three, a tubby man with fading red hair answered first. "Her Highness and her lady-in-waiting, her handmaidens, and some Master out of Sadai."

"Exactly. So knowing that, who would I be?"

"Well, you'd either be someone we missed, maybe someone come to harm Her Highness, or one of those from inside."

Adelei nodded. "If I was someone here to harm Her Highness, you'd already be dead. I'll make it easier on you though—I'm Master Adelei, here at the King's orders. You may see me come and go at all hours and often in odd dress. Don't let that stop you from making me identify myself if you don't know who I am, because you're right. Someone here to harm the royal family is going to do their best to blend in. Always watch who comes and goes, understand?"

"Yes, master."

Where she was going she didn't know, but that was the point. *Walk the halls. Draw a map of the layout. Learn where you are seen and where you are not.* A well-practiced mind sought out the shadows and corners as she traveled down the hall. She wasn't interested in talking or making friends. She wasn't out to be noticed this evening, choosing instead to hide in obscurity and listen. *Do so now before everyone knows who you are,* prompted Master Bredych's voice in her mind.

A turn brought her to a lengthy corridor which should've led to the stairwell. Instead she found a storage closet. Adelei retraced her steps until she found the staircase. She would work from the ground up, so she followed the stairs down to the first floor and down another hallway until she reached the entryway. Masses of people gathered as they waited to sup in the great hall. She doubted the assassin was hiding—in fact, she bet it was someone in the hall, someone in plain sight.

For now, she passed by the crowd of people as she continued her map making. As she moved, most ignored her entirely, deeming her the peasant or servant she appeared. Someone not worthy of acknowledgement. A few women nearby commented loudly on her appearance. "Who let *that* in?"

"Who does she think she is to be here, walking amongst us so freely?"

"Did someone's serving girl get lost?"

I've never understood why people of class and blood think themselves so far above everyone else. I could slit their throats as easily as a prince in finery. Once past the entrance to the great hall, she roamed into the kitchens where a corpulent woman with arms the size of fire logs loaded her down with a pile of dirty mugs for the scullery. Adelei used the excuse (and the disguise) to pass through the kitchens and into the scullery where she dropped off the dirty mugs with pleasure.

Beyond these rooms lay a back entrance to a smaller courtyard with a well and the back pathway to the stables. Adelei didn't spend long outdoors and moved back into the castle. She passed the cellar, a larder, and several other rooms for the making and storing of the castle's food and drink. Around the corner were the servants' quarters. The majority of the rooms were little more than closets, but she made an internal map of each one. When she tried to go down the stairwell at the end of one hallway, a brute of a guardsman stopped her. "Dungeon's down here, milady. Ye not be needin' ta go down here for naught."

She would have to give it a good explore once she was recognizable to the guards. A few guest rooms for the commons finished up the first floor, and she moved on to the second. By now, the mass of people had moved into the great hall, leaving her free to climb the staircase in peace. The second floor was simple: guest rooms, a shared bathing house on each end, and several ambassador suites.

At first, she thought the third floor similar to the second as she encountered more guest rooms, but near the great chamber lay the castle library. It wasn't the book collection, albeit vast, that caught her attention, but the two women who stood in the back corner, deep in conversation. *Ladies like this will be missed at dinner. What business do they have here at this hour?* Adelei moved to a shelf on the other side of them and crouched down to listen between a crack in the bookshelves.

The woman facing Adelei's direction said, "With all the rumors I've heard about him, I wouldn't let my dog marry him, let alone my daughter." Her pink-tinted grey hair stood out as did the string of rubies at her neck—one the size of Adelei's thumb.

I wonder if they're speaking about this prince. More rumors, perhaps?

"Shhhh…" Her companion, a woman in green too bright for her pale skin, waved a hand.

"What? I'm not afraid to make my thoughts known."

"I thought I heard the door earlier. Could be stray ears about, Millicent." The woman wearing green cast a look about the library but didn't see Adelei through the bookcases. "I've heard he leaves a trail of bodies behind him, and no matter where he goes, no one can stop him. Just look at what happened with your—"

The woman in rubies pressed a thin finger to her companion's lips. "I miss her, Angelina. I don't understand why the Boahim Senate won't do something."

"How could they? Would you want to go up against something—someone like that? That much money and power, he could buy the entire senate."

Millicent sighed, and when she glanced down, her gaze fell on Adelei. At first, Adelei held her breath and didn't move, but Millicent's eyes widened. Her hand flew to her chest as she let out a slight squeal, and she backed up a few paces. "Angelina, there's someone there." She pointed at the space where Adelei's head had been. Her fingers gripped the bookcase's corner as Adelei leaned back on her heels out of sight.

"Where?" asked Angelina.

"She's gone. But there was someone there, peeking through the bookcases at us." While Millicent explained what she'd seen to her companion, Adelei tiptoed away from the stacks and toward a rear door that would take her near the state rooms. At this hour, all state guests would be at supper, and the hallway was blissfully empty.

As she turned the corner, a voice called out, "Please wait. Why are you here?"

Adelei took the corner with much faster steps than the girl of her disguise would do, and she rushed toward the stairwell. For a woman of her age, Millicent moved with remarkable speed. She called out to Adelei from the base of the stairwell. "Are you here to stop the wedding?"

Her hand stilled on the banister, and Adelei faced the woman. She kept her voice light and airy as she spoke. "I-I don't know what you mean, my lady. Is there a reason the wedding should be stopped? Being new to this land, I am unaware of local customs." The disguise wavered as the lady's strong perfume tickled Adelei's nose, roses and the hint of something sweet. Her nose twitched unbearably at the scent.

"Oh. My apologies, my dear. Something about your face, I mistook you for…" The woman's eyes rested on the scar along Adelei's jaw. As her companion in green caught up, the younger woman's breath came in haggard gasps as she leaned against the archway for support. The woman in rubies gestured toward her friend and said, "This is Lady Angelina de Gant of Hersh, and I am Lady Millicent Sebald of Loughrie. Who might you be, dear?"

Fairly prominent houses. "I'm afraid I don't recall my name, as odd as it sounds," said Adelei as she fell back on the ruse Ida had used as they traveled.

"What were you doing in the library, child? And why were you spying on our conversation?" Angelina said, and she pursed her plump lips. "I don't believe for a second you don't know your name. Sounds more like a servant who doesn't wish a sound lashing for being where she ought not to be."

She could ask them the same thing—why weren't they at supper with the rest of the court? Instead of the retort on her lips, Adelei shrank in on herself like a terrified child. "I-I was only looking at the books. There are so many, and—and I thought they might help me remember. Captain Warhammer found me wandering the forest and thinks I must've hit my head or been accosted by highwaymen." The women gasped appropriately, and Adelei continued to lay the trail. "I have no memories before she found me, naught but a fuzzy memory of this man." Adelei shuddered, blinking her eyes rapidly as if she were fighting back tears.

"Oh, you poor thing. That must be ghastly." Lady Millicent patted her shoulder.

"I'm sorry I startled your ladyships," Adelei whispered. "Did you recognize me? Maybe you know who I am?"

"Your face. It's similar to someone I saw earlier in the day. I mistook you for another, but unfortunately, I have little knowledge of your house or name. Whose colors are those?"

"Captain Warhammer brought this dress from the launderer. No lord's colors, I suppose."

"You speak well enough. And despite your...dress, your manners are good, and your looks noble. You must be of a house of some repute. Though you move more like my master huntsman than a lady. Do you recall any training you may have had?"

Damn, I'm more out of practice with this than I thought. "I-I do not, my lady. As embarrassing as it is to say, I was found with naught a stitch on. Only wearing scratches all over—and I know not where I got them." Adelei rubbed her arms and pulled up part of her sleeve. Light scratches healed beneath the fabric. Luckily for her the rush through the forest lent her tree scratches enough.

Both ladies glanced around the stairwell as if expecting more ears to be listening in. "Have a care, dear, who you say such things to." Lady Millicent's voice shook as she hooked her arm through Adelei's elbow. "No need to mention that again. I'm sure the captain did the best she could for you. You say you remember a man? Do you recall his looks?"

Time to find the kernel.

Adelei closed her eyes and pretended to visualize the scene. "He bore black hair like ashes. And his eyes...brown again, b-but terrible. They held such cruelty, but I know not why. And the scratch under his eye—a jagged thing, all puffy and white."

The two ladies traded looks, and Lady Millicent asked, "Are you sure?"

"Yes, my lady. It stuck out so from the dark brown of his skin."

"Do...do you remember anything else about this rogue's appearance?"

Adelei allowed her shoulders to slump. "His frame was large and strong. It made me want to trust him, but then he changed. Those eyes. His clothes were nice. No offense to your ladyships, but much nicer than yours. His long tunic was soft and bore a tiger on it. I think it was a tiger—I mean, I've never seen one, but my father used to tell me stories of them, animals of living flame from the south—"

"So you recall your father?" Angelina asked, and Adelei shook her head.

"No, my lady. I only remember this now because I thought of the tiger." Adelei wrung her fingers and swayed on her feet.

"Oh Gods, the images my brain paints for me, surely I must be trapped within a nightmare."

"Here now, it's all right. You are among friends," said Lady Angelina, who wrapped a thick arm around Adelei's shoulders. Adelei twisted away from the woman's grasp. "I c-can't bear it—his eyes on me."

"Come." Lady Millicent ushered Adelei down the stairs and through the short hallway into the lady's guest chambers. The room was warmed by a private fireplace, lavish where Adelei's room was not, and Adelei kept her expression neutral. If these were Lady Millicent's rooms, she carried higher status than Adelei had originally thought.

Adelei took a hesitant seat on the edge of a chair that cost more than Adelei's battle steed and shuddered as if holding back great sobs. "I know the man of which you speak, though he is no man, but a monster. A horrible creature that spreads fear and death wherever he walks," said Lady Millicent.

"Then...then these things I see, they're true?"

"They may be, child. I've heard of other girls such as you, found wandering with their minds and bodies broken after meeting The Monster."

Ah-ha. So they did know something. Adelei stuck her bottom lip out and blinked rapidly.

"If you saw this man again, do you think you would recognize him?" asked Lady Angelina.

"I'm not sure, my lady. So much in my brain is fuzzy, so confusing. I just want to go home to my father, but I don't know where home is." This time a few of the tears that fled down Adelei's face were genuine. She used this momentary weakness to her advantage. "Can you help me, my lady? I hate to ask it of such an important person. I'm sure you're busy, but I don't know who else to ask."

This time, when Lady Millicent glanced at Lady Angelina, Adelei watched from underneath wet lashes. *She wants to use me to go after Prince Gamun, but she's not sure if I'm genuine. She's still thinking of who she thinks I am. Damn. Does she think me the Princess or Amaskan? I'm not sure which is worse.*

"Please, my lady, help me. Help me find who did this to me." Adelei cried, and she raised more sleeve to expose healing lashes left by tree branches. Several days old, they could pass for whip welts. When her hands moved to raise the hem of her dress, Lady Millicent's hands covered hers. "I believe you child—you don't need to expose your injuries."

"Maybe you should fetch your husband," Lady Angelina suggested, and Adelei cringed.

Her reaction cemented something in Lady Millicent's mind. "My husband's brother serves on the Boahim Senate. My lord won't harm you, but should he agree with me on your story, this may be the evidence needed to stop the Monster from harming anyone else."

By the Thirteen, the Boahim Senate. She was highly connected. Adelei clenched her fists in an effort to remain calm. She needed information, not the Senate. *Not yet anyway. I must tread carefully.* The last thing she needed was for them to discover her identity and bring her up on perjury charges, much less murder. *Only unjust and unholy beings defile their tongues with untruths against those that protect them.*

This time, Adelei's shiver was real. She couldn't let Lady Millicent summon the Senate. Most of Sadai ignored the Order's use of murder to seek out justice, but that was because the Order took great pains to hide themselves from the long sight of the Senate. A few faces popped into Adelei's mind. She couldn't think of the number—wouldn't. Didn't matter how many she'd killed as long as justice was served.

Lady Millicent stepped outside her rooms. Alone with Lady Angelina, the woman stared at Adelei as if she could see straight through the makeup that disguised her face: full cheekbones embellished by rouge, shadows across the eyelids to narrow them, and a powder to give the appearance of being younger than her twenty years. All of it subtle, and yet not enough.

The wig itched, and Adelei tucked a strand of hair behind her ear as they waited. Her hands returned to her lap as the door opened a few minutes later, and a man in a thick overcoat squeezed through the doorway, gut first. Sweat lined his face and upper lip.

He might fall over and roll across the room rather than walk the distance. She bit her tongue on the laughter and changed it into a slight hiccup as she feigned more tears. Adelei retreated as far back into her chair as possible, wrapping her arms around her thin legs as she stared at the floor.

"Is this the girl?" He moved across the room with more finesse than she thought possible for one as grotesquely large as he was, and when his stubby fingers touched her chin to tilt it up, she screamed.

"I'm sorry, good sir. I'm sorry—I don't know why I did that."

"You say you don't recall who you are?"

When Adelei shook her head, the lord turned to his wife. "What would you have me do? For all I know, she's an escaped servant or a runaway."

"But she described Prince—"

"You don't know that. There are many men out of Shad who fit that description," he interrupted. "Besides, you said yourself that her memory's fuzzy. I can't go to my brother with something as weak as that." The fat on his arms jiggled when he shook his fist in the air, and he returned his narrowed gaze to Adelei.

Every curve of her shape, every scratch and scar noted, and she squirmed in her chair, an action only half-feigned. "If you saw this man, would you know him?" he asked.

She took her time answering, brows furrowed in concentration. "Maybe, my Lord."

This is getting me nowhere. Certainly not information.

"As you said," Adelei whispered, "There are many men of that description."

"See? Even the girl seems unsure." She couldn't keep her eyes from his jiggling arm, which escaped his sleeves with several rolls. "I'm needed elsewhere."

Whatever this prince may or may not be guilty of, it may not be related at all to the assassination attempts. With hope Lady Millicent can piece some of this together.

"I'm sorry for his curtness, child," Lady Millicent said as the door shut behind her husband. She seated herself in the chair beside Adelei, and patted Adelei's hands. "The Boahim Senate has to be very sure before they seek justice for a crime against the Thirteen. Is there anything else you can remember about this man? Anything that can help?"

Adelei faked a yawn. "Not at the moment, my lady. Maybe I will remember more on the 'morrow."

"Of course. Forgive me, my child. My manners have escaped me in all of this. Have you somewhere to rest?"

Adelei nodded. "The Captain made arrangements with someone in the castle to give me a room in the servants' quarters."

Lady Millicent sniffed. "I guess a room amongst the staff is better than no room at all. Still, someone with a good name should be housed somewhere more appropriate."

"I think the rooms are full with the wedding," said Lady Angelina. "Have you seen the healers yet?"

"I'm to see them tomorrow as well."

"Good. Maybe you will recall what has happened to you. And by whom," said Lady Millicent.

With another jaw-cracking yawn, Adelei stood and bowed. "By your leave, I will retreat, my ladies."

"We shall talk again, child. Come see me after you've seen the healers."

As Adelei turned to the leave, Lady Millicent called out, "Wait. We must have something, some name by which to call you."

"I remember not my name."

"Let's call you Alethea." Adelei flinched, but the woman continued without noticing. "It means *truth*, my dear, for surely we will find the truth in all of this."

I know what it means. The room suddenly felt cold. *I hope my truth isn't found. That could get everyone killed.* At the woman's dismissal, Adelei retreated to the hall where she sought the shadows. The fourth floor map would have to wait. For now she would avoid the people returning from supper as she sought the stairs.

The number of guards on the third and fourth floors was astounding. She was asked to identify herself ten times on the way to her own room. Tomorrow she could get started on the job. Right now, she wanted to fall into bed and away from all the thoughts chasing themselves around her heart and brain. Focus on the job before her, and how she was going to track down the killer in their midst.

Just before she passed through the door to the Princess's suite, the glint of gold caught her attention as it reflected the light in the hall. Adelei followed it down to a head of thinning grey hair and ducked into the sitting room before her father could speak with her.

She didn't have time for that. She had a job to do.

CHAPTER TWELVE

The chair was normally comfortable, but this evening, the plush reminded Leon of the age of his body as his joints ached in rhythm to his heart. The drawing room was empty for the time being, but King Leon waited for the betrayer. *I don't know whether to be proud or aggrieved by what has become of my daughter. Ah, Iliana, where did you go?*

When the door opened, he didn't need to look up to recognize her light steps. "You took your time getting here," he said to the former captain.

Ida Warhammer knelt before him, and he waved an idle hand in her general direction. She said nothing for a time, leaving him to gather his thoughts before speaking. *I used to appreciate that trait. At least before she—* In the back of his mind, a small voice asked, *did what? Told the truth? Would you rather she had lied and remained hidden?* Leon shifted his attention to her and away from his own double-crossing mind.

The grey in her hair had multiplied in recent months, and her shoulders slumped. It was a look of defeat, something he'd never seen in her, and for a moment, he ached to hold her.

The tiled floor stretched out for several horse lengths, the stone gilded with hints of silver and gold, and yet the empty room was too crowded. Leon whispered, "Did I make the right decision fifteen years ago?"

"Goefrin brought a very appealin' choice before ya and your advisors. Said it was the only way to keep Alexander from ruin. What else could ya do?"

Her words made sense. They were thoughts he'd worked out himself many times, but they didn't keep the doubt from eating at him. Leon shut his eyes. "Despite my wishes for her, Iliana has returned, but she's not who I thought she would be. I thought that surely she would remember me, remember Alexander. That maybe, despite being a killer, I could save her somehow."

When Ida said nothing, he continued, "How did this happen? All I wanted was my daughter back, safe and sound. Instead they send me this...this assassin. I'm afraid of my own child."

"You fear her 'cause she returned Amaskan."

"Yes."

A sea of blue met his earthy gaze as she sat beside him. It was Catherine's chair, now Margaret's, but he didn't mind Ida being there. Her eyes reminded him more of the ice of the Cretian Mountains than the Harren Sea, and he shivered. *How does she do that? How can she make me feel like a child with just a look?* And then her words reminded him.

"Are ya afraid of me? I was Amaskan, and yet I recall times when there was more between us than fear and loathin'."

He flushed to remember and then cursed her under his breath. It was a reminder his loins enjoyed more than his heart these days. "Only an assassin could speak of love and death in the same sentence with little distinction. And no, I'd not forgotten your betrayal."

Ida flinched and removed her hand from his arm. "Have ya decided whether or not to kill me?"

"As much as I'd like to, I can't. I never could," he whispered and patted her hand. "But I can't trust you."

"I brought her home."

"Yes, you brought Adelei of Amaska to Alexander. I fear that my child, my Iliana is dead. Gone these past fifteen years."

"Leon," she said, and her image swam in his tears. "I'm sorry. I can't ever undo what I've done."

"I know."

"What would ya have me do?"

King Leon sighed. "I'm removing you as sepier. You will retain your former captain status, but I need someone I can trust in that position."

Ida nodded. "I expected as much. Will ya give it to her instead?"

"No. I can't trust her either." King Leon removed the silver circlet from his brow and stared at the thirteen amethysts as they pulsed in the sunlight streaming through the window. He felt the circlet's weight like he carried his horse across his brow, and for a moment, he resisted the urge to dash the object upon the stones outside. Instead of chucking it out the window, he set it aside and massaged his temples which pulsed with the beginnings of a headache. "I'll make her Margaret's sepier for the time being. Maybe the ranking will help her finish the job, so she can return home."

"Give it time, Leon. Give her time."

Time was one thing he did not have. Leon cupped his head in his hands. "The blood on her hands must not touch Margaret. We need the treaty that this marriage will bring. Iliana's identity must remain a secret, even from my advisors."

"Do ya doubt her ability?"

"Not at all. That's the problem. I want my little girl back," the father said. "I miss the little girl I sent away and grieve the loss of her all over again. This person who has returned is hardened and angry. I worry how much of this anger is directed at me. Did I make the correct choice in having you bring her back?"

"Only you can know that answer, Your Majesty, but I'll say who better to protect Margaret than her own sister?"

"Iliana doesn't look upon Margaret as a sister. When we spoke upon her arrival, she acted as if Margaret's a piece of cattle she's protecting. It's unnerving, the detachment."

"It's necessary, Your Highness. Emotions are a weakness on the job."

"And you would know?" He internally cursed the grin he felt grace his lips. Ida rested a hand on Leon's shoulder, her fingers tracing circles across his tunic. It was a gesture he'd missed of late. *She betrayed you*, his mind spoke, and he argued back. *Yes, she did.*

"Adelei will protect Margaret, no matter her personal feelings."

He sought out Ida's face and saw a tiredness living there that was new. *Neither of us is getting younger. I wonder which of us will go first? With this poison in me, I figured it would be me first to die.* Leon knew well the scars that decorated her body, but there were new ones along her face that reminded him of the dangers of being sepier.

A position I'm giving to Iliana.

He ran a wrinkled finger across the light welt above her brow. "Who has been using you as target practice, hmmm?" It was a touch driven by instinct, and he pulled away as if burned.

"Tribor."

Fear washed over him, then anger as images crossed by—the women he loved in this life fleeing and having fled such monsters. His fingers sought her wrist and tightened their grip. "Were you followed?"

"No, Your Majesty. Your talented daughter made very sure of that."

The statement did not relieve him. If the Tribor were involved, maybe there was more to the rumors about Prince Gamun of Shad than he had originally given credit. Maybe this wedding *was* the disaster he had worried it was.

Ida interrupted his thoughts, her smile as fake as his own. "This wedding should be a joyful occasion—the joinin' of two families. If it is advice ya seek, I would tell ya to forget all else for the time and allow Master Adelei to do her job. Enjoy the time with your daughter."

Of course, if you're betraying me still, you would say that. You would want this wedding to proceed. But her smile hung crooked, and her muscles tensed beside him. She wanted this no more than he did.

She left him alone in the room, alone to press the circlet back into place, its weight none the lighter. He stood then, shoulders back as he pushed his personal feeling aside. Today he must be king as he met with his advisors. He must be king first, and father second, if only for a brief time. Then he could enjoy time with his daughter, as Ida had recommended.

It was then that he realized she hadn't said which daughter.

The serving girl who entered screamed as her foot connected with Adelei's bed in the dim light that streamed in from the hallway. Furniture in the wrong location and a glint of steel sent her voice higher. The young girl's dark outline was all Adelei could see in the darkness.

The girl's hunched shoulders spoke her fear, and Adelei relaxed. An assassin wouldn't be afraid and certainly wouldn't trip over her bed. Adelei slid the dagger beneath her pillow. The servant's eyes caught the blade as it moved, and she stumbled over something else as she backed out of the room.

Adelei groaned as she fell back against the bed's mattress. Two guards dashed into her room with swords drawn. "Are you all right, Master? We heard a scream."

"That would be the serving girl," she muttered, her arm thrown over her eyes to block out the light. She listened to their footfalls withdraw and the door close behind them. Only after they retreated did she allow herself to fall asleep.

The next knock on her door arrived after Adelei had dressed, her clothes a mix of swordsman gear as she donned black leggings and a deep blue tunic. Instead of a hood, she wore a scarf wrapped around her head. While the look was Sadain, it didn't scream Amaskan or so she hoped. At least these were styled after the Amaskan fighting gear. Just to be sure, she moved both arms and legs to test the outfit's stretch and flexibility. *It'll do.*

When the next servant entered, it wasn't the frightened girl but a woman more than three times Adelei's age. The woman braced thick feet in the door frame as she frowned at Adelei's rearrangement of the furniture. *I guess they decided to send me someone's grandmother in hopes I wouldn't kill her on sight.*

"Name's Charleena, master. I'm to see to your needs today."

The servant's lips pressed together in thin, grey lines as she eyed Adelei's attire. "I'll be needing a new chair." Adelei pointed at the crippled chair in the corner.

While Charleena nodded, her lips remained pursed. "Anything else?"

"There are a bunch of knickknacks in the trunk here. See to it they're removed."

"As you will, master."

Adelei thought back a moment to her walk of the castle grounds the night before. "Has His Majesty spoken to the staff about watching the guests?"

"Yes, master. We're to keep our eyes and ears open for anything suspicious." The old woman leaned close to Adelei as she waited.

Curiosity killed the serving girl, or it will if she continues to stand in my personal space. Adelei hid the smirk behind her hand. "I assume the wedding dress is already made?"

"Well," Charleena played with the edge of her apron. "It keeps going back for adjustments. The Princess doesn't eat much these days."

"Is she ill?"

"Oh no. Just nerves, master."

Great, that's going to make it even harder for me to fit into her dress. Hopefully she's not lost too much weight. "How would you describe Her Highness's frame?"

"Master?"

"Her build. Is she fat? Thin? Tall?"

"Oh. She's a bit smaller than you, master. Less...broad in the shoulder, bit thinner in the thigh. But she's about the same height."

Adelei released the breath she was holding. "I need someone to take my measurements and have the dress adjusted to fit them. Can you arrange this?"

"I don't understand—"

"Can you arrange this?" Adelei repeated. When the woman nodded, Adelei continued, "Tell no one of this. Understand? Her Majesty's life may depend on it."

The woman drew a fluttering hand to her chest. "Truly? Is that why we're to watch people come and go?"

"I can't answer that, only His Majesty can, but I speak the truth when I say that you can't tell anyone, no matter how much you think you can trust them. This stays between us."

"Yes, master." The servant gave Adelei a hesitant smile. "Is there anything else I can help you with, master? Breakfast can be brought to your room, or something else if you have need of it?"

"What is Her Highness's schedule today?" The serving woman rattled off a long litany of wedding plans, meetings in the audience chamber, and afternoon tea in her bower with noble ladies. The list continued, and before Adelei could pull her teeth out in frustration, she held up a hand to stop the breathless expression. "I understand. She has a busy schedule then. Are her days normally this busy?"

"Yes, master."

Adelei took a deep breath in through her nose and exhaled through her mouth. *I'm going to regret this.* To the servant, she said, "I need to speak with the Her Highness as soon as possible."

"I'm afraid Her Highness is still asleep. She likes a good lay in and won't be rising for another hour. And after that, she has an appointment with the Duke of—"

"Yes, yes, I know. Busy day. But I must insist. Wake her up now if necessary."

The servant shook her head. "I'm sorry, master, but Her Highness left strict orders not to be disturbed."

And she outranks me, at least to you she does. Adelei strode past the woman and into the hallway. The door itself was locked, and she ordered the guard outside to open it.

"Master, I can't. It's the royal bedchambers."

"I don't care if it's the royal bedpan. His Majesty left orders for you to follow any and all commands I give, and I said open the door."

The guard nodded and knocked. When the knocks went unanswered, he tried the doorknob. Three shakes and the door remained closed. "I'm sorry, master, I don't have the key, and the door won't open."

"What would you do if it was an emergency?"

"Master, we'd knock the door down. Is this an emergency? Should I get Captain Fenton?"

Captain who? Must be head of the guards. Adelei shook her head. "I'll take care of it. Step back." With the roll of her palm, Adelei pulled a small metal rod from a hidden pocket in her sleeves. The lion's mouth served as the keyhole, and she rolled her eyes. Not exactly the best disguise for a keyhole.

Careful fingers threaded the rod toward the roof of the lion's mouth until she felt the spring. The metal rod bore narrow notches across the top and when pressed upward, the spring compressed until a light clicking sound announced the unlocking of the door. Behind her, Charleena gasped, and the door swung open to reveal a room more purple than anyone had a right to enjoy.

Adelei shut the door behind her and glanced around the giant room. Amidst a sea of lilac and royal blues, her sister slept in tangled covers. Her pale, smooth legs stuck out from beneath the mass, one hanging over the bed's edge. Adelei didn't recognize the room but figured its decor had changed in the fifteen years she'd been absent from the kingdom. Changed as much as her own room in Sadai over the years, if not more so considering the money at the kingdom's disposal.

The face before her was like her own, so much so that Adelei's outstretched hand shook as it halted over her sister. Margaret truly looked like her twin. *And my brain remembers her not.* A slight pang caught her off guard, and Adelei ached to touch her sister's face to see if her eyes were the same brown as Adelei's own.

Would Margaret know her? Would she scream to see her own face before her? Even bald, the two women would look similar enough to pass for one another. By the look on Charleena's face, she had maybe four minutes before the King himself arrived. Maybe less. *Do I tell her who I am? Or will that only make guarding her more difficult?* On the one hand, Margaret's knowing might make it easier to accept Adelei's orders, but knowing would paint a bull's-eye on her back. A target for every enemy Adelei or the Order had.

Margaret shifted in her sleep, the innocence on her face giving her the blessing of youth, whereas Adelei's face bore scars and lines from a life of hardship and violence. *Maybe not yet. This is going to be hard enough for her as it is to accept.*

Adelei gave Margaret's shoulder a brief shake. Her mouth flew open, and Adelei clamped a hand over it. Breath warmed her fingers as Margaret tried to both exhale and scream through the hand. "If I remove my hand, will you remain quiet, Your Highness? Your father sent for me. Take a good look at me," she said. Margaret's gaze landed on the dagger at Adelei's side.

Margaret nodded, and Adelei loosened her hand. "Why has my father sent for you? And who are you to be in my bedchambers?"

"My name is Master Adelei of Sadai, formerly of the Order of Amaska." A blank stare met Adelei's words. Then Margaret's eyes flitted to the bolted door of her bedchamber, and she sucked in a deep breath to scream. Adelei clamped a hand over her mouth again. "Do your people not talk of the Amaskans here? Great Gods, if I wanted you dead, you'd already be so; now hush, we don't have long."

"You are...an assassin?"

"Amaskan," Adelei corrected. "Your father sent for me to protect you."

"You're here to kill me." Margaret tried to move too quickly and slipped. When her hands grabbed for the bed curtains, several boxes and glass figurines tumbled to the floor.

I don't have time for this. Adelei seized hold of her sister by her shoulders and leaned close to her ear. "Look, I'm not here to kill you, you ninny. The King brought me here to protect you as your body double."

Margaret's breathing stilled for a moment, her round eyes reminding Adelei of a tempest, a dark black whirlpool amidst a sea of brown. "Truly?" Color returned to Margaret's face with a flash of pink.

Wow. She goes to trusting that fast? We're definitely going to have to work on that. Still gripping her sister by the arms, Adelei braced herself for the protest to come and spoke again, a hushed whisper amongst the footfalls outside the bedchamber door. "There's a real threat on your life—an attempt has already been made. It's because of this that I'm here."

"Surely not. No one would be so foolish as to attack me. With Father—"

"Can you recall when you met Prince Gamun of Shad?"

At just the mere mention of this name, Margaret flushed bright red and her lips parted in a sleepy smile. "Of course, his hair—"

"Please spare me his accolades. Do you remember how quickly you were forced from the drawing room?"

Her sister's smile faltered, and her brows furrowed in exactly the same layout of lines that spread across Adelei's own face when worried. "Y-yes, but they said the Prince took ill suddenly and—"

She stopped and stared at Adelei. "Oh. That was why they hurried me away?"

"Yes, Your Highness. Your father brought me here because I'm the best. I can protect you like no other."

"As my body double." She stumbled over the words and paused as her gaze traveled across Adelei's face. "How could you resemble me so? You have rougher skin and scars, but your similarity is bewitching."

A pounding on the door caused them both to flinch. "Listen," said Adelei, "My looks aren't important. Right now, I must tell you something. Something no one else can know, not even your father. Your life may depend on it." Guards attempted to knock down the solid wood door and failed. The thud shook Adelei's teeth.

"I must take your place in the wedding."

"No." Quiet words whispered between something hard dashing against the door. Margaret crossed her arms over her chest and glowered at Adelei.

"I'm taking your place in the wedding, Your Highness. You'll be present, but hidden. This is not optional, and if necessary, I'll make it a royal order."

Margaret's quivering bottom lip stuck out. "You can't make it a royal order. You're not royalty. You're nothing more than a dirty assassin, a murderer. I should call for the Boahim Senate right now."

Don't think about it. Deal with the job. Something slammed into the door again, and she withdrew her dagger. "It will happen, with or without your help, Your Highness. If you want to live, you'll keep this knowledge secret."

It's probably the guards, if not His Majesty. Probably summoned by the servant. But just in case, I can't take a chance that it's the Tribor. Adelei held her dagger as she unlocked the door. As the knob turned, she put her back to the wall and waited.

Three men wearing royal guard uniforms rushed in, their own swords drawn. As one of them passed, Adelei tripped him and used the distraction to grab the second one from behind. She twisted his arm behind his back, and the third man skidded to a halt.

King Leon followed, his feet still bare and hair damp. Behind him, Charleena poked her head around his arm. Adelei kept her dagger available, but bit back laughter as her father slid a small kitchen knife in his robe. "Put up your weapons," King Leon ordered everyone.

The guards listened. Adelei didn't.

She released the guard, but positioned herself between the group and Margaret. "Captain Michael Fenton, this is Master Adelei of Sadai, and sepier to Princess Margaret," King Leon said to the tallest of the three guards. The man's blue uniform bore not only the royal insignia but also the trio of swords, showing him as the Captain of the Guard.

Captain Fenton bowed. "My apologies, Master Adelei. This woman swore there was an enemy to the crown present." Fenton nodded toward Charleena, who bowed deeply and fled.

King Leon frowned at the dagger still in Adelei's hands. "It was a misunderstanding, I'm sure. Captain, if you would make sure that *all* of your men know of Master Adelei's new rank so that this doesn't happen again. I was in the middle of a bath."

"Yes, Sire."

"Master Adelei, I am not the enemy," said the King.

"Everyone is a possible enemy, Your Majesty. Until I know who is a danger, that includes kings." She ignored Margaret's gasp behind her and sheathed her dagger. "I apologize for that show of force, but it's necessary to prove the point. I owe my allegiance to Princess Margaret and the protection of her life."

"Leave us," the King ordered, and Margaret sniffed loudly. When only the three of them remained in the room, Adelei gestured for the King to sit without thinking much of the action. Yet King Leon raised an eyebrow at the role reversal.

"Who are you to tell the King what to do?" Margaret hissed.

Adelei sat in the chair beside King Leon and ignored Margaret completely. "Have you told her nothing of the Amaskans?"

"She knows enough to know who they are and what they do."

"But nothing of the code of honor they follow, nor the work they do to ensure the safety of kingdoms."

The bubbling laughter made Adelei grind her teeth as she promised not to slit the spoiled brat's throat. Margaret's foolish grin could have set the calmest Holy Woman on edge. "A bunch of murderous thugs having honor?"

"Stop." The sharp word from King Leon ceased all talk, and he wiped sweat from his flushed face.

"If I'm to protect her, she must be able to follow any and all orders. If she's unwilling or unable, it may cost more than her own life. I won't walk into a suicide mission, no matter what Master Bredych promised you," said Adelei.

He nodded. "She will follow orders. I'll make sure of it."

"But she wants to take my place in the wedding. My wedding. It's the day of my dreams, and now you're both saying I can't even participate." The unlit candle she threw came within a foot of hitting Adelei, who made no move to dodge it.

"Poppet, I know this is a lot to take in, but Master Adelei's here to protect you. I've appointed her your sepier."

"I don't want a sepier." Margaret wrapped her robe closer about her and stood with her fists on her hips.

"I'm sorry, but you need one. I need her here to protect you."

"What happened to Captain Warhammer?"

"She has been stripped of that rank." When Margaret opened her mouth, he interrupted her. "I'm not going to discuss this with you, Margaret. You must follow whatever order Master Adelei gives as if it is my own—it's for your safety."

"But—"

"Someone is trying to kill you. Do you think I wish to see you dead, like your mother?" The words zapped the air in the room, and Margaret startled upright, her face flushed as if burned. "Adelei will serve as your body double during the ceremony at the cathedral, though you may endure the rituals beforehand yourself. Master Adelei will be present to guard you during those. You will do this, by my order if I must make it so. On my life, you will do this." Hatred in Margaret's gaze reminded Adelei of the "fit" she had heard through the door when she had arrived yesterday—a spoiled princess throwing a temper-tantrum because she'd never been told "No."

"Yes, Your Majesty." Margaret was no wildfire today—she channeled Adelei at her best, a slow-stirring beast whose spit flecked bits of flame in warning.

This appeared to be nothing new as King Leon merely shrugged before standing to place a kiss on Margaret's crown of black curls. "Today's a busy day of meetings, and I have much to attend to. Mind Adelei and Nisha as they watch over you today, and I'll see you at dinner." As he left, Margaret made a face at his back and retrieved the candle from the floor.

How am I going to survive these tantrums? Adelei sighed.

"You sound like my father."

"What do you mean?"

"When you sighed just now, you sounded like him. And you will address me as 'Your Majesty.'"

She couldn't help the second sigh and tried to shift her mind elsewhere. Margaret moved like a fragile person—no defensive stance, no awareness of her body at all. When Margaret stood, her flimsy nightgown parted to display long, pale legs with muscles used to slight steps when walking the castle instead of fighting or horseback riding. *Poor Hero. I bet she's barely even ridden that poor pony. I doubt she can sit a horse, much less anything else.*

Small footsteps took the princess to a dressing shade where she rang a bell. Several handmaidens rushed into the room to dress Margaret. They removed and retrieved clothing with a speed that left Adelei dizzy. "Do you enjoy watching people dress?" Margaret said, her tone insinuating a certain impropriety in Adelei's watchful stare. "I've heard there are people that enjoy such pursuits."

Adelei ignored the jibe for what it was, an attempt to chase off the new bodyguard. Many deft hands wove the laces of Margaret's corset, and when she stepped out from behind the shade, her narrow waist had lost several inches in the process. The princess sat on a stool before a tall mirror. A few sapphires decorated the mirror's crown, and when Adelei's gaze traveled further down, she caught Margaret's reflection staring back.

Margaret's handmaidens brushed her thick, black hair as they counted the strokes. When her comment garnered no response, Margaret tried again. "My hair is most beautiful, would you not agree, Master Adelei? Women covet it. Or maybe you'd rather speak of my body—the body of a princess. But I doubt you'd understand such feminine things." Adelei counted under her breath as Margaret tried to puncture the hardened exterior of Adelei's shell. "Do you even have breasts under there? Oh Gods, I never even thought to ask—you are female, right? I mean, I can't have a man in my bedchambers, let alone in my wedding dress."

"Leave us," Adelei said. All at once, four pair of feet withdrew with a scamper across the stone floor.

"Wait. Where are you going?" Margaret cried, and when her handmaidens ignored her, she fell back onto her creaking stool.

Another unlit candle flew toward Adelei, and she caught it one-handed. Adelei crossed the room in half a dozen steps and set the candle back in its place before turning to Margaret. *I need to stop thinking of her as my sister. She knows nothing of who I am, and besides, anyone this spoiled could no more be related to me than the goat in the stables. Besides, I don't remember her at all. Blood does not family make.*

She leaned over Margaret, whose back pressed into the dresser's hard wood. "I made it very plain that my role in your wedding was to remain a secret, something you just revealed to your handmaidens."

"They're nobility. And besides, I didn't tell them what role. They won't tell anyone—"

"Listen you stupid twit, servants—even ennobled ones—are the biggest gossips in the Little Dozen. Anything you say to them will spread across the land like a plague. Not even five minutes in, and you've told them that I'll have a role in the wedding. Do you want to die, you fool?"

Margaret sputtered, but Adelei didn't give her the chance to respond. She withdrew her dagger and held it against Margaret's bosom with a grand smile. "Here—if you really wish to die, I can make it possible. Isn't it what I'm best at? Murder? You said so yourself. So if you want to die, let's make it fast. I have a home to return to."

Princess Margaret tried to wriggle away from Adelei, but weak arms did little to move Adelei's strong frame. Movement brought the dagger closer, so Margaret grappled with Adelei instead. Her fingers fought to find purchase in the silk tunic. When she failed, she tried to claw the dagger from Adelei's grasp.

Margaret released Adelei's hand. "So will you watch as my husband makes me a woman on my wedding night? Is that part of your duties, too? Or will you take my place in that role as well?"

The dagger inched closer to Margaret's throat as Adelei's patience wavered. The only way Margaret would follow her is if Margaret understood the risk as well. "No, Your Highness, that will be one of the few times you'll be alone with your husband in these chambers. I hope for your sake he is not the assassin, for if so, you'll be dead before the sun rises. Or maybe that would be a blessing if he's the monster people say he is."

She dropped the dagger in Margaret's hands, which fell through the softened fingers and into her lap. The blade tore a small hole in the overskirt's light layers. "Go ahead, princess. If you want me gone, save the assassin the trouble, and I'll be gone by noon."

"I don't want to die. Stop it." Margaret cried. She stared at the dagger as if it were a large spider, and she squirmed in place. When her fingers dared touch it again, Margaret swept it from her lap with shaking fingers. "Please. Please, get it away."

Finally hearing the word she wished, Adelei returned her dagger to its place. Sweat glistened across Margaret's brow, and when she tried to stand on shaky legs, she fell back against her stool.

"That's better. You and I have no reason to like each other, and that's fine. I'm not here to be your best friend. I'm here to save your life. You will do as I say, or I will have you bound and gagged. Whether or not you enjoy this experience is no concern of mine. I'm paid either way."

Margaret frowned, her fingers clenching the laces of her corset. "You called him a monster."

"Did I ruin your precious image of him?"

She shook her head. "It's just...I've heard things. Never mind, you must be mistaken." Margaret smoothed out her skirts and frowned at the tear. "You said you have a home to return to. I've never heard of an Amaskan having a home before, yet you speak as if you have family and friends."

"I do, Your Majesty. Hard as it may be for you to understand, I have a father, too, and friends who miss me very much. If I die defending you, it is an honorable death, but if I die because of you, because you fail to follow my orders, they will not be happy. A blood feud may be declared." Her sister paled at this. So she was at least aware of blood feuds. *Good.*

"So how does this work, then? You're protecting me?"

"Most of the time, I'll follow you, watching and listening for signs that someone is planning to harm you. At large events, such as your wedding, I will play you. If someone were to attack you, they'd really be attacking me."

"Why can't you just watch and listen at the wedding, and...and take them out if they attack? I don't understand why my day has to be ruined."

It was a petulant sob that escaped pouting lips, which Adelei ignored, much to the princess's frustration. *Good lord, if that normally works on Father, no wonder she's so spoiled.* To her sister though, Adelei said, "Large events have more people. More chance of attack. If someone came at you, you wouldn't have the first idea how to fight off an attacker, but I would. If they assault me, I can diffuse the situation quickly and safely."

"How do you know I couldn't escape them? I've had some defense training—"

Adelei's eyes rested on the unused candle beside her, its wax long dried from burning last night. She snatched the candle from its holder and tossed it at her sister's head before Margaret had finished her sentence. Startled, Margaret saw it only after it was airborne. Too late to do anything about it. The hardened wax bounced off the side of her head with a thud before dropping to the floor.

"That's going to bruise."

"If I'd wanted that to hurt, I would have thrown it harder, and trust me, it would have left a mark. And that was just a candle." Her fingers deftly moved and before Margaret could blink, Adelei held one of her throwing knives. "Imagine if that candle had been this." Sunlight bounced off the knife, and sparkles danced along the wall.

Margaret swallowed hard.

"It's good though that you have had some training, Your Highness. Some training is better than no training, though I intend for you to have more instruction in self-defense as well. We'll need to clear a few things from your day."

"When?"

"As soon as possible." Margaret's mouth opened and closed when Adelei raised a brow. "Is that going to be a problem, Your Highness?"

"No, Master Adelei. Only, please don't schedule it this afternoon. If possible. Please?"

Much better. Adelei nodded. "I'll see what I can do. Now, what's on your schedule for the day?"

Gods help me, it's going to be a very long day indeed.

CHAPTER THIRTEEN

Adelei ignored the shocked glances that occasionally came her way from the embroidering ladies; idle chitchat passed their lips in the afternoon activity that was Princess Margaret's indulgence. With so many highborn women arriving with their lords for the wedding, Margaret felt the ladies "needed time to chat."

Embroidery over tea left them the opportunity to catch up without the formalities of the royal court. *Though I bet everything said here will reach other ears as soon as they leave this room.* Adelei balled her hand into a fist and resisted the urge to scratch the itch under her head scarf.

If they continue discussing the wonders of Prince Gamun, I may go mad from sheer boredom and assassinate myself. She leaned back against the wall where she sat on a cushion thrown in the corner. Adelei crinkled her nose at the smell of wet dog exuding from the cushion, which probably belonged to some royal mutt or another. *Fitting that they left it for me, though it's another reason they stare beneath their lashes when they think I'm not looking.*

Margaret thought it a joke when she offered Adelei the cushion or a seat in the circle. "I've even brought an embroidery square if you wish, Master Adelei."

One look at the women who treated gossip as the latest morsel at the dinner table, and Adelei chose the dog's bed in the corner. *I think I'd rather be dead than sit as a member of this circle.* She rubbed a hand along her lower spine. While the cushion was comfortable enough for the hound, the lack of feather stuffing left her lean backside aching after an hour.

Lady Millicent tore at a stitch in frustration and avoided looking at Margaret, who spoke of the prince in dulcet tones. *She knows this marriage is a bad idea, yet she lies before my sister.*

Lady Angelina hung over the sides of her chair, her elbows bumping with the women on either side of her. She, too, focused her attention more on the stitching and less on the conversation. No one else appeared uncomfortable with the topic as the ladies laughed at Margaret's "precious naivety."

"What other reason could there be for the existence of husbands than to care for and protect their loves?" Margaret asked. Her fake smile eroded only when she glanced at Adelei.

And so it went for the next hour—Margaret gushed over her upcoming wedding, while Adelei fought to keep her legs from falling as asleep as her mind already was.

Most of the high court ladies were Margaret's age or older, though one duchess from the hill lands couldn't have been more than thirteen or fourteen. She sat in her chair as manners dictated, but every so often, her legs bounced as she peeked at Adelei. Unable to contain her curiosity any longer, the young woman interrupted Margaret. "Your Highness, I'm sorry for being blunt, but I noticed the visitor with us. Might we be introduced to this person? Her outfit bears such a foreign look that I find myself curious about its origin."

Several ladies gasped while others chuckled. Adelei bit off a laugh as her royal *highness* tried very hard not to murder her needlework. The veins on her face stood out as they throbbed in rhythm to her heartbeat, and Margaret said, "Master Adelei, Sepier of Alexander, this is everyone. Everyone, this is Master Adelei. Now, on the topic of Prince—"

"It is unusual in this country for a woman to be employed as a sepier. Such a manly role—" the young woman said, and Lady Angelina elbowed her in the ribs. "What? Well, it is."

"Hush. Captain Warhammer served as sepier for a long while. Plenty of women take the role," Lady Angelina said.

She's not afraid to speak her mind. I like this girl already. Maybe I can get some information out of her, with a flapping tongue like that.

"If the King feels the need for an additional sepier, especially one who sits guard in a woman's own bower, things must be grave indeed." Lady Millicent sought out Adelei's face. "Tell us more about why you are here."

Margaret's lower lip jutted out as she jabbed her stitching needle into the fabric. Brown eyes glared at Adelei across the head of a dozen women. "Big weddings tend to bring large groups of guests. I'm here as a precaution and nothing more. Please, return to your sewing, ladies."

"There now, nothing to worry about. Let's move on to brighter topics." Margaret's voice cracked, but she rattled on about topics of little importance. While the ladies returned to talk of the courts, Lady Millicent stopped sewing altogether. She stared outright at the two sisters, an odd expression across her face.

She thinks she knows something. Damn. Adelei stilled her tapping foot. *I can't see how similar we'd look with the amount of makeup I'm wearing or our clothing differences.* Where Margaret was soft and warm, rouge scattered across her high cheek bones and light purples painted on her eyelids, Adelei's face resembled stone: hard and unyielding with taupes and dark sages lining her lids and lips, leaving her cheek bones blunt and bare. The stark contrast of the coal lining the edges of her eyes darkened the brown of her irises until they resembled black holes rather than mud.

Not even my posture is gentle like Margaret's. I'm sitting on a smelly cushion on the balls of my feet in the corner of the room. And yet Lady Millicent's convinced there's something to see.

The women paused briefly as a servant entered bearing a tray laden with fruit and light wine. Adelei took the opportunity to stand in a slow, full-bodied stretch, after which she stepped outside to watch the change of guards.

Difficult enough to protect Margaret from an unknown assailant, but more difficult still to find out who he or she was when Adelei was busy playing nursemaid. There was movement behind her, but she ignored it. The footfalls weren't hidden, only soft; she figured it for the servant and tensed when a hand touched her elbow.

"Master Adelei..." said Lady Millicent and the partially withdrawn blade returned to Adelei's sleeve. "Master Adelei, I must speak to you immediately. The marriage must not happen—"

"Not here," Adelei interrupted. With a finger flick, she called several guards over to the bower doors. "I need to escort Lady Millicent to her rooms. No one is to enter or exit the bower until I return, is that understood?"

"Yes, Master Adelei."

"This way, my lady."

Lady Millicent followed Adelei into a tiny, rarely used room Adelei had discovered in her sojourn through the castle. Probably once used as a closet, it now held extra pieces of furniture and random bits of household goods. The lady paused upon entering the room, then uprighted an overturned chair and settled into it as if it were completely normal for someone of her station to be consorting with an Amaskan in a closet. "I'm sorry for the necessity of meeting here, but there are too many ears in this castle."

Lady Millicent's fine green gown rested against a chair that used to be of the same shade before dust coated it in gray. "The wedding cannot happen. Prince Gamun Bajit isn't the man people believe him to be, and he can't be allowed control of the throne."

Adelei overturned a short stool and sat, glad to be resting on something other than a dog's cushion. "I was told Alexander royalty held a joint leadership."

"Yes, but we both know that the moment the Shadian family marries into this kingdom, the royal family's days are numbered. And with the Princess and her father out of the way, it's only a matter of time before Prince Gamun would rewrite law to allow himself control."

"If it's so easy to rewrite the law, I'm surprised this hasn't been an issue before." Despite a solid background in the histories of the Little Dozen, she could remember no time where such a concern had existed. *But then, I can't think of very many instances where the royal family married outside their own kingdom either. Not since long before the war.*

"Prince Gamun is different. Crueler than most and ruthless. Certain laws can't be changed without the agreement of the King's advisors—the Alexandrian council. But if members of that council were to suddenly disappear or die before they could be replaced, or if they were replaced by members of the Shadian bloodline, then those laws could be changed easily enough."

Lady Millicent swallowed hard, the lump in her throat causing the ruby on her necklace to bounce like a clump of blood resting on her breast.

"What makes you think this prince is capable of such lofty goals?"

"Don't play coy with me." The lady's eyes flashed. "An Amaskan within our midst can mean only one thing—an attempt on the royal family's lives. What else would bring someone as detested as you into Alexander? That's why you're here, is it not?"

Adelei said nothing. When she continued her silence, Lady Millicent sighed. "I know you can't discuss details with me, but you can't hide from me either. Why not come outright and ask me for information...Alethea?" Adelei's eye twitched. "I thought I finally had the evidence needed to take before the Boahim Senate and lock that monster away. But I don't, do I? There is no girl, no victim here. Only an assassin seeking information."

"I'm sorry, Lady Millicent. It wasn't personal."

The way the lady's rigid frame sat straight in the chair, her fingers in a white knuckled grip on her hem, gave Adelei pause. When she spotted the unshed tears, she swore. *Something isn't right here.*

"Lady, I will help anyway I can. If this man is a perceived threat in the eyes of the Boahim Senate, he is on my map as well. Tell me what you know—let me help." The anger fled from Lady Millicent as a few tears leapt over her eyelids and rolled down cheeks that had been rosy only moments before. *Whatever monster she thinks exists in this prince, it's not just about Margaret. This is personal.*

"This Prince of Shad has a history, but it's all gossip. Whenever the Boahim Senate gets close to a victim, they disappear—sometimes permanently. Sometimes just the victim's memories are missing."

"So when 'Alethea' came before you, you thought—"

"I thought we'd found another victim, this one in time to save my—to do something about this monster of a prince."

Adelei noted the slip. "I apologize for the necessity of that. After I heard Lady Angelina and you in the library, I didn't know whether you would be willing to speak with me. I do wish to talk with you further, but I fear leaving Her Highness alone for too long."

"I understand. I'll leave you to your job then."

"Wait—" Adelei touched the woman's arm as she brushed past. "Tonight, when the Princess has retired, seek me out in her sitting room. We'll discuss this further."

If the woman thought it odd to be invited into royal chambers, she said nothing of it, nor did she give any exterior sign of surprise. She nodded curtly and excused herself, kerchiefed fingers blotting at her eyes as she retreated.

That made one ally in Alesta. With hope the information was worth the price. Adelei strode toward the bower, tension twisting her muscles. The laughter inside set her on edge. *Back to the torture chamber.* Adelei nodded to the guards before she crossed the threshold into the room of women that made her skin crawl.

"Where is Lady Millicent?" Lady Angelina asked, and all eyes returned to Adelei.

"She didn't feel well so I escorted her to her rooms. Carry on, ladies."

While the others returned to their sewing, Lady Angelina's gaze met Adelei's. While she didn't make the connection Lady Millicent had, she studied every false line painted on Adelei's face. *How long I can carry on this façade, I don't know. Too many people seem preoccupied with my appearance.*

Adelei returned to her seat on the dog bed in the corner, a brief prayer on her lips. *Let me survive this long enough to ask my questions of my master. If too many people put together the clues, this is going to be the shortest lifelong job in the history of the Order.*

She expected swords. Big, metal things with sharp edges for butchering people. Or maybe some throwing knives like the ones Master Adelei carried. Or that horrid dagger Adelei had used against her. When Margaret followed Adelei into the practice room after tea, she'd expected at least some weapon or another. But what she got was a room full of furniture.

While the quality left much to be desired, the layout felt familiar, and Margaret pursed her lips together as she spun about the room. "I thought you wished me to learn self-defense."

"I do."

Margaret picked up a familiar-looking candle from a short table. The purple candle still held the dent from earlier that morning, and she rubbed her finger across the indention. "This is my candle. From my bedchamber."

"It is."

"You were in my room. Who gave you permission to enter my room—" Adelei wore a look that stilled Margaret's tongue, the same look she'd worn earlier when she'd held the dagger against Margaret. "My apologies, Master Adelei, but I don't understand. How is this candle going to help me defend myself against an assassin?"

"It probably won't, at least not against a Tribor or some other assassin. But if you're attacked by someone else, it might save your life."

Margaret returned the candle to the table and crossed to a chair by the open window. "Wait—this room. It's set up like mine. It's not my belongings," she said and crinkled her nose at the well-aged, well-used pieces. "But the layout is like my room."

Adelei nodded. "I want you to get familiar with how to escape from rooms you're commonly in, as well as those you aren't. Take that candle for instance." When Adelei picked it up, she hefted it like a ball, and before Margaret could move, the candle came hurtling at her. Margaret covered her head with her arms and tucked her shoulders in closer to her body. When nothing made impact, she cracked open one eye and then another.

Master Adelei's hands were empty. Puzzled, Margaret turned to her right where the *thunk* had sounded. A large splotch of purple wax stuck to the wall in a clump, while the rest of the candle lay misshapen on the floor. "That could have hit me," she shrieked.

"Not in my hands. I knew exactly what I was doing when I threw it." Adelei waited a heartbeat, then turned her back to Margaret.

"What are you doing?" Margaret leaned over to see around Adelei, but the Amaskan's hands were hidden in her pockets.

The woman's feet shifted on the stone floor, and she held something in her fist. "Your Highness, be honest," she said as she faced Margaret. "If an enemy came, you'd be unable to fend them off at present. King Leon has done you a great disservice in not having you learn more self-defense. It's not enough for you to know how to run, though that's a good start. You have to know how to defend yourself."

"So you said." Margaret gestured to the room. "But there aren't any weapons here."

"You're surrounded by weapons."

Margaret frowned. "Are you expecting me to carve a sword out of a table?"

Adelei kicked the wobbly chair beside her. "You could, but there's no time for you to learn sword work—"

"Good. It's too manly a sport anyway."

They were the wrong words. Margaret barely caught the shift in Adelei's stance as the woman came at her, dagger in hand. "Wait, stop," she cried, but there was no time. Her feet stumbled over the footstool behind her, and she fell on her rump beside it.

The dagger's edge quivered near her chin, and she squeezed her eyes shut. "Closing your eyes won't save you. Won't make you any less dead. Now get up."

When she opened her eyes, Adelei sat in the rickety chair from before. "Your first mistake was not running."

"But—"

"Your second mistake was not using the chair beside you. Kick it at me, so I stumble. Throw it at me. Wood in the face hurts."

"But the chair will break."

The Amaskan sighed, and Margaret bit her trembling lip. "Stop thinking of this furniture as important. It's all garbage— stuff the Stewart was throwing out. It's here for our use, so use it. Besides, in a real attack the assassin won't care two pennies for your precious candle. Use whatever you have to escape. If you're dead, it won't matter anyway."

This time when Adelei rushed Margaret, she had more warning. *At least this time I know she's not going to kill me. I don't think.* Lost in thought, she barely had time to kick the chair. It moved a scant foot, and she hopped on one leg. "Ow."

Adelei rolled her eyes. "You're going to have to toughen up, Your Highness. Do you participate in any sport? Hunting? Riding?"

"I ride my pony in the spring. And when the Duke of Ceras visits, his lady and I play *paille-maille*. Have you heard of it?"

"It goes by *mai-dur* in Sadai. You hit little balls through arches on the ground, correct?" asked Adelei.

Margaret clapped her hands together. "Yes. Most of the other sports are too rough, but *paille-maille* is genteel enough."

The Amaskan stood before Margaret and grabbed her hands. "These are soft hands. Hands that don't work. Hands that don't know a blade." She leaned close to Margaret's face and stared at her. "An assassin doesn't care what is and isn't genteel."

The princess tugged her hands from Adelei's grasp. "And when this assassin is gone? Would you have me return to my position with the rough hands of a...of a farmer?" Margaret picked at the tie at the base of her braid. Tears stung her eyes, and she stared at the floor so Adelei wouldn't see.

"I don't want to be a fighter."

A gentle hand rested on her shoulder. "And I don't want to be here. Sometimes, the Gods don't care what we want, Your Highness, any more than assassins do. I'm not asking you to be a fighter, but you need to understand how to defend yourself and your kingdom."

"Father handles that. Or Captain Fenton—"

Adelei whispered, "And when they are gone?"

The swift intake of air made her cough. "No, I refuse. This isn't necessary." Margaret strode to the door and as she reached it, a chair exploded into a dozen pieces of wood as it slammed into the wall beside her.

"One day, they won't be around to protect you, Margaret. And if you don't learn something, people will take advantage of you until there is nothing left of you to take advantage of."

Margaret let the door close behind her. She made it to the third floor before the tears fell in earnest. Several servants nearby averted their glances, but the whispers moved down the hallway as she fled. Once in the safety of her room, the door securely shut and locked, she fell into her bed and cried.

I don't have to be strong. I don't.

Heavy footsteps sounded outside her room, too heavy for Master Adelei, and Margaret scrambled upright. Her eyes dashed around the room. She needed a weapon. Something. No swords awaited her in her bedchamber, nor daggers or knives. *Oh Gods, please save me.*

Whoever stood on the other side of her door jiggled the door handle, and Margaret covered her lips to muffle a scream. The handle shook again, and then an odd sound like a kitchen knife on a spoon. Margaret ran to her bathroom and leapt into her bathing tub.

If I stay here, maybe they won't find me. She crouched down in the tub as silence reigned outside her bedchamber. *Oh Gods, of course they'll look here.*

She stumbled out of the tub in her rush. Margaret raced to the bathing room door and put her back to the wall where she wouldn't be seen. Her gaze landed on the stool near the tub, and Adelei's words floated through her mind. *Kick it at me so I stumble. Throw it at me. Wood in the face hurts.*

Margaret dashed over to the stool and snatched it with both hands before returning to the door. Footsteps outside, quieter this time. *As if they're tiptoeing. Oh Gods, someone is trying to kill me.* The shadow crossed the doorframe, and she held her breath. The person stepped away. Margaret exhaled, and they leapt through the door. Margaret's stool hit the attacker straight in the face, and the person fell to their knees.

When she stopped running for the tub long enough to look back, it wasn't an assassin who lay groaning on the ground, but Captain Fenton. "Oh, oh, oh. I'm sorry, Captain. I thought you were an attacker."

The man wiped a streak of blood from his cheek as a second shadow fell across the floor. Master Adelei stepped around Michael and nodded. "He could have been. He still could be. Anyone in this castle could be your assassin. Don't drop your guard because they're down. Now is when you should be running."

"No, not Captain Fenton. He's been a family friend for years—"

"So was your father's Grand Advisor, Goefrin."

Margaret frowned, and Captain Fenton shook his head. "She doesn't know, Master Adelei."

Adelei swore.

"I don't know what?" asked Margaret.

"Later," said Adelei. She handed Captain Fenton a cloth, which he held to the cut on his face. "You did well to throw the chair in his face."

"I thought he was an assassin."

Captain Fenton stood and gave a quick salute to Master Adelei. To Margaret, he bowed before retreating from the bathing room. "I wanted you to think that because he could be. If you hear someone where they shouldn't be, or you think you're in danger, save yourself. Run. Defend yourself if you must." Adelei picked up a piece of the broken chair. "I'm going to add some lessons to your day, Your Highness. Some weapons work with the captain."

Margaret opened her mouth, but Adelei shook her head. "Nothing too heavy. You won't wield a sword for a long while, but it will lay the groundwork for skills you may need later in life. Especially if war breaks out."

A bubble of laughter escaped. "War? There hasn't been a war here since I was a child. With the Boahim Senate, who would dare?"

The way the Amaskan looked at her, Margaret wished she could crawl into a hole somewhere and hide. It was Adelei's *are-you-really-that-stupid* look, the same one Margaret's tutors sometimes gave her, and she flushed under it. Chair pieces in hand, Adelei gave Margaret a short bow. "You will still meet with me for self-defense training. Anyone can be a killer, Your Highness."

"No one can live that way. I can't see shadows in every light in front of me. It'll drive me insane."

Adelei grinned, showing too much of her white teeth. "Now you understand more about Amaskans," she said, and she was gone. Margaret squatted on the bathing room floor and wrapped her arms around her knees. She didn't want to understand the Amaskan.

All I want is for things to go back to normal. Please.

CHAPTER FOURTEEN

Exhaustion was not a strong enough word for what Adelei felt as she folded her frame into the largest chair in the sitting room. Her legs stretched out closer to the fireplace as she leaned her head against the cushion. How Margaret maintained her smile all day long through such boredom was a mystery.

It wasn't that guarding the princess was exhausting—watching and waiting was something Adelei excelled at, something she'd done over and over again for many jobs over the years. But the constant boredom of moving through social circles—greeting, gossiping, greeting again, and smiling—it was enough to drive her insane.

An entire day of doing nothing. How could anyone live like that? Her eyes closed as she soaked up the fire's heat. Princess Margaret had retired for the night. After seeing her rooms were secure and safe, Adelei had shooed out the handmaidens and settled down to wait for her guest.

Now the real job begins—figuring out who is after royal blood. In the meantime, the rest will do me good. Adelei focused on her breathing and allowed her body to release stress with each exhale. One ear listened for changes in the suite's normal sounds while the other tuned out. She fell into an unsteady trance. *Wish I could afford the time for a deeper meditation, but I'll take what I can get.*

The footsteps outside the door shifted from the guards' normal pacing to a lighter step and then silence as they stood still.

Adelei waited for the knock to announce the Lady Millicent. It wasn't the lady who entered as expected, but King Leon.

Adelei was still seated when he walked through the door, though less casually once she recognized the footsteps as much heavier than a woman's. She bolted upright. "I'm expecting a visitor any moment now—"

"I asked the Lady Millicent to give us a few moments." He claimed the seat across from her and winced as he settled into it. "Captain Fenton tells me your mere presence has ruffled a few feathers, especially Margaret's. How went today? Did you perceive any threat?"

Adelei sighed and rubbed her temple with long fingers. "Many, Your Highness, though none I'd care to name just yet."

He gestured for her to continue, and she reported on the many instances throughout the day where guards were derelict in their duty or areas of the castle that were too exposed or open to being breached. "Worse still is that Her Highness has no idea of the precariousness of her life, or care for guarding herself. She claims to have had some self-defense training, though I saw no evidence of it this morning when we...approached the issue."

"When you chucked a candle at her spoiled rotten head, you mean." King Leon half-laughed, half-coughed his way to his next breath. "Yes, I heard about your attempts to instill some sense of self-preservation in her. Good on you to establish order early on. Something I never learned to do with her, sadly. Tell me though, what does Lady Millicent want with a visit to an Amaskan?" Wrinkles decorated his forehead, frowning in sync with his lips.

"Former Amaskan."

"Does that bother you?"

She kept her muscles still, but her toe twitched despite her efforts. "Yes. Would it matter to you if you found yourself suddenly not king?"

A genuine smile lit up his face. "Not at all. I would enjoy the leisure, I think. So what does the lady want with a...former Amaskan?"

"She believes the alliance between the Shadian family and your own is a trap."

"It is."

His answer startled her, though she supposed it shouldn't have. *Any king worth his weight in gold would be well aware of such traps. Such is the risk in alliances.*

"Then why go through with it? If you've proof of such a trap, why not go before the Boahim Senate and cry foul?"

"If I had such proof, I would, but I have nothing more than conjecture. My hope is that in your search for our assassin, you'll find me proof enough to call off the wedding."

Adelei nodded. "I've nothing yet, but with hope my conversation with Lady Millicent will give me what we need. She knows something, something important. I just have to gain her trust enough to hear it."

"Good," King Leon said, his body rocking slightly with his nodding head. "Iliana—"

She held up a finger to her lips. "Adelei. Even in this room, it has to be Adelei."

"But—"

"Your Majesty, if I'm to protect Margaret, there can't be anything to use as a weapon, do you understand? I can't be...who you want me to be, nothing that can be used against you. I must be who you hired and nothing more." Her voice shook at the end as an internal voice whispered, *Coward. Hiding behind an excuse.*

No, she answered. *Emotions are a weakness.*

And if you had to admit to yourself that you're curious about this father? That you remember...something? That you want to remember more? That would be a weakness? You're hiding.

"Ili—Adelei?" asked King Leon. He leaned close enough for her to smell the roast pig on his breath. "Are you well? What's wrong?"

"Nothing. I'm tired. Too long in the saddle."

Another excuse. Another lie.

Her father touched a finger to her cheek long enough for her to blink twice before withdrawing it. "I-I wish we had more time to speak. I've missed you..." The knock at the door startled them both, and Adelei leapt up.

A guard stuck his head inside, nodding by way of his apology. "I'm sorry for the intrusion, Your Majesty, but Lady Millicent still waits to see Master Adelei. Would you like her to return another time?"

"No, no, we're finished," said King Leon. All traces of her father washed from his face in a moment. "I'll leave you to your business, Master Adelei."

Outside the door, Lady Millicent bowed low to the King as he passed. She strode inside with a raised brow and shut the door behind her. "Interesting company to keep so late in the evening."

While the lady seated herself, Adelei gathered her composure. Her mask had fallen—just for a moment as her father had reached out to her. *A weakness. Lock it away, shut it down.* Such a conflict *couldn't* exist. *Shouldn't* exist.

"Tell me about this prince."

"He's a sadist, Master Adelei. He finds girls of a certain age, young but not little children, and he lures them in with promises of nobility, land, or trinkets of great value. Then he breaks them. Sometimes they come back with such damage. Unspeakable things on their flesh. If that's how they're found, they are lucky."

"How so?" Adelei asked and swallowed the bile in the back of her throat.

"In the worst cases, their minds are gone. I don't know what magics or evils are used, but they aren't there anymore. Any trace of who they were is gone. And this is in addition to the body's physical condition."

"How do you know for sure this is what he does?"

Lady Millicent's eyes went flat, and she blinked slowly, wrapping her arms around herself as if trying to hold all the horrors inside. Adelei had seen it before in other victims, and she asked, "Did he hurt your Ladyship?"

"Not me," she whispered. "My daughter. My only daughter."

Adelei could smell the bile in her throat. Again she swallowed it down. "I would think this proof enough for the Boahim Senate."

Tears smeared the lady's well made up face. "I thought so, too, which is why when we found her, broken and beaten, I rushed her before the Senate, but they wouldn't see us until morning. But by then, my Alethea—" Adelei flinched at the name. Puzzle pieces clicked into place. "My Alethea, she'd found a knife and...and..."

"She took her own life."

"Yes."

Adelei handed Lady Millicent a kerchief which she used to blow her nose indelicately. "How do you know it was him?"

"Our manservant found her. In an alley in the city's lower quarters. When he found her, Prince Gamun's name was the last word she ever spoke."

"I know this is difficult for you." Adelei clumsily patted the woman's hand. "But I must ask you more questions if I'm to stop this from happening again." When the woman nodded, Adelei continued. "You said he's left a trail of bodies behind him. How did you come by this information?"

"After Alethea, my husband hired some men to find information, to find out more about this prince. We knew who he was, of course, as he visited our city on his tour of the Kingdom of Alexander years ago."

"When he first met the Princess."

"Y-yes. He flirted openly with our daughter, and while we knew he was promised to Her Royal Highness, we thought maybe he might take our daughter as a second wife or a mistress. We thought, the mistress of a King is better than naught—it would be a chance of royal blood in our line. So when he invited her to dine with him, we thought her safe. We thought her happy and our future secure."

Adelei grimaced at the picture being painted. As highborn as her ladyship was, no royal blood graced her family tree. Adelei could picture it now, how happy Lady Millicent and her husband must have been at the idea of a grandchild of such prestige—bastard or no.

"My husband searched for information and found similar tales all over, though most were in the Kingdom of Shad itself. Tales of girls disappearing, never to be seen or heard from again. And each time, before the girls were missing, their home was visited by Prince Gamun Bajit on his tour of his kingdom or ours."

"How many?"

"My husband stopped asking after three dozen."

Thirty-six girls he'd used and discarded.

"Why hasn't the Boahim Senate stopped him? Their entire purpose is to stop crimes against the Thirteen. The temple is a gift from Adlain. To kill another is to kill yourself. Not even royal blood would protect him from their reach."

"Evidence. There isn't any. Just gossip. Stories. Any lead they've had just disappears forever."

"Have you ever thought to hire the Amaskans?"

Blue eyes focused so intently on Adelei's jawline that her toes curled in her boots. "Not in this kingdom, Master Adelei. Not since—"

"Iliana."

"Yes. The death of the princess . There is no help to be had. And now you understand why this wedding must not occur. He must not gain entrance into our kingdom as King." Lady Millicent's voice doubled in volume, and Adelei waved her hands at the distraught woman to quiet her. Outside, the guards shuffled in place.

"I understand, and now if you don't mind, I must attend to another matter. Thank you for your information." Adelei guided the woman from her seat by the elbow.

"So you believe me?"

"I do, which is why I must attend to something immediately," said Adelei, and Lady Millicent hurried out. Once away from ear range, Adelei turned to the nearest guard. "I need to see His Majesty immediately. Please take me to him."

King Leon's rooms backed up against Margaret's, but his sitting room made her feel impoverished in comparison. "Wait here," the guard said, and Adelei stood. If she sat in the chair, it might wilt or tarnish. The number of blue hues tripled that of the sitting room she shared with Margaret. The guard returned and ushered her into a private study where more blues colored her vision by way of a large tapestry—its subject, a woman she could only assume was her mother.

The thread's thinness and colors' brightness spoke of great wealth. Not to mention the labor to create such a thing. *I wonder who made it?*

Her father cleared his throat, and she bowed. "Rise," he said, without looking up from the paper before him. Leon wiped the pen free of ink and gestured for her to sit. "Stunning, isn't it?"

"Your Majesty?"

"The tapestry."

"I hadn't noticed," Adelei lied.

King Leon tilted his head. "Come now. Be honest—you wouldn't be formerly Amaskan if you didn't notice. I'd wager you've counted the number of objects in the room that would serve as a weapon."

"Forty-two, but only because your bedspread is dusty enough to choke one to death."

Adelei's nose crinkled, and he laughed. His rich, brown eyes turned wistful. "Your mother was quite the beautiful woman, although a bit scatterbrained. Still, you have her smile, you know."

When she frowned, Leon waved a tired hand at her. "I take it your conversation with Lady Millicent was fruitful?"

"It was, Your Majesty, though maybe not as fruitful as I'd like."

"And yet still, you hurry before me late at night."

"Yes, Your Majesty," she answered.

"Tell me what you'd have me hear, Master Adelei."

Adelei spoke with a level voice that didn't tremble as she retold the information she'd learned that evening. "Lady Millicent is convinced, as am I, that harm would befall Princess Margaret if this marriage moves forward. Price Gamun may or may not be involved in the assassination attempts, but whether he is or isn't, her life is in danger. This wedding cannot occur." She kept her gaze on the floor while waiting for his response, and when there was none, she sought his face. Weariness stared back at her.

"Prince Gamun is not responsible for the attempts on her life." The hair on Adelei's arms stood on end, and she rose before backing away.

"Explain."

King Leon said nothing at first, and Adelei repeated herself. Fire sparked in those brown eyes, eyes she shared, and she flinched when he grinned a dark grin. "And who are you to order the King, hmmm? Just know it was not him," he said sharply. "That still doesn't excuse the evils he's been inflicting on my land. I share your concern in regard to the royal wedding."

It was a risk. It was treason, and yet her job was to protect Princess Margaret. No one else. Everyone else was expendable, right up to the King himself.

Adelei withdrew her dirk in a swift motion. "You will tell me what information you have on the assassin."

"You dare draw arms against me?"

"You hired me to do a job, to protect your daughter. Something I will do 'til my dying breath. And if it means I must protect her from a treasonous king, so be it. Now explain yourself. What have you done?"

King Leon rose up, fury inferno one moment, and then as suddenly, the man shrank in on himself. All the fight drained out of him as his sorrowful eyes begged forgiveness before he spoke a word.

Her skin, suddenly too tight across her bones, itched as the hair along it moved. "No," she whispered. "How could you—"

"I needed you here. It was the only way I could ensure you would come home," he cried. The anguish scrawled itself across every feature her fuzzy memory identified as father. "Master Bredych needed a cover. A reason to release you from the Order in such a way that you wouldn't expect—"

"Expect betrayal? Treason?"

"No, I needed you home, dammit. So I arranged for someone to pretend—"

"To pretend to kill your own daughter? How could you hire the Tribor? Did you think they'd stop after one attempt? How stupid are you?" King Leon gasped, his mouth working while no words escaped. "Your Majesty?"

His shaking finger gestured at the table next to her where a cup of warmed liquid sat. She handed it to him and watched him guzzle it. He spilled a few drops on his lap in his rush.

The smell was familiar. The plate on the table held traces of green powder. "How long?"

"W-What?"

"How long have you had such fits?" The pallor of his skin. The weakness of his frame. *I should have noticed this earlier. Damn. Double damn.*

"Long enough. You know what it is?"

"You've been poisoned. Long enough to cause permanent damage to your insides." Her anger drained away with a second look at the powder. *He's dying. He brought me home because he's dying. And by the look of him, he doesn't have long.*

She didn't know whether to hate him more or less. He was right though; Master Bredych would have had no other choice.

"How much longer do the healers say you have?"

King Leon placed the cup on the table beside him. His hands shook less this time. "Days? Months? Years? No one seems to know, but not long enough. There are things I would clear from my conscience before I pass from this plane, and I'm sorry to say this was necessary. But I didn't hire the Tribor. I swear to you that was not my doing."

"Any chance that whomever you hired did?"

"No, none." When she raised a doubtful eyebrow, he shook his head. "It was Ida. She did it by royal order. The dagger was fake. Margaret was never in any real danger."

"She does all the dirty work, doesn't she?" Adelei shook her head. "Sorry, I'm just tired." Adelei returned to her seat and rubbed the bridge of her nose.

"Ida told you her part in your kidnapping?"

"She did."

Silence stretched between them like fifteen years, funereal in feel. Adelei studied her mother's tapestry again. When she pulled her eyes away, King Leon's own were damp. "I'm glad your mother never knew you were in danger. It wasn't her idea to send you away. In fact, we fought about the decision before I sent her elsewhere."

"Was it Ida's?"

"No. I didn't meet Ida until the day she took you away. When she returned, I didn't recognize her. Hells, I didn't know who she was until last year." Her father rubbed his hand across his face and covered his eyes. "What a mess this has all been. Poor Ida has tried to make it right—to make amends."

"And what about you?" Her anger flared up, new wounds too fresh to ignore.

"You tell me. Will it ever be enough for you? To say I'm sorry you were kidnapped? I didn't know, Adelei. I swear it."

"I-I don't know. I have too many questions, too much to think about right now. After, maybe. I can't promise anything," said Adelei. The hope in his eyes pierced her armor, and she shifted the conversation. "So you arranged for Ida to make a false attempt or two on Margaret in order to bring me here. But what were you going to do when I found no assassin?"

His fingers relaxed their grip on the arm of his chair. "Honestly, I was hopeful that by then you'd want to stay."

"It's not as simple as that. I was sent here to do a job, which only ends if there is no longer a threat, or I fail. If I succeed, I will return home to await new orders."

"You would, were you Amaskan. But you're not now. There are no new orders for you."

Adelei touched her finger to the scar on her jaw. Puffy but healed, it was a reminder. "I would still go home to await new orders. It's my duty to the Order."

"So it doesn't matter what you want?"

"Does it matter what the father wants when the King must act?" When he frowned, she continued, "I thought not. It's the same with me. I have a job to do, Amaskan or not. Part of what makes me the best is that I do my job because it is right—just. If it were any other way, you wouldn't want me here to protect the Princess."

King and father battled for a moment, his shoulders tensing as he shifted in his seat until he slumped forward, more defeated than ever. She thought the King had won out until he spoke. "How you are so wise at such a young age, I'll never know. It couldn't make me prouder, though I wish your sister shared some of that wisdom."

It was a father's joy that spread across his face, lighting up his eyes like fireflies and tripling the wrinkles around his eyes. It was a familiar joy. Master Bredych had been a wonderful father, if light on the praise at times, and now both men shared the same look. One before her, and the other in her memory.

"I'm sorry I brought you here under false pretenses," he added, and his smile faded. "Ida mentioned an attack by the Tribor. Tell me about it."

Watching this man shift from father to king so rapidly left a bad taste in her mouth. Her head was spinning. *I never know who I'm talking to. Even worse—just when I feel like I'm getting to know the father, the King undercuts me and leaves me vulnerable and exposed. What a dangerous man he is.* Adelei glanced up at the King through thick lashes.

He did it on purpose. The King moved across her father's skin, a hidden creature just out of reach. *When I think it safe, he strikes. No wonder people find him such a deadly enemy.* She hated being used like that but admired the skill nonetheless.

"As we passed through the forest a day's travel before Menoir, we were attacked by a Tribor assassin. I held him while we questioned him, but he gave us little information. All we know for certain was that he was sent to stop me from reaching you. Before we could get details, he killed himself on my blade."

"So a real mark has been placed on Margaret's head."

"Not necessarily," Adelei answered. "He was sent to stop me from reaching this city—the mark may well be on me. If it is, I can't take Her Highness's place in the wedding. It'll put her in more danger if she's me."

"Margaret will be happy with that." She shot him a dark look, and he shook his head. "That's not what I meant. She'll be happy to be in the wedding again. I can't see her rejoicing over your death."

"Are you sure about that?"

"What do you mean?"

"Nothing," she muttered.

King Leon drummed his fingers on the chair's arm, the pads of his fingertips thumping the carved wood. "Why would they want to stop you?"

"They want this marriage to move forward, and they know that if I'm here, I'll find out information that could lead to the end of the peace treaty. Chances are they were hired by the Shadian family to ensure things move forward, despite the rumors regarding Prince Gamun."

"I assume this one bore the mark."

Adelei nodded. "'Twas fairly new though."

"Why the ankle?"

"Your Majesty?"

"Why the mark on the ankle?" he asked.

"The ankle is easily hidden. Unlike Amaskans, the Tribor wish to remain anonymous since they are hired to commit acts against the Thirteen." Adelei's eyes flashed as she stared at King Leon. "Amaskans are proud. They bear their mark openly and are not afraid to do their job."

Footfalls moved outside, and Adelei held a finger to her lips. She tiptoed to the door, one hand on her dirk's hilt. Adelei waved at her father then, miming talking with her fingers.

"Oh...um...that makes sense, I suppose, though I can't see what the Shadians think they will gain...by such a plan," he said.

She pressed her ear against the door. Outside, the guards still paced. Whoever it was, he or she was high enough in rank for the guards to maintain their silence and not be startled.

Adelei waved in her father's direction again, and he cleared his throat noisily before speaking. "Do you think yo—the princess is in danger?" As he spoke, Adelei yanked open the door. She reached through it and seized the eavesdropper by the shirt. Adelei hauled the person into the room before slamming the door shut again. Without a glance, she shoved the would-be-assailant into the chair she had vacated, and it was only then that she got a good look at the person before her.

"Margaret. What are you doing here?" King Leon asked, color flooding back into his cheeks.

"I-I couldn't sleep. A-and I decided to take a walk, when I saw *her*—," she said, jerking a thumb in the direction of Adelei, "—come in here. And I thought you were in danger." Margaret held up a small dinner knife, one used to spread jam and with all the sharpness of a hair comb.

Adelei burst out laughing.

"What? What's so funny?" Margaret dropped the knife in her confusion, where it clanged against the stone floor and skittered under a chair. King Leon's lip trembled as he bit back laughter, which only served to make Adelei laugh harder.

Unable to breathe, she sucked in a gasp. "I'm sorry, but seeing you holding that knife—" A small laugh tried to escape her lips, and she bit her tongue to stop it. "I shouldn't laugh. My apologies, Your Highness."

"Father, I truly thought you were in danger. I don't see what is funny about that at all. Besides, I did what she said. It's a weapon."

The truth of it sucked the humor out of the situation, and Adelei sighed. "You're right, Your Highness. All of us are in great danger, which is not funny in the least. But my directions told you to run, not come defend the King."

"I was speaking to my father," Margaret snapped.

When his fist crumpled the paper beside him, he tossed the ball into the lit fireplace where it crackled and burned. "Enough," he said. "Margaret, your disdain for Master Adelei has been noted, but it doesn't change the fact that she is here to protect you, to protect us all. If you will not do your part as princess and help by following orders, then how do I know you are ready to rule this country? What future as Queen do you have if all you focus on is yourself?"

From the look on her face, I'd say that's possibly the first time he's ever raised his voice to her. Her Highness's lips curled down, teeth visible from the grimace that painted her face an ugly shade of confusion, and then shock as she realized he meant it.

"Too bad, Father," Margaret said in a spur of inspiration. "I'm all you've got. And once I'm married, the law will be on my side."

Leon's eyes met Adelei's, anger and sorrow mixing the brown into muddy waters that threatened to spill their banks. "I think it may be time that Margaret knew."

"Knew what?" asked Margaret.

"This isn't a good idea, Sire. Knowledge is power. And this could endanger her more."

"But she refuses to listen to you. If she knew—"

"Knew what?" asked Margaret.

"It's not a good idea," Adelei said. "Trust me on this."

King Leon held up his hand in protest, and Margaret stood, her hands on her hips. "Know what?" she shouted. Her face reminded Adelei of a berry, flushed red and purple as she stomped her foot.

"Margaret. Poppet. Master Adelei is your sister."

Silence followed the announcement, until Margaret tore her eyes away from her father long enough to study Adelei's face. "She cannot be. My sister is dead."

Adelei knelt in front of her, her face before Margaret's, and removed her head scarf. She used it to wipe away the makeup that hid her looks behind false wrinkles and almond-shaped eyes. "Look at me closely. I'm not dead."

Margaret's irises shrank as they moved across Adelei's face. "It's not possible. How—why—when—" she sputtered.

"That's not a story I wish to repeat. You tell her how it happened," answered Adelei. Anger seeped into her. Always there. *I don't know where my loyalties lie anymore.* "By your leave?" she asked and bowed to King Leon. He nodded, and she secured the scarf before fleeing the room.

Her feet took her past her own rooms and down corridors and stairs until she found the stables. A familiar nicker greeted her. Midnight stood in his stall happily munching oats, and she ran a hand across his neck.

Master. Father. Why did you send me into such a situation? You had to know this would end up this way. You had to know this would tear me to pieces. She refused to give in to tears again. Midnight nosed her, nickering softly. *Do I protect the sister who hates me for a father who played me, or do I return to the father who kidnapped me and stole me away from a chance of knowing this family of mine?*

Adelei kicked at the straw below. *I don't know. I thought I knew what I was doing, coming here, but I don't. And I get the feeling, Master Bredych, that you didn't either.*

The crunching of twigs under the boot heel of another caught her ear, and she froze. *Behind me.* She pressed her palm against Midnight's neck. He responded to the touch and the tension in her body by shifting in the stall. Once he was in a better position to kick, he quieted. Adelei stepped right, out of his way, and watched him.

When the scuffing of a boot toe sounded, it was closer than before, and she leaned against the stall's wall, dagger in hand. One foot at a time, she slid closer to the door until another footfall sounded.

A gloved hand reached over the stall, feeling for the latch. The person gently pushed the door open. Adelei held her breath, eyes moving between the hand and the ground where a booted foot stepped just left of one of Midnight's droppings. When the figure entered, Adelei didn't waste any time. She ducked.

Midnight flung both rear hooves into the chest of her assailant. The kick hurled him through the swinging door and across the stable, where he slammed into the frame of another stall. Horses nickered loudly at the disruption, and Adelei rushed to his side.

The heart beat faintly beneath his flesh, but he remained unconscious as her deft, gloved fingers rifled through his clothing. While his pockets were empty, hidden at his wrist was a small piece of parchment bearing a sketch of her likeness. "Damn," she whispered. "What do you want to bet he's Tribor?"

Her horse whinnied in reply from his stall. He would alert her to the presence of others as she continued searching the body. This time when she found the tattoo, it was worn and faded, marking him an older member despite his baby face. The man, dressed in black, carried a small knife but nothing else.

Her mind pictured Princess Margaret, and she winced. Knowledge was power, even if the assassin had come ill-prepared.

The man moaned, and she tugged him into a sitting position by his muddy shirt. Adelei slid his knife into a pocket of her own and crouched down beside him. She was confident in her ability to keep him immobilized. When his eyes fluttered open, he tried to lurch forward, but his ribs set him coughing.

Dejected, he leaned back against the wall. "My horse probably broke a rib or three with that kick," she spoke in Shadian. Adelei leaned close to his freshly shaven face. No night grease covered his skin, giving her a clear picture of him, and she studied his features as she talked. "I wouldn't move too much—I don't know if those broken ribs are near any internal organs." He shrugged, hazel eyes wide as they watched her.

"I see you were coming after me." She held up the piece of paper she'd pried from his wrist cuff.

"Not you." He coughed, then leaned over to spit blood upon the ground.

Damn, looks like something did get punctured. Adelei pursed her lips together. When his words connected, she grabbed the paper and held it up close to her face. "Yes, me."

"Similar, but...not you." A cough shook his frame. Then another. "You have no hair."

Oh Gods, he was after Margaret.

He glared at her with eyes green one moment and blue the next. His cheeks puckered, and she leaned back, dodging the mixed saliva and blood he spat at her. It landed on the floor with a fizzle. The stone remained untouched, but the strands of loose hay bubbled and hissed when the mixture connected with it. When she looked on him again, foam dribbled down his chin from between pale, thin lips. His eyes rolled backward as his body seized beneath her.

"Dammit," she yelled and rolled away from his poisoned body. Behind her, Midnight danced in place, a concerned whinny catching her ear. She ignored him for the moment, more concerned with the poison foaming out of the Tribor's mouth. It hit the floor, leaving a foul smelling trail of bubbling hay in its wake.

"Hey," she shouted. When a stablehand came stumbling sleepily from around the corner, his eyes popped out of his skull at the sight of the dead man. "Stop. Don't come any closer." She waved a hand in warning. "Go fetch a guardsman, preferably Captain Fenton."

As he scampered off, she grabbed a nearby shovel to push the untainted hay away from the pool of liquid gathering outside his body. The ooze seeped through his clothing. There were poisons, and then there were poisons. This was like nothing she had ever seen. Adelei twisted on her heel to keep from stepping in the stuff. If it could eat through his clothing and skin, it could eat through Adelei's as well.

The ooze ignored the stone as it continued to eat its way across the stable floor. Footfalls in the distance alerted her to the approaching guards, and she shoveled the mix of hay and manure until she had created a wide circle around the body. A hiss behind him meant the poison had reached the stall he leaned against.

Inside the stall a frightened horse whinnied.

"Oh Gods," she whispered. Her eyes darted around in search of an axe. None. Nothing to break the damned wood and stop the spread. Kind eyes peeked over the stall's gate. Kind, brown eyes that were widened to the whites as the hissing ooze ate away at the wood. The mare backed against the rear wall where she found no escape.

"W-What is that?" Captain Fenton stopped at Adelei's outstretched palm.

"I don't know, but whatever it is, it eats through anything but stone. We need an axe—we may be able to stop its path."

"There's another way," a familiar voice croaked, and Ida Warhammer strode to Captain Fenton's side. She reached out an arm to snag the stablehand by the shirt. "You, go fetch me the biggest pail of goat's milk you can get. Tell the shepherd it's by my orders, but get it here as fast as ya can. Understand?"

The boy's knobby legs fled the stables for a second time that night. "Goat's milk? You know what this stuff is?" Adelei asked. Another startled whinny from the stable took her attention away as the ooze leeched across the floor.

"Get the other horses out of here," Ida shouted to the guardsmen as the animals cried out in fear. Adelei tiptoed across the floor, careful to step where the ooze was not, and she opened the gate to Midnight's stall. He danced beneath her grip as she eased him out and edged him around the growing circle of goop.

She tugged his lead and found it taut. All four hooves dug in, and he braced himself for battle. But when she sought the enemy, none appeared. Except the ooze on the floor. The moment her hands were free of the reins, Midnight leapt over the poison and pivoted around to kick in the partially eaten door with ease.

"No."

Too late. Midnight's hooves made contact with the acidic ooze. He backed up and gave the rear wall two swift kicks. A light whinny from Midnight was all it took, and the mare escaped through the hole in the rear wall. Just as quickly as it had spread across the wood of the gate, the poison frothed across Midnight's hind quarters. It bubbled and hissed its way across his flesh, and he cried out.

"Oh Gods," Michael whispered, his eyes glued to the scene before him.

Adelei ached to reach out to Midnight, to touch his quivering flank and soothe him. Instead, she could only remain a spectator as it crept across his flank. He screamed a brutal sound out as his rear legs failed to support him, and the battle steed fell to his knees. Bloody foam scattered across the stone floor.

"You did good, boy," she whispered. Adelei stretched her arm across too far a distance, fingers stroking the air. Her mind remembered the touch of his black mane beneath her long fingers and the warmth of his breath as he inhaled her scented palm. Adelei fell to her own knees as Midnight cried out in agony. Beside her, Michael withdrew his sword and moved toward the battle steed, but Adelei placed her hand against the captain's leg. "No. You can't touch him. It'll spread."

Ida's hand rested on her shoulder, a light sympathetic squeeze along her collarbone. "If the goat's milk gets here soon, we can—"

"It's too late."

Adelei gestured at the horse's rear quarters, a mess unrecognizable in the bloody foam. When Midnight cried out again, bright red foam erupted from his mouth and nose. Captain Fenton balanced on one foot as he leaned forward. He gripped Ida's shoulder for support and stabbed Midnight through the heart.

Michael left the sword where it was, quick to release it lest he be contaminated as well. Midnight whinnied softly, the sound more a gargle than anything else. His eyes rolled toward Adelei, and then he stilled.

The ooze continued to devour Midnight's corpse, and Adelei returned her dagger to its sheath.

"Worth the sword. No one should suffer like that, be they beast or man."

"I have the goat's milk." The bucket knocked against the stable boy's knees as he approached.

Adelei ignored him. She watched her battle steed's body instead.

The first time she had seen him, a foal among a field of horses. Each one to be trained as a battle steed. He was a beast of solid black, a creature meant to replace Master Bredych's fallen mount. Before anyone could tell her otherwise, Adelei had clambered over the fence and into the field. Never mind the battle postures of the horses around her, she bee-lined for the foal.

"Adelei, come back," Master Bredych had cried. Only the Horsemaster and his crew had been given clearance to the field, and for good reason—all those half trained mounts. *I'm lucky I wasn't killed. Which was exactly what Master Bredych said when he got a hold of me. But by then, that foal was convinced I was his second mother.*

No one could explain why we bonded so well, only that we did. She had visited him daily until Master Bredych had gifted him to her. Adelei's first battle steed.

Milk spread across the floor, and the hissing ceased. Ida scooped cups of it out of the bucket and sloshed it across the stall doors and walls. Anywhere that was infected. When the milk touched Midnight, Adelei watched, part of her hoping that somehow he'd rise up, whole and fixed again.

But the body didn't move. He lay still. A foul mix of decay, ooze, and goat's milk. Bile rose in the back of her throat as she turned away. On hands and knees, she crawled into the nearest stall where she lost her dinner like a war-green soldier.

Midnight's stall.

The hay still fresh with the smell of him, his saddle slung across a side-wall. He was a gift. He was family.

"Master Adelei," Ida called softly from the door. "The poison's stopped. It's safe now for the stable boys to clean up."

"That's fine."

Ida shifted back and forth in the remaining hay. "We...we didn't know what ya wanted us to do with Midnight's body."

Adelei glanced up and met a sea of blue holding back unshed tears. "His body should be sent back to Sadai, but...but I don't think that's possible now. There's not enough left to..." A lump rose in her throat, and she swallowed. "I'll take care of it."

"Are ya sure? I can help—I know what it means to lose—"

Of course. Ida had been Amaskan, too. Adelei nodded. "I thought to burn her body here, at home, but is it safe? The poison—"

"The milk stopped it, so the body should be safe enough. Just in case, I'd recommend we do this outside the city walls— maybe in an open field nearby."

Outside the stall, half-awake stablehands chopped at the damaged wood and carried pieces of it away. "You recognized this poison," Adelei said, eyes hardening. "You knew how to stop it. What is it? Tell me what you know, please."

Ida sighed and leaned against the corner frame of the stall. "Bein' so close to Shad, Alexandrians know much more of the

Tribor than we do of Amaskans. There are rumors that they use dark and evil techniques to kill, unclean ways to damage a body and remove evidence of their murders. One way is through a thrice boiled plant said to grow only in the high reachin' mountains of Shad. Something about this plant creates a bubblin' plague that eats through most things."

"But you knew how to stop it."

"Yes." Ida's eyes darkened. "While on my first mission, my mark was a Tribor who'd killed a Duke. He used a similar poison cap to kill himself when I found 'em. The ooze burned down half the inn and killed several people before 'twas stopped, and then only 'cause it started rainin'. Rain doesn't normally stop it. Not completely or anything, but this time, it poured so heavy that the rain washed most of it away. What I didn't know at the time was that some of it ran into the town's water well. People drank the stuff."

Ida shuddered, her blue eyes haunted and lost as they stared at nothing. "A friend's child touched what was left of her mother's body, her screams bringin' half the town to her door. In pain, the child knocked over her glass of milk while thrashin' about, and when her burnin' hand touched the milk—"

"—It stopped the poison."

"Yes, it did. It's called *adenneith* in Shadian. I'm not even sure there's a word for it in Alexandrian, and I'm certain there's not one in Sadain. I'm not even sure the order knows much about it."

"Didn't you report it on your return?" The chopping of wood had stopped, and the clopping of horse hooves sounded as horses were returned to the remaining stalls. Adelei gathered Midnight's gear without looking too closely at it. She couldn't.

Ida hefted Midnight's saddle over her shoulder. "I did, but I don't think they believed me all that much. My own brother swore there was nothin' in the Order archives about such a poison, so they wrote it off as the overactive imagination of a journeyman."

When Adelei stepped out of the stall, Midnight's body had been removed, and she stared at the lightened stone where her battle steed had fallen. "I had them wrap him in burlap and haul him to the city gate. We can take him by cart to a field for burnin' when ya wish, though I recommend sooner than later," Ida said, and she followed Adelei through the stables.

"We'll stow Midnight's gear in my room until...well, a replacement won't be sent. Not anymore." Adelei rubbed her jaw with a finger. Outside, the air was quiet again, but hints of light called out across the horizon. Soon the morning sun would rise, and Adelei would report to the King about this latest attempt by the Tribor assassins.

And all too soon she'd be back to guarding her Royal Highness. No sleep tonight. Adelei wearily climbed the stairs to the fourth floor. Each step set her chin to rub against Midnight's saddle blanket. The smell of horse and grass brought tears to her eyes. Soon though, she would find the person responsible for the mark.

Princess Margaret's sitting room remained silent at this hour. A light snore bumped against the door and drifted through the cracks from Her Highness's rooms. Adelei opened the door to her small room. The decorations from before were gone from the storage chest, and Adelei set Midnight's gear inside. Ida passed her the saddle, which didn't fit, and Adelei tucked it across the desk's chair.

"Come, let's go honor my horse before Her Royal Highness wakes to complain about lumpy beds and silly rules," she said with more humor than she felt.

Let's go honor my horse, who was more my family than my own sister. What does that say about me?

CHAPTER FIFTEEN

Heavy bags beneath sagging eyes told Adelei that King Leon hadn't visited his bed either this night, now day. When she spoke of the attack, he hung his head. "I'm truly sorry about your horse," he said. "But I like even less that another attack has been made on your life. Were you able to ascertain anything from this hired-thug before he killed himself?"

She shook her head. "He knew I'd try. This one came very prepared."

When he raised an eyebrow, she spoke of the adenneith. "Your Majesty, it burned like nothing I'd ever seen before. If Ida hadn't known how to stop it, I'm not sure it would have stopped at all until everything but the stone belly of the castle was left."

"Would it have truly devoured everything?"

Adelei nodded. "It burned everything it touched except the stable's stone floor, be it hay, wood, or...or horse. It certainly dissolved the Tribor's body. I never even got to search his body properly."

"You said Ida was familiar with this?" He summoned a page by hooking his finger. "Fetch Captain Warhammer." To her he added, "We will wait for the captain to discuss this further."

When he gestured for her to sit, she claimed a cushionless stool. Of several, it looked most stable. The corners poked her rear, and she shifted in place. *If I didn't know better, I'd say this was intentional to hurry along audiences with unwanted guests. Master Bredych had used this same trick.*

Two men in two different kingdoms—yet an abundance of similarities between her two fathers, though neither would admit to such a connection. As much as it pained her, they were both her father.

She glanced up at the King's face to find him watching her as well. If anything, he looked ten years older this morning. Familiar creases tripled in depth, especially those across his forehead as his brows tried to dig themselves deep into his pale skin.

Several squires and pages idled in the background of his audience chamber, giving them no privacy. For once, Adelei wished it, shifting the weight from one hip to the other and back again on the stool. *I'd be willing to bet that's why he hasn't slept—the talk with Margaret. I don't think that was a positive conversation.*

Adelei itched to ask about it. *I don't need another reason for my sister to hate me. This job is difficult enough without the situation growing grimmer by the minute.*

The rear doors opened, and Captain Warhammer closed the distance quickly before bowing to the King. "Ya called for me, Your Majesty?"

"I did, Captain. Master Adelei tells me of a...a poison that is a great danger to my kingdom. I would hear your knowledge on this subject." Tired eyes grew bleak as Ida divulged what knowledge she held. Adelei watched them from the discomfort of her stool.

When Ida spoke, the King leaned forward in his chair, and his gaze followed her every move. When speaking to him, Ida's voice softened, though with the gravel-like timbre of her voice, not even when soft could her voice be described as delicate or feminine.

The way their eyes lit up and the corners of their mouths danced with each word made Adelei nod. *Ida spoke the truth about their relationship. He loves the woman who kidnapped me. And she loves a deceptive fool.*

The mix of pain and joy pierced her armor. It was a relief when Ida finished, and King Leon turned his attention to Adelei. "Do you think this was an isolated use of the poison? Something he used when backed into a corner?"

"Normally, I would think this what it appeared to be—a last minute, desperate tactic to escape capture. But with the closeness to the wedding, I can only think it's not. They intend to stop me any way necessary as long as I am here."

"But why? What is so important—" Adelei stared at her father, and his words fell from his mouth as understanding spread across his face.

"I am a danger to Her Highness and Your Majesty as long as I remain here."

It was a truth they both knew, and yet the father bled through the King. "You cannot leave. I—"

Adelei held up her hand and gestured at the others still in the room. "I can't leave because doing so would leave Her Highness in danger as well. Even if I left, I would not take all of the danger with me. Besides, I think they are more concerned with me stopping the wedding than my protecting the royal family. That poison comes out of Shad, which can't be a coincidence, Your Highness."

"You believe the rumors about a plot by the Shadian royal family to seize my crown?" When Adelei tilted her head in the servants' direction, King Leon clapped his hands once. The servants and pages withdrew and shut the doors behind them.

"I've already told you what Lady Millicent disclosed to me. I find it much more likely that she is correct. Why else the need to stop me? If all they wished was me dead, send enough assassins and even an Amaskan will get unlucky. Most of the time, the Amaskans and Tribor ignore each other. There's nothing to be gained by starting a war between the two groups, but now I'm endangering their plans for Her Highness. If she doesn't wed Prince Gamun, they have no way to continue their scheme. But something the Tribor let slip—he wasn't after me."

"Explain."

"He had a picture of what I assumed was me, but he claimed it wasn't. He seemed rather shocked when I held the picture up to my face and it matched."

The chair creaked as Ida leaned forward. "Are ya sayin' he's after Her Highness? But that makes no sense with your theory."

"They can't want the wedding and want her dead. We're missing something." King Leon leaned his chin on the palm of his hand, his elbow burying itself in the cushion of his chair's arm.

"I wish I knew what, but right now we're all in danger," said Adelei.

King Leon cleared his throat. "I wonder if they changed their minds. Maybe you were getting to close to something? Do you also believe what they say about Prince Gamun's...proclivities?"

"I wish I could give you peace of mind and answer no, but I can't. I believe it possible. Until I meet him, I can't say it for fact."

"I've heard the rumors as well, Your Majesty, but I've not seen any evidence of their truth," said Ida. "But then, I've been in Sadai more than Alexander these days, so I may not be the best person to ask."

The mask wavered, and the King returned. "Master Adelei, you will have that opportunity as I'm told the Prince should arrive here tomorrow. With the wedding in little more than a month, we have little time to gather evidence, not if we wish to cancel the treaty."

"And if you're to do so, you'll need solid evidence to go before the Boahim Senate," added Ida.

"Indeed."

King Leon stood and walked over to where Adelei sat on the increasingly uncomfortable stool. He knelt before her, his hand brushing her cheek. "What a wise and strong daughter you have grown to be," he whispered. "Can you find me the evidence I need and keep yourself safe? It's not worth losing you again. Surely we can figure something out."

His trust in her abilities was humbling. His love for her was crushing. *Even as a killer, he's found a way to love me. Not the daughter he envisioned, but me. Master Adelei of Amaska.* Her mind still separated the father from the King—it had to. *The King I can forgive, but the father I can't. Marry the two, and where does that leave me? And yet here he is, having loved me anyway—doing what I cannot.*

It chafed and ached at the same time. Adelei stumbled away from his touch, knocking over the stool. His pain drove her to stare at the floor as she bowed before him. "I will do my duty to the Kingdom of Alexander, as I have sworn to do. I will find the evidence Your Majesty requires. But I will find it, however I have to, and I'll not have a care for anyone's sensibilities or rank."

The Captain stood stiffly and leaned between the King and Adelei, her hand on her blade's hilt.

"Peace, old friend." King Leon met Ida's gaze. "She's only reminding me of the folly of my own design. Having you fake an attack on Margaret it seems has brought a real threat to our door."

Adelei said, "Wishes are fishes. Once caught—"

"—They are forever changed," Captain Warhammer finished. "He only meant to bring ya home, but I understand your meanin'."

"As do I, Master Adelei. Watch the Prince and get me the evidence I need. You are dismissed." King Leon peered right through her then. The unfocused stare shifted around her, to settle on anything except the person before him.

She bowed slightly before retreating. How long could she maintain balance? Adelei barged into the sitting room she shared with Princess Margaret. Who was she kidding? She kicked a floor pillow as she passed on the way to her room.

Empty and cold, she huddled beneath the blankets on her bed. She allowed herself that moment to finally respond to the chaos, and like a breached dam, the emotions poured forth.

She wanted to cry, then stab something until it died. Adelei propped up a pillow and casually tossed a throwing knife at its center. *Once upon a time, there lived a princess.* The next throw was not so casual, and a pillow exploded with a mass of goose feathers.

The princess was loved, until she was whisked away to a faraway land. She was loved and taught the way of things by her new family—the balance of life and self. Until she was abandoned again.

Adelei tossed another knife at yet another pillow, though this one resisted her assassination attempt with aplomb. *Lost, she stumbled around in a maze made of uneven ground and waterfalls. Her balance destroyed, she hid herself away in her rooms to assassinate pillows. Damn you all.*

Equal parts frustration and self-loathing, she leaned her head against the wall and cried.

"Ida—a moment if you will."

Leon scribbled bits of nothing on the parchment before him. He had nothing important to say, only that at this moment, he couldn't look at her. In the past twenty-four hours, he'd defended her, touched her, and loved her again, all while his brain urged him to cast her aside and be done with the traitor.

Her return with his daughter was wonderful.

Her return and his forgiveness were nothing short of a miracle.

So why couldn't he face her?

"Sire?"

By the sound of her voice, she stood behind him. *Damn.* She probably had seen the scribbling mess he made with this ink. Leon set the feather pen down on his desk.

"I need you to run an errand."

"Fetch ya another sheet of parchment?" she asked, and the corners of his mouth lifted against his will.

When he turned, she was close enough that the scabbard of her sword brushed against his knees, and he inhaled deeply of the scent that was uniquely hers. Sweat, flecks of steel, and the tiniest amount of lilies.

"Your thoughts are far away this early mornin'."

It wasn't that her words were a whisper; more that he was so far away just then, the sound reaching out to him from a hundred leagues. "I'm sorry, Ida. Too many creatures walk my mind, too many not of my own making."

She nodded. "What do ya need?"

Leon memorized her face. If he never saw her again, he wanted to remember it. Just as it was—every wrinkle and scar. "I need you to set out for the Shadian border as soon as you can ride. I must know if these tales about the Prince are true. Something factual. Anyone who can testify to the rumors' validity."

"The prince will arrive sometime tomorrow or the next day," she said.

"I know, which is why I need you to leave today. I'd prefer he not cross you on the road into Alesta. Further out among those traveling the Meridi Pass, you'll hardly be recognized in the throngs, but at the city gates, everyone knows you. Leave now. Spend no longer than a month away or send word of whatever you find before the wedding."

"As ya wish, Your Majesty."

When she turned, he caught her arm and pulled her closer to him. "I-I can't completely forgive your role in all of this, but I'd like the chance. Return to me, Ida. Don't risk yourself more than you have to."

Leon was the first to break eye contact, and she pulled away from his grasp. Her footfalls were heavier than normal as she retreated. "Wait," he called out, but she'd already fled the room.

Neither of them was ready for things to be normal between them. But maybe, once all of this was behind them, they could find their way back to one another.

No candlelight left the windowless room pitch black. Adelei thought it night until her sister's scream reached her. The near hysteria spurred Adelei forward. She paused at the door when the cries grew less shrill. No sounds of an assassin—just a fight different from what she expected.

"I can't possibly wear that. He's arriving today, and I have to be *per*-fect," Princess Margaret shouted, stretching out the last word as her voice jumped half an octave.

I wasn't asleep long enough. With a sigh, Adelei propped the murdered pillows across her bed and rose. A splash of water from a bowl woke her, and Adelei redid the scarf about her head. One deep breath later, and she stood before the doors to Margaret's suite.

Probably shut because of the tantrum inside. Several guards stood nearby, slack expressions speaking out that this was nothing new. Every time Margaret's voice jumped, their eyes glazed over a little more.

I would pity them, but at least they get some break throughout the day from her, whereas I might not. She strode into the room bearing her chaotic sister. Without knocking.

Her sister stood behind a screen with several of her handmaidens, all of whom were pulling and tugging at something while Margaret swatted at their hands. "Tighter," she ordered, and several grunts passed through the room as the servants continued their quest. When Adelei let the door shut with a loud clatter, all motion ceased behind the screen, and Margaret's head poked out around the corner.

"I ordered the guards that no one was to enter."

"An assassin would hardly ask permission of your guards, Your Highness. Besides, my orders trump yours when it comes to your safety."

Another tug and Margaret advanced from behind the screen. The deep blue dress washed out any color from her skin. The corset, which Adelei supposed was responsible for the tug-of-war, shrank Margaret's already small waist to almost nonexistent. "How in all the Thirteen Hells do you breathe in that? I'm surprised you can even move." Adelei watched in amazement as her sister moved with ease across the room where she stopped before Adelei.

"Breathing isn't important." Margaret leaned forward to study the scar on Adelei's jaw.

The invasion of Adelei's personal space made her skin itch, and the hair on her arms stood up beneath her clothes. "Like looking in a mirror. Except for that ugly scar," whispered Margaret. She waved a delicate hand, and the handmaidens all but fled the room. "Father says you are indeed my sister. He tells a pretty story of it, but I say my sister died many years ago. The person standing before me is a killer, a murderer who finds joy in carrying out evil deeds. No sister of mine could ever be involved in such...such affairs as this."

Adelei allowed the words to roll off her like sand from the desert. "I'm glad we understand each other." Margaret's grin faltered. "What? You expected to upset me with your words? I'd rather be related to a donkey than to such a spoiled child."

Margaret's mouth opened wide as she prepared to shout, but Adelei wasn't finished. She tapped a finger to Margaret's lips. "Despite your apparent hatred and jealousy, I will do my job because that is what I do best. I will protect you, even with my life if necessary. I truly hope you live long enough to understand the sacrifices others are making on your behalf, Your High-*ness*."

She executed an elaborate bow, her arm flourishes mocking Margaret while her petulant voice did the same. Adelei retreated to the door and stood like a member of the royal guard, eyes unmoving and her face a wall of neutrality.

At first, Margaret tried shouting, and when that garnered no response, she tossed another candle. This one missed the mark so wide that Adelei didn't even blink. Eventually, Margaret took to ignoring Adelei's presence as well. Dressed and ready, the Princess retired to a corner chair to read until a bustle at the door sent several pages scurrying in. Adelei stopped all three as they shouted their messages with all the tact of children given a new duty.

"Prince Gamun—he's here."

"The Prince is here. You must come."

"King Leon says hurry. The Prince is here."

Margaret dropped her book and ran her fingers through her long, black hair. Several braids twisted in circles near the top, but the bottom portion hung free. She snarled at a few tangles, then fixed a smile on her face as she rose. Adelei stopped her before she reached the open door.

"His Highness gave you orders this morning, orders to obey me for your safety. Whenever you leave this room, I go first. Before you enter another room, I go in first to check it. Can you follow these instructions?"

"If I can't?"

"Then you don't leave this room."

Margaret nodded her compliance, though she stuck her tongue out at Adelei. The slow process of searching each room before Margaret's entrance, even if just a visual check, delayed their journey across the castle to the front doors where the royal family would await the approaching Prince Gamun of Shad, soon to be of Alexander.

By the time they arrived, Prince Gamun already waited at the entrance, still astride his horse. Upon sight of his bride, he dismounted and stared up at the clouds. King Leon shot a nervous glance at them both. Adelei shrugged and jabbed her thumb in the Princess's direction.

Margaret ignored her father completely. She strode across the cobblestone courtyard to Prince Gamun himself. The break in protocol was the action of a love-sick child, something most of the courtyard found sweet as they smiled knowingly at their princess, but Adelei caught the smirk on Prince Gamun's face. His spotted Paloda skittered when the wind caught Princess Margaret's dress, and its ruffles fluttered like birds before the nervous horse. Adelei kept her distance from the spirited horse but moved closer to the couple in case the horse reared.

Prince Gamun bowed low to the Princess, his black hair glinting in the sunlight. He remained on one knee as King Leon approached and rose once King Leon's voice rang out across the courtyard. "Welcome to the crown city of Alesta, Prince Gamun Bajit of Shad. May your Way guide you."

"Thank you, Your Majesty. May your Way guide you as well," Prince Gamun replied in perfect Alexandrian. "I see a few faces I do not recognize from my last visit." While he gestured toward members of the high court, his gaze rested on Adelei.

She ignored him for the most part, choosing instead to study the men and women in his entourage. Prince Gamun kissed Margaret's hand, an action that elicited a giggle and a flush from head to toe as Margaret declared him to be the "perfect gentleman."

Adelei bit her tongue and counted to ten. Twice. *If she swoons one more time, I may not be able to restrain my sarcasm.*

As the King introduced other members of the high court and visiting dignitaries, Adelei spotted a young girl in the Prince's party. Her cloak glittered in the sun, and her smile matched. When she caught Adelei watching her, she ducked down in her saddle.

She couldn't have been more than twelve. What possible reason did he have for bringing her here? There were servants aplenty in the castle. *Though with a hooded cloak that nice, she couldn't possibly be one. A second wife perhaps? Fits his type.*

The young girl clung to an older, heavy-set woman. *Tutor perhaps? Old nursemaid?*

"I see your kingdom has acquired the services of the Amaskans." Prince Gamun stepped in Adelei's line of sight.

"Prince Gamun, allow me to introduce Sepier Adelei, formerly of Sadai," said King Leon. Prince Gamun reached out a hand and grinned wider when Adelei didn't offer her own in return. She wore a face of boredom and neutrality.

"Does Master Adelei speak Alexandrian?" Prince Gamun stepped a foot closer to Adelei, the gleeful grin dazzling Princess Margaret. "Do you speak Shadian, perhaps?"

"She possesses quite the brawn, Prince Gamun, but I've seen naught by way of brains," answered Margaret. "Yet my father is convinced it is time for me to have my own sepier, so here we are." She blushed when he smiled again, though his eyes darted to Adelei.

"As well you should, Princess. These are dangerous times we live in."

Adelei raised a brow. "Indeed, Your Highness. And with the wedding bringing so many strangers into Alesta, it would be all too easy for an enemy to slip into the castle. Right through the front gates even."

"They might even be welcomed by some. Dangerous rumors followed us on the road to Alesta."

"Prince Gamun, allow me to introduce to you my grand advisor..." As King Leon spoke, Gamun's fingers brushed Adelei's elbow. Her body cried out for her to flee, to step back, but she remained still as he tightened his grip. *Let him think he has you scared.* Truth was, her legs fought not to tremble as she stood on display.

"Similar, yet different," he whispered, and Adelei couldn't help but follow his glance.

The sun lit Margaret until she glowed. She pursed her rosy lips and fluttered her eyes like a simpering idiot. Despite looking the fool, Margaret's brows furrowed as she noted Gamun's grip on Adelei's arm. "Maybe she's not the fool after all," Gamun whispered to Adelei. "But then, how could she be? With an Amaskan by her side? You and I must talk later."

He released Adelei's arm. "Such an intelligent princess I am to marry," Prince Gamun called out, and he raised his hand in gesture to the nobles. "Her wit doth flatter me more than her beauty. Already, she loves me."

Margaret blushed and hid her meek grin behind her hands. Most of the gathered guests smiled, while a few ladies simpered and fluttered long lashes at the prince. "I thank His Majesty for such a grand welcome. Though I did think Alesta a smaller city last visit. Maybe it was the eyes of a child that colored it, or did your kingdom grow, Your Majesty?"

King Leon stiffened, and Adelei rested a hand briefly on his arm to halt his steps. She tapped her foot three times, a signal of danger, and her father schooled his face with a deep breath.

"Did I say something wrong?" Prince Gamun asked as his smile faltered.

"Everyone is quite prickly today, Your Highness. Must be the stress of planning such an event," said Margaret.

That jibe about the kingdom growing. I wonder if he knows about the border change rumors or whether it was truly a faux-pas? I've only heard the rumors about him in this kingdom. Could they use the rumors to hide their own deceit and treachery?

Her father watched the prince, but Adelei watched her father. His frame remained tense as everyone stood silent.

"I don't understand what's wrong with everyone," Margaret whispered.

"Don't worry, dearest. I often joke when nervous. Truly, Your Majesty, I meant no harm. It must be a child's eyes that misremember such a grand kingdom." Prince Gamun smiled at Margaret, who melted under his gaze. "After such a long wait in the sun, I'm hot. And famished, honestly. Maybe we could sit and discuss our future?" he asked Margaret, and with a break in protocol, he led her by the arm through the courtyard arch and into the shade.

The nobles followed the royal couple inside the castle. Adelei searched for the young girl she'd spotted earlier. A wisp of red hair under a hood was all she saw before the girl was gone, whisked away by her overbearing protector. Adelei swore and several highborns skittered away from her foul tongue.

"The gall," King Leon snapped behind her.

Adelei eyed the scattering crowd and finding nothing, spun around to face her father. "We have bigger issues than that," she said.

"He twice insulted this kingdom and in effect, me."

Adelei nodded. "Yes, though he claims he meant nothing by it. Intentional or not, he knows you won't do anything about it. To do so would upset the peace treaty. Did you see the redheaded girl amongst His Highness's entourage?"

"Is that what you were tapping about?"

"No, but it may be related. Why would a prince bring a child on such a cross country trek? What possible use is she to him?"

King Leon frowned. "Do you think...?"

"It's possible. If he's brought one of his *toys* with him, he's committed a serious error in judgment. I may be able to get the evidence needed for the Boahim Senate," Adelei said. "But worse, I'm positive he knows what he should not." When her father only frowned, she continued, "I've heard rumor regarding the party responsible for the death of your daughter, Princess Margaret's sister."

This time, his eyebrows kissed the sky. "This is a dangerous game he plays."

"Indeed, Your Majesty. And he plays to win. But win what, I'm still not sure. I feel this is about more than just your crown."

"How did he know?"

"I don't know, but we must tread lightly with him. I fear I made the wrong move in responding with nonchalance. It seems to have fascinated him more."

King Leon chuckled. "That would be the family blood coursing through those veins. I never could control my temper either. Let's see if we can find out who this girl is, shall we?"

"Let us hope she lives long enough to be found." Adelei suppressed a slight shiver. She'd never admit it to her father, but the worry growing in the pit of her stomach intensified as the wedding day grew closer.

This close to the big day, I need to find proof. I need this girl to stay alive. May the Gods be with us all.

Nothing could be more boring than a hundred people paying tribute to His Smugness and Her Bratty-ness. Captain Fenton stood watch in the audience chamber, along with his best soldiers. It was a risk, but Adelei *had* to know the identity of the child in Prince Gamun's entourage.

The hallway was packed with people. Some were already settled guests as they made their way to the audience chamber in a flurry. Others were newly brought from Shad and ordering servants to carry baggage up the stairs; some would say they were integrating into the castle staff—Prince Gamun's personal servants and pages, his advisors, and whatever the Shadian equivalent of a sepier was, if they even had them. *Which are you, little girl? A play thing? Servant's child? Bastard child of His Highness, perhaps?*

Adelei was stopped several times on her way to the third floor housing the state rooms, including a suite set aside for Prince Gamun. Guards asked her to identify herself, and with the throngs of Shadians shuffling through the hallway, she didn't blame them one bit.

She knocked on one set of doors and then another. No one answered either one, and she moved on to another set. The fourth one resulted in an odd little man answering. His pinched face reminded her of sour lemons, and he frowned at her Alexandrian.

"I was wondering if you could help me," she repeated in Shadian. "I'm making a list of guests for the dinner this evening for the table arrangements—"

"No. You're not."

"Excuse me?"

"What? What do you want? Truthfully?" He peered up at her through tiny spectacles as he rubbed his arms. "Saw you clear as day. When I arrived. You be that sep-thing for His Majesty. So I ask again. What do you want?"

Damn. Adelei inclined her head. "My apologies, sir. You're correct, though I am making a list of guests."

"What for?"

Her toes curled in her boots. "Does Shad have sepiers?"

"Depends. What's a sepier?"

Ladies and lords of great importance moved through the hallway as their rooms were given, and the steward brushed by Adelei in a rush. "No, no, not that room—the Rouge Room I said—" he called. For a moment, the cacophony muffled her words, and she waited until the group followed the steward to the other end of the hall.

"From what I gather, it's a special assignment to the royal family. Doing odd tasks for them. Ensuring their safety. Those sorts of tasks," she said.

He tilted his head and peered at her. "I imagine all sorts of odd tasks pop up. For one with *your* skills." His hand held a small, wooden staff whose top was decorated by thirteen blackened spires. He reached up with the tip to touch the scar at the base of her jawline.

The staff bothered her, but the little man held such fire in his eyes, she couldn't help but laugh. "Master Adelei, formerly of Sadai," she said and held out her hand.

He accepted it, his grip strong for one with hair so white with age. "Master Echon of the House of Echana."

She left her hand in his through will alone. "I-I hadn't realized His Highness brought mystics with him on his journey."

"Master Adelei, forgive my bluntness. You seem unnerved to see me." She swallowed hard and kept her gaze on him. "I know other masters of my trade roam Sadai freely. What about my presence bothers you?"

"Forgive me," she said with the incline of her head. "Our mystics serve the House of Sharmus, God of healing and protection. To serve Echana..."

"The Goddess of Chaos is, I would think, more aware of people's needs than Sharmus. These times—bad times they are." He struck his staff upon the stone floor once. "But I'm not a mystic. Not yet, anyway." The old man pointed to the top of his staff with bony fingers. "If I was, the spires would be lit by Anur's fire."

Little old to be a trainee. Adelei glanced over his head at the clang of metal behind him, and Echon pulled the door closer to his back as he stepped partially into the hall. "Echon. That isn't a Shadian name."

"Adelei isn't a Sadain name either."

"True. I was wondering, though, I saw a young girl in the group with His Highness. Does the prince have a daughter?"

The old man pursed his lips together. "He does not. If there's nothing else?"

He didn't give her time to respond as he stepped back inside and closed the door behind him. *Interesting.* Adelei knocked on several more doors, but her knocks went unanswered.

Who is this child? And why would the prince bring mystics here? And one serving Echana no less. Adelei left the state hall by way of a now empty staircase. *Nothing good comes from chaos.* The palm of her sweaty hand still tingled from his touch, and she rubbed it across her long tunic.

Her not-so-casual stroll through the servant's wing left her no clues. In fact, the moment one of the castle staff spotted her, a dozen heads ducked back into their rooms, leaving the area mysteriously absent of people. Adelei could have entered their rooms at will, but chose not to make more enemies than necessary. Not yet anyway.

Though I have a feeling that will change.

CHAPTER SIXTEEN

Prince Gamun's welcoming feast arrived with all the fanfare Adelei expected but little else. Everyone smiled at the royal couple. Everyone laughed at Prince Gamun's jests. And everyone utterly ignored Adelei, who hovered nearby. She had several opportunities to politely inquire about the new guest and his court from Shad, but rarely did she speak a word before the person was caught again in the web of His Highness.

The creepy grin he shot her way when no one else was looking didn't help. Adelei rubbed her arms as she sat before the fireplace in the King's sitting room. A brief chill stood over Alesta. Windows were shuttered in the spring evening. She rubbed her fingers over her temples. It would have been nice to shutter her own eyes for a bit.

King Leon echoed her motion and took a sip of wine from his cup. "It's creepy the way people are reluctant to discuss him," said Adelei. "You can see the information on the tip of their tongues, but the minute they open their mouths to speak, their eyes gloss over and they forget, or they shrink in on themselves, afraid of him more than me. And that's saying something."

"Have you heard back from any of your Amaskan contacts?"

"Yes, I got word from a friend at the Order just before the dinner. But the information isn't much better, I'm afraid. The rumors out there about this Prince are...are downright disturbing. I thought the rumors limited to Alexander but apparently not."

"That's an odd thought."

Adelei bit her tongue. *Not really, not if you are stealing land from neighboring kingdoms.*

She gave a tired smile and continued, "But again, he covers his tracks. Anyone who's a witness doesn't live long enough to say anything. Not even the Amaskans have evidence on him, though that wouldn't stop us from acting if necessary."

"I thought the Amaskans followed an honor code of justice."

"We do. Amaskans are like the local peacekeepers, just not limited to a specific locale. We often step in, especially when someone can't be reached by the local law." When her father's frown deepened, she continued, "Let's look at this Prince— everyone seems to think he's guilty of great crimes, but proof hasn't been found to one hundred percent confirm this. If you were to contract out the Amaskans on this, because the knowledge we do have leans toward his guilt, they would probably accept the contract and take care of him for the safety of the people of all the Little Dozen Kingdoms."

"So you would execute a man with no real evidence? Just conjecture?"

"People's words count for more than you think, Your Highness. How often do you rely on the opinion of others before carrying out justice in your kingdom?" Adelei glanced up at her father, a triumphant smile on her face. But his shoulders sagged and flesh stretched too tight across thin bones. Her smile fell. Why did she care though what he thought? He stared at her as if she were a stranger, which only confused her further. "You look ...concerned."

"I didn't realize the Amaskans held life in so little regard."

Anger swept away some of her confusion. "Your Majesty, we are the only ones who hold it in such high esteem. Before the Order of Amaska takes a contract, we research. We study. We make absolutely sure we come down on the right side, that whoever our contract kill is, that the person is evil. That it's a necessary killing."

"So what did you do?" he whispered.

"I don't follow."

"What did you do that was so evil that the Amaskans called for your death? Surely Ida told you."

Adelei stood and put the chair between them. He didn't look at her. He didn't need to. Something grew in the pit of her stomach, some terrible knowledge, and the room spun. She gripped the chair's back with whitened knuckles. "She was sent to kidnap me, yes."

"She was sent to kill you."

"I think she misunderstood. Master Bredych would never harm a child, nor would any in the Order."

Her father laughed, but his fisted fingers betrayed his façade. "The man slit the throat of his own sister. Yet you doubt his ability to kill a child? Why else do you think you were taken?"

"For a peace treaty," she muttered. Adelei wrapped the lie around her shoulders in the chill of the room.

"You still believe that lie?" His cup flew to land on its side before the fireplace. "I never sold you, child. Peace treaty be damned." A guardsman peeked into the room and darted back out at Adelei's narrowed glare.

"What Ida told you was truth. She was sent to kill you but could not. Don't you see? The honor code you seek is what saved you. Ida knew it went against the Order's supposed code to kill a helpless child, so she refused. And for that, her brother tried to kill her. Your own people whom you call family—they aren't as justified as you think. They talk a good talk in the recruitment room, but when it comes down to it, they aren't much more than hired thugs on a zealot's quest to eradicate his idea of evil."

Her own fist curled. She wanted to hit him.

Wanted to rip the lying tongue from his mouth. The battle rage fell on her, and she tasted blood where she'd bitten her tongue. King Leon stepped toward her, his hands outstretched. "Adelei, look at yourself. I speak the truth—you know it—and yet they have you wanting me dead. I can see it in your eyes, child. You want to kill your own father for speaking truth. What kind of person does that? Certainly not a peacekeeper of justice."

The throwing knives were within reach. Her finger rested on one at her wrist. She could have it out and halfway to this throat before he could call for the guards. But that would be wrong. He was the client, not the enemy.

Before her body caught up with the direction of her thoughts, Adelei tumbled out the door. Her feet carried her in the stable's direction where she lost the contents of her dinner. *What is wrong with me? Why am I so off-kilter?*

She touched a hand to her clammy cheek. By the time her mind stopped swimming enough to recognize her surroundings, the lump in her throat had grown. Adelei stared at the stall her horse had once occupied. The mare, not Midnight, whickered at her lightly and sniffed her shoulder in search of food. "I'm all out of carrots," she muttered.

In the absence of a treat, she scratched the horse behind the ears absentmindedly. *He's right. Damn him, he's right. Why did Master Bredych want me dead? How could he accept a contract on a child? And who had ordered the contract? I don't know him at all—my own father and he's nothing like the man I grew up knowing. Can I trust anything he's ever said?* The questions came fast and hard, relentlessly hammering on her psyche.

Boots scuffled the stone floor. *Another assassin?* Adelei spun on her heel until she faced the stall's entrance. A single candlelight provided little illumination. She scratched the mare and gave the impression that all she wanted was some one-on-one with a horse. But her muscles quivered in response to the battle rush.

Another candlelight approached. Prince Gamun leaned over the stall's half door, all smiles. "I thought I saw you heading this way. How curious to find you in the stables, considering your horse is dead."

Words meant to hurt only angered Adelei. *I've had a lot of shit thrown at me today, and you've picked the wrong person to mess with. I'm itching for a good fight.* She clenched her teeth and said, "Curiouser still to find Your Highness here, among the horse shit."

Adelei snatched the brush from the wall beside her and had the joy of watching him flinch. She groomed the mare, the soothing motion helping to control the boil beneath the surface.

"I was always taught that the Amaskans were the ultimate in the practice of neutrality, their justice carried out in swift impartiality and calm. And yet you are an enigma. Considered the best of the best—despite having a temper like thunder. How is it that you gained your place amongst the Amaskans?" The corners of his mouth curled up in half-smile, half-grimace.

She didn't answer, but the brush's motions sped up. He continued, "Maybe you gained your place through your father.

Having a parent in high places, even an adopted one, is useful, wouldn't you say? I've always found it to be quite helpful indeed."

When his hand touched the mare's neck, she shook her mane and whinnied. Adelei patted her. "I earned my place through the same training as any other," she said. "There is no favoritism amongst the Amaskans."

"And yet you feel it necessary to defend yourself. Something has you walking on a blade's edge. I've seen you before, you know. You once were in Shad to kill a man—my cousin in fact. You moved with a confidence and strength that I admired. I said to myself, 'Now there's a warrior who knows death. Who isn't afraid to die, but seeks it out like a lover.'"

"I don't—"

He interrupted her, holding his hand up beside her face. "Moved, past tense, Master Adelei. The person standing before me now is no Amaskan. You seem unsure of who you are these days. And I can't help but wonder why that is."

"I am Amaskan—"

He tapped her scar. "Former Amaskan. Does it confuse you? The struggle of loyalty?"

"What do you mean?" She allowed her fingers to tremble as they brushed the mare.

"I mean, does it pain you that you're going to have to choose?"

She faced him, trying to read him, but the smile that lit up his eyes in the candlelight covered any truth that could have hidden amongst his features. "Either speak plainly or leave. I came out here to be alone with my thoughts." Adelei returned to brushing the mare, leaving her back to him.

Come on, take the bait. She leaned over the horse and allowed her shoulders to slump. He'd been right about her knowledge of death, but it wasn't lost knowledge, despite her inner turmoil.

"Do you still love him like a father, even knowing what he ordered done to you? What he tried to do to his sister?"

Adelei fought then to remain in her vulnerable position. Her body screamed out to move. When she didn't, he leaned his frame against her backside, his lips so close to her ear that she could smell the wine on his breath. "I know more about you than you do, Master Adelei. Information is power, as well you know. What will I do with this information, hmmm? You have to be asking yourself that," he whispered, and his arm encircled her waist. She allowed the contact, though her nerves screamed.

"This marriage will happen, or I will take my information to the highest bidder. Be that the Boahim Senate or the Tribor, it makes no difference. Either way, you will still be dead, as you should have stayed, Iliana Poncett of Alexander."

"And what makes you think this knowledge is unknown? Or correct? Threatening an Amaskan is never a good idea." She tried to face him, to prove she was calling his bluff, but he held her in place.

"Now, now—it doesn't have to be like that, Master Adelei."

Cold fingers stroked her cheek. She shut her eyes and willed herself to remain calm. *He's toying with you—ignore it. Get the information. Let him think he's winning.* Adelei allowed herself a slight shiver, which elicited another chuckle from the prince.

"I'm a powerful man, Master Adelei. I could buy your contract, set you free of all of this. With you and me together, no one could stop us. We could shape the Little Dozen as we like."

"And why should that tempt me?"

"Because with me, you know what you're getting."

"I don't follow."

"Sure you do," he said, "I've been nothing but honest with you. What I know. Who I am. I could keep these things hidden, but I don't. I am what I am. Can you say the same about...your father?"

Adelei held back her wince.

"Your father sent you away and into the hands of those who wanted you dead. What if I told you this same father has plans for you yet?"

She froze. The action this time was genuine. "What do you mean?"

The mare butted Adelei's hand, and she absently brushed the mare's shoulder. "The Little Dozen. Why do you think I want this marriage? King Leon has plans to seize the kingdoms—all of them—and I'm here to stop him. For the good of the people."

"You're mad," she muttered.

"Am I? Think about it. Why else would he bring you home after all this time? If not to strike an alliance with the master you call father, the man who stole you away. Bring you back home so you can help them both."

Her hand paused mid-stroke. "I don't think so—"

"Think of it, Adelei." He hugged her closer. "One could spread the Amaskans further than before, and the other has an Amaskan princess to lead the way and conquer the Little Dozen."

His words carried enough truth to stir the doubt within her. "You have proof of this?"

Prince Gamun grinned against her neck. "I have proof that the King has been changing his borders. The rest, not yet. With your help, we could change that."

"Where's the proof on Alexander's borders?" She tilted her head to see his face, but his eyes were closed. Relaxed. Where her body was shoe tacks, his was a calm river.

"In my suite, of course. I don't make a habit of carrying around documents like that in enemy territory. If you wish to pay me a visit, I would be willing to show you these documents—"

"And Princess Margaret?"

"A simpleton. A dressed-up waif. Easily broken and discarded."

Interesting choice of words. I wouldn't visit your rooms for all the money in this kingdom. His fingers stroked her cheek again to the line of her jaw down and middle of her neck. Adelei tensed, a reaction he felt through her clothing. He released his grip a small amount, and she asked, "And your previous plans to kill me? The Tribor?"

"My father's plans, not mine. But I can convince him you are worth keeping alive. Long enough for you to kill him. Surely it won't be the first king you've taken out."

Wrong move. Adelei slid sideways and out of his grasp. "You couldn't afford me if you tried, which I suggest you don't."

Prince Gamun tossed a coin into the hay by her feet. Its bronze face was vaguely familiar. "Well, your company has been enjoyable, Master Adelei, but I have someone waiting for me. Enjoy your evening with your thoughts. Think about my offer."

"Wait—" she cried out, but he'd stepped back into the shadows and was gone.

I should go after him. But that was what he wanted. Adelei bent over to retrieve the coin, an old coin, its edges worn. She wiped the mud off with a fistful of hay and gasped when her own childhood face stared back at her. When she flipped the coin over, the other side bore her sister's face: her nose just a tad smaller, and her brows less dense.

She'd not seen these coins in use before, not in the past ten years she'd traveled the Little Dozen Kingdoms. The coin must have been from before the war. *How'd he get a coin like this? More importantly, how does he know who I am?* While she shrugged it off for the moment, her skin still crawled where he'd touched her. She took her time leaving the stall. *I've got to get a hold of myself. If I don't, someone is going to get killed. Maybe me. Probably my sister.*

By the time Adelei reached her rooms, she didn't want sleep. Not after that. She sat cross-legged on the cold floor with only one candle to light the room. She remained dressed but had shed anything she carried.

Weaponless and vulnerable.

"I come before the Gods, an empty vessel. For guidance, for balance, for clarity and neutrality," she whispered and closed her eyes. She pictured the candle flame in her mind and breathed deep of the herbs burning beside it. "I am not myself. I don't know who I am, and all these questions only further the confusion in my mind. If I'm to do my job, to succeed and do what is best for all peoples, I need your help. I don't normally ask for it, but I find myself adrift."

Adelei focused on the inhale and exhale until she slipped into a trance state, ready for whatever the Gods saw fit to bestow upon her. An hour passed. The lack of burning herbs caught her attention first. Her legs tingled, but nothing filled her with a sense of peace or comfort. The knots remained in overly tense muscles. The old, confused self remained intact, brimming with a million questions that had no answers.

She bit her lip. *Damn. Double damn. I'm on my own.*

"Duke Remy and Duchess Nadine Dauphena of Brussell," called out a young squire. The two approached the dais where Adelei stood.

Instead of merely hovering behind the royal family as one of the guards, Adelei was the center of attention this early morning. She hadn't wanted this. Her job was to protect Princess Margaret and seek out the truth about Alexander's borders, but King Leon had *insisted*. *Required* it even.

Instead of the black, tight fitting clothing she preferred, King Leon had adorned her in this blue get up, like she was little more than a guard. A blue tunic that reached halfway to her knees was tied off around the waist by a thick, black belt. Darker blue leggings tucked into mid-calf boots. And to top it off, a white, silk sash with silver stars marked her as Alexander's sepier.

He'd refused to allow her a head scarf. "Besides, your hair has grown back enough. Bit on the short side, but most females in the royal guard wear their hair rather short."

"There's short, and then there's this," she'd said, pointing at her head. "I look like a freshly shorn sheep."

The King hadn't helped matters by laughing, but in the end, her black stubble stood out with the rest of her. The kingdom's new sepier—on parade for the kingdom's nobles.

Good old Remy looked like he was older than the castle. The man's head was balder than Adelei's now, and his joints creaked as he and his wife approached.

"May I present to you, Sepier Adelei," said King Leon, and Adelei presented her dirk as instructed. He'd told her to wear the sword he'd presented her with at the ceremony's start, but she had given it to Captain Fenton.

I may not get to wear my own clothes, but by the Gods, I'll wear my own weapon. While the Duke grinned at her, the Duchess scowled as her husband not only bowed, but kissed Adelei's hand, ignoring the dirk altogether. "By the blessing of the Thirteen, may your...dirk serve this kingdom well," the old man said, and his wife mumbled his words.

Behind her, Prince Gamun yawned. *Even he's bored with all this pomp and circumstance. And a prince should be used to it.*

The couple moved past, and the squire announced a single name, the Duchess of Verdon. She moved through the motions as quickly as possible and stepped on the hem of her long skirts when she ambled away. Most opportunities to dabble with the nobles brought a large crowd, at least thus far it had, but today it seemed the only ones present were those required to witness King Leon naming her as sepier.

And most of them would rather have been elsewhere. Her outfit wasn't fooling anyone. From the stubble to the scar, the highborns of Alexander knew exactly what she was. *I'm just lucky they turned up their noses at me rather than stoned me to death.* At least the makeup disguised her other identity. *No need to loosen that squall upon the highborns.*

The squire moved on to introduce the earls and barons of Alexander, the first of which was Lady Millicent Sebald and her portly husband. At least the lady she knew, well enough to smile in greeting despite sore cheek muscles.

Other than those required, the royal guard stood watch over the proceeding and a scattering of city folk stood far in the back. Bright sunshine streamed through the windows, and Adelei sighed. "Not too much longer," King Leon whispered.

She could almost wish for an attack, just for the distraction. She bit the inside of her cheek and sighed. *No use temping the Gods. Forgive my impatience.*

If the Gods forgave her, they showed no sign. The sun continued to tempt her, her feet continued to ache, and her heart continued to pound with each approaching footstep across the soft, blue rug that ran the audience hall's length.

After a long litany of highborns, the presentations moved on to the members of the King's own council. Adelei's feet were falling asleep in shoes a pinch too small for her, and she shifted her weight back and forth.

When that didn't distract her, she gazed at the mural painted across the audience chamber's back wall. King Boahim himself stood in a field of green where he planted the blue flag in the ground, its silver star held aloft by deer's antlers as it looked to the heavens. It was difficult to believe the Little Dozen Kingdoms were once one land under one man. Adelei paused in her thoughts to acknowledge King Leon's Grand Advisor as he touched her dirk and welcomed her.

Beside King Boahim stood thirteen mystics: advisors and healers for his castle in the new city of Alesta. *The entire history of this land began right here. I wonder if these are the original stones from long ago, or if war and rebuilding has changed them, too.* As she studied the nobility as they came and went, she frowned. Any one of them could be behind the Tribor. And yet, her gut told her she already had her culprit.

He had all but admitted it in the stables.

When the last of the ennobled presented themselves, sweat decorated her brow. An irritating trickle ran between the inch-long hairs on her scalp. Her fingers twitched, but she resisted the urge to scratch her own head.

Everyone knelt as King Leon left the audience chamber. Adelei followed behind Princess Margaret and Prince Gamun, the latter of which slowed his steps every so often to turn around. "Beautiful tapestry," he mumbled, but he never once looked at it, nor the statue in the hall or the painting hanging in the stairwell.

His eyes were always on her. Or so it felt.

As hard as she tried to ignore him, her skin crawled as they walked. The royal family retired to private chambers for a brief break. The King had his meeting with the council after noon. Adelei had another "practice session" with Her Highness around the same time. She yawned as they climbed the stairs to the fourth floor. Once her sister was secured in her own rooms, Adelei strode straight into her bathing chamber.

Hot water. And lots of soap. Water flowed from the wall into the small tub, and she dropped a bar of soap into the water.

It wasn't the sweat that bothered her as she stripped of the sepier outfit. Not at all. For the second time that day, Adelei scrubbed her skin pink in the stone bathtub.

"Another report has come in from the Shadian border, Sire." Leon's Grand Marshal handed him the parchment. His eyes skimmed over the numbers, and he resisted the urge to crumple it up and toss it across the room.

More small villages and farmers begging for his protection. More landowners pleading with him to annex them into his kingdom. Every time he opened his court to hear the complaints and concerns of his people, there was always someone else who pushed the boundaries. Or wanted him to push them in a literal sense.

"What reasons do they give this time?" Leon asked as he rubbed his temples.

"More of the same, mostly," said Grand Marshal Levon Doublis. The man pointed a finger at one in particular. "This one here—it's a Baron Akash near the Meridi Pass—he claims his cousins, the royal family of Shad, are employing evil men. He's got quite a list of reasons he needs protection from us."

"Hmmm, that one may be worth investigating."

The Grand Marshal nodded. "Captain Warhammer passed our herald on the road. Said she was heading that way anyway and would look into it.'"

Something about this news set Leon on edge, and he ground his teeth. "What else?"

Lady Mara Britus cleared her throat, and Leon repressed a sigh. *I must replace her.* The old bat couldn't give decent advice if someone gave it to her first. She still wore the necklace her husband had given her last year, just weeks before he died. Died and left her sitting on his council. Leon sighed as she cleared her throat again. The slightly chipped ruby hung on a dirty chain. Bits of yesterday's dinner still stuck to its links.

Gods, none of us are getting younger.

The lady rubbed the thick ruby that hung between her breasts before she spoke. "There's something else, Your Majesty, something none of them—" she said and gestured at the rest of the council, "—wished to tell you. Not before the wedding."

"What is it?"

"A body has been found."

Leon stiffened in his chair. Five members of his advisory council sat around the old table, but two were missing. Princess Margaret held a reserved seat upon the council, though she rarely used it. But the last seat belonged to his sepier. Adelei now served as the royal family's sepier, but when Leon glanced at the empty chair, he kept waiting for Ida to claim it.

Ida. The woman he'd sent to the border. *Please don't let the body be hers.*

When he opened eyes, his physician studied him. Leon waved a hand in the man's direction and asked, "Whose body?"

"We're not sure," said Mara. "It was a child's body."

"There's a problem, Your Majesty," the Grand Marshall added. "The child arrived with His Highness of Shad."

His fingers gripped the table's edge, and the five faces before Leon swam. He released one hand long enough to ring a bell. "Go find Master Adelei. Have her brought here immediately," he told the page.

"Is that wise?" Lady Mara asked.

"She's sepier. I want her here for this." When the woman scowled, Leon asked, "Do you have some reason for not wishing her present?"

This time the lady remained silent. His Grand Advisor, Dumont, rubbed his hands along the carved table. "She believes your sepier may be responsible for the child's death."

King Leon let loose a hearty laugh. *Oh Gods, this will be an interesting day indeed.* No one shared in his humor, and when he raised an eyebrow at Dumont, the man shrugged and stared at the table.

"Think on it, Sire. Amaskans are known killers," Lady Mara said.

"So are Tribor."

The lady touched her hand to her forehead. *I've done enough hiding this week. How can they advise me if I keep secrets?*

"There's something you should know," he said. Leon downed an entire cup of chilled wine without blinking. "The Tribor are in Alesta."

CHAPTER SEVENTEEN

Margaret held the dagger like it might turn around and bite her, and Adelei bit back a laugh. "Again," she said and watched Margaret tap the stuffed figure with the dagger's tip. "Your Highness, I've seen you poke fruit with more force than that. If this figure is trying to kill you, and you can't run, you're going to have to do more than stick it."

The princess tried again, this time with force enough to dent the coarse muslin. Adelei seized Margaret's elbow and thrust the blade forward until it sunk into the stuffed figure. "Like that, Your Highness."

"So hard? That feels unseemly."

"It is, Your Highness. You're trying to possibly kill someone."

Margaret dropped the blade. "I'll not kill. It's against the Thirteen."

"If someone is trying to kill you, would you stand there and allow them to do so?"

"No, I would scream."

Adelei sighed. "What good would screaming do?"

"It would bring help."

Her sister's lip trembled. Adelei handed her the blade once more. "If you're somewhere alone, no one might come. By the time you've sat there and waited, you'd be long dead. Try again."

Round and round they went, Margaret putting up protest after protest as to why she couldn't and wouldn't stab the straw man, while Adelei ground her teeth and tried yet again to describe the danger they were all in. *Gods forbid I take her away from time with her precious betrothed. It's enough to make me kill something.*

When the knock interrupted them, Adelei was grateful for the interruption. The page bowed to them both. "His Majesty requests Master Adelei's presence in the council chambers. Immediately."

"Am I needed as well?" asked Margaret, and when the boy shook his head, the princess smirked.

Adelei stopped her at the door. "Wait. You'll need an escort." When Margaret opened her mouth, Adelei continued. "Any time I'm not with you, you will be accompanied by Captain Fenton or several guards. We've already been over this, so no argument."

She summoned the guards just outside and as Margaret passed, the princess merely frowned. *No ugly face? We've made progress then.*

While Adelei walked in the opposite direction of her sister, she couldn't help but laugh at Margaret's feeble attempts to stab the hay-stuffed figure. *Gods help her if she's ever attacked for real. She'll probably try to offer them tea.*

By the time she reached the council chambers, her humor was gone. Six faces watched her, all grim and tired.

The council chambers reminded her of her own room in that it held no windows and had only a single means of escape. The plain decor emphasized the importance of the room—nothing to detract from the people within it. Grand Advisor Dumont sat one end and her father at the other. Their grim faces gave her more answers than they knew.

Something is wrong, or worse—someone is dead. King Leon gestured for her to take a seat in the chair squeezed back into the corner.

"This afternoon, one of the guards found the body of a young girl in an alley in the lower circle—a child with red hair," said King Leon. He coughed then, a spasming cough that shook his massive frame and stopped his speech momentarily. A quick swallow of liquid and he continued. "They brought her body here, and I believe her to be the child you and I saw yesterday."

The child from Prince Gamun's court.

"How was she killed?" Adelei asked.

Dumont nudged King Leon's glass, and he took another long sip, the thick liquid calming the spasm. "Her body was mutilated, Master Adelei. Someone beat her, and then carved across her skin until she died." Dumont stared at the table as he spoke and avoided looking directly at her.

Adelei glanced at her father. "I'm surprised you were able to recognize her if her body was cut up that much."

"That's what you were hoping at least," said an advisor to Adelei's right. The advisor leaned across the table. "The marks on her—circles. Nothing but circles. Told you this was the work of an Amaskan."

The statement was so silly, Adelei laughed. She held her sides as she continued to laugh in their silence. "Lady Mara, is it?" she asked, and the woman nodded. "My lady, Amaskans don't kill children."

As the words left her mouth, she paused. *Or do they? After all, they were going to kill me.* Her father nodded in her direction, as if reading her mind, but she waved it aside. "Besides, no Amaskans are here."

"You know this how?" An advisor, a Lord Jovoni if she recalled correctly, peered at her. The flush on his olive complexion tried to match the red hat on his head. "Are you yourself not Amaskan?"

Adelei stared at her father, but he, too, avoided looking at her directly. She tucked away her irritation and faced Lord Jovoni. "My employer of the past was once the Order of Amaska, but no longer. That is a contract I've been cut from. This knowledge is to remain secret as many lives are at risk by your knowing."

"Master Adelei, our job is to advise the King, which we can't do if he's keeping information from us. His Majesty felt it necessary to speak on your...past as you put it. If not you, who else would defile this child so?"

"I have no reason to kill a child, nor would any Amaskan. As for who—"

King Leon shifted in his seat. "And yet they ordered the death of my daughter, Iliana, did they not?"

The air left the room for a moment. Adelei inhaled deeply through her nose. "I can't comment on that, having no knowledge as to the why, but I can assure you that I did not kill this child.

Your Majesty knows this, just as you know very well who *did* kill this girl."

"I've explained to my advisors our concerns with Prince Gamun." King Leon sighed long into his cup as he took another sip. "But Lady Mara feels there is more at work here, as do the others. I've done a great disservice to my kingdom by propagating the idea that the Amaskans are no better than Tribor. While I am not comfortable with the idea of assassins, Master Adelei has shown me that they are not all cut from the same cloth. But I cannot discount the possibility of another Amaskan."

"I promise you all that the Amaskans are not responsible for this. Had this child been the work of the Order, the Amaskan would have slit her throat cleanly or stabbed her in the heart, not played with her corpse like evil beings better left unnamed." Adelei stood, leaning her frame slightly over the table. "Trust me, this prince is sneaky. He knows things he shouldn't and plays with people. Toys with their heads, makes them confused. People like that are bad news."

King Leon asked, "Where were you last night?"

Adelei flinched. He was having her followed. Worse, she hadn't noticed. *So caught up I've been in figuring out who I am that I was blind to something right in front of me. Dammit.*

"You could have left on horseback for all we know," said Lady Mara. "Why are we wasting time waiting for excuses? Who else would have done this?"

"My lady, my horse is dead from an assassin's poison. And as for where I was, I was in the stables getting some air. Which is where Prince Gamun cornered and threatened me."

A cacophony of protests, laughter, and gasps covered up whatever King Leon said. Despite his skin still bearing the pallor of his coughing fit, King Leon stood and silence swept across the room.

Adelei shook her head. "How do you stand this woman? How in all Thirteen Hells did she gain a seat on your council of advisors?"

The lady gasped, but King Leon shot her a warning glare. "Purely accidental, I assure you. Her husband recently died, and she holds his seat in proxy until I replace her." Any protest on the Lady Mara's lips died with King Leon's reminder.

"And you've taken this long to do so because...?" Adelei asked.

He smiled, but the emotion didn't reach his eyes as he waved a hand at her. "Enough. Tell me what happened between you and the prince."

Prince Gamun Bajit was not the first sexual deviant or psychopath to cross her path, but the things he said—close enough to truth to set her insides aflutter. She told the council what had transpired, editing out his knowledge of her birth name. After she finished, King Leon remained quiet for a time. "So he tried to bribe you and when that failed, he took it out on the girl?" he asked.

"I would assume so, Your Majesty."

"Why didn't you come to me immediately with this information?"

"I honestly didn't think he would go after her. With me here, I thought she'd be safe, at least for the evening. I certainly didn't think he'd be so obvious about it, and I'd hoped I'd shifted his focus to me."

"The man knows who you are and all but threatened to turn you in to the Boahim Senate. Or sell you off to the highest bidder. Or take you as his bride, or slave, I'm not sure. I don't think he fears you at all."

The words stung.

"I'm sorry, Your Majesty. I've failed to protect this victim and gain the information you asked of me, though I'll certainly continue to try. But I will remind you that my primary job has been and will continue to be the protection of Her Highness, Princess Margaret. I can't be at her side at all times if I'm sent on other tasks."

He took the truth as well as she did, which was to say with a wince and a frown. "I'd hoped we'd find a way to stop the wedding, but you are correct to remind me of your duty. Are you sure it was him?"

"I'm not, but so far as we know, this prince has done a very good job of cleaning up any 'messes' that may remain behind. It does seem too obvious—too easy. It bears investigating further," said Adelei. "I'm worried at how he's gained the information he has."

King Leon nodded. To his council, he said, "Leave us. I would speak with my sepier alone."

No one protested, though Lady Mara still scowled at Adelei as she left. Once the door shut behind them, Adelei asked, "Did you really think me capable of killing that girl?"

"No, but my council did. I needed them to hear from you, to understand you weren't the culprit. However, the idea that another Amaskan could have done it—that is possible. It's not something I've ruled out."

Already it felt like an old argument between them, and despite Adelei's confidence that an Amaskan wouldn't kill the little girl, her brain reminded her of her own kidnapping. *I can't trust anyone.*

Her father whispered, "I'm sorry."

She nodded, but it didn't change anything. They were empty words. An idea struck her, and she asked, "Who knows my identity?"

"Us. Margaret...and Ida."

"Ida. Who betrayed us both before." Adelei grimaced. "I hate to think it, but someone has told this prince very specific information that is not public knowledge."

"There's no way Ida would betray me again."

Adelei reached over to touch his hand. "I—I know you two have a history, but Prince Gamun knew things that Margaret doesn't. Either you told him, or she did. I'm sorry."

"She can't have done it. Someone else must know." His frown dragged his brows down with it. "I sent Ida out on a small task before Prince Gamun arrived. When would he have encountered her?"

Goosebumps ran across Adelei's arms. They both inhaled sharply in unison. "Where did you send her?" Adelei asked.

"To the Shadian border to see if she could get some answers about the Tribor and the Shadian royal family."

"Then our lovely prince passed by her on the way out of the city. I assume she's to report her findings on a regular basis?" When King Leon nodded, she continued, "Good. It's possible she's still alive then, assuming she hasn't run into any Tribor."

King Leon stood and paced back and forth. "They've failed twice to take me out," said Adelei. "With their client breathing down their necks, their next attack will probably be against Ida or Margaret to get to me. In the meantime, send for Ida to come back with all haste."

He nodded when another cough shook him. The King fell back into the chair, and he lunged for his cup. The liquid sloshed over the side before he downed several gulps, and his breathing eased. "I hate this. The war is over—the treaty was supposed to protect us, to prevent this. I wish I could send you both away until—"

Adelei closed her eyes as his words trailed off. "That didn't work very well the last time."

She hated to hurt him, but she needed the King right now, not the father. "Order Ida back. I need to return to Margaret's side. By your leave...?" Moisture lined his eyelids, but he nodded permission for her to withdraw. He didn't look up from the crown resting on the table, the candlelight casting tiny sparkles across the walls like fireflies.

Duty first. Family later. She held onto the words like a mantra as she fled the council chambers.

I may not be able to ease his pain, but after finding that girl's body, the least I can do is my job. And do it well. Adelei squared her shoulders and lifted her chin high. At first, no one noticed when she entered the courtyard where Her Highness sat watching a game of sport.

Prince Gamun smiled at her as he held the ball aloft and winked before returning to the game. Adelei kept her mouth shut and focused on the crowd that seemed to have grown in her absence. *Keep her safe. Duty first. Vengeance later.*

She didn't even care that she'd thought the word. He would pay for his crimes, justice be damned.

One month.

Exactly one month until the wedding, and still things were a mess. Adelei was no closer to finding evidence on the child's murder, nor evidence to connect Prince Gamun to anything criminal. Worse still, no word came from Captain Warhammer, and lack of sleep was driving Adelei into the ground. She rose before sunup and crashed into her bed shortly after midnight.

Instead of eating supper, she roamed the city. Adelei wore neither sepier nor Amaskan clothing, trading both in for the clothes she'd worn as Alethea. As a middle-class lady, tongues wagged around her, and she was able to pass through markets and streets with ease.

She bought an apple from a vendor in place of the feast going on in the castle and leaned against a stone building to eat. Business trickled to a crawl as families sought their homes to prepare the evening meal. Even the vendor packed up his goods as she bit into her apple.

The man didn't say more than a simple greeting to her, so after he'd set off for home, Adelei found a nearby inn and settled down at a table to wait.

It wasn't long before one of the more unscrupulous patrons cast a shadow across her, and she glanced up to find him grinning down at her. "A lady such as yourself should never be alone. There're dangerous folks about."

His breath stank of ale, but his looks were nice enough and his clothing mostly clean. She gestured at the empty seat across from her. "But I'm not alone. I'm at an inn full of patrons. Alethea," she said and held out her hand.

"The name's Garret, milady. Are you visiting Alesta for the big wedding?"

"What makes you think I'm visiting?"

When he grinned, he was missing a tooth. "Your accent isn't from Alexander. Figured you must be visiting for some reason or 'nother."

"Good call. I took a caravan over from Sadai. Curious to see this prince everyone's in a frenzy over."

The barmaid dropped off another mug of ale for Garrett, and Adelei pretended to sip her wine. "Now I know you're not from around these parts."

Adelei laughed and pursed her lips together in an imitation of Margaret's pout. "Now what did I say?"

"Only folk I know lookin' forward to a Shadian joining the royal family are them highborn ladies who don't know no better."

A few customers at nearby tables grew quiet in their conversations, and Adelei frowned at Garret. *Interesting*. This was the third time she'd heard citizens of Alesta point out that no one was looking forward to the wedding.

"I heard there was still a feud between the two kingdoms, though I always figured the War of Three settled all that business." Garret laughed and took another swallow of drink. "But over in Sadai, people don't pay much attention to the politics of others. Could be I'm wrong. It's not like I encounter many folks on my daddy's land."

His eyes widened at the mention of property. "What does your father do, if you don't mind me askin'?

"The family farm grows grapes. Fact, this wine here is my family label. Last year's crop—not as good as two years ago. Drought hit us pretty hard. Still, least I'm able to choose the man I marry, whoever he'll be," said Adelei, and she smiled broadly at Garret.

He leaned over, picked up her glass of wine, and gave it a sniff. "Eh, wine's wine to me, but its good business, I hear. Profit to be made for them that provide to the highborns."

"Indeed. My da's been wanting to expand some, ship some goods to Shad and further out. I figured if I could maybe meet His Highness—"

Garret leaned back in his chair, the feet scraping against the inn's floor. Conversation around them ceased, and the innkeeper stopped cleaning the glass in his hand. "You don't want to do that."

"Why ever not? I mean, I'm sure everyone must be dying to meet him—"

"That's just it. *Dying*. Take my word for it, milady. Keep away from that monster. It was nice meeting you."

When he stood to leave, Adelei called out, "Wait. I don't understand—"

As he passed, he leaned close to her ear and whispered, "The man is a mean bastard. When I said there be dangerous folk about, I was talking 'bout him. Just—just don't bother with the likes of him. Not if you want to see your daddy again."

He nodded to her and left the inn, his ale unfinished.

Damn.

Every time she ventured out into the city to gather information, the scenario went the same way: pretend to be someone else, ask about the prince, person freezes up and leaves by way of a warning. And that was if she was lucky.

Some people got up and left the minute Prince Gamun was mentioned.

The wedding approached and so far, Adelei had no way to stop it. Not without breaking the treaty and sending them into civil war.

Maybe I'm asking the wrong people. Maybe I need to hit the slums.
Or maybe I'm in over my head.

Weeks had passed since her encounter with Garret at the inn, and while Adelei was no closer to finding the answers she needed, at least Margaret had made progress in her lessons to defend herself. Albeit *slow* progress.

The princess stabbed the hay figure hard in the chest and spun around to face Adelei, grinning. "I did it," she called out.

Adelei nodded. "Now we work on a moving target."

Between some hand-to-hand training, where Adelei tried in vain to teach Margaret how to escape, the two sisters met as often as Margaret's schedule allowed to focus on work with small daggers. Margaret's eye-hand coordination hadn't improved. She still threw candles in wide arcs and completely missed hitting Adelei, but she could stab a stationary hay man. Adelei sighed and picked up the chain mail across the chair.

She didn't like the heavy armor, but with Margaret's aim, she needed it. *Last thing I need is for her to stab me. And knowing her, she'll try by complete accident.*

Adelei pulled the hay man out of the hay bale and carried him by the pole. "Okay, Your Highness, same plan. Only this time, I'll be moving."

At first, Margaret stood still—dagger gripped between her fingers as she watched Adelei pace back and forth. It wasn't until Adelei shoved the hay man near Margaret's face that the princess jabbed the blade forward. The thrust lacked drive enough to do more than bounce off the head, and Adelei didn't give Margaret time to recover. She kept ramming the figure closer to the princess.

When the figure's stick arm touched Margaret's shoulder, she squeaked. The dagger struck the air twice before the hay man knocked Margaret in the head. "Look at my feet," Adelei said as she moved. "If I step forward with my left foot, chances are, I'm going to move left. Strike left."

Margaret wiped her sweaty brow with her bare arm. "This is impossible. I can't watch your feet and the straw man at the same time. No one can." The princess retreated to a hay bale, and Adelei leaned the target against the wall. She stuck her head outside the practice room door.

"You," she called to a guard. "Come here for a moment."

The man was easily twice Adelei's size at the shoulders. When Margaret spotted him, she stumbled over the hay bale. "You can't possibly wish for me to fight him."

"Arm yourself, guardsman." Adelei withdrew her dirk. Margaret let loose a sigh, but Adelei *tsked*. "Watch our feet."

The guard looked down, and Adelei tapped his sword. "Not you," she muttered. "You, I want to attack me."

"Master?"

"Her Highness needs to watch our feet, so attack me already."

He couldn't have been more than five years past her twenty, yet he eyed her with a weariness that spoke either of fear or wisdom. If it were the former, he kept it well-hidden as he watched her shift her weight from side to side. At first, all they did was scrutinize each other. But after a few minutes, his impatience got the better of him.

The guard led with his right foot. Adelei could have trapped his blade in the slit at her dirk's hilt but instead leaned to her left and parried. She read the surprise on his face and waited for his next strike. His shoulder straightened as he met her gaze, and he tried a quick feint before attacking again on her left. She sidestepped to the right and held her dirk up to his throat. The lack of space left him little room to maneuver, and while his sword brushed her armor, he lacked the leverage to do any damage.

Rather than press further, the guardsman released his sword. *If you were under my command, I'd smack you six ways to Sathday for dropping your weapon.* Adelei nodded at him, and he grabbed his sword before retreating.

"So, what did you see?" she asked Margaret.

Thought lines bunched up across her brow. "When he attacked, his feet led on the same side."

Adelei nodded. "Not everyone will. A real pro might not, but most fighters do. Or if not with their feet, they lean with their shoulders."

"But how can you watch that and watch their weapon? You knew where his weapon was enough to stay out of his way or block him."

"Practice."

"Great," Margaret groaned. "Something I don't have. How is any of this going to protect me?"

As she said the last word, Adelei moved. She crossed the distance between them in four steps and brought her dirk up. Margaret scrambled with her dagger but managed to block Adelei's blade. Margaret's eyes widened at the halt of Adelei's dirk. "If I had wanted to harm you, my blade would have injured you. But you deflected some of the force, which would have given you longer to get away, get help, or even hurt me. No move is a wasted move."

The guardsman from earlier stuck his head in the practice room and cleared his throat. "It's almost time for Her Highness's meeting with the Duchess."

Adelei stripped the chain mail off and hung it over the straw man.

"Thank you," Margaret whispered. When Adelei turned, Margaret waited for her at the door. The princess glanced at her with a flushed face. "I know I'm not good at such pursuits as, well, fighting or stabbing people, but you didn't have to do this. I know you're trying to help."

Only by biting her tongue, did Adelei prevent her mouth from falling open. She exited the practice room first and escorted Margaret to her suite. Strands of Margaret's hair tufted out of its braid in places, and sweat left lines down her made-up face. Nisha, her lady-in-waiting, rushed forward, her fingers unwinding the braid with deft movements. "And you meeting with the Duchess in ten minutes," Nisha muttered. She snapped her fingers, and six handmaidens brought powders, perfumes, and brushes.

The crew set to work on making their princess presentable again, and Adelei used the distraction to duck out of the mayhem. She stopped into her own room long enough to strip her own clothes. Not that she'd worked up any real sweat against Margaret, but for the job she had in mind, she needed a completely different outfit.

Rags borrowed from the laundress and then "modified" by Adelei would disguise her today. The coarse, muslin dress smelled of hay and barns and bore several holes at the shoulder. The matching sea-green corset's threads did little to give her a waist, though it did shove her flat breasts up and give the suggestion that she had them.

Barefoot would have been best, but Adelei didn't want to risk the chance of injury. The slippers she pulled over her feet were a size too large, and she hoped she wouldn't need to do any running in them. Just in case, she pulled the leather laces at the side as tight as they would go.

She closed her door and stopped short of Margaret, who was exiting her suite with an entourage of handmaidens. The princess stopped to stare at Adelei. "Where in the Thirteen did you get such a hideous outfit?"

Adelei pursed her lips. "I need to go down to the city's lower circle."

"In that?"

"What would you have me wear, Your Highness? If I wore something like your dress, I'd be robbed the moment I stepped foot off the main road. Besides, I need to blend in. You know, with the impoverished people of your city, Your Highness."

Margaret flushed, and Nisha hurried her out the door. Her honor guard followed her, while Adelei turned the opposite direction. She avoided the main stairwell and took the servant's stairs instead. When she popped out in the servant's wing, a few of the pages stared at her a moment before continuing on their way.

The fewer eyes she drew, the better.

Once in the stables, she rubbed dirt and hay across her face and arms, then scurried out before she was spotted. A guard stopped her at the gate to the upper circle of Alesta. "Where do you think you're going?"

Adelei pulled the silver signet from her pocket. His eyes widened at the sepier star, and he ushered her through without another word. The majority of people gave her wide clearance as she passed, doing so until she reached the second to last set of city walls. It was easier to blend once she crossed over into the lower circle.

She'd tried walking the streets as a member of the royal army. The moment the prince's name had passed from her lips, people stopped talking to her. Before long, word had spread through the lower level that a "guard" was looking to "hang someone for talking about His Highness."

There were several seedier inns down toward the middle of the lower circle, away from the city gates and most of the guards. When Adelei walked into the first one, the innkeeper said, "No beggars." She held up half a notch and slid into a table. The sleeve of her dress fell down to reveal a round, pale shoulder, and she ignored it. With no stockings, her dress exposed the hint of an ankle as she sat and waited.

She didn't have to wait long.

Within a moment or two, a woman with a much healthier chest and hips strode up and tossed a penny her way. "Clear out," she muttered, and Adelei rolled her eyes up to meet the woman's gaze. "This be my turf. Ye not welcome here."

Adelei slid out of the table with a shrug, but left the coin behind. The ample-chested woman needed the money more than Adelei did. Back out in the daylight, she crossed the street to an alley that led to yet another inn. This time when she claimed a seat, the only two who took notice were the barkeep and an old man at the bar. She fell into the same routine, exposed shoulder and a hint of ankle, when the old man hobbled over with a glass of watered-down wine.

"Surely someone as hard workin' as you could find work in a city of this size," he said as he slid into the seat across from her.

"One would think, but things are changin' wit' the new prince 'n all." Adelei took a sip of the offered glass and hid the grimace from her face. *Watered down piss is more like.*

"Aye, you be right 'bout that, I wager. Still, girl like you—jus' askin' for trouble in a place like this."

"Probably. Seen my fair share o' trouble of late. Do you think things be better under the Shadians?"

The old man touched his fingertips to his forehead a moment. When he peered at her, his eyes settled on the dirt on her cheek and the hole in her dress. "Nothin' good'll come of this."

"That's just it," Adelei said. "No matter where I be, none can tell me why. Everyone says, Alethea, you get out of this city whilst you can. But where would I go? Least here, public girls and the like be legal and—"

He laid his hand across hers gently. "You aren't a public girl. I agree with them that told ya to get. Head west. I hear Sadai treats folk kindly."

Adelei shook her head. "Isn't any use. Not enough coin to get to the border. Besides, how you know I'm not what I says?"

"Too innocent. You aren't broken yet. Not like them he leaves behind."

"He?" Her heart raced in her chest, and she leaned forward.

"The one few want to talk about."

Please talk to me. Come on, give me something I can use. She took another sip of the wretched wine and breathed slowly. "You seem willin' enough to talk."

The door to the inn slammed shut as two patrons left. The barkeep glared at the old man, who lowered his voice to just above a whisper. "People be scared. Too many rumors runnin' 'round 'bout this prince. I don-wanna see you tossed away like garbage. Figure if I talk to you, maybe you'll listen to them folk that told you to flee. Alesta's not safe no more, not for young girls like you."

"How do you know that?"

Her voice trembled, and she held her breath for a beat or two. He bought her act and pushed the wine toward her. She faked a sip, and he continued. "Thing is, no one knows. Like I said—just rumors. But these rumors, too detailed to be lies. Must be true, I say. Once heard he's got powers. Things right outta the stories of old."

"He be a mystic?"

"Don't know. Never seen it meself, but heard plenty who say they have. Someone like that, he keeps souvenirs. Don't let you become one." The old man pulled a few coins from his pocket and pressed them into her hands. "You must be goin' soon, tonight if ye can manage."

Adelei opened her mouth to call out to him as he hobbled to the door, but a young boy slid up to her table before she could move. "What?" she snapped at him, and he flinched.

"Beggin' ye pardon, milady, but Verlan wants ye out." He thumbed in the direction of the barkeep before running off. But by the time she reached the door, the old man was nowhere to be seen. In her hand were two full notches—enough to catch a ride with a caravan at the least.

Tempting. Would be so much easier if she could just leave. She stared at the coins and sighed. There were still a dozen more inns she could try before sundown. Before she reported back to the King about her failure. *You were right, old man. I should've left when I had the chance.*

When Adelei asked for a formal audience with King Leon, he raised an eyebrow at his steward but scheduled the meeting in the drawing room after supper. Margaret was in seclusion before the wedding, and supper had been oddly quiet without her nervous chatter. The candle mark came and went without the arrival of Master Adelei, and he thought her not coming at all. Or maybe having forgotten their meeting. After he finished the last of his glass of wine, he rose from the comfort of his chair to retire when a knock sounded on the door. The guard announced Master Adelei, and had he not known her looks well, he might have doubted his guard's ability to see.

The outfit she wore looked like something more fitting a beggar. *Or a public girl.* King Leon shuddered. While the sleeve of her dress was torn, the blood on her lip concerned Leon more. Leon fetched her a glass and offered her some wine as she rubbed her knee.

"You look as if you've seen better times."

Adelei nodded and leaned back in the chair. "I went in search of information."

"Where? A brothel?" When she merely shrugged, he leaned forward and clenched his fingers around the arms of his chair. "Tell me you didn't—"

"No, so you can calm your thoughts, Your Majesty. The integrity of your sepier is still intact." She swilled back the rest of her wine. "If there is one thing I've learned in the past month, it's that the citizens in your kingdom are absolutely terrified of Prince Gamun and the royal family of Shad."

"So you made progress, then?"

She shook her head. "The other bit I've learned is that absolutely none of them will talk about him, or if they will, they know nothing more than contradictory rumors. Nothing more behind them than the wind."

"Is that how you got the bleeding lip?" he asked.

Adelei touched a finger to her mouth. "Must have been when I bit my tongue. Don't worry about it—I didn't even notice." Dark circles hung suspended under her closed eyes, and when she stretched out in the chair, her movements were stiff. He thought her asleep when she picked up her train of thought. "I think I've been inside every inn and brothel in Alesta this past month. No one in the upper or middle circles would speak ill of His Highness, so I ventured into the lower circle disguised as a desperate beggar."

"How desperate?" One eye cracked open to glare at him, and he winced. "Sorry, continue."

"Everyone I spoke to told the same story. The Prince is bad news. He hurts girls. Get out of the kingdom while I can, get out while I'm still whole. Your Majesty, people are sending their children away."

"Just in the lower circle or—"

"All three circles. Those not ennobled anyway. Unmarried girls are being packed up and sent outKingdom and fast. The majority of people wouldn't speak at all about him, but the few that did were willing to give me money to get out of Alexander."

Leon frowned. "I'm glad you didn't take them up on their offers. Still, how'd you end up injured?" Her hand stilled on her knee, and he pointed. "You've been favoring it since you walked in."

"I was asking too many questions. Several barkeeps and vendors decided they wanted me gone from the city." Adelei said nothing more on the topic, and while Leon wanted to know the details so he could stick a sword through the men, the look on her face warned him against such action.

"So your questioning was unfruitful."

"This prince is good, Your Majesty. But one man hinted that the prince was a mystic. Also mentioned that he kept souvenirs. Definitely worth looking into."

"I can't risk the treaty by sending you to search his rooms, at least not yet. Dammit." Leon clenched his fist. "I need more than rumors on the wind."

"Maybe there's something we've missed in Shad, something Ida will find. Have you heard anything back from the captain?"

He shook his head. Something was wrong. Despite the dread in his stomach, he plastered a half-smile on his face. "I'm sure a messenger will arrive any time now. Or Ida herself."

Adelei picked up her empty glass and stared at it. He offered her more wine, and when she nodded, he poured a healthy amount for her. Both sipped their second glasses in silence until she apologized. "I've failed you."

"What in the world would make you think that? You haven't failed me."

"The wedding's tomorrow, and there's nothing I can tell you that gives you power to stop it. The peace treaty will proceed."

King Leon held up a finger. "Wait, didn't you say you were taking Margaret's place in the wedding? In case of an attack?"

"Yes, but I don't see—"

"Tomorrow, the prince will be marrying you. Not Margaret."

At first, her brows furrowed in concentration. When she got it, Adelei's mouth fell open into a wide grin. "You are quite devious, Your Majesty. What the prince doesn't know, won't hurt him. I like it." She smacked a hand across her thigh and laughed. It was the first time he'd seen genuine joy on her face, and the contagion spread to his own as the corners of his mouth lifted.

"We may find a way out of this yet, Adelei. Keep looking for information. Somewhere out there is the truth," he said.

Adelei finished her wine before she left, but not even their deception held them back from the cliff's edge. She left the room with a limp and slumped shoulders, though less so than when she sought out the audience with him. Leon bit his tongue as he watched her leave. *It's my treason tomorrow. If Gamun discovers our ruse, he could go before the Boahim Senate. And if he does, this will not touch her.*

She's risked enough.

Leon spoke the words in the chapel when required and celebrated the holy days as expected, but he didn't hold much faith. Whether the Thirteen existed or not, they certainly hadn't been here when his Catherine had been killed, nor when Adelei herself had been kidnapped. But as he watched the fire in the fireplace burn down to cinders, he held up a glass of wine.

"Gods be with my kingdom," he muttered and downed the drink in one swallow.

Gods be with you, Ida, wherever you are.

PART II

CHAPTER EIGHTEEN

The morning of the wedding didn't so much dawn as cascade in a torrential downpour. The rain flustered the servants, whose mud-caked feet tracked across the castle's stone floor as they dashed about. Some tried in vain to remove the mud, only to have it return five minutes later.

Everyone sighed in relief when the skies cleared two hours later. The sun poked out from clouds less grey, and still Margaret's shrill voice noted her displeasure. The two sisters sat on opposite sides from one another in a room no larger than a closet.

Steam rose from the floor where logs of wood burned red hot as the Holy Woman poured small amounts of water over them. The temperature was cooler than summer days in Sadai's deserts, but the humidity difference stifled Adelei. Her skin tried to leap away from the hot coals.

Neither the distance, nor her own meditation kept Adelei from wishing she could pluck her own eyes out. *Or cut off my ears.*

"It's so hot in here. My skin might melt off before the wedding."

"Why does *she* have to be here?"

"It's *my* day."

"The sun certainly took long enough to show itself." For the past hour, Margaret's tirade had assaulted their ears while her perfumes assaulted Adelei's nose. The Amaskan sat on her hands to keep from scratching her nose.

Each time the grating whine failed to elicit a sympathetic response, Margaret's pitch rose. Adelei's back muscles seized each time the princess opened her mouth. Between Margaret and the heat, Adelei was ready for the day to set. She glanced at the water clock and sighed. Four more hours until the ceremony, if the disaster actually happened. The time was both short and long, a relief and a burden.

Sweat covered her nude body, and she reached down to pat a weapon that wasn't there. "I need to remain armed," she'd said, but Her Holiness would hear nothing of it.

"This is a sacred ceremony that would be marred by both clothing and weapons of any kind."

Not that she minded nudity—Hell, half the Order bathed together in the communal tubs—but being this exposed when an attack was coming was dangerous. Adelei shifted, her skin peeling from the wooden bench beneath her.

And then there was the prince. She may not have been his ideal mark, but he was still a danger. Especially if he kept talking to her in half-truths. *I know better, and yet—*

Adelei shook her head, his words on her like his hands had been. *"With me, you know what you're getting. I've been nothing but honest with you. What I know. Who I am. Can you say the same about your father?"*

His arm wrapped around her waist, and she leapt up from her seat. Her Holiness frowned. "Is everything well, Master Adelei?"

"An ember must've hit my leg and startled me." The lie rolled off her tongue easily. His arm was gone, and she returned to her seat.

He wouldn't know honesty if it hit him. Besides, he's got nothing I want. Nothing to offer me. He'd be in for a hell of a shocker thinking to break me—I haven't been virginal or helpless in a long time. Whereas the princess is both down to her toes. Adelei sighed. She was everything he could want in a victim.

Adelei had elected to skip the "examination." She had chosen to stand guard outside during the barbaric ritual. Made her glad she wasn't a princess. The Holy Woman released another trickle of water across the coals to release more steam.

Margaret had blushed crimson when Adelei had stripped off all clothing and weapons with practiced ease. Where Adelei was all whipcord and muscle, Margaret was thin and supple, close to childlike in appearance. Just what Prince Gamun enjoyed most.

She pushed the thought of him away and focused on deep breaths. The sweat had long since washed away any trace of makeup Adelei had used to disguise her appearance. The Holy Woman eyed both sisters but said nothing. Nor would she.

Bored, Adelei's thoughts swirled like the heated mist. She missed home. Her real home. The sea cliffs along the trails, the hills nearby, the common rooms—she could picture it all.

"It's my wedding day." Margaret's flat voice erupted from her nose in the most unladylike fashion. "Why does everything have to go wrong? Why can't I enjoy my day and participate in—"

Adelei's foot "slipped" on the smooth floor and connected with Margaret's shin.

"Ow. I'm going to bruise now. Not only do I have a guard, but a clumsy one at that. How is she to protect me if she can't control her own feet?"

One. Two. Three. She's upset. Damn, keep counting. Four. Five. Six. She's spoiled and isn't used to not getting her way. Patience. Seven. Eight. Clear your mind. Nine—Teeth clenched, she made it to twenty before the tirade was interrupted.

"Your Highness, this room is a place of healing, of cleansing—a place to expunge all negativity of the old life as you prepare to enter the new. May I suggest that you use this time silently to reflect on your past and your future?" The Holy Woman's gaze met Adelei's, and she winked.

Only the Holy Few could have made a suggestion like that. Or an Amaskan. Adelei touched the scar near her ear and sighed. Margaret's lip stuck out, but she remained silent, and for that alone, Adelei sent her thanks to the God of Silence for the respite.

The last twenty minutes dragged. As the three women stepped out of the room, the air's chill splashed against Adelei's skin like a frozen pond, and she sucked in a sharp breath. Her sister did the same, goosebumps decorating her pale flesh in the Holy Sanctum's outer chamber. Only Her Holiness seemed unaffected by the temperature difference as she dried off with an available bath sheet before wrapping herself in a thick, red robe.

Once clothed, the comfortable weight of Adelei's weapons settled some of the building tension. Margaret slid the ceremonial robe's red silk over her damp skin, before tying her hair back in a quick knot at the nape of her neck.

The Holy woman led them into the antechamber. Several servants waited with dishes of peeled fruits and watered wine. It was well past noon, and Adelei's stomach growled at the sight of food.

No meat amongst the bowls and plates of food, or any fruits bearing their skin. It wasn't something she recalled from her studies on Alexandrian wedding ceremonies, but then, there had been only the one book. It had done little more than dip a toe into the less obvious parts of wedding rituals. And usually about the male's role—nothing on the woman's.

Adelei eyed the mounds of fruit and asked, "Your Holiness, why are all the fruits peeled? And why only fruit?"

They gathered around the simply carved table and each sat upon the floor cushions. The Holy Woman took a peeled apple for herself before passing the bowl to Margaret. "Marriage is the union of souls, as well as the union of skin. Until the latter has occurred, the princess shall eat no food that has a skin or contains blood."

More barbarism. *I hadn't realized this kingdom still held to the original teachings of the Thirteen. Still, it's a chance to eat fruits I've only read about—fruits from the far reaches of the Little Dozen.* While Margaret nibbled daintily on a piece of orange, Adelei helped herself to a kiwi, moaning aloud at the taste. Sadai lay too far to the North to grow kiwis. By the time any were shipped that far west, they were moldy sweet messes. Master Bredych would have killed to taste a kiwi.

Juice dribbled down her chin as she grinned. A similar expression showed on Margaret's face as the orange's sticky juice ran down her fingers, which she licked greedily.

Margaret broke the spell with her frown. She picked up the cloth next to her and wiped her hands. The orange's remains lay on Margaret's dish, forgotten as if diseased. *I guess sharing a smile is too much to ask of Her Highness. More fruit for me, I suppose.* She attacked another kiwi with fervor.

"What happens after this meal?" Adelei asked.

"Her Highness will take refuge in her chambers in solitude to meditate until sunset. It is a sacred time to reflect and pray. Once the sun has set, the chapel will be lit like the day's sky. Her servants will prepare her for the ceremony itself, bathing her in Holy oil before being dressed." After a moment's consideration, Her Holiness asked, "Do members of the Order of Amaska marry? Or can they, I should ask?"

"It's not forbidden, Your Holiness, but it's not encouraged either. Most members' lives are too dangerous to protect a family and too short to attempt to have one."

"Sounds miserable...and lonely," said Margaret.

"In some ways, we are our own family, each one of us caring for the other." A moment of homesickness swept through Adelei. This time of day, her friends would be training just before evening meal. She pictured Master Bredych swatting a young trainee with a practice weapon and smiled.

"It's similar in that regard to the Holy Few, as the sisters and brothers here are my family as well."

Margaret opened her eyes wide at the Holy Woman's disclosure. "It can be quite lonely at times to be Amaskan," said Adelei. "The job is everything, which is why you'll never see a family man enter our trade. It's usually loners. People who have no family at all."

"How can you be a loner when you were born—?" Margaret stopped herself short and cast a quick look about the room. Her Holiness raised her sharp green eyes from her fruit.

"While born in a...unique situation, the Order is all I've ever known. There are a few fuzzy memories from before, but nothing solid. It's a shame that I never got to know more about my first home, but my Sadain family has been very good to me. I miss them greatly."

Whereas she'd complained all morning, Margaret remained quiet as they finished eating. When it was time to leave, a heavy, thick outer robe was draped around Margaret. Its hood covered most of her face from view. A similar robe was draped over Adelei. With a nod to the priestess, Adelei broke custom and exited first.

Guards lined the walls outside, their eyes forward and backs straight. As the procession passed, Adelei sought out the guests' faces as they crowded the halls for a glimpse of their princess. Stairwells and dark corners hid little from her, but she frowned as the guards ignored them all.

Guards who looked straight ahead would find nothing unless the assassin decided to step out in front of them shouting, "Here I am. Shoot me."

Even though Margaret remained covered, her ears must have been able to hear the buzz of conversation for she basked in the warmth of people's gazes, smiles, and good wishes. The princess stood taller, slowed her pace, and smiled beneath her hood. Halfway down the long hallway, a hand reached out for Margaret.

Adelei stepped between them and grabbed the thick wrist. Some of the audience stepped away as Adelei's hood fell back, but others pushed forward—closer to the fuss. "Step back," she ordered in a sharp tone.

The wrist belonged to a woman holding flowers, and Adelei released it before they continued forward. Margaret's shoulders drooped and the healthy glow she'd borne gave way to slight creases at the corners of her mouth. Her eyes were hidden from Adelei, but she bet a royal fury was brewing there—a tempest that would spill out later in private.

I'm sorry I've ruined your little popularity party, but you'll thank me later when you're still alive.

No one else approached as they returned to the royal suite. Word had spread through the crowds before them. After Adelei checked and found no intruder, Margaret trudged into her bedchambers and sprawled across her bed.

"Why did you stop that woman from approaching me? How dare you presume—" Margaret's vocals climbed as did the color across her cheeks as she lay there, hood thrown back.

Red hood. Red cheeks. Fitting for a brat bride.

Adelei interrupted the tirade. "If you continue, you'll go hoarse. How will you talk to your beloved husband if your voice is gone?" Her sister's mouth shut with an audible snap.

And now we wait for sundown.

Adelei seated herself at the door and propped her feet on a stool. *I pray sunset comes quickly for your sake, sister of mine. Otherwise, I might be tempted to save the Tribor the trouble and kill you myself.*

"Hold still."

Margaret tugged on the corset until Adelei thought she'd die from lack of oxygen. Rather than give an excuse that would please Her Highness, Adelei said, "If you tighten that much more, I won't be able to move enough if an attack should come."

"But if it comes loose, you'll fall right out of the dress," said Margaret. The princess grinned at Adelei's discomfort. "Besides, you're the Amaskan. Quit whining and hold still."

Her sister tugged on the laces several more times, and when the deed was done, short breaths were all Adelei could manage. Margaret ducked behind the screen to put on the sepier's uniform. While she prattled on about the "horrible look" of the outfit, Adelei loosened the laces on the corset's sides. She couldn't reach the one in the back very well, but the sides were enough.

She could breathe again.

Margaret stepped out from behind the screen and scowled. "Here, let me help with that," said Adelei, and she wrapped the shawl around Margaret's head with practiced hands. Only Margaret's eyes remained visible.

Adelei belted the dirk at Margaret's waist. Even seated, the clothes rested wrong. The leggings protruded at awkward angles, and the dirk at her side looked less at home than a broom.

Hidden throwing knives were tucked away in the pockets Adelei had ordered sewn into the wedding dress. She'd told them Margaret needed to hide her fidgeting hands, a simple lie they accepted with furrowed brows. The hideous gown's sleeves had originally been too tight until Adelei had "adjusted" them, slitting some of their seams with her dagger after the handmaidens had been sent from the room.

She was glad she'd seen the handmaidens lace Margaret into the dress the day before when they'd checked the dress's fit. Otherwise, Adelei would have had no idea how to dress herself. As it was, she'd had to order Margaret to help.

The chemise itself was more of the same ruby red fabric Margaret had worn in the Holy Temple, but held much more complexity to its layers. Laces pulled the fabric shut at the sleeved upper arms and wrists, and the corset itself. The corset alone took ten minutes to lace up, and the soft, full skirts were several swords heavy.

Not that she'd worn many skirts. Too hard to move in them. *I can imagine it now, me trying to scale a wall in these.* Adelei pulled soft red slippers onto her feet. *I'd fall through the window rather than climb.* The thought made her giggle, despite the nervousness running through her veins. It wasn't that she worried about an assassination attempt—more that her sister wasn't capable of pulling off her end of the plan. If they couldn't fool the public, the plan would fail before it had begun.

Margaret stared at her, opened mouthed. "You look like a princess."

"That's the point. How else can we exchange places?"

"I—I didn't think you would look..."

"Princess-like?" Adelei asked.

"So much like me."

Adelei stopped fidgeting with the dark wig on her head. Thirteen different braids, each one woven into a larger braid gave her a princess's hair. The men in the market had sworn by the powder that kept it in place.

"I suppose I do look like you, though you don't look enough like me. That's a problem." Adelei poked Margaret in the shoulder. "Stand up taller."

Margaret pulled at the long tunic and scratched where the sash made her neck itch. Adelei had rarely seen a mirror. They had them in Sadai, but only the wealthiest possessed one. The princess's bedchamber held three, and Adelei couldn't help but peek at her reflection while her sister continued tugging on the sepier uniform. The woman before her was a princess, someone born to rule, and her stomach twisted. She pulled herself from the vision of what could have been.

The setting sun cast shadows about the room. Margaret's eyes didn't leave Adelei as they waited for sunset. Adelei whispered, "I'm sorry. Truly I am." The princess held up a hand. "That Tribor said it was you he wanted. If it was me they were after, I'd gladly allow you your rightful place in the ceremony. Do

I look like I want to be in this...dress?" Adelei plucked at the corset, and the corners of Margaret's mouth tilted up.

"I'm sorry about your horse," said Margaret. One moment her face looked pensive, and the next, she wore her princess mask again as she looked in the mirror and frowned. Despite the practice, Margaret still moved like a princess. Her tiny steps crossed the large room with grace and delicacy.

"Big steps. You have to walk with larger steps than that. And look around. Pretend you're looking for a rose and you're surrounded by a field of tulips. Search every tulip to make sure it isn't a rose. And don't speak to anyone," Adelei repeated. She'd never move correctly, but it would have to do for now. With hope everyone would be too busy looking at the royal couple.

Once Adelei had unlocked the door and the servants were allowed entrance, they'd found exactly what they'd expected—a princess in her wedding dress and the sepier guarding the door with an angry scowl on her face. *At least I didn't have to teach her that part—her frustration with me has given her my expression to a tittle.*

Adelei's ribs itched, the corset digging into the places she didn't know could hurt. She tried to scratch beneath it and wheezed. The handmaidens checked the dress. "You should have allowed us to dress you, Your Highness. These laces are too loose." When one moved to tighten the corset further, Adelei slapped her hand away.

"Leave it."

Her body was too muscular. They'd know it was her. They dressed Margaret every morning. Even standing, the dreaded corset jabbed her rib cage, so she paced.

"Begging your pardon, Master Adelei, but it's uncanny the way the two of you look. So similar. I can see why His Majesty hired you," the handmaiden said to Margaret. The princess frowned.

Not even the makeup hid it. A few wrinkles, thinner lips. It wasn't enough when they were side by side and up close. The confusion of the morning kept the handmaidens from asking too many questions, but Adelei prayed the day would move faster, and that they'd all survive it.

Both sisters started at the knock on the door, and like mirrors, they turned at once. A handmaiden allowed King Leon entrance before all the servants took their leave.

Once the door closed, he approached Margaret and kissed her forehead through the shawl. "I know this is not what you pictured for this day, poppet, but it's necessary to protect you. You'll learn as co-ruler of this kingdom that sometimes—" He glanced at Adelei. "Sometimes sacrifices are made for the greater good, to protect those we love."

Adelei tried to take a deep breath to calm her racing heart and failed. "Sometimes a king or a queen must make difficult decisions, even if they aren't what we want for ourselves."

"Papa, I...I know this is to help me, but must I dress in these clothes?" Margaret's fingers plucked at the leggings that clung to her body in a way that showed every curve she had. Curves that Adelei did not have.

If I didn't know how much she hated this, I'd almost be jealous. She looks better in that outfit than I do, and it's my outfit. While the dress Adelei wore was lovely, the restricted movement and bulk made her long for her own clothes. And pretty though it was, she paled in comparison to her father.

His silk fabric shimmered when he moved, various shades of blues and purples reflecting the ambient light. Movement lit fireflies across the silk, and despite his gray hair and worry lines, he looked younger than ever. His royal circlet was the only reminder that he'd served as king for over four decades.

Another pinch in her side, and Adelei was tempted to pull apart the dress then and there. Certain improvements had been made, Margaret blissfully unaware of such things. *She'd probably give birth to a litter of hounds if she knew how many daggers and throwing knives are hidden in these ruffles.*

"If I can't move, I better be well-armed," she'd said to King Leon. The seamstress cried when ordered to "modify" the dress.

King Leon didn't approach Adelei or address her. Everything he gave of himself was for Margaret, but subtle glances and half-halted gestures gave him away. He wanted nothing more than to dote on her. His daughter in a wedding dress—something he would never see on Adelei again.

He knew as well as she did the lifestyle of an Amaskan. When King Leon finally did rest his eyes on her, the worry returned. "It's time." He held his hand face up in front of him. Adelei placed her hand on top of his and waited.

When Margaret didn't move, Adelei nodded her head toward the door. Playing sepier, the princess exited first. This was the part Adelei hated most. She was the least protected this way, but it couldn't be helped. Still, Adelei watched and waited for the inevitable.

Outside of the room, Margaret carried herself gracefully, and the guards furrowed their brows at her bright smile. Adelei flicked the princess in the back. "Angry, remember?" she hissed.

The hallway outside the royal chambers was empty of all but guards as the guests and visitors amassed in the castle's chapel. Those that couldn't gain access to the main room would fill the halls and flood outside where they waited for word.

The shadows held no signs of an assassin, but then, Adelei didn't think the attack would happen in the hallway. Her sister had been wrong when she'd thought no one would try to kill her in front of so many.

If they had changed their minds, Margaret was safer masquerading as Amaskan. The Tribor wanted the princess's death in public, in front of the world. To show the master that while they had failed with Adelei, they had achieved second best. They wanted notoriety and forgiveness.

In the distance, heads bobbed as the wedding party approached the great hall. The assassin's need for success made him more dangerous than ever. If he failed, the Shadian royal family would have the Tribor wiped out, removed from Shadian lands, or brought up before the Boahim Senate. Ticking off the people who sheltered you, those willing to harbor criminals, was never a good idea. It was part of the reason Master Bredych always accepted jobs from the King of Sadai.

Their trip to the chapel was uninterrupted from that point on, though Adelei barely noticed between her search for an attacker and watching Margaret to ensure she played her part. Then there was making sure her own feet minced their steps. Thick crowds vied for a glimpse of her as she strode to the great doors of the chapel.

Engraved wood held patterns and symbols known only to those of the Holy Few. Carved centuries ago, these doors had withstood wars, and a few scorch marks marred a symbol or three. The castle itself, even after intense repair, wore its battle scars from the past. But the chapel's interior lay untouched, as though protected by something greater than mere stone.

Adelei whispered to Margaret, "Remember, you'll enter first and stand on my right during the ceremony. Keep up the angry face as you look around, and you'll do fine."

From inside the chapel, hundreds of voices chanted ancient words of hope, welcome, and peace as they greeted the kingdom's future; few outside the holy orders knew what they said, only that it was done and had been done that way for generations. Adelei listened, but none of the four languages she spoke told her the words' meaning.

As Adelei reached the doors, her red dress flamed the light of the candles and torches, and the chant swelled in volume. It reached the throngs of people in the hall; those that knew the words added to the sound. She looked to and fro, but the room was too thick with people to even begin a proper search for trouble.

Her Holiness stepped upon the dais, and silence rolled across the room. During the wait, Adelei's hand left her father's, and he waited again, palm up. When she placed her trembling hand on his, the lines on his face multiplied.

In Sadai, lutes and song would have welcomed them, but here the walk through the chapel felt funereal. Rather than keep her hand flat, Adelei curled her fingers until she held her father's hand in a strong grip. Margaret's steps faltered, and Adelei searched the dais for the reason.

The prince.

His feral grin unnerved her, and she sought strength in the chapel's beauty. Gorgeous colors bounced off the colored panes of glass windows, each one depicting a scene from the history of Alexander. Even the walls reflected the light, which bounced ever dancing color across the stone.

But even in the candlelight, a room of people made of shadow greeted her. *This was a mistake. Too many people—too many possible enemies. I should have found a way to cancel the wedding.* Only her father's brief frown and reminder tug moved her forward.

King Leon knelt with her before Her Holiness. She unrolled the peace treaty, and Prince Gamun stepped forward to witness, leaving Margaret alone in her sepier disguise. *I don't like having my back to Margaret. Dammit, I can't see anything.* Adelei swallowed hard as Her Holiness droned on. *I didn't think this through.*

Once witnessed, King Leon released her hand, and left her to sit on the throne beside Her Holiness. Prince Gamun held his hand, palm up, and waited for her. When she hesitated, his brows furrowed, and he seized her fingers. The contact zapped her.

Every hair on her body quivered in response. Teeth whiter than most smiled at her, and she resisted the urge to rub the hair on her arms. When she stood, the edge of her dress caught beneath her slipper, and she stumbled into the prince. The powder on her face left a smudge on the collar of his blue jacket.

He grimaced and released her hand to wipe futilely at the smear. It must have taken a year to have woven something as fine as his jacket. People were struggling to feed themselves, and his jacket alone could have fed all those in the lower circle of Alesta for a year.

Alexandrian blue made up the bulk of his jacket and pants, but the subtle pale green of Shad was counter-woven across the threads. In the light, the ensemble was mostly teal. The color clashed with the deep red of her dress. *An intentional slight, perhaps?*

Adelei openly stared at the man they called the Monster while she flitted her lashes like a lovesick bride.

And he pretended she didn't exist.

His hands were soft in hers, betraying his years as a pampered prince, and his face almost perfect, as if chiseled out of ice by a master artist. Only the danger in his eyes shattered the image. While Margaret believed him perfect, tiny movements betrayed him further—the slight rolling of his eyes during Her Holiness' speech, the twitch in his hands as she held them. A bump near his boots that told her a blade was tucked inside. She couldn't fault him his protection.

"Marriage is not just the joining of two countries or two bodies, but a joining that impacts everyone, from King to servant to farmer. As ruling King and Queen of Alexander, your decisions will impact its people and their livelihoods."

A movement in the crowd to her left—brief but movement all the same as people stepped aside for the smiling face in brown. The smile was a façade, its corners up too high, teeth showing too much. A grimace more than happiness.

Adelei darted glances between Margaret and the man, but the princess was oblivious. She only had eyes for Prince Gamun. Thankfully, her shining brown eyes were visible only to the wedding party. Gamun caught the look and dropped his hand. Then he chuckled.

Not a single guard moved to halt the grinning man in motion. Adelei fanned herself and forced her legs to wobble. "Are you well, Your Highness? Do you see something?" Her Holiness whispered.

The way it was worded, Adelei bit her tongue. *She knows it's me behind this dress.* When Adelei shifted her eyes in the direction of the moving figure, the Holy Woman frowned. Adelei rolled her eyes in the back of her head and faked a fainting spell as she tumbled to the floor.

Her eyelids cracked enough to watch as the figure approached, his grin widening with each step. Prince Gamun and Margaret both knelt by Adelei's side, the former touching her cheeks and neck to check for breath. Adelei grabbed Margaret and tugged her to the floor. "There's an assassin here. Stay low," she whispered.

"Halt." The Holy Woman pointed a long finger at the man fifteen feet from the dais. Guards near the doors blocked off the exits. The bulk of those in the front formed a ring around the wedding party, blocking them from view.

"You will explain this later, I take it," Prince Gamun whispered to Adelei, who had time to do little more than nod as another shout rang out.

Captain Fenton wedged himself between two guards and bowed to King Leon. "Your Majesty, the man has been detained. He carried several daggers and a hand bow. We checked for poison but found none."

Adelei chose that moment to officially *wake*. "Don't move Your Highness, you may have hit your head," a guard spoke. With

Prince Gamun's help, she rose, her breath shallow with the corset's tightness.

"Your Highness, perhaps you should lie back down." The guard moved to intercept, and she waved her hand. "I—I'm fine." Adelei shifted her voice to mimic Margaret's dulcet tone. "What has happened?"

"Nothing to worry about," said King Leon. He faced Captain Fenton. "Take him to the dungeon. We'll deal with this intruder later. He's ruined enough of this wedding ceremony." King Leon broke through the circle of guards to stand before the crowd of guests. His overly cheerful voice carried throughout the chapel. He smiled with cheeks too tight and eyes pained.

"All is well, just a misunderstanding. Let us return to this joyous occasion."

Prince Gamun leaned close to Adelei's ear. "Did you actually faint? Are you sure you're all right?"

"Is this genuine concern, or just part of the act?"

He stepped back a pace and glared until Her Holiness gestured for them to return to their places. Adelei fought the tension in her muscles. Adrenaline called for her to fight, to chase after the guards and interrogate the attacker. Instead, she feigned a relaxed stance and fluttered her lashes at the Monster.

Too easy. Too pat. It was like the attacker wanted to be caught. Adelei would rather die than be taken. No one else in the crowd forced their way forward. Just a sea of eyes waited for her.

No adenneith on his body either. I supposo I should be grateful. How easily would it spread through this castle—like a plague? Adelei craned her neck around. Margaret glared at her and tilted her head in the Holy Woman's direction. *Damn. What was I supposed to say?*

Prince Gamun mumbled under his breath, and she repeated, "My honor for Alexander, my breath for its people, my soul for the Gods, and my life for the crown."

Margaret mouthed the words with her, the whisper audible to the Holy Woman. She paused before she continued, and Prince Gamun swore his oaths.

"This unified pair is blessed by the Gods. May they live and rule forever," Her Holiness said as she handed the royal circlet to the prince.

He kissed her hand before placing it on her brow. The cold metal felt odd, much like the prince's hand in hers—a delicate, yet firm grip by a stranger. She resisted the urge to touch the circlet. Her father cleared his throat, and she brought her hand down to rest alongside her thigh.

If anyone could, King Leon understood the conflict within her.

The prince tugged at her arm, and she remembered how to walk. One foot before the other. Small steps. Her lungs remained behind as she took quiet little gasps through her nose. The moment she could, the corset would come off.

In front of her, Margaret took exaggerated steps as they exited the chapel. The group spilled into the main halls where more people gathered. Some cheered. Others cried. The mass hummed with excitement, and Adelei's smile faltered under the strain.

Playing what she was, and what she could have been. Never again.

A small voice in her roared at the injustice. It didn't matter that she couldn't recall her time as a child here. It was the knowledge that silenced her mind and twisted her heart with doubt.

At least she'd ordered the Walk of the Family cancelled. A carriage ride through the entire city would have been a nightmare. *One I'm not sure I'm up for honestly.* Prince Gamun led her to a balcony that overlooked the main courtyard. They stepped forward and waved at the cheering masses below. A quick appearance and they popped back indoors. Adelei kept her hand on Margaret's elbow in the crowded halls.

Like the grubby hands of toddlers, eyes crawled across Adelei as people examined her and weighed her worth. Before, she'd been a daughter. A princess. She was married now—a future ruler. Now she had value. Adelei grit her teeth to keep the scowl from her face.

When they reached the royal suite, Adelei refrained from wilting in relief. Prince Gamun spun her around by the elbow, but whatever he would say was interrupted by the entrance of King Leon. Her father patted him on the back. His hand hit too hard, and his handshake released too fast. Like patting a snake.

"Congratulations and welcome to the family."

Margaret brushed past her father and threw off the head scarf. "My prince, I am sorry for the deception, but I am the princess. I am your wife."

CHAPTER NINETEEN

The viper stilled, unsure of his target or his strike as he wavered between Margaret and Adelei. One wore the wedding gown and one did not, yet their faces were the same. Adelei swore he'd figured it out during the ceremony—he'd made a few jibes in that regard—but his face flushed.

"What treachery is this?" He stepped back from Margaret's outstretched arms. "You mean to invalidate the treaty?" His feet found the chair behind him, but not soon enough to prevent his hard tumble into the chair.

"Prince Gamun," King Leon reached out his hand to his son-in-law. "There has been deception, yes, but not what you think. Several attempts have been made to take the life of my daughter. In an effort to prevent today's attack, we thought it best to switch their roles."

Adelei stepped forward. "It was my idea, Your Highness. Had the man taken into custody today been successful, he would have only killed me and not your wife. With me in her place, it was unlikely he would have been successful at all."

I didn't even want him aware of this role reversal, you silly, silly brat. Adelei shot a sidelong glance at Margaret.

Gamun's eyes rolled over her as if she were a fellow predator competing for food. Then he winked.

He *had* known. So why the game? The muscles in his jaw twitched, giving his face a more chiseled look, while the veins along his temple throbbed. "I appreciate your concern, Master Adelei, but your services aren't needed any longer."

Margaret's face spelled mild panic, and she touched a hand to Adelei's arm. "*I* require her services. She is my sepier."

Adelei didn't know who was more shocked at the sudden declaration.

"Surely you can do better than some former Amaskan bodyguard. I can put my people on it, Margaret. You'll be safe enough."

"No, I formally request her services until my father feels they are no longer required."

The King had coached her, that much was obvious, but it took nerve to stand up to her husband, and Adelei resisted the urge to applaud the princess's growing backbone. Adelei bowed to Margaret. "Your Highness is wise indeed. One can rarely spot the enemy amongst one's friends. They are the hardest to locate with their masks."

Gamun tried to hide his smirk behind the brush of his hair. "I know you don't have sepiers in Shad, but here, they are more than mere guards. They are advisors. They run tasks entrusted to a select few—those who have the crown's trust in all things."

"They are spies," Gamun muttered. "But as you will."

The words were as choppy as his steps as Prince Gamun left the sitting room. "Where is he—?"

Adelei interrupted Margaret. "He's probably returning to his state rooms."

"I don't understand. Did I do something wrong?" The wind of emotions across her face threatened to spill her tears. "This was supposed to be my day."

"You did just fine, poppet," said King Leon as he rested his hands on her shoulders.

"Ass. Probably going back to his mistress or his mystic." The swift intake of breath told her this was news to them both, and Margaret's mouth popped open.

King Leon chided her with a single look before he kissed Margaret's cheek. "Don't worry, Margaret. All will work its way in time. And you—" He faced Adelei. "You and I will speak on this mystic business later." He excused himself, leaving the two sisters alone.

"Come on," Adelei said to Margaret. "We might as well trade places again. I think I can guard you better as myself. I know I can certainly move and breathe better."

Margaret stared off into nothingness, and her bottom lip trembled. "He doesn't love me."

"Help me out of this dress, will you?" She thought distraction would help, but when Margaret didn't move, Adelei placed a light hand on her shoulder. "What is it?"

"H-He w-was supposed to be perfect."

The inane sentence almost shocked Adelei. *Almost.* If not for those words, Adelei could believe them sisters. Margaret held a fragility and naivety about her that was so very childlike. Exactly what the prince desired—a child rather than a woman. *No wonder she's falling apart on me.*

"Let's focus on the now, shall we?" Adelei said.

Margaret didn't struggle—her small frame relaxing against Adelei's own as she lost her composure. Tears landed on the dark sepier fabric. After a few minutes, Margaret whispered, "I missed having a—someone to talk to."

"You have Nisha. I thought you were supposed to be close to your lady-in-waiting?"

Her sister shook her head. "Nisha's new. I-I don't know her all that well. Besides, it's different. You understand, well, some things. It's not your fault you weren't raised here."

Memories stirred in Adelei's mind. Fuzzy images of another time when they held each other and cried. When they were leaving for safety. It wasn't a full memory—just a flash. This may not have been the family she grew up with, but it was a family nonetheless.

And either way, Adelei would break their hearts. Either because the job was done and she left, or because the job was done and she was dead.

It took an hour to change clothes. Margaret had returned to the silent consternation of before as she stood in a simplified version of her wedding gown, still red and ornate in its decorations, only shorter. The silk gauze bore fewer ruffles and was loose enough for freer movement. Adelei spent most of the hour learning how to lace up the parts of the dress as she helped Margaret into it. Her Highness didn't want Nisha, or her handmaidens. For the moment, she was content to be alone with Adelei.

Having never acted as a servant for anyone but herself, much less a princess, Adelei only made it through the ordeal successfully because of Margaret's implicit instructions. As Adelei wrapped her head with her scarf, Margaret caught her wrist. "Adelei," she whispered, "You will protect me? You swear it?"

Margaret hunched in on herself. Her brown eyes reminded Adelei of Midnight in his moments before death, afraid and yet so trusting. *So knowing.* Something about the attack earlier or maybe Prince Gamun's attitude had Margaret believing everything now. *I wish I knew which changed her mind about me.*

"I swear to protect you from any and all that would harm you."

"You swear by the Thirteen?"

Adelei nodded. "Even if it means my death. No harm will come to you if I can help it."

Her sister tightened her grip on Adelei's wrist for a moment. "He's going to hurt me," she said. "There is something foul, something evil about his face...something wrong." She released her grip and continued smoothing out her dress.

Even the deer knew not to trust the wolf. Adelei had worried Margaret lacked brains enough to recognize the danger. When the knock sounded, Margaret remained in place, giving Adelei wide berth as she approached the door. She opened it a crack. King Leon and his honor guard waited to accompany the princess to her wedding feast. But instead of a newlywed on her way to a party, Margaret resembled a mourner, her downcast eyes focusing on slow moving feet. Drooping shoulders added to the dread in the pit of Adelei's stomach.

The feeling intensified as Prince Gamun joined them. He seized Margaret's hand in a tight, possessive grip. A mass of people crammed along benches in the great hall. Heads bowed at the entrance of the royal family and remained so until King Leon was seated at the grand table up on the platform. The very center of the hall was empty of benches and people. In the corner of the clearing, a grand harp awaited its harpist.

Smells assaulted Adelei's nose, and her stomach growled in response. Remnants of a fruit meal were long gone, and Adelei's tongue ached to fill her stomach with the roast boar fresh from the spits. Runners carried trays amassed with chunks of carved meat to the grand table first. Food would be served to the royal family before it reached the other nobles and guests in the hall. Guardsmen, staff, and servants would be served last, and only after the celebration was long over. Adelei stood behind her sister with a rumbling stomach and set about watching the people in the great hall.

Boredom set in early—her largest opponent in the job, especially when waiting or serving as a bodyguard. People ate and drank. Chatter echoed through the hall. Yet Prince Gamun said little more than four words to his new bride, something that set the servants' tongues aflutter with gossip. Once the royal family finished feasting, the formal dances began. Prince Gamun led his wife in a partnered dance, and Adelei chafed at watching from afar.

While Gamun shone like the stars, Margaret stumbled and blundered her way through the steps. Despite having a reputation for hosting great dances, her feet found his toes often enough that even Adelei winced in sympathy.

She heard more than felt the person who approached from her right, shoes tapping an off tempo beat on the stone floor. His labored breathing was familiar at this point, so the bump at her elbow didn't startle her. "All's well thus far, Your Majesty," she said.

"You must be starving, Master Adelei."

"I am, but the job comes first. Besides," she said, laughing, "this isn't the first time I've had to wait a long stretch between meals."

"Margaret and Gamun will soon be joined in their dance by other members of the high court. After another dance with him, Margaret will rotate through the various high ranking guests. How will you protect her in such a throng of moving people?"

"Easy. I'll shock them all and be out there with her, even have a few dances."

The man next to her chuckled. "And shock my court you will. The idea that an Amaskan can dance is shocking enough, but to join in on the high court dances as if their equal—tongues will be wagging tomorrow for sure." The merriment in his eyes when he glanced at her was contagious, and she smiled in return. With a wink, he set off to charm his way through the dance clearing.

The King's advisors sat to her left at a long table with the ambassadors from several other kingdoms. *So few present. Is he disliked by so many? Is there any truth then to the border disputes? His own council mentioned them, so there must be.*

The honor guard shadowed King Leon's movements as her eyes shadowed Margaret's. Captain Fenton hovered near the ambassadors, and Adelei move herself around tables and stools until she reached his side. "Captain, I wondered if you might be able to help me out a bit," she said, her gaze never leaving Margaret.

"What can I do for you, Master Adelei?"

"I was wondering if you could tell me more about the advisors and ambassadors."

Without breaking his line of sight, Michael described those closest to them, injecting bits and pieces of personal opinion with facts. He was bound to have heard rumors and gossip from his own men, not to mention what he was able to pick up on his own. Most people ignored those they thought beneath them and were freer with their tongues. "Duke Hughes is one of the oldest. Very quiet until he's got reason to speak, and then, well, let's just say he's quite vocal."

A man in pale green crossed the room. The edges of his tunic and pants darkened to an emerald green before flecks of gold embroidered the hem. A difficult effect to do well. Adelei tilted her head in his direction.

"That is the Ambassador from Shad," Michael answered.

"Is it necessary to have an ambassador with Prince Gamun here and part of the family?"

"Of course. While the treaty makes him the future King of Alexander, the two countries are still separate lands. So an ambassador is still needed." Michael's tight lips compressed in pale lines.

"You didn't have much to say about him," said Adelei. The music shifted to a light waltz, and people moved to the floor to join the dance. Adelei twisted around to watch Margaret be handed off to Lord Philip Sebald, Lady Millicent's husband.

"There's little to say. He arrived the day before you did."

"That's odd. I would think an ambassador was needed here before then." Michael remained silent, and she asked, "Any others in the bunch I should know about?"

Michael tore his gaze from the group and stepped directly in front of her. He didn't block her line of sight any more than she blocked his, but his lips were now hidden from the Shadian Ambassador should he happen to look. "We've had ambassadors pop in and out from all of the Little Dozen for the past thousand years—except Shad. This is the first time they've ever sent an ambassador. A fact I find quite odd indeed. More so, if I were looking for someone behind a murder attempt, that would be the first place I'd start, assuming I was allowed to do so."

He ground his teeth. With a last glance at the table, he said, "Maybe that nothing in the dungeon could tell you more about his master." The Captain turned about face and walked away. Adelei eased herself into a corner and leaned in what she hoped was a relaxed position.

Hmmm. So the Captain believed the ambassador and the attacker to be in collusion. As she watched others glide across the floor, she wondered if there was any validity to the theory. People danced, and she waited. *Patience abounds.*

Her sister was thirty feet away in the arms of her father as the dance shifted yet again. Emerald green moved in the corner of her eye, and she pivoted to her left. The Ambassador of Shad flinched at her sudden movement. Despite his obvious fear, the corners of his mouth twitched. Her bored expression made his eyes twinkle all the more.

"My apologies, Master Adelei." She failed to place his thick accent—though it wasn't Shadian. "I am Chortez of Treques, Ambassador to the Kingdom of Shad."

She nodded her head but did not accept his outstretched hand. "I've not heard of Treques in my travels. Is it part of the Little Dozen?"

"Non, I mean, no." With a slight frown, he withdrew his hand. "It is far to the west of Naribor, across the Harren Sea. It's an intriguing story. And one I might tell you if you would do me the honor of dancing with me."

It was the perfect excuse to get closer to the royal couple. And he knew it. But then, if he was behind the assassination attempts or worked with Prince Gamun, this would at least keep him where she could see him and give her a chance to pick his brain.

Her nod surprised him and this time, it was her turn to chuckle at his expense. Chortez proved an able dance partner as his steps led them closer to the royal couple. Most dancing stopped as Adelei passed. *Quite the odd pair, this foreign Ambassador and me.* Adelei grinned widely.

In the stifling heat of so many bodies, she had left the head scarf behind. Her ear-length hair stood out in stark contrast to the lengths and styles of hair around her. Highborns found their steps again, but most women stared at her with open hostility. A word whispered in passing stung Adelei's ears red, and Chortez cocked his head. "Excuse my boldness. I don't know this word—this *gouime?*" Laughter left a flush across the Ambassador's face. "What does it mean?"

"It's a rude word, slang." He continued to frown, and she said, "They are saying I'm a man and not a woman."

"*Samlaing.*" He repeated the word in Shadian.

"Yes, that."

"Their loss. It is a rare treasure when a woman is both beautiful and strong. In my lands, you would be a queen." His eyes flashed with irritation as he looked across the floor of dancing nobles.

Adelei could have been. All this could have been for her. She followed his line of sight and shook her head. "I would never be queen. Seems like a complete waste of time to sit around telling others what to do, rather than going out and doing it yourself."

"I would agree. This is not for me," he said. Chortez spun her in a circle, and she sought her sister's head in the crowd. Margaret's dark hair popped up a dozen couples away, and Adelei fell back into the dance.

"When I was a child, my father was interested in expanding his lands, so he sailed across the Herran Sea in hopes of finding hospitable people to conquer, or if nothing else, trade with."

His teeth gleamed against his dark tanned skin. A handsome smile she could appreciate. Chortez's eyes narrowed as they passed by Prince Gamun. *A dangerous smile.*

"When he reached land, he found the Kingdom of Naribor. Seeing as their troops far outweighed his own, he traveled east until reaching Liallan."

"Let me guess. He found the kingdom well-established."

"Indeed, he did. Everywhere he traveled on this continent, he found lands well-settled and defended; more so than our own which had nothing like your Boahim Senate. Instead of returning to lands full of chaos and war, he remained here and reestablished our home."

Four feet away, Margaret chatted idly with Gamun, who wore a look of utter contempt. Odd how Margaret had gone from terror to animated so easily.

The ambassador leaned with her. "They make an interesting couple," he said before continuing his story. "My father chose to return to Nicen and settle there. I helped him run what he deemed 'Our own little kingdom.' Once I was of age, I traveled to Shad with the intention of applying for membership in the Boahim Senate. The idea of twelve kingdoms all working together in peace, well, it interested me. It seemed like such an impossibility. Of course, by then, Shad and Alexander were deep in the Little War of Three. The Boahim Senate laughed at me."

"Because you believed in peace?" she asked.

"No, because I thought I could apply to join them. I didn't understand how exclusive a group it is, requiring patrons, nominations, and the blessing of kings. In my attempts to curry favor, I ended up the Ambassador to Shad. Though I admit I am worried."

The song changed to a faster piece, but he did not release her. "Are you worried about something in particular?" she asked.

Chortez nodded. "No one has remained a Shadian ambassador longer than a year and never here. That His Majesty of Shad would select me and send me here..." He shrugged as he trailed off. Adelei stepped on his toes again as she fought to maintain sight of her sister and keep her feet stepping in tempo. "Now that I've told you my story though, what is yours? What brings you to Alexander, Master Adelei?"

Ah, so *there* was the reason for this dance. He knew damned well why she was here—what was he fishing for? To him, Adelei said, "I was hired to protect the royal family. To serve as sepier."

His fingers tightened a moment on her shoulder and despite his clenched jaw, he didn't miss a step, his feet moving smoothly across the floor. "But of course. Protection is something everyone seems to need these days, with assassins roaming about unattended."

He's a viper indeed. Trying to hook me with that line about being worried. He steered them closer to the royal couple, and she asked, "You mentioned how interesting a couple they are. What makes you say that?"

His wry grin lit up his already charismatic face. "I do not wish to speak ill of your country..."

"It's not my country," Adelei replied. "I'm from Sadai, so please continue."

The volume of his laughter led several nearby dancers to misstep. "I like how blunt you are, Master Adelei. Indeed, I find the princess a stifling bit dull. Flighty. I can't imagine someone as active and adventurous as the prince choosing someone that dimwitted. Now someone like you—someone with a mind and a body to match it—you would be more fitting to our prince's tastes. I imagine you have no trouble hunting or making a variety of sport."

There's no way he could know of the prince's offer. Or could he? Adelei missed the next step.

It was a risk but worth it. "Alas, I am not royalty. I'm afraid your prince will have to make do with Her Highness. Besides, he didn't choose either. The treaty has created this union." She met his stare with a confidence she didn't feel, and this time when he smiled, it was with malice more than humor.

He said nothing. A shiver ran from the tips of her toes to the base of her neck, where her scalp tingled. "There does seem to be a slight chill in this room." Ambassador Chortez tightened the arm about her waist.

Warning signs rang out like flares in her mind. It wasn't safe to be in the presence of this man any longer than necessary. Despite this, she had a theory to test. "I would have thought them an odd couple as well, until certain knowledge was made known to me. Her Highness is certainly a few years too old for his tastes, but she's fairly childlike."

His warning squeeze was enough. He leaned close to her ear and whispered, "You play a dangerous game, Master Adelei. One wonders if you know *how* dangerous." As suddenly as he held her, he released his hold, and the distance between them gave her room to catch her breath.

"I do, but I have to wonder, do you even know what game is being played?" The polite mask returned to his face as the music ended with a final flourish of harp strings. There was a brief pause before the next song began with an arpeggio of rapid notes. Groups gathered, pitting women against men. She took the opportunity to steady herself, and dancing guests bumped into her. The ambassador was forced to retreat a step.

King Leon waited to the man's right, and Adelei bowed. "Thank you for the dance, Ambassador. May I, Your Majesty?" She held out her hand, which he accepted with slight trepidation. It was one thing for her to dance with a foreign ambassador and quite another to dance with the King. By accepting the dance, he named her an equal to members of the high court. Adelei had forced King Leon into a tough decision, but Chortez left her little choice.

"Have you enjoyed the feast thus far, Master Adelei?" he asked.

"It's been interesting to observe, Your Majesty. Just a moment ago, I was able to enjoy a dance with Ambassador Chortez, who seemed intensely interested in me."

She waited a beat or two, and he inclined his head once before they separated to make a circle around the dance floor. It was several minutes before the dance brought them back together again, but when it did, he replied, "Did he find it so unusual for us to have a sepier?"

"No, Your Majesty, but he did find it odd for that sepier to be me."

This time, he missed reaching for her hand as they circled, the falter telling her he'd taken the hint. "I, for one, am glad to have someone so trustworthy in my employ—with your presence, Ambassador Chortez can be rest assured that his knowledge and concerns remain his alone."

When they joined hands, he squeezed hers gently. Neither spoke for the rest of the dance and as the song ended, Adelei extracted herself from the crowd to sit on an empty bench. No one else approached her for a dance. Not that she wanted to—it was tiring enough trying to keep after Margaret, let alone carry a conversation and dance.

Her Highness danced with a dozen men, most courtly group dances and upbeat pieces meant to keep the wine flowing and the smiles lighting the room. Margaret's smile faltered every time she found Gamun, whose flirtatious voice carried well through the great hall. Adelei stifled a yawn, and her stomach growled audibly. When a nearby serving boy offered her a leftover piece of boar, she removed it from the plate with her knife.

Stomach placated, Adelei shadowed behind Margaret as she dragged herself back to the royal table. Prince Gamun walked arm and arm with another ambassador, and Adelei resisted the urge to trip him as they passed. Margaret sank into her seat, her skin white in the candlelight. Her Highness reached for a cup and lurched forward. Her frame sagged across the table. "Your Highness, are you all right?" Adelei asked.

Her sister's eyes fluttered, a flush marching across her cheeks. A giggle escaped too pale lips, as she reached for her glass. She missed it completely, and the maroon spread across the table.

She was drunk. Wonderful.

Across the room, Prince Gamun's scowl was visible as he cut his dance short. When he came within sight of Margaret, she stood on wobbling feet. Margaret lurched for him and missed him by a good foot. Her eyes were too bright in the darkness, and Adelei frowned. More like she'd been drugged.

Margaret's smile was a crack of lightning. "Issit time for us...for us to retire?" She touched a pale hand to Gamun's cheek.

He flinched like he'd been burned. "Take her to her rooms. She's had too much to drink." Adelei nodded. "So much for being her protector," he muttered as he strode away, and she bristled at the insult. The moment his feet landed in the dancing square, ladies surrounded him as they vied for his attention. Several leaned toward him in a half-bow, their best assets visible from the platform.

Margaret opened her mouth in protest. "That's—"

Adelei clamped a hand over her sister's mouth. "The last thing we need is a scene," she hissed and snagged a passing servant. "Give Her Highness's regards to His Majesty. Let him know she has retired for the evening."

The servant nodded, and Adelei guided her sister toward the back passage behind the stage. Margaret stumbled, and Adelei all but carried her through the tiny alcove. Adelei didn't like the pathway's deep shadows, but she trudged on, glad her sister weighed so little. The passage released them next to the stairwell. Each step Margaret took was exaggerated as she wobbled around like a drunkard. The only people to witness Her Highness's state were the royal guards, none of which batted an eye with Adelei beside her.

Once inside Margaret's chambers, Adelei laid her sister on the bed, clothes and all. Margaret giggled as she rolled over, and only Adelei's hands saved her sister from rolling off the bed. Margaret wrapped her arms around Adelei's neck. "My prince, are you now t'make me your princess?"

Adelei pried clumsy fingers from her neck and rolled her eyes. "Your Highness, it's Adelei. Not Prince Gamun. What have you had to drink tonight?"

Margaret's unsteady gaze wavered in the candlelight as her head weaved. Her eyelids bunched up. "There you are," she said as she reached for Adelei. Her Highness giggled in drunken hysteria. "How'd I get here? Where's my prince?"

"Still at the banquet. Stay here." In her own room, Adelei dug through a bag for the packet of *thwaite* leaves, and returned to find Margaret attempting to stand. She balanced precariously at the foot of the bed, her arm wrapped around its post for support.

"Wha' is that?"

"*Thwaite.*" Adelei chewed a few leaves to break the skin. She spit them into a cup of water near the bed and waited for the liquid to turn a pale green. "Drink this. All of it."

"Why? What's Thwante-Thwaite-whatever?"

"An herb. Helps you gain clarity."

"Never heard of it." Margaret set the glass aside, and Adelei shoved it back into her hand. "It's an herb used by the Order. Drink it. It tastes horrible, but it will help sober you up."

Her Highness tossed it back and gagged. She coughed and then pursed her lips at the bitter aftertaste. When she leaned back against the pillows on her bed, Adelei stationed herself at the door.

With hope this will counteract whatever's in her system. The stuff works on drunks, but this is more than too much wine. Someone laced her wine with something, and I don't know what. It doesn't seem deadly, just intoxicating and then some.

She leaned against the door frame. Light snores sounded from the bed's direction, and Adelei sighed. Margaret flung her arm across a pillow and smiled a lopsided grin in her sleep. Adelei's stomach rumbled.

It was past midnight when *Prince Charming* returned. He stumbled toward the royal chambers with less coordination than Margaret had possessed. The herb hadn't done much. Her Highness had fallen into a deep sleep. When His Highness returned, Adelei first thought them under attack.

Finding the bedchamber locked, Gamun tried to forcibly remove the door from its hinges. She held her dagger to his throat on his first step through the door, and he halted midstep. He cursed loud enough to wake the dead. Seeing who it was, Adelei released him and backed up as he stumbled toward her, fists clenched.

She dodged his misplaced throws. "Your Highness, it's Master Adelei. Please stop attempting to hit me." He scrunched up his eyes as he tried to focus swimming vision on her face, and he dropped his fists.

"Leave us."

She hesitated. Leaving Margaret with him was a bad idea. Especially if he was the one who had drugged her. But then, she didn't want to watch two newlyweds drunkenly grope at each other, either. With a curt nod, she left the room and closed the door behind her.

The night couldn't be trusted—too many secrets in the wrong hands and questions in the air. Not to mention the odd behavior of both Their Highnesses. Adelei propped a chair in front of the door and settled in for a long evening. One of Margaret's handmaidens brought up food for her. While cold, it hit her growling stomach easy enough as she enjoyed her sister's wedding feast.

A noise outside woke her from a light doze a few candlemarks later. King Leon and Captain Fenton walked in, their bodies moving as heavily as their feet. "Good, you're here," said Michael. "Your skills are needed in the dungeon."

Adelei stretched stiffened joints and stifled a jaw-cracking yawn. She wished she dared a pinch of *thwaite* herself, though the risk of addiction and the resulting headache persuaded her otherwise. She rubbed the sleep from her eyes and with a longing look at the chair, she stepped into the hallway with her father.

"It's time to interrogate the assassin," he said.

Suddenly, she felt much more awake in the predawn. Much more.

CHAPTER TWENTY

Adelei smirked as she entered the cell. The man sat on the ground, his ankles and wrists shackled to the damp stone wall. She didn't say anything, just pulled in a chair and sat in front of him, crossing her legs in complete relaxation as if it were a sunny afternoon outside, and she was picnicking with friends rather than interrogating an assassin.

While a search of him showed no Tribor triangle, it didn't mean they hadn't hired a hit man for the attempt. After all, if he were caught attacking the royal family at such a celebratory event, they could claim they weren't responsible since he wasn't Tribor. No one wanted to be tied to an attack on a day that involved the fulfillment of a major treaty. As she circled the cell, she allowed him a good view of her clothing.

"Change into your Amaskan clothing," the King had ordered before they had left the royal suites.

"You won't fool him."

King Leon had given her a weary-eyed stare. "You may have hair on your head and a scar on your jaw, but trust me. He'll know you for who you are."

As she stood before the assassin now, his eyes widened in the candlelight. Hair too short for most, black silk from head to toe with no embellishment, and then there was the scar. Her father had been right. Even with her tattoo gone, anyone with half a brain could put the pieces together on who she was—or who she'd been.

His thinning hair was more noticeable through the sweat that poured down his face, leaving paths clear of dirt in their wake. Even in the dungeon's chill, dark circles grew at his armpits. His chains rattled like chattering teeth as he tried to retreat.

It was he who spoke first, his Alexandrian broken and weak. "Why here you?"

Adelei stared. His medium-build strained against the chains which clattered loudly. When he tried to melt into the wall, she stood and took a single step in his direction. "You know what I am, yes?" When he nodded, she continued. "You are no assassin. No threat. Who sent you?"

The man shook his head and shut his eyes. Adelei touched a hand to his chin and lifted his head. "Who sent you? You will speak."

No reply. She switched languages to Sadain and then Shadian. When he thrice refused, she withdrew a dagger from her sleeve. At the sound, his eyes popped open. She leaned forward and pressed the dagger to his chin. In Alexandrian, she whispered, "I won't kill you. Not yet. But I will make this last until you speak."

A puddle grew beneath the man, and the acidic smell of urine hit her nose. *Definitely not a real assassin. Just a hired thug, more like.*

Adelei split the seams on his clothing, removing every stitch until he shivered before her in the chilly air. The man's teeth chattered along with the sound of the chains that bound him.

No tattoos. No identifying marks of any kind. She ran a calloused hand over him, and he grinned at the touch. Adelei jabbed a knuckle at his rib cage. A sound croaked out of his mouth, a smaller dialect of Shad being his language of choice. "I am Javas. I will not talk to a murderer." With this, he spit at her, missing her completely, but the intent was clear.

He must truly be scared of me. Interesting though that he chooses Shadian. Could be a false trail. "I don't care who you are, you'll answer to me. Who are you to speak of murderers, coming here to commit such a crime yourself? Who sent you?"

His eyes flashed a moment and behind her, the door creaked open. "You will speak, or I will cut the tongue from you," King Leon shouted, his rapid steps bringing him close to Adelei's side.

"You shouldn't be here."

"I will see him answer." King Leon refused to meet her gaze, staring instead at the naked prisoner.

He's fine with the job I'm doing, but not that it's me doing it. It was understandable, yet it stung. Javas set his mouth in a grim line of determination, which opened when Adelei's dagger drew a shallow line down his chest. It wasn't particularly deep. If she'd wanted to hurt him, she could have easily enough, but it was surprise that pulled the shout from his lips. King Leon closed his eyes against the sight of her knife moving through flesh.

"Your Majesty, please leave. It will be easier to do my job without an audience."

Instead of waiting to see if he was going to follow her request, she drew another line down the man's chest, this one running from the neck to the belly button. The footsteps behind her hurried their pace as Javas screamed out again, this time with some pain behind it. "You will speak as your tongue will be the last thing I remove from your body. Speak, and your death will be quick. Your master will never know you ratted him out."

White circled his irises, and his head bobbed up and down. "I don't know who-who hired me direct-like. He sent someone to meet with me. Offered five crowns if I took a shot at the princess."

"Did the person you meet have a name?"

He swallowed as Adelei's dagger rested in her hand, his own blood gleaming in the light as she twisted it this way and that. "He never said. Jus' paid me half up front."

"Why'd he want Her Highness out of the picture?"

"To break the treaty. Said there were too many failures—didn't know what he meant an' I didn't ask."

"Questions get you killed."

He nodded, swallowing behind his thick tongue. "We met in an alley in Drehsmä in Shad. Near a bakery where I was to do some side jobs. He told me to kill a princess. Seemed to think there were two, crazy man. I've not seen none but the one."

Thin streams of blood mixed in with his urine on the stone floor. She ignored his pleading brown eyes, interested only in his sudden willingness to talk. "Who hired you?" she asked again. He shook his head, and she placed the dagger behind his ear. This time, she didn't have to mar his skin before he spoke up.

"I told you—I don't know. But-but I can describe him."

Adelei listened to his generic description that could have been any man in half a dozen kingdoms, a response he was trained to give. But who trained him? He lacked most assassin training, and yet, someone had taken the time to plant suggestions into him, so he wouldn't betray his master.

More questions with no answers. Adelei patted him on the cheek and left him sagging in relief. She shook her head as she turned her back to him. "*Tsk, tsk.* This won't do."

Javas cried out, "I know more. Heard'im talking about some weapon."

"Go on."

The man swallowed hard. "They—"

"They? You mentioned one master."

If he could have wet himself more, he would have. His chains shook as he backed away from her. "There was only the one, but someone came to the alley while we was talking. I only heard bits of the conversation. Man I met, never let me see who he was talking to. Other one was cloaked, I swear it. But he was talking about some kinda hammer they were keen on getting. Said it was important to the King, but it was being moved or something. Once it crossed the border, they were..."

"What?" Her voice trembled, and she shook him by the shoulders.

"They were going to make sure King Leon never saw it again."

He was lying. He had to be.

King Leon waited in the hall, surrounded by several members of the royal guard. "Is there somewhere nearby we can speak, Your Majesty?" Adelei asked and followed him into a lieutenant's office. The man vacated the room after a brief bow to His Majesty.

"Did he speak much?" her father asked, his eyes boring holes into the desk's dark wood.

"Javas says he was hired indirectly in the city of Drehsmä to assassinate 'one of the princesses, doesn't matter which.'" His fingers squeezed into fists. "He claims he only knows of one princess, that he doesn't know what the client meant by that. He implied that the client was impatient and decided against the treaty at the last minute."

"Do you believe him?"

"I...I'm not sure, Your Majesty. He doesn't have assassin training—I doubt he would have made it past your honor guards to be honest—but he's been...mentally prepared."

White knuckles flexed as he stretched stiff fingers. This time when he looked up, there was a coldness along the line of his chin that stretched up to meet his eyes—brown eyes almost black as no light reflected back from them, no warmth. Adelei shivered. She'd seen that look before—the look of death in another's eyes.

I used to see it in Master Bredych, before I knew what an Amaskan was. It was the look that had me hiding under my bed in fear, unsure what I'd done. Twenty years old, and I find myself wishing I could hide under my bed right now. King Leon crossed the small distance between them, his face so close to hers that their noses stood one inch apart. "Details. What did he tell you?"

"Not much. But he didn't have to, Sire. His hands are rough like a blacksmith. He's worked hard his whole life, but he lacks the muscle tone of one assassin trained. He was sent here as a last resort, because the Tribor failed. They wanted someone expendable to try. But he's never been tortured—his pain tolerance is abysmal, and he spilled information too easily, especially considering that the mental preparation should have averted that. He told us exactly what they wanted us to know and nothing more. But he said something. Something about Captain Warhammer, but it has to be a trap."

The way he watched her, she didn't want to tell him. Her father moved for the door, and Adelei stepped in the way. "Wait, Your Majesty. Please. He only mentioned her because it's what they wanted us to hear. This enemy of the crown wants to lure you in with hints about the captain. The assassin, he knows *nothing*, Sire. He won't tell us anything more." Before King Leon could interject, she continued, "This man must be killed, Your Majesty. He will tell us nothing more, but not knowing what they have done to him, he is a great danger to the crown. He could turn on a moment's notice and be an instant danger to himself and others."

Adelei unsheathed her dirk, but her father's hand reached out to grab her arm. "I would not have you do this deed—Amaskan though you may be. The royal guard will handle him."

He wanted to see if they could get more information out of the assassin. *Damn.* He was falling right into their trap. Her father's face hardened as his own fingers caressed the ceremonial eating knife at his waist.

"No, Your Majesty. Javas won't tell you anything more."

"You will not be the one to sully your hands with this filth." He leaned close enough to touch her. Adelei thought him angry until she saw the sheen in his eyes. He didn't want her to do it because she was his daughter.

"It's my duty to complete this task, Your Majesty. Is it not why you called me here? To protect the crown?"

Father and King struggled, their agonies playing across his face. "I am honor bound to carry out this execution, if for no other reason than his being a danger to the Order of Amaska."

The King won the internal struggle, but the father wasn't done. The way his worry lines bunched up, it aged him twenty years in a moment. She looked away, not wishing to cause him more pain in an already difficult situation. "Do as you will," he whispered.

She hated being there. She'd been warned that family complicated everything, and they were right.

A flash of purple in the corner of her eye betrayed her father's presence as he followed her into the cell. "Please, you must kill me. He can't find out I told you anything," Javas pleaded.

"If you don't know who hired you, how can you fear him so?" she asked, and Javas paled, his face a canvas of sickly yellows and light peaches. Another chill washed over her.

"Please, kill me now. Quickly. They are here. They are watching."

The hair on her neck stood as the air hummed, and the would-be assassin's eyes doubled in size. "Damn. Mystics," she whispered.

"What? Where?" King Leon's eyes darted around the cell, and he tripped over the chair.

Adrenaline crashed through her veins like ice water, giving her clarity and focus. Before the prisoner had done more than blink, her dirk was through his heart and out, blood running from the wound to pool on the floor beneath his corpse. She wiped her weapon clean on his cast aside clothing. The feeling of being watched vanished.

"You said he was mentally prepared? Explain."

She jumped. She'd forgotten his presence in the moment. His words were an order meant to catch her off guard. Adelei opened her mouth to answer. Then her brain caught up, and she shut her mouth just as fast. The flash of lightning across his features warned her, but she shook her head. "I'm sorry, Your Majesty, but some of what you wish to know cannot be known to you. But I will explain what I can."

"You will explain it all."

Adelei shrank inside herself. Was this the man who ordered her return? She could see why Master Bredych had complied. King Leon was a dangerous man indeed. But she couldn't give away Amaskan secrets. For all that he was her father, she couldn't betray the Order—not even for him.

"When Amaskans are trained, there are certain mental practices used to ensure that if captured in a particularly high risk job, the Amaskan can't betray the client. I've heard rumors that the Tribor use a similar technique."

"You mean they're brainwashed to protect the people at the top."

"You may call it brainwashing, though it is more complicated than that."

"So when you were sent here, were you conditioned like this? To ensure that your loyalties remained with the man who stole you from me?" The desk's wood cracked when his fist smashed into it, the wood splintering down the middle.

She didn't answer him, couldn't. The conditioning in her mind went deep—implanted since childhood, longer than most. Access to the vast library and schooling usually afforded by only the wealthiest came with a price.

Absolute loyalty.

Her doubts and fears since arriving had eroded the trusted foundation, and for a moment, she came close to betraying herself. Her mouth opened again with the words on her tongue. He must have seen her fighting, her mask slipping and cracking in places visible to him, because he gripped her shoulders and shook her. "You have information that could be vital to the job. How can you protect Margaret if you don't tell me everything you can?"

The tactic almost worked, but Adelei shook her head. "You don't need information to protect her. You aren't the protector. I can do my job without telling you a thing. I'm sorry," she said. And truly she was. While he growled in frustration, her mind screamed.

This man was her father, too. Did it mean nothing? *Master Bredych, what have you done to me?* She'd thought the conflict was that of the prodigal daughter returning to a family she barely remembered, but flashes of...something...like an odd dream, filled her mind. Master Bredych's fingerprints lay on her memories, his hands on who she was. He had messed with her memories. Her mind.

The realization brought her to her knees. Her fingers dug into the dirt floor as bile rose in her throat.

"Adelei." Her father knelt at her side. When his hand touched her shoulder, she flinched.

Memories came rushing back—her father's face as he hoisted her up on his shoulders, running through the courtyard with Margaret as they chased their loose ponies, and her mother. Her face as King Leon took Adelei from the room. "It isn't safe. I have to send you away," he'd said, and her mother had screamed until her white face was shut behind the door. Adelei remembered the Amaskans, Uncle Goefrin, and the gag's taste in her mouth. The bits and flashes from before bled through until they were real enough to touch. To smell. Adelei gagged.

"Oh Gods." she cried. "I'm swimming in memories. Whose memories? Mine? Is this who I was?" She grabbed her head between her hands, fingers pulling at her short hair. If she removed it, would she be Amaskan again?

Chaos that wanted action. Her legs fought to move, her hands sought a target, but she refused, forcing herself to remain still despite the commands racing through her brain.

"Please, what's wrong? What can I do?" asked King Leon.

Adelei's breath came in rapid gasps. "I feel like I'm breaking into pieces." She grabbed hold of his shoulders and clung to him as the room spun. "What did he do to me?"

"Who? What's wrong?" King Leon held her. "Guards."

Several rushed into the room, and he ordered them to fetch a healer. From inside the cell, Adelei could hear the dead assassin's laughter, a sharp-pitched giggling that rose and cadenced in rhythm to her pounding heart. "Master Bredych—he…he did something to my mind. He took away my memories. Who am I?" Her vision swam, though from her spinning head or tears, she didn't know.

"Am I Adelei or Iliana?" she whispered, and her father glanced at the door. She followed his line of sight and caught a glimpse of the healer standing in the doorway. His brows wrinkled as he tried to work out the newfound knowledge. Before she could do more than wave a hand in his direction, her vision went dark, and she passed out in her father's arms.

King Leon paced the length of his bedchamber, his eyes glued to the well-loved and worn carpet. It was the only place he could think to bring her without too many people seeing. Lucky for them all, the hour was very early, and few roamed the castle. "What's wrong with her?" he asked as he studied the small hole in the rug beneath his feet.

"I'm not sure. What did Master Adelei say to you before she fainted?" asked Roland, Leon's personal physician.

"Nothing that I can repeat."

Roland laid a hand on Adelei's brow, and tilted her head as he bent over her to listen to her breathe. The man listened for her heart and nodded to himself before turning back toward Leon. "I understand that there is information vital to the kingdom's safety—information I'm not meant to know—but what she said could give me a clue as to whether I'm dealing with something physical, mental, or even mystical in nature. I can't do much for her without determining that, and honestly, there's nothing physically wrong with her that I can find."

King Leon quickened his pace and kicked at the hole. "She was trying to tell me about our prisoner. She said something about being *mentally prepared*. I asked what that was, and when she tried to answer, something happened. Master Adelei grew confused and began talking about her Master doing something to her mind."

Roland cursed, an action that gave Leon pause. The healer pointed a finger at the chair near the bed. "Sit."

When Leon ignored him, the physician stood, gesturing again. "You're ill, Your Majesty. The last thing I need is for you to collapse as well, now sit."

Leon claimed the chair, but his foot tapped a solid beat on the floor. Irritating rug. Always in the way. "Catherine made this rug," he said, offhand. "What do you know of this mental conditioning?"

"All Amaskans receive it. A fail safe to make sure they don't turn on their masters and clients," Roland replied. "As far as I've ever seen, it only activates if they're captured and close to spilling vital information. Why it would trigger in Master Adelei is beyond me—certainly not usual. She has no connection to Alexander, and no need to betray the Amaskans. I mean, you weren't asking her for anything privy to the Order were you?"

"I asked her to explain the mental conditioning to me."

Roland frowned. "That in and of itself shouldn't have done anything. Not really. She would have answered without giving much detail, but certainly not disclosing anything that would cause this mental collapse." Roland studied Adelei's face and inhaled sharply. "Your Majesty, at the end, she-she said something. And now I see—is she—no, I'm not sure I wish to know."

The physician's fingers shook, and Leon pursed his lips. Adelei's skin was pale beneath her tan and her features jumbled up in either fear or pain, though he didn't know which. He ached to hold her, to return her to the carefree child he recalled in his memories. "She is my daughter, Iliana."

"How is that possible, Your Highness?"

"The Amaskans kidnapped her. Through Goefrin. The traitor told me they killed her. Captain Warhammer's the one who discovered she still lived. The Amaskans raised and trained her. I brought her home to...to protect Margaret."

"I understand the law against harboring Amaskans now." Roland's brow furrowed. "I'm no mystic. Nor am I trained in mental conditioning either, but if I had to take a guess, I'd say that her loyalty to the Amaskans must have shifted. Something made her question her loyalty. I think it snapped her mind into two pieces—one side Amaskan and the other Alexandrian."

"She mentioned that he played with her memories. I think she was recalling her time here as a child." Leon's eyes were drawn to the rug again. Damn old thing. He wished Ida was here. *She was Amaskan. Maybe she'd know what to do. Where are you, love?* "I'm to blame for this state. This is all my fault, as is everything."

Roland dug through a bag and pulled out a small stopper of liquid, which he poured into a small bowl. The physician ground up something else until he made a paste. He fed some to Adelei, and Leon asked, "Will that make her better?"

"I don't know, Sire. I'm hoping it will help her relax. Help her struggle less. Maybe that will help her come back to us, but I'm not sure."

Leon's foot ceased tapping. *Bad enough to have lost her once, but to lose her again?*

"This isn't my area, Your Majesty. I'm sorry, but it would be better to call for a mystic."

Leon wrinkled his nose at the thought. "There hasn't been a mystic in Alexander in over a hundred years—evil things set upon evil works. There has to be another way." Adelei breathed, her chest rising and falling like normal, yet she winced in pain as she slept. "Wait, Adelei—she said Prince Gamun had a mystic with him. Could he help her?"

Roland's eyes widened. "Your Majesty, if what you've told us is true and Prince Gamun seeks your control of Alexander, I don't think any mystic he brings will help us. What we need is one sworn to Sharmus, a mystical healer. I've seen the man she spoke of, Sire, and he's no healer."

"So Gamun brought something foul into my castle."

"I believe so, Sire."

"Speak of this to no one," Leon ordered, and Roland nodded. "Dammit. If only we had evidence. Something to take to

the Senate. Margaret's married to this monster and now Adelei..."
His voice cracked on her name. "Leave me."

"I'll come back later to check on her. By your leave."

Once alone, he gathered Adelei in his arms and held her head
against his chest. "You were always my favorite. So like me. I
don't know what they did to you, but come back to me. We were
just finding each other again," he whispered in her ear. Her face
was so like Margaret's that he could fool himself into believing her
a princess and not a killer. But scars marked her flesh and muscles
covered her in places they did not on Margaret, whose gentle
frame had never known battle. *Gods hope she never does. Iliana's paid
enough for them both.*

He held hands calloused from years of weapons work instead
of soft, manicured hands. The differences were subtle but enough.
And he didn't care.

She was his daughter. No matter what sins of the past, no
matter who or how many she had killed, he loved her.

King Leon removed his crown, setting it gently on the pillow
next to him. The king stepped aside for the father—the father
who held his child until he fell asleep.

CHAPTER TWENTY-ONE

Where there was shadow before, bright sun bathed the room. Brighter sun than expected when she cracked her eyes open. Well past a reasonable hour to be awake anyway. Without thinking, Margaret sat up in bed, placing bare feet to the cold stone floor before her head caught up with the motion. The pounding in her skull matched the waves of dancing in her stomach. *Last night...*

She remembered part of the feast. She remembered drinking too much. Someone talked her into another dance, and then her mind clouded over with a grey mist that refused to budge. Adelei had given her something to clear her head. She'd been sleeping, then Gamun... Heat rose to her cheeks. A quick glance to her right showed him passed out, his fingers tangled in the sheets. Her flush became anger.

Drunk and frustrated, he'd tumbled into bed. That much she remembered clearly. He hadn't wanted a wife. He'd wanted a play thing.

Margaret caught her reflection in the mirror and turned away. A stranger's face had looked back. She was changed, though truth be told, she'd expected to awake somehow wiser, if not more beautiful. Laughter bubbled at her lips, a desperate laugh as her trembling hand touched skin marred by bite marks, tender to the touch. Red and puffy, they marked the anger her "perfect prince" dealt last night.

All the stories spoke of tenderness, of love breathed into a woman's body. But that had not been the case. Not last night. She returned to the mirror and found brown hollow eyes shrunken in their too-large sockets. The bruises on her cheek bones struck a contrast that left her face more gaunt than before.

He smelled like soured wine. Her bed smelled like it as well. And as she moved shaking hands over her tender head, her skin smelled of his drunkenness.

The wine had burrowed itself into her bruises and his bite marks. People had said he was a monster; that he hunted women and girls, leaving them broken, if not dead. "And I ignored it," she whispered. "He was so perfect." Tears smeared the reflection of her battered self. *But surely Papa wouldn't have allowed me to marry a monster.* Even as she thought it, she chastised herself. Her father's wishes held little choice in the matter. Treaty marriages were for the sake of state, not love. And she had been fool enough to believe otherwise.

Margaret's cheeks flushed. Oh how they must have laughed at her. The women of the high court—the knowing looks they gave before the wedding. Her teeth chattered, and she wrapped her arms around herself.

Why hadn't Adelei stopped it? There was no one in the room but the two of them. She stood carefully and winced as she approached the door. Margaret fumbled with the lock, and the doorknob squeaked. Her fingers clenched her robe tighter about her shoulders. Meaningless against him, she supposed.

A quick peek showed Gamun remained sleeping. She bit her lip to prevent the cry of relief from escaping. When she poked her head out the door, the chair beside it was empty.

"Do you need help, Your Highness?" A servant leaned her head out of Adelei's room, and Margaret's heart raced.

"No, I was curious where Master Adelei was."

The servant averted her eyes. "I hadn't seen her yet, Your Highness. I was just going into the room to freshen it up."

Her robes couldn't hide the bruising across her face and neck; her teeth chattered enough she thought her jaw would break, and she closed the door against the servant's knowing look. Margaret stumbled into the bathing chamber with its stone tub. Dials above it opened the torrent of water. It was here that her lady-in-waiting found her curled up in the cold water. Nisha's eyes traveled over bite marks and bruises, welts swollen in the water. It was bad enough to be seen in such a state by anyone, but worse that Nisha said nothing as she gathered up towels and the robe from the floor to be taken to the scullery. Nisha helped Margaret out of the dirty water and wrapped blue towels around her body. Gentle hands dried her and treated her wounds with aloe salve.

Margaret tried to step into her chemise, but her muscles refused to move in the directions her mind dictated. It was only with Nisha's careful hands that she was able to don more than a simple bathrobe, and even then, her corset bit into irritated wounds. She winced every time she breathed, and she bit her bottom lip as she gripped Nisha's arm for support.

"You haven't said anything about any of this."

"Beatings are common place in the lower class. Nothing I haven't seen before. When my mother was the earl's mistress, he beat her daily. At least until he got her with child. After his wife died, and he married my mom, things changed."

The nonchalance with which it was stated, startled Margaret. *How many of the servants in this castle have suffered the likes of this? Why has Papa done nothing to stop it?* Then she froze, eyes wide.

"What is it, Your Highness?"

"My-my father. He cannot see this." Margaret stood too fast, and bruises assaulted her with sharp, painful protest. "Maybe I can say that I'm ill. I was up too late last night with too much drink. That is expected of us after all, right?" Margaret moved with slow determination toward the table and stool where her powders and makeups lay strewn.

Her clothing would cover most of his handiwork, but she would need all of her skill to cover the bruises on her face and neck. Brush in hand, she set to work in recreating her face, covering the purple bruises with the pale skin and pinked cheeks she normally wore.

"You can barely see it at all, Your Highness." The woman bowed and backed out of the room.

Silence. Margaret lurched upright on the stool. The lack of snores told her what Nisha had not. He was awake.

His shadow fell across the floor, and her throat seized up as fear trampled across her body. Gamun touched a hand to the bruise on her cheek, barely visible beneath the makeup. "This is good work," he said, still stroking the bruise. "I can't have you seen in public looking like a walking eggplant, can I now?"

She pulled away from him, pain in each step as she crossed the room to her reading chair. Margaret gave it a bewildered stare. Her mind held no interest in the books before her, but only sought to flee her husband's caress. He waited to see what movement she would take next as his look was upon her. Margaret swallowed hard before she retreated to the bedroom door.

"Where are you going?"

"I would speak with my father this morning. Master Adelei has not been seen since last night."

This time, she didn't imagine the breath on the back of her neck. Gamun came up behind her and wrapped a possessive arm around her waist. His lips pressed against her ear as he whispered. "Maybe the little princess-turned-assassin found a worthy opponent. But feel free to go check on her."

Margaret tugged helplessly against the arm encircling her, and he laughed as he released her. She ignored the cries of her bruises as she rushed past several stunned guards. Their footsteps followed her until she reached her father's suite. His guards stood aside, and she breathed a sigh of relief once in the safety of her father's sitting room.

Her fingers tucked a stray hair back into place before she knocked lightly on the door to his private chambers. The muffled speech of two men reached her and soon after, her father's face peered out at her. "I thought—oh, what can I do for you, poppet? I didn't expect to see you this day." His frame filled most of the doorway as he held it open a crack.

She stepped forward, but her father held the door in place. "Papa, what's going on? Why can't I—you aren't entertaining a woman, are you?" Her cheeks grew warm, and she pulled the high-necked overcoat tighter across her shoulders.

"No, no—I'm just in the middle of something with Michael and—"

"Perfect. I need to talk to you both. It's urgent, Papa."

King Leon stepped away from the door with a sigh, and she squeezed through the opening. Bruises brushed against the door's wood frame, and she bit her lip to keep from making a sound.

"Now what is it that you needed to tell...?" His words trailed off at Margaret's shocked expression. Adelei lay in her father's bed, two healers at her side. Her stomach twisted like a river.

"He said she found a worthy opponent. By the Gods, I didn't think he meant it." Her words brought four sets of eyes to her face, and then everything moved at once. Healers rushed to her side and her father's mouth moved frantically, though she heard none of the words. "She can't die. Who will p-protect me?" Margaret cried out. All four voices stopped.

"Your Highness, are you hurt? That bruise..." Roland reached for her cheek, but Margaret stumbled away from his hand.

"I-I'm fine. What's wrong with my sister?" The moment she uttered the word, her hand flew to her mouth. "I'm sorry, Father, I didn't mean—"

"I didn't hear anything, Your Highness," said Captain Fenton. "None of this is my business. With your leave?"

King Leon nodded. "Not a word, Michael."

The veins on her father's face stood out against the pallor of his skin. "What did he do to you?"

The words were a whip, and she flinched. The healers busied themselves with fluffing Adelei's pillow. "It's nothing. What happened to Adelei?"

"She is in a deep sleep or coma, Your Highness," Roland answered.

"Did h-he do this?" She didn't want to ask the question, but she had to know. Margaret brushed past her father to sit on the bed beside her sister. Both of them—two little girls sitting on this same bed as their mother braided their hair. *Now we're older, and here we are again. Only it's two healers tending you. What happened?* Worry lines decorated Adelei's young face, and Margaret tried to smooth them out with a shaking hand.

"This isn't from Gamun," King Leon said, "But this is." He reached out to touch the bruise on her cheek, but she pulled away. "What did he do?"

Her father's curt words threatened to open the tidal wave beneath her façade. She clenched her fist in her skirts. "If he didn't hurt Adelei, why is she in a coma? How long will she stay in it?"

"Your Highness, Master Adelei has suffered a mental breakdown," Roland said, "And we don't know how long or why. Are you sure you are all right?"

Margaret shifted in her seat, away from their stares and questions. *Her face looks pained. Why does this sleep hurt her? Is she dreaming?* Her father's hand on her shoulder shouldn't have startled her, shouldn't have made her insides scream with the need to flee, but they did. When she met his eyes, only concern and love reached out from them. The battle against tears was lost, and she fell into her father's embrace.

It hurt when he held her; his arms resting across her tender shoulders smarted, but she needed his strength. "I'll be fine. But I need Adelei. Who will protect me now?"

"He's a dead man." Her father spit the words from between his clenched teeth.

"You can't, Papa. He's my husband. Think of the treaty. Besides, he only did this because I—"

"Your Highness, is that what he told you?" Roland asked, and when she nodded, her father's grip became too much. Margaret tore away from his embrace.

"Don't even tell me you think this your fault." The nearby vase on the table beside him leapt from its perch when his fist slammed on to the table. "Surely this should be against the Thirteen. Where is justice now?"

"In a coma," she whispered.

"I'll have him hanged."

"Papa, why? Because he—" She couldn't say it. The words made it real.

"Yes, by the Gods, yes."

His rage frightened her, but Nisha's words rang in her ears. "Papa, if this angers you so, why have you done nothing to stop it from happening in your own castle? Your own kingdom?"

"Explain yourself."

Margaret repeated Nisha's words to him, but he seemed unperturbed. "You know how servants talk, poppet. Besides, what happened to Nisha was in Shad, not in Alexander. You don't know for certain these events have happened to her, let alone something similar in this castle."

"And you don't know that they haven't. I've never given a single thought to Nisha's family. I don't look twice at my handmaidens. I've never thought about the servants. Why should I? How closely do you look at those who attend you, Father? For all that the Thirteen exists to protect all people, it surely does more protecting the highborn than anyone else."

Just the thought of Nisha watching her mother beat—the way I—poor thing. No one should have to go through that. Ever. Not when I'm Queen. Margaret closed her eyes a moment. Gamun's strong hands held the straps, and she shuddered.

"When I'm Queen, no one will fear like that." She'd expected praise for her wisdom, but King Leon's eyes held only sympathy as he glanced again to her cheek. Margaret cursed his ability to make her feel so like a child.

"At least let the healers take a look at you."

"Who is going to protect me? Adelei's been the only thing between me and death this past week, so who will stop these Tribor now?"

"Captain Fenton is in charge of that. He will have the guards on alert for any attacks. In fact, he had an interesting idea, though I'm not sure it would work. Especially now."

"Now that I'm all bruised up?" Her father winced, and Margaret's mouth fell open when the thought caught up to her. "You wanted me to pose as her."

She didn't know why it made her angry, only that it did. *She goes into a coma and even still manages to ruin my life in some way. Next thing you know, they'll have me running around attacking people or something.*

Irrational anger was swallowed down when she observed her sister's motionless body. *She'd do this for me. She said she'd protect me, even if she was killed.*

"Captain Fenton thought if you walked around like her, people would think nothing of it. They wouldn't notice her disappearance."

"Your Majesty, her bruises actually might work to the benefit of us all. Who would the people expect to wear bruises? The princess or the Amaskan?" Roland asked.

Her father's fists clenched the blanket beneath him into wads of satin, and Margaret laid a hand on his. "I'll do it," she whispered.

"Poppet, you don't have to."

"Yes, I do. She'd do it for me."

Roland removed a jar from one of his many bags. "I have something that may help you walk with less pain, if Your Highness would allow?"

Margaret cast a hesitant glance at her father. "Papa, could you leave us for a bit?" His jaw clenched, but he acquiesced.

"No more false bravado, Your Highness. Let me see what I can do for your injuries." The healer helped her out of the overcoat, and once she was down to her chemise, he rubbed salve on the bruises that peppered her legs and arms.

An eggplant indeed.

He was gentle, but despite his healer's hands, just his touch on her back left her clenching her fingers around the quilt. "Your Highness, it may not be my place, but as your father's healer, it's my job to oversee the royal family's health. These wounds are not against the Thirteen, but if he...took you by force, that would be. Charges would be brought up—"

"No."

"But His Majesty and Master Adelei have been seeking evidence against him. If he did something to lend evidence to his being a monster, then—"

Margaret spun so quickly that Roland dropped the jar of salve, its glass bouncing harmlessly off the rug where it hit the stone floor and cracked. "Listen to me, this man is my husband. I did not marry a monster."

Tears welled up again, and she brushed them aside with the back of her hand. "It is my duty as future Queen to keep this treaty intact, else we will plunge into war yet again. I provoked him. Once he loves me, I know I can keep it from happening again, so no, I will not hand myself over like a piece of cattle so the Boahim Senate can ogle at the stupidity of me. Let alone send the Little Dozen into war. As my healer, you will keep this information to yourself. You will not share it with my father, do you understand?" When he nodded, she said, "Now help me back into this... No one else need see me."

Once dressed, she retreated to her rooms, walking the halls rather slowly. It wasn't the bruises that drove her to mince her steps, but *him*. The rooms were empty, and with a sigh, she eased herself into a chair before closing her eyes. The strength left her.

She was such a fool. She played at being Queen, but what did she know of it? She certainly didn't know how she was going to impersonate Adelei. What was it Adelei had said? *Take larger steps? Look around a lot?*

She opened her eyes, and Prince Gamun sat before her on one knee. Margaret thought it a dream at first. He smiled at her, a smile that held love and affection, not malice or hatred. The sun bounced off his damp hair, casting a halo about him. The smell of her soaps hit her nose, and her smile faltered as she bolted upright in her chair.

"I'm so sorry, my lady. It was not my intention to startle you, only you looked so peaceful just now."

The shift in his demeanor confused her. She scooted to the edge of her chair and glanced at the door. When he didn't laugh or attempt to stop her, she frowned. "What you did last night—"

"Was inexcusable, I know. I am deeply sorry. Sometimes I don't know what I'm doing. I drink, and it's like this other person takes over. They call me a monster. Maybe I am."

He hung his head down, rubbing his face with damp hands. Softly spoken words. The words of another man. She reached out to touch his face and tilted it up to look on him better. "Are you truly sorry?"

"I am, Your Highness."

"Then I forgive you. We won't speak of it again," she answered. "I will help you—we can mull the wine, water it down. There are surely herbs a healer would know to help—"

"No healers. Just you. Only you can help me, my lady. Only my perfect princess can save me."

When he wrapped his arms around her waist, she couldn't help but twitch, muscles tense despite their shared words. She didn't doubt his sincerity, not while he held her so gently. Margaret held him like one would hold a child as he repeatedly begged for forgiveness.

"I forgive you," she said, and his smile pierced the room like sunshine.

My perfect prince.

Gamun left.

For where, Margaret didn't care. While she forgave him and believed his sincerity, she needed him gone if she was going to impersonate Adelei. Nisha helped Margaret dress in her sister's clothes. The first time she'd worn the sepier's garb, Margaret had hated it. But with the bruises aching across her body, they allowed a comfort her own clothes did not.

"How do I look?"

Nisha scowled. "Like a ruffian, Your Highness. We need to tuck your hair back though. Your face looks too much like you."

Her lady-in-waiting braided Margaret's waist-length hair and wrapped it into a tight bun. The head scarf covered her head, though a wisp managed its way free and Margaret tucked it under. "Is this wise, Your Highness?"

"If I want to remain safe it is. You wouldn't understand. Trust me." When Margaret stood, the dirk knocked her on the knee, and she winced. "Go check the door."

Nisha poked her head outside and waved Margaret over. Instead of the smaller steps her bruises allowed, Margaret forced a gangly pace. "Tell no one where I've gone," she whispered to Nisha, and fled the sitting room.

One of the royal guards barely kept the smirk off his face at her movements. "Master Adelei, do you be needin' a healer? Too much to drink last night?" he asked, and Margaret scowled.

My steps are drunkenly. How does she walk like this? Her frustration lent itself to her scowl, and he apologized before standing back at attention. Adjusting her gait was harder than wearing the uniform. Even with the small changes, her steps were sloppy and exaggerated. By the time she reached the first floor, she gave up and continued with the idea she was recovering from a night of too much ale. Rather than approach anyone in particular, Margaret stood in the entrance hall and glared as people passed. Like Adelei had told her, *dart your eyes about.* Margaret's didn't rest on anything in particular.

After ten minutes, boredom drew her away from the entrance hall. The courtyard smelled of spring and roses and all the things Margaret loved, but she figured even Adelei had to enjoy the outdoors sometime. She claimed an empty bench in the sunshine. Three minutes passed before Lady Millicent approached. At first, Margaret flinched and her heart raced. *She'll know I'm not Adelei. What do I do?* But the lady passed after a brief nod in Margaret's direction.

The roses had bloomed early, and several ladies of the court knelt to smell them as they talked. As they passed, several turned their noses up at her and hurried their steps. Anyone who passed displayed similar reactions. Their responses helped harden Margaret's expression, but inside, it hurt.

A shadow crossed over her shoulder. "May I?"

Without thinking, Margaret nodded, and Lady Millicent sat on the bench beside her. "I was wondering if you could tell me something, Your Highness?"

"What is it?" Margaret asked. A skipped rock later, she gasped. "Lady Millicent, you mustn't speak—"

"What's happened to your sepier?" the lady whispered. "If I may be blunt, Your Highness, I wouldn't dream of divulging this information. But if you'll allow, I may be able to help."

"How did you know it was me?"

"You aren't a fighter."

Margaret's face grew warm. "But how could you possibly know this from my sitting in the gardens?"

Lady Millicent poked Margaret in the arm. "Easy. You didn't try to remove my finger just now. You don't react like an Amaskan."

"And what would you know of Amaskans?"

The lady remained silent and pursed her lips. "Your Highness, please. Tell me what's happened to your sepier."

Margaret glanced around, but the majority of people in the courtyard had found reason to be elsewhere. She and Lady Millicent were alone. "She's fallen ill. Something I don't understand, and my father won't speak on it. But there is danger, and to show we are without our sepier—"

"—Is a great weakness." Lady Millicent pursed her lips. "Nisha does good work. I'd almost believe that bruise to be real."

Her back ached sitting on the stone bench, and the sun irritated her eyes. Still, Margaret waved off the comment as well as the pain. "She knows tricks from the Shadians of how to paint a face quite accurately. Plus, we had help from my father's physician."

Lady Millicent accepted the answer, though she stared at Margaret's cheek a moment longer before she nodded. "If you want to fool people, stop expecting them to notice you. To the people of your court, Master Adelei is beneath them. She's a murderer and dangerous. Notice how members of your court have treated you since you arrived in the courtyard."

"They fled."

"Indeed. People are afraid of your sepier, as they should be."

"People didn't treat Captain Warhammer that way," said Margaret.

"But they did. With her as close to His Majesty as she's rumored to be, there was some level of respect. Fearful respect, but respect nonetheless."

The lady waited to see if Margaret would let slip anything about the rumors, but Margaret merely shrugged. *The things these gossipers will come up with. Next they'll be saying I'm already with child.* The thought tensed her muscles, and her bruises cried out in protest. *Delorcini, do not bless me with life. Not until I know...if I have indeed married a monster.*

"Are you well?" Lady Millicent asked, and Margaret swallowed a lump in her throat.

"I am, my lady. Just surprised. I don't think I realized how much Master Adelei is hated here." Or how very much alone she was.

A group of people scurried by. Not even Lady Millicent's presence granted them calm. One duchess pointedly whispered about "consorting with such people" as the group passed, and Margaret made note to speak to the woman the next time they met. Lady Millicent excused herself shortly after, and Margaret remained alone again in her own garden.

Her thoughts drifted. Margaret recalled living with her sister, playing with her and hiding from their nursemaids and tutors in the castle's hallways. But then there was the horse ride. Her mother's death. Events grew fuzzy, and when they shifted again, Iliana was gone from her memories.

For a while, Margaret had thought her sister little more than a dream, but now that Adelei was here, Margaret's head spun. Another shadow passed over her, and when she looked up from the past, Prince Gamun stood beside her. Margaret pulled the head scarf closer, trying to hide the bruise across her cheek. He stared across the rose bushes with a grin on his face.

"It's a beautiful day. Spring in this country always amazes me," he said without looking at her.

Margaret scowled.

"You disagree, Master Adelei?"

She tilted the bruised side of her face away from him, feigning interest in the roses. "The spring is nice, but I prefer the heat of Sadai." Still too high a voice. She needed to lower it, more manly she supposed.

He placed a hand on her shoulder, and she scraped her knuckles along the bench to keep from wincing. "Have you given any more thought to my offer?"

"I don't know what you mean."

"Come now, wouldn't it serve justice more to protect the citizens?" Margaret tucked her hands behind her back and balled them into fists.

"The work I do does protect them."

Gamun sighed. "You've sat in the council meetings. Have you heard His Majesty's excuses for seizing land from the helpless? They *give* him the land—"

"My—" she bit off the word *father*, but he continued without her.

"—Surely you don't believe such a lie."

"Better than what you speak of. Spinning falsehoods and fear."

"Adelei, when have I ever lied to you?" He caressed her cheek, and she tried not to shiver at his touch. "You and I together, the things we could do—"

Margaret couldn't maintain her composure and spun around to face him. His hands stroked her jawline and up the other cheek until they found the bruise. "What is this?" Gamun scrambled back. "What game are you playing, Margaret?"

"My prince, I-I wanted to see what the world is like through a sepier's eyes," she lied and reached out for him. "I apologize for my deception. If I understand what life is like for those in my kingdom, then I can better serve them as Queen. Would you not agree?"

"Will you pose next as a stablehand?" Anger flashed across his features as he struggled for control. Eyelids eclipsed dark eyes and when he opened them, her prince had returned to her. "I'm sorry, my love. You caught me off guard," he said as he bent down to kiss her hands. "You really do make a very good sepier."

"I hope not. This life doesn't suit me one bit, and everyone today has been so rude. They hate Master Adelei."

He laughed at her genuine surprise. "She's a killer. Of course she's hated."

The frown on Margaret's face faltered. "But you mentioned an offer. What offer have you made to my sepier?"

"I asked her to become my sepier as well, but openly, as the Amaskan she is. Maybe if people saw our strength, yours and mine, and knew that we held such dangerous allies, people who would do evil would think twice about visiting it upon this kingdom."

"Really? You wish this?"

Gamun took her hand, and a passing dignitary coughed as he passed. "I do."

When her prince gently kissed her, she smiled against his lips. *He means to change. I must make Adelei and my father see. He's not The Monster. He's not.*

But he is *lying to me.*

Leon watched Adelei breathe as his physician wiped her brow with an herb-soaked cloth. "I could order you sentenced for treason," he whispered.

He wished the man would flinch or show some bit of remorse, but Roland continued wiping her brow as if everything between the two men were perfectly normal. "I would tell you if I could, Your Highness, but it's my job to take care of your daughter's health as well. If she's sworn me to secrecy, there is little I can tell you no matter how much you glare at me."

"Stubbornness must run in the family."

At first Leon thought Margaret returned from her venture, but the voice was too low and roughened. His eyes flicked down to Adelei's body. Her eyes, though groggy, followed his paces. "Sharmus' blessing."

"How do you feel, Adelei? What is the last thing you remember?" Roland asked.

She blinked a few times and sat up even though the healer tried to prevent it. "I feel a bit wobbly, like I've been drugged. Where am I? What's happened?"

"You're in your father's bedchamber. What's the last thing you remember?"

Adelei's brows furrowed in concentration, and a cascade of worry lines made their way across her young face. "I was having a conversation with you, Your Majesty. And I was explaining the Amaskan conditioning. What did they do to me? My own father. He played with my mind."

"You mean the man who raised you?" asked Roland.

Leon paced the floor in front of his bed, shoulders hunched. He ached to hug her, to hold her and tell her everything was going to be all right. Like he had when she was but a small child. Tears rose in her brown eyes that pled for Leon to deny what she said, but he couldn't. Adelei ran her fingers over the well-worn quilt, its blue and green plaid pattern one his Catherine had woven just before Iliana's birth. He'd forgotten Catherine had made it.

"Mother made this," Adelei whispered. Her fingers buried themselves in the fabric. "Everything in my life has been a lie, hasn't it? They raised me as a weapon. To get to you."

Leon stiffened, then sat hard on the bench at the foot of the bed, his legs no longer supporting his weight. "This conditioning—I thought it was just to protect the Amaskan Order. Could they order my death from afar?"

"If I understand it correctly, the mental conditioning keeps Amaskans calm during situations that normally wouldn't illicit a calm response. It can also keep them from talking, from giving away secrets that could harm the Order, is that correct?" Adelei nodded and the healer continued, "If it's hypnosis or brainwashing, they could easily plant suggestions for further action, though I would think it to require activation. Can you explain why you think they wanted you to kill?"

Adelei swallowed. "When we were talking, something clicked in my head. Like a candle suddenly lit. I could remember." Upturned eyes sought Leon's as she blinked back tears. "You, Mom, Margaret. Being taken away.... Having those memories back—Bredych lied to me. He kept me from you. I wanted to protect you, but the Amaskan in me said you were a danger to the job. I needed to kill you immediately to protect the Order."

A chill crept over Leon as she spoke. There was an honesty in what she said, no mask between him and his daughter. "My legs and arms, they moved on their own—I could barely control myself. I thought I was actually going to kill you. But I didn't want to. You must believe me," she pled.

Leon brushed past Roland's outstretched arm and took her hand. "I do."

"I made myself stay still. I refused to follow orders." She exhaled as if the words took great effort, and her shoulders slumped forward.

They had sent a weapon into his kingdom, told him she would protect Margaret. *But they placed a weapon within her that would destroy me if I got too close. Or if she did. She remembered enough to care. To think on me as a father again.*

But the pain. He had never wanted to hurt her. He touched her quilt-covered foot, patting it gently. "I'm glad that you chose not to kill me," he said and forced a slight laugh.

"But you're worried. I can see it. I'm a weapon we have no control over."

Leon said nothing to his daughter. *If she's a danger to this kingdom, she must be destroyed.* The voice inside his mind was that of

King, and he shook his head. *No, I cannot. I won't. Surely there's another way.*

He looked on Roland. "Can conditioning of this sort be broken?"

"That's what I was saying. If the conditioning is truly just suggestive, it's possible. Knowing the Amaskans, probably difficult as all Thirteen Hells, but possible. Problem is, I'm no mystic. Master Adelei, do the Amaskans employ mystics?"

"Yes, but only as healers. Sharmus' path." Her furrowed brow matched her father's. "I shouldn't have been able to tell you that. Huh."

"Does that mean the conditioning is broken?" Leon asked.

"I don't think so, but that's interesting. This isn't my area, Your Highness. I heal bodies, not minds." Roland stood and gathered up his supplies, which he tucked into several plain bags. "I should go. There isn't much more I can do here, and I'm sure you two have other things to discuss. Try to rest, Master Adelei. We don't know whether the conditioning is broken, and..."

"And you don't know if I'm dangerous."

Roland tilted his head toward the door. "I'll be right back," Leon said, and he followed his physician outside into his study.

The physician twisted his mouth into a long grimace. "She's dangerous, Your Highness. I know that's not what you wish to hear, but she could lose control at any moment and kill you or me before we even blinked."

"How likely is that to happen?"

"Very. She's fighting it for control even now."

Leon leaned against the door frame, his body feeling every day of his fifty-five years. "What caused her to fall into the coma?"

"I think, well, this is only speculation. But I think she chose her loyalty to you over the Amaskans, which triggered conflict where there shouldn't have been one. Maybe it's built into the conditioning—put the assassin into a coma before they can betray their people. I don't know. But I would think that's what caused this. Either way, we don't know which she'll choose if put in that position again, which makes her very dangerous."

"She'll choose her family. I know her, Roland. No matter what they put in her head, she's still my daughter."

Roland shifted from one foot to the other. "I hope you're right, Sire. For all of our sakes." With that, the man bowed and left, leaving Leon alone in his study. He stuck his head outside the room and spoke to the nearest guard. "I want the guards in the royal hall doubled until I say otherwise. Inform Captain Fenton immediately."

When King Leon returned to his bedchambers, Adelei was already out of bed. The old bed robe clung to her slight frame as she stood bent over a trunk. Adelei scowled as she ruffled through it. His wardrobe stood open, as did the screen to his bathing chambers. Leon cleared his throat, and she flinched. Her eyes were wide for a moment, and then identifying him, she relaxed. "You don't happen to recall where my clothes might be?"

"They aren't here."

"And why exactly is that?"

"Margaret's wearing them. We thought it best that no one know you were ill, so she's—"

"—Pretending to be me. Gods help us." Adelei laughed, though the sound was strained as she paced across the same rug worn thin by his own tread. "How long was I out?"

"Luckily, you were only out for two days, but that was long enough. I fear for Margaret's safety."

The pacing stopped as she turned sharp eyes on him, and he felt like a bird in the line of feline sight. "Has something happened? Tell me."

He relayed the events of the past two days, or what little he knew of them. She didn't move when he finished, just stood stone still as she stared off in the distance.

She's fighting it even now. Roland's words boxed in his skull as he watched his daughter.

"If we could get her to talk more about what happened, it may be enough evidence to have the treaty nullified and the prince brought up before the Boahim Senate. But we still won't know who's behind the attacks. As much as I don't like the risk, my opinion would be to hold tight. Let me refocus and see if he and the Shadian family are behind everything."

"Won't that leave Margaret exposed?"

"I'll do my best to protect her while I search for evidence, but have Michael double the guards just in case."

He didn't tell her it had already been done and not for the reasons she thought.

She will pick her family. The Order will lose this fight. But even as she resumed her pacing, his stomach clenched in knots. *Admit it, old man, you don't trust her—not the Amaskan part of her anyway. And it eats at you to admit it, or even think about what might have to happen if you're wrong.* He didn't voice his concerns to her though.

The King knew better.

CHAPTER TWENTY-TWO

The idea of forgiveness wasn't a new concept to Adelei. She'd forgiven the bully, Min. After the fight that day, Adelei's busted nose wasn't the only thing to heal as the two became friends. In part, she'd even forgiven her birth father. But watching a bruised Margaret idolize the Monster was enough to set her nerves on edge and then some.

She swore he hadn't meant it. "It was the drink," she had said while holding his hand.

Almost as bad as claiming she had asked for it. Adelei worked her jaw as the couple put on quite the performance. Margaret's strained smile was tarnished compared to the one Gamun paraded around. Smashing his face into the nearby wall sounded like an excellent idea. Again, and again. And again.

The royal couple prepared for their first state dinner while Adelei waited with less and less patience.

When Adelei had first appeared in the sitting room, only the number of guards in the room had kept Margaret from rushing to Adelei's side. Gamun, on the other hand, paled and refused to acknowledge her presence.

Margaret chattered about the gowns the women of the high court would be wearing until the group reached the great hall's entrance. Adelei stood behind her sister as they awaited the announcement of their arrival. If Adelei had had it her way, she would have gone first, but not even she could convince King

Leon the risk was worth an "incident." Damned politics and their status dictations.

The page called out the names of the royal family. Adelei was merely *Their Highnesses' Sepier.*

Guests and dignitaries rose as Margaret and Gamun took their seats on the platform where King Leon waited. Adelei stood behind Margaret while Captain Fenton stood behind His Majesty. The majority of those present welcomed the couple with enthusiastic applause. But half a dozen heads down the long table, Lady Millicent tapped her fingers together three times before she returned them to her lap. A few other faces withheld their lack of enthusiasm long enough to be polite. The great hall's walls were lined with guards, and behind the platform, the honor guard swelled to impressive numbers. *A full show of force tonight.*

The royal couple joined the high court at the table. The wedding feast had been a smaller affair, and even it swelled in numbers. But the couple's first state dinner brought in the majority of nobility in Alexander, ambassadors to the Little Dozen kingdoms, and anyone who knew someone enough to gain or bribe a seat. Tables lined the floor and were wedged into every possible corner. Several benches bumped right up against the central square set aside for entertainment, and the musicians' backsides sat inches from the backs of those eating.

Supper was served and the wine flowed, as did the tongues. Those sixteen seated with the royal couple chatted mostly of trivial topics such as fashion or family bloodlines, but Lady Millicent met Adelei's glance head on, her voice carrying slightly over the din of voices. "I do worry about the storm that's coming. From the east they say. A foul wind indeed. I worry it might do harm to the people outside the castle walls, people like our Captain Warhammer. No one likes nasty weather."

"Why would you concern yourself with a retired captain, my lady?" Gamun asked as he stabbed a piece of venison with his knife.

"Captain Warhammer has been of great use to this kingdom. I'd not see her harmed," said Lady Millicent, who glanced over Gamun's head to stare pointedly at Adelei.

The prince stifle a false yawn as he looked over his shoulder. "Ah yes, the sepier. Master Adelei, what do you think of all this?"

"The captain seems quite confident and able, but ill weather can catch even the best off guard."

"I would think it important to check in, but perhaps the captain has found someone more interesting to occupy her time." Gamun shrugged and turned his attention to the ladies across the table. King Leon took a long swallow of his wine. Adelei caught the glint in his eyes before he hid it behind a cough. She stepped away from the table and leaned closely to Michael's ear. "I think Captain Warhammer's in serious danger. Have you heard from her yet?"

He shook his head. "Not recently. There was word a while back. A short message that said she was making good time toward the border, but that was before King Leon called for her to return. Do you take what Lady Millicent has said seriously?"

"I do. She has been a reliable source before, and I've little reason to doubt her. Besides, the assassin mentioned that the man who hired him was seeking her. To kill her. I thought it nothing more than a trap, but now..."

"I'm sure the captain is fine." Michael returned to the task of watching nothing at all.

He didn't believe her. He was concerned, but something had changed. Adelei peered out across the crowd. Not one guard at the walls watched the bulk of the guests. Instead they watched the table with the royal family. She turned on her heel to count the honor guard and stopped at twenty.

Michael followed her movements as she walked the long table's length, and she caught the honor guard doing the same when they thought she wouldn't notice.

They weren't just there to guard against assassins; they were there to guard against one in particular. Adelei.

King Leon returned her stare with a slight nod. She wanted to be indifferent, but a small knot in the center of her gut told her that despite her better judgment, she cared, and she swore under her breath.

Quiet interrupted her thoughts. Those seated at the long table waited for her. "What?"

"I asked if you had someone back home, or whether it was forbidden to Amaskans." Prince Gamun simpered at her as his fingers traced the condensation built up on his goblet. When he took a swallow of wine, Margaret's smile faltered.

"It is not forbidden, no, but it's unusual." Adelei refused to look at the bastard. If she did, she'd seize his knife and end him for the fading bruise on her sister's cheek.

"So you are Amaskan." The words were from some lord further down the table.

"Formerly."

"I didn't think such a thing was possible," said Lady Millicent.

"It's not," said Adelei. She noted the wine glass in Gamun's hand as he took another swallow. *Look somewhere else. Anywhere but him.*

Margaret grew pale under the pounds of makeup used to poorly cover her bruises. No one said a word about it—the entire table of highborns prattling on as if it were completely normal for their princess to be sporting such a mark. He was going to pay for that bruise. And each and every bruise unseen.

She flinched when Gamun laughed. "Come now, you completely dodged my first question, Master Adelei. Anyone you're sweet on back home? Or are your blades all you need to keep you warm at night?"

Several women tittered nervously at his boldness. "No one, Your Highness," said Adelei. The women gazed longingly at him. They flirted with their lashes, with the turn of a shoulder or the purse of their lips. Not a single one of them knew what game he was playing.

Adelei spent the rest of the meal on a blade's edge, waiting for him to make a move or mess up. But the prince smiled his way through dinner, completely ignoring her as he wooed the women at the table. Much to Margaret's distress, he ignored her just as much, and as the wine flowed, so did his mouth.

"Do you miss your family back in Shad, Your Highness?" The countess who asked this wore makeup as colorful as Margaret's bruises. She fluttered her long lashes at the prince and toyed with the beetle-sized ruby on her finger.

"I thought I would miss the women of my father's court, but the ones here are so fascinating and beautiful that I find I miss very little at all." Gamun laughed and waited for the rest of the lengthy table to join him. Margaret was not alone in her silence.

When the servants rushed in to clear the remains of dinner, some of the tables crowding the stage area were pushed aside. Musicians struck an upbeat piece, and Prince Gamun escorted a rather stiffly moving Margaret to the floor.

Adelei felt for her sister. Watching the bastard flirt with everything with legs at a dinner celebrating their new marriage was disgusting, if not embarrassing, and yet Adelei understood the audience's ambivalence. It was a marriage based on a treaty. No one expected the prince to love Margaret, no one except Margaret. Poor thing didn't understand that she wasn't his type. He liked things with spirit, things that could be broken, and Margaret wasn't a fighter.

Margaret was rescued from a second dance with her husband by King Leon. The Shadian ambassador shadowed Gamun. When he caught Adelei watching him, he retreated to the crowds and was lost amongst the sea of color.

"He's unhappy because he can't stop me from dancing with all the pretty women," a voice at her elbow said, and Adelei faced Prince Gamun. If she forgot herself, she could believe his charismatic grin which was a shade shy of genuine. His hand locked around her elbow, and she held her breath. "Do me the honor of a dance."

Adelei dug in her heels. "I'm busy."

"I won't accept a no." He leaned close to her ear. "After all, I'm supposed to dance with all highborn present. It's only good manners that you honor me with a dance as well."

His whispered words hadn't caught the attention of anyone else and out of curiosity, she acquiesced. Several guards moved with her, staying within a few steps' reach.

"Only one dance. I have a job to do." His only response was laughter, which carried across the hall. People noticed who Gamun chose as his dance partner. From five couples away, Margaret's voice rang out, a high pitched whine which sharpened as it rose.

"Ah yes, it seems my darling bride is none too happy to see us together. I do believe her to be jealous. Excellent." Prince

Gamun gripped her waist tighter as he matched the diamond patterned dance steps.

Adelei barely kept up with his rapid pace as the dance intensified. She lost track of Margaret seven steps in, but when she whipped her head around to search for her sister, the song increased tempo and his grip tightened. Sweat beaded on her brow, and Margaret's voice reached her. *Shrill sister, ten steps back.*

The song called for an exchange of partners halfway through. Adelei came face to face with Margaret and the King. When Gamun refused the exchange, several folks bumped into Margaret. One constant in an expanse of moving stars. When the princess resumed her dance, she spent too much time watching Gamun and not enough on her footing. "She's going to leave His Majesty with broken feet," said Gamun as he whisked Adelei closer to the middle of the floor.

He flicked his eyes in Margaret's direction. "I wasn't behind the attack on her."

"Why should I believe that? You've already made it known you sent the Tribor after me."

"My father, not me." She rolled her eyes. "Think about it, Adelei. I wanted this treaty to succeed. To get into Alexander where I can do more to prevent the egregious overuse of power by His Majesty. Why would I try to kill my own wife and break the treaty? Why not have her killed beforehand and be done with it? That is, assuming I wanted her dead."

"And the little girl?"

It was the first time he misstepped. The flash of anger across his face surprised her, and he squeezed her fingers too hard. "She was my niece. A favorite of mine."

"So you grew tired of her and broke her?"

Gamun halted his steps completely. "She was not some plaything, Master Adelei," he snapped. "Tasha was the child of my dead sister, and someone I'd sworn to protect. I didn't kill her, and when I find whoever did, they will die very, very slowly."

"You're mourning." His focus shifted on her when she spoke.

"Did you think me the monster rumors make me out to be? I thought better of you, Master Adelei. Even I have people I care about, people I'm willing to die to protect. Can you say the same about yourself? Who exactly does an ex-Amaskan have?"

The conflict rumbled under the surface as the mental conditioning screamed to answer, but Adelei clenched her jaw and refused. "I have people who love me. And those I love in return," she whispered, and he frowned. "Besides, you did try to kill my sister, remember? On her wedding night."

His shoulders sagged. "It was the drink. I have apologized for my behavior to Her Highness and earned her forgiveness."

"I'd be a fool to believe that."

"Love makes fools of us all," he murmured.

The knot in Adelei's stomach grew. She studied the well-preserved mask for signs of cracking and found none. He was like two people in one. Master Bredych had spoken of mystics who had fallen upon evil spirits. Mystics who had found themselves with two souls—one the original person and the other a demon. When he touched her, her body reacted as it should not. She had no idea how he was doing it, but he was no mystic. She would know.

The music carried them further away from Margaret, and Adelei tensed. *Or would I? Could Master Bredych have sent me into a much deeper trap that I suspected?*

Gamun smiled at her and for a moment, she could almost believe him a *pieges*. A trapped spirit. *Almost.*

As the music's recapitulation peaked, even Gamun spoke very little as he concentrated more on the steps and not losing her hand. In the song's last notes, Adelei misstepped, her boot heel coming down on his toes. She stopped and apologized, more out of habit than actual concern for his well-being, but he waved it off. "It's fine, I don't think I needed that set of toes anyway. Though dancing with all these beautiful women may prove difficult after such an injury."

Adelei bit back a laugh. "You could always tell them that Amaskans have two left feet, which is excellent for confusing one's mark but horrible for dancing."

The way he peered at her sent a flush across her cheeks. She backed up a step and swallowed hard. "I need to return to my duties. Thank you, Your Highness," she said, and bowed.

As she turned away, he caught her arm and pulled her close. "You've given me the perfect excuse for not dancing with more of these simpletons. Please, at least come sit beside me and keep me entertained. We can discuss my earlier offer a bit more, and I can prove to you that I mean you no harm."

She had to hold her sides as she laughed. Whatever warmth she'd felt at his touch, dissolved at the mention of the offer. "Prince Gamun, I'd be more likely to accept a deal from a snake than from the likes of you—one driven to proclivities of the most heinous kind."

"King Leon means to take land by whatever means necessary. Surely you see this—"

"I know what you speak of yes, but most of those people come to him willingly—" *I hope.* "—And only because they seek to flee Shadian lands to escape the Monster."

"Are you going to let injustice reign over all the Little Dozen and its people, Master Adelei? All over one person's sins?" His voice was a touch too loud, even over the raucous drumming, and several nobles turned their way.

"Your sins are hardly singular, Your Highness, but thank you for sharing with the members of the high court. Now they can see you for exactly who you are." This time when she brought her heel down, it was on his instep. Though not as hard as she'd liked, he hissed in pain. *That's the prince we know so well.* "Return to your followers, Your Highness. I already have a job."

Adelei refused to turn her back to him. She backed into the crowd of dancing couples until she was one face among many. He scoured the crowds for her a moment or two before giving up.

"Just what do you think you're doing?" Margaret hissed, almost bowling Adelei over.

"What I'm doing? I'm not sure I understand your meaning, Your Highness."

"You. You're flirting with my husband." Margaret's voice carried too much, and Adelei pulled her aside. Her face shushed the protest. "Look you ninny, this husband of yours is trying to kill you, or have you forgotten?" Adelei jabbed Margaret's bruised cheek.

Margaret covered it instinctively, and Adelei pointed. "See? He flirts with anyone—anything to get what he wants." The prince's laughter carried. He stood near the edge of the dancers, his face leaning close to another woman's. "He alternates threatening and flirting with me to try and get to you. And you're playing straight into his hands by acting like a child."

"But he's my husband. He loves me."

"Did he tell you that?"

When Margaret nodded, Adelei poked her in the side where another bruise hid. "Ow. Why—"

"Remember that? Tell me again that he loves you."

"But he—" When Margaret spoke, Adelei poked her again, this time on the thigh.

"Look, he's telling you what you want to hear. He's using you. If you want a man like that, you can have him. I have no interest in bedding a monster."

Margaret's scowl deepened, her eyes scrunched up close to her nose. "And what would you know of such things?"

"Plenty, Your Highness. I'm not a princess, remember?"

Gamun strode toward the door, his followers left behind. Adelei was several steps into following him when at her elbow, Margaret asked, "Where are you going?"

When she followed Adelei into the hallway, not even the makeup could hide the mottled reds and yellows of the bruise. Adelei winced at the picture her sister painted for the court. *She's so naïve. In love with love. She can't help how she feels.* Spur of the moment, Adelei touched her sister's hand. "I'm following your husband. If you are so sure he's innocent in all of this, follow me. See where he's going, who he's meeting, and what is said. It's about time we got to the bottom of this."

Adelei exited through the doors vacated by the prince a minute before. His footfalls in the gardens trailed, as did Adelei's. *Mother planted these gardens.* Memories of playing amongst the roses, feet wiggling in the dirt as she tossed something at her sister flashed across the surface of her mind, and she shook her head. Gamun's hair bobbed above the bushes to her right, and she tiptoed closer. When voices sounded, she ducked behind one of the potentilla bushes. Slow hands pried the branches apart. Two men stood beneath the moonlight that peaked out from behind dark clouds.

"That was risky, you fool. Dancing with the Amaskan," Ambassador Chortez hissed, his beady eyes darting around the garden shadows.

"Relax, I know what I'm doing. Besides, she's fascinating," said Gamun.

"You take great risks. Your father—"

"—Is not here to tell me what to do."

"But if he were, what would he make, I wonder, of the work you did on your new wife? I thought we were supposed to keep a low profile so that the Tribor could do their work." Chortez gesticulated toward the sky. "By the Gods, you're a fool sometimes."

Gamun seized the man's tunic before he mumbled something Adelei couldn't hear. Then louder, he said, "—Besides, the little fool bought my apology. She thinks I love her, that everything is wonderful. Marital bliss and all that garbage. She's too stupid to know otherwise, which is exactly what we need."

"But the plan—"

"The plan's going forward just fine."

The way Gamun's lip curled upwards, reaching for his nose as if it too, believed itself infallible, made her itch to wipe the sneer from his face with her bare fists. Adelei didn't need her knives—five minutes alone in a room with him, and she'd have all the proof she needed. A choked sob from a nearby ivy caused both men to halt their conversation.

Prince Gamun swore when his seeking gaze followed the stream of moonlight. A pale blue dress's hem rested on the soil below the ivy, which led upwards to a teary face. The prince snarled, three footsteps into a flee before he spotted Adelei. As he passed Adelei, he paused, his voice strong enough to carry over the distance. "Remember my offer, Adelei."

Adelei didn't try to stop him as he left. How could she? Her word against his. Even Margaret's bruises weren't enough for the Senate. Besides, empty threats weren't against the Thirteen any more than a good beating was. The sob from the tree caught her attention, and she stood up from her crouch with a sigh.

"He—he really does want to k-kill me."

Adelei could have smacked Margaret. *I feel decades older than her, rather than five minutes.* She held out her arms, which her sister tumbled into.

The way we fell into Mom's. She didn't know why the memory came to her then. Maybe it was the garden. Or maybe it was the vulnerability of her sister just then, but she remembered her mother's brown hair cascading over both of them as she swallowed them in her embrace, the bright sunlight streaking through the trees of the garden that day. *The day they sent me away. The day she and Margaret fled for their lives. Did she know then that I was leaving? Is that why she hugged me so long?* Adelei could smell the tulips that were crushed beneath her little booted heels as she clung to her mother, sounds of battle reaching them even within the castle's inner gardens.

Margaret pulled away. The tulips fled with the memory. "I've been a fool," Margaret whispered, wiping away another tear as she stared across the gardens. "I thought he loved me, but he only wants to use me. To kill me. Why, Adelei? What did I ever do?"

"I seriously doubt it's about you, Mae-Mae. I think he has another agenda in mind."

Her sister's hand dropped into her lap. "I-I haven't heard that name in a long time. In fact, I didn't even remember it until you said it," said Margaret.

"I'm not sure where it came from—it popped across my tongue. I used to call you that, didn't I?" Adelei shifted her weight from one foot to the other, the night's silence grating on her. Adelei itched to move, to go after what she needed to catch Gamun. But with her sister before her, all tear stains and bruises, she was torn.

"He mentioned an offer. He's mentioned it before, when I was disguised as you. What was he talking about?"

"He offered me a way out."

"Out?"

"A way to leave the Amaskans."

"But you've already left, right?"

Margaret touched Adelei's scarred jaw. "They removed the tattoo, and yes, my name has been stricken from the histories, but once Amaskan, always Amaskan."

"I don't understand. You can't retire or leave?"

"No, that's just it. I can't. If it was that simple, I would've never come here." *Never learned the truth.* "I'm Amaskan, tattoo or no. Will be until I die." Adelei looked at the toes of her boots as she shifted soil around with the point. It wasn't common knowledge, and it wasn't something she was supposed to disclose, and yet the conditioning didn't fight her.

"I don't understand."

Adelei sighed. "I know. I can't explain it—only that I serve Anur. I serve Justice to protect others. It's not something that can be taken away from me. It's something I have to do."

"So if you can't leave the Amaskans, how can he offer you a way out?" Margaret asked.

"Gamun wants me to join him. With the resources of his kingdom and the Tribor, he figures he can defeat the Amaskans. He wants me to betray my family, both families, and side with him. "

"To commit treason. But how does he expect you to do that? He's married. It's not like he can just seize the crown—" Her eyes widened, two smaller moons echoing the larger one beneath the canopy of trees. "Oh. He means to marry you after he has offed me." Margaret's jaw clenched. "Why have me when he can have the killer princess?"

Poisonous words. Adelei winced and shook her head. "I told him no. Besides, it's my job to rid the world of creatures like him, not marry them."

The smallest hint of laughter escaped Margaret's lips. A gust of wind blew gently through the private gardens, sending the fragrance of a dozen flowers around them in the moonlight. The roses in particular were pungent, and their soft smell tickled Adelei's nose as well as her memories. Lost in thought, she almost didn't hear the scuff of a boot heel in the dirt some distance away. A twig broke as he passed the bench nearby, and Adelei held a finger to her sister's mouth.

The Shadian ambassador stepped around the hedge, and Adelei fingered the knife in the sleeve of her wrist cuff. He held both hands in the air as he turned around. "I mean you no harm, Your Highness. Nor you, Master Adelei. I have much information. Information that would please everyone."

Adelei kept her sister's body behind hers as her eyes sought any weapons he might carry. She found no lumps where there shouldn't have been, but the loose fitting garb he wore could easily disguise smaller weapons. "Don't come any closer," she said and stepped near Margaret.

"I am armed." He moved his hand to his waist where he slowly withdrew several darts from a hidden pocket near his hip bone. Chortez tossed them to the ground. "If you wish to search my person further, I will submit myself for search."

"Stay here," she told Margaret as she approached Chortez, her hand never leaving her weapon. She seized him by his arms and pulled them out to the sides. Experienced hands moved lightly across the folds of his garb. She checked his wrists and his waist. Every pocket was turned out before she checked the tops of his boots. The first search revealed nothing, and she said, "Open your mouth wide."

He hesitated, and she rapped his jaw with a knuckled hand. Chortez acquiesced, and Adelei slid a finger under his tongue and around the sides of his cheeks. No adenneith. She couldn't guarantee that he was weapon free, but it was as close as she was going to get short of stripping him down. Adelei wiped her finger on her breeches.

"What do you want?"

"Asylum. Protection."

"And why would you need such a boon?"

"Because I can retrieve the evidence you need to go before the Boahim Senate. To dissolve this marriage and end the Monster."

"Go on."

"I would rather disclose this information to His Majesty, if you would be willing to grant me an audience."

She shook her head. "Nope. You tell me first. Here. Now. Or not at all."

Chortez frowned and looked over his shoulder at the path that led to the door. Whatever he expected to see wasn't visible to either of them as he returned his attention to her. "The King of Shad has engineered the downfall of the Poncett family. A plan since before the Little War of Three. He has contingency plans in place in case the Tribor fail, including setting up Gamun to take the fall."

"He would set up his own son?" Margaret stepped forward and placed her hand on Adelei's shoulder.

Gamun said he didn't kill his niece. That he wasn't behind the attempt on Margaret. Could there be truth to this? To Chortez, she said, "Gamun claims he's already been set up."

The ambassador's teeth flashed bright in the moonlight. "Of course he's told you these things. He wishes an alliance with you to kill his father, does he not?" Behind her, Margaret gasped. "The King of Shad is planning to take down everyone of royal blood. Including you." He pointed a finger at Adelei.

Adelei ignored the comment. "Yes, yes, so I've heard. You said you have proof."

"Not on my person, but as I said, I can retrieve it. The prince keeps certain documents in the ambassadorial state suite, which I have access to."

"How do I know they aren't your documents?"

"You will know when you see them." Sweat drowned his eyes, which blinked rapidly as he shifted on the balls of his feet. Chortez cast another worried glance over his shoulder before continuing. "You won't be able to read the documents without my help. They aren't in Alexandrian. Or Shadian," he added when she opened her mouth to interrupt him again. "They're in code."

"Why can you read it?" Adelei asked.

"Because I taught him this code—it's an old cryptography used to send messages in my father's homeland."

"Does he admit to killing those girls in the documents?" asked Margaret.

"The documents are journals. He details names and places of his sport. How they were killed. Things he shouldn't know, Your Highness, unless it was his hand that harmed them. Notes of payments made to the Tribor by both His Highness and his father, King of Shad."

"And why would you share this information? Why betray your country?" Adelei asked. It was too easy. Something wasn't right about it.

"Shad is not my native country. I owe no allegiance to that land any more than I do to this one. With Prince Gamun Bajit and his father, my days are numbered."

The wind stirred up the leaves overhead, and Chortez fell to a crouch. "It's the wind, Ambassador. What makes you think I won't take the journals and kill you right here?"

"I've watched you, Master Adelei, and I know you for a justice seeker. The rumors of Amaskan justice are correct it seems, and so I beg you for help."

"We must help him, for the good of all the Little Dozen kingdoms," said Margaret.

Adelei winced. She would have preferred to leave him hanging for a while. See what else shook loose. "I'll take this information and offer it before His Highness myself," said Adelei, "But I can't promise you anything, let alone asylum. You've watched him commit crimes against the Thirteen and until now have done nothing, which is a crime itself. When I know of his decision, I'll contact you."

The ambassador sucked in a quick breath. "But—" Adelei shook her head, and he gave her a curt bow before fleeing the gardens. She turned to chastise her sister, but Margaret was nowhere to be seen.

CHAPTER TWENTY-THREE

Margaret was exactly where Adelei thought she'd be: sitting outside King Leon's formal audience chamber. She didn't flush or avert her eyes as normal, nor did she slump in her seat. Margaret remained stiff backed and eyes forward until the page announced the arrival of His Majesty.

Their father paused in the doorway. He noted Margaret's serious expression and opened the door to the audience chamber. The memory was less fuzzy now—Adelei at her father's feet while royal dignitaries came and went. Margaret beside her as they watched their father "play king." The disconcerting memories bugged her. Not because they were a connection to the Poncett family—she'd already acknowledged her birth family—but because they interfered with her job. The images had overcome her at random points since waking, leaving her unaware of what was before her in the now.

King Leon sat on his throne and waved a hand at Margaret. "Poppet, you've pulled me away from an important feast. Is this something I need to know right now, or can it wait until morning?" Lines crossed many paths along his face, and his skin wore a grayer coat than usual.

Margaret bowed before her father in a well-practiced motion. "Your Majesty, I come with information vital to the survival of the Kingdom of Alexander." She remained on one knee before him until he motioned absently for her to rise.

"I see this is more formal an occasion than I'd thought it to be. Does this require the presence of my council?" He rubbed trembling fingers across his forehead.

"I-I don't believe so. At least not yet, Your Majesty."

He gestured for her to continue, and Margaret reported the ambassador's request as well as the information recovered during the overheard meeting, all the while holding a steady voice. Adelei's brows rose higher, a motion caught by King Leon as he stared at her over Margaret's head. When Adelei nodded, he rubbed his eyes. The façade of King shifted back into place, but not before she glimpsed a hint of sorrow there. *He was hoping maybe the Shadians weren't behind it. He's too old for another war, and he knows it. But that's what this will mean. Civil war will spill across our lands again, only you won't be here to save the day, will you, Father?*

"For all that the Boahim Senate may believe they hold these lands together, the Shadians clearly think otherwise," he said.

"There's more, Your Majesty. Something Prince Gamun said to me..." Adelei swallowed. "He said that there was a movement by many of the Little Dozen rulers to dethrone you. He claims that the Poncett family has been expanding their borders and seizing the lands around them by force."

His crown slid to rest lopsided across his brow. "Your Majesty," she said and stepped forward, "Is there any truth to this? Does Alexander wish to expand its borders?"

"How can you ask that?" said Margaret, but King Leon shook his head.

"It isn't that simple, Adelei. Some of these landholders— farmers, smiths, and the like—they're suffering under their current lords. They come to me—they offer their land and fealty to me if I will free them from their lord's tyrannical rule. What am I to do?"

"When the land is whole, then will the people burn with righteousness,
The truth will mark them and Justice be served by blood across the land."

Adelei whispered the words. Holy words marked down at the split of Boahim. A dozen little kingdoms united whole by the blood of war and the might of the Senate.

"What did you say?" Leon asked, and Adelei shut her eyes from the fear in his.

"Do you know what you've done?" she asked. "The Little Dozen cost the lives of so many. To break a holy contract, one made with the blood of thousands—it's heresy. If the Boahim Senate knew—"

"They do."

His words silenced her. The Boahim Senate knew. *The Thirteen forgive us.* "It will mean war."

"War was destined to be, it seems." King Leon sighed and took a deep swallow from his cup. The blue jeweled crown bore heavy lines on his brow. "Your training has made you into a worthy successor, Princess Margaret. The crown thanks you for this information. You have our permission to withdraw."

Margaret stumbled on her feet. "Papa?" a hesitant voice called, a daughter's eyes finally noticing the sheen of sweat over his ashen skin.

"I'm just tired, poppet. Go back to your rooms and give me a moment with Master Adelei if you will."

For a moment, Adelei thought her sister might ignore the dismissal, but after a moment's hesitation, she bowed and turned to leave. Adelei caught her arm and whispered, "Be careful. Ask the guards if he's there before you enter those rooms and lock them behind you. He can stay in his state suites tonight."

Her sister's footsteps weren't as steady as they left the room. Adelei approached the throne, and her fingers reached out to wipe the sweat from his brow. They stopped inches from King Leon, hanging uselessly in the air.

Face it, you hate being useless. There's no enemy here to defeat. No justice in this man dying before you. Adelei dropped her hand back to her side.

"Do you think the ambassador has the evidence we need?" King Leon asked after taking a long swallow of wine.

"I'm not sure he has it, but he certainly seems to think he can get us the evidence—the journals and records of the payoffs."

When he coughed, the sound was the stormy tide dashing upon the rocky coast near the Order—a sound both great and terrifying all at once. That he had the strength left for such a cough was hopeful, but the ragged bark frightened her. When he continued, his voice carried less strength than before. "You've said little in regards to this. I would have your council on whether we should trust this traitor in our midst."

"When he first spoke to me, he was a snake in the garden for sure. Now he seems to have shed his skin to save himself, which causes me concern. I would say let the man worry for a bit while I try to gain what evidence I can. With your leave, I will follow the prince. Maybe he is meeting with others. Maybe I can lay a trap too good for him to pass up, and then we won't need the ambassador at all."

"You would leave Chortez to hang for his crimes rather than grant him amnesty?"

Adelei shuffled her feet under that gaze. For all that he was ill, those eyes could make her feel like a child. *Master Bredych had that way about him as well.* She replied, "I would. '*A snake may shed its skin, but it is still a snake within.*'"

"So bitter for one so young. But your meaning is noted. Go. Do what you must to find the evidence needed."

She bowed before his waving hand, but she, too, hesitated before leaving. "Father, is there anything I...the healers can do to ease your pain?"

He smiled tiredly, yet for a brief moment it lit up the darkened room as he looked upon her. "Nothing, but thank you for your concern. And...and thank you for calling me Father."

Both brown pairs grew moist, but she glanced away first, retreating into the darkness lest he see how much his illness affected her. She wanted nothing more than to seek out a good brawl, but instead, she sought out the nearest guard. "Have you seen his Highness, the Prince?"

"He has retreated to his personal chambers for the evening."

Which set of chambers?

"Which?" His answer indicated that the man had some brains after all, having sought his state chambers rather than those he shared with Margaret. Still, Adelei's steps hurried to the royal suite. The door was locked, her sister alone behind it.

Adelei's hands were on the knob to her own room when the door swung open behind her. "He's dying, isn't he?" Margaret whispered. When Adelei nodded, her sister asked, "Why? What's causing this? Has he seen the healers?"

"He has, and there's nothing they can do against a poison of this type."

"Poison? Who would dare...?" Margaret's hands balled up into fists.

"Goefrin. He told the King that I was dead. He was the reason for our mother's death." Margaret's fingers dug into the chair's cushioned back, the crushed blue like a choppy ocean beneath her fingers as she squeezed it. "He had a hand in the death of Grandsir and has been poisoning our father for years. At this point, there is nothing we can do. I'm sorry."

"How long does he have?"

"I don't know. Weeks? Months? There's no way to know."

The fabric tore under her sister's fingers, and the wool stuffing fell to the floor to land at her feet in a pile of light grey fluff. "You're lucky, you know," Margaret said, her eyes staring at the mess she'd made. "Someone gives you orders, and you take them. People before you are either right or wrong, and you move forward to serve justice. The rest of us are stuck in a world of grays, constantly wondering if we've made the right choice, if the decision we make will end in someone dying or starving, or worse, war." Margaret met her eyes boldly then, and the fierce determination settled across her young shoulders. "It must be nice to live so simply."

Adelei bit her tongue to keep her bitter laughter from spilling out. "As if it's that simple. Have you ever killed someone, and then had to wonder if what you'd done was truly justice? If the man before you, whose family is crying at his funeral and mourning him, truly was the monster everyone made him out to be? The blood on your hands never goes away. To call that simple, it's naïve, and a ruler should know better than to fall before such ideals."

"I may not have killed someone, but one day I may have to order someone's death. I think you have the easier path."

You don't understand. This blood. The Magistrate stood before her again, and the chair's wool transformed into blood. Margaret wouldn't understand, not until it was too late. She would make a mistake as a ruler that would cost someone his life, and then she would see. Too late to stop it, too late to do anything more than carry the guilt of the crown.

Margaret interrupted her thoughts. "You aren't going to rule a kingdom. You follow orders like a guard and nothing more. Your decisions impact very few. How could you possibly understand the weight on our father's shoulders? A weight that will soon be mine?"

Adelei sighed and counted to ten. "I understand it more than you know, and I truly hope for our kingdom's sake that you find a way to selflessness sooner than later. A queen has to think about more than the immediate future, about more than herself. A queen can't be afraid."

Margaret opened her mouth to protest, but Adelei held up her hand to stop the words. "Don't. I can see it in the trembling of your shoulders, so don't lie to me, Mae-Mae. Father dying means you will receive the crown much earlier than you thought, and with it, you'll likely inherit a war, something you know nothing about. With your prince removed by the Boahim Senate, the decisions will rest on your shoulders alone. Only a fool would say they were unafraid of such a task, but you can't allow that to drive your decisions or your words."

When the question came, it wasn't the one Adelei expected, and she winced when Margaret whispered, "How do you do it? Swallow back the emotions to do what you must?"

Adelei could have lied. She wanted to. *I wish I had an easy answer. I used to.* She swallowed hard before the truth. "I wish I could tell you one just pushes it back, tucks it away, and moves on. It's what I did for a long time in fact, but I don't have the answers anymore. Everything I thought I'd been doing right, doing well, was a lie. You can't look to me for answers, sister. I don't even know the questions anymore."

"I don't understand."

"Me neither." Behind Margaret, a dozen candles lit the bedchamber like the sun's surface, and Adelei tilted her head in their direction. "Trying to stay awake?"

"Sometimes...I don't want to sleep."

"I understand," Adelei said. "Ever since the coma, I remember things…"

"What things?"

"You're better off not knowing."

My childhood. What I lost. The faces of the dead—and the people I've killed on the orders of a man I called father. A man I trusted, who played with my mind. Oh yes, sister, I know. Adelei leaned her head against the doorframe. "Every time I close my eyes, I have to wonder if I'll open them come morning." She hadn't intended to speak the words, but the whites of her sister's eyes told her she had.

"Can I tell you something?" Adelei asked, and when her sister nodded, she continued, "I don't think I ever want to sleep again."

Her footsteps left light marks in the dusty cobbled road. Adelei kept her eyes glued to the figure before her whose purple hem hung just low enough to peek out from beneath the grey hooded cloak. The prince moved through the shady marketplace seemingly at random, moving too quickly to shop or browse, but slowly enough to be noticed.

If he was looking for his next victim, it was surely an odd way to go about it. Most of the merchants didn't recognize him with the cloak pulled down over his face, but if he straightened his posture, as he had at one booth, then his clean, polished features and clothing marked him as someone of high rank.

Adelei stopped at the merchant shortly after the prince, but the men said he'd bought nothing and said nothing either. Just stood there a few moments before moving on. No foods or supplies bought in these streets would lead to anything good, and she wished he'd purchase something so Adelei would have information to tell her father.

Every major city had their black markets, but following Prince Gamun through Alesta's left her more puzzled than anything else. If only he would give her something to work with. Ah well, what else would she do with her time? Not like she slept much anyway. So Adelei followed him, night after night. Waiting for him to slip up. It wasn't until he stopped at a fourth booth, his chin tilted in her direction, that she confirmed he'd spotted her.

This time when he moved on, she hung back and waited until he turned the corner before she left the shadows. When she reached the corner, he was out of sight. Adelei cursed under her breath and turned, only to find the prince leaning against the frame of a rickety building. His smirk was visible beneath the dark hood.

He beckoned for her to approach. She did so, albeit hesitantly. She mimicked his relaxed posture and leaned against the door to the shop whose merchant disappeared upon sight of her. "What do you want?" she asked.

"I should be asking you that, considering you've been following me most of the night."

She could hear the smile on his lips and repressed a shudder. "I've never been to the Alexandrian marketplace. This evening seemed like as good a time as any to explore it."

He arched a brow. "The mighty Amaskan perusing the black market? What could you possibly need here?"

"I imagine the same thing as the Prince of Shad."

When his hand touched her arm, tendrils of cold flame crawled up to her shoulder and toward her heart. She stumbled sideways, wresting her arm away from him, but the burning cold remained a moment longer before fading to a dull throb. The pendant around his neck still held a bluish glow, matched by his normally brown eyes.

Magic. Holy Thirteen. It wasn't just a possibility that the Shadians employed mystics, but that the prince himself was one.

"Lying to a prince can be a dangerous occupation, Master Adelei," he said, his voice completely level and calm as if he hadn't just tried to kill her. "Have you given any more thought to my proposal?"

"I will not be taking you up on your offer, which I believe you already knew. I have a job already."

"Yes, justice at the hands of murderers who kidnap and kill in a zealous attempt to right wrongs. Except those that they commit. How do you sleep at night? Or do you sleep anymore these days?"

He laughed at the expression of fear she wore, despite her attempts to school her facial features. *How did he—? Of course. Last night.* Exhaustion had driven her to a few hours' sleep after Gamun had returned from his trek through Alesta. Deeply asleep, she had walked through a crowded room, so tightly packed with people that she brushed shoulders with every man and woman she passed as she sought the exit. Very little light illuminated the room—just thirteen candles that flared to expose the dirty, rotting faces of the people around her. Their clothes stank of death and clung to their shriveled bodies like desperation as they moved toward her, their feet trudging across the dirt floor.

She'd caught a glimpse of one portly man's face as he bumped into her, and even in her dream state she'd gasped aloud in terror. *Magistrate Meserre.*

He faced her and grinned, his rotted teeth black in his mouth where dirt caked his gums. Someone had buried the body, and his clothing carried the dirt of his grave with him as he moved among the throng of people. As each one approached, they bumped into her and grinned before moving on, and she recognized them as those she'd killed. Each man and woman she brought to death stared back at her, judging her.

At first, she merely walked among them until an intense pain in her shoulder caused her to cry out. When she touched the wound, her hand came away bloody; she sought the attacker only to find more bodies standing in her way as they lined up to receive her. Something sharp cut into her bicep, and she screamed. Her cries brought more bodies as they surged forward, their knives glinting in the light of the thirteen candles which floated in mid-air. Another stab—this time in her thigh—and then another. Adelei couldn't move without another blade robbing her of thought. Finally she crouched down, using her arms as a shield as they each attacked her, one stab for every life she'd taken.

"Please. Stop."

The words were mere whispers in the darkness, which echoed amongst the shuffling feet of hundreds of bodies who never spoke, only stared at her with empty eyes. Dead eyes. "Please. Stop," they mocked.

Small legs bumped into her knees—legs too small for a man or a woman. The child's brown eyes stared back at her for a moment before they rolled out of their sockets, leaving empty holes in their place. She screamed and pushed the child away. "I never killed children." she shouted into the emptiness. "Amaskans don't kill kids."

Laughter bounced around the room, and she clamped her hands over her ears. They all vanished, leaving her alone. Laughter erupted from the darkness and her shoulder ached. An ache that should have disappeared with the rest of the wounds when the spirits vanished. Adelei had awoken in a pool of sweat. Upon rising, she had found no wounds. She chalked up the aching shoulder to an odd sleeping position.

As Adelei stood before the prince now, memories of the nightmare fresh in her mind, her shoulder throbbed. The intensity worsened until finally, unable to stop herself, she was compelled to touch the shoulder. Her hand came away bloody.

Gamun's hand shot forward, and he gripped her shoulder with his bare skin through the flesh wound. His fingers dug into the hole. She cried out as blood gushed from her shoulder, and her eyes flitted around the marketplace in a blind panic.

No merchant moved to help. Every one of them found themselves busy with cleaning imaginary dust from their storefront or shuffling objects around for no reason at all. They ignored her cry and averted their eyes, their faces pinched with fear.

"Please. Stop," she cried. Words out of her dream and just like then, his laughter echoed across the tiny distance between them. The world fell away as other wounds from the nightmare were made real on her body.

A moment longer and he released her with a whisper. "Don't toy with me."

She only heard his footfalls as he strode away, her vision swimming as she curled into a protective ball. She probed the stab wound on her thigh and hip with cautious fingers. Both had closed up, but the blood on her clothing lingered. The wound on her shoulder remained open and hot to the touch. Adelei winced as she stood on shaky, booted feet.

One of the merchants cleared his throat. The man held a cloth in one hand and a pitcher of water in the other. "If I may?" he asked, and when she nodded, he poured the water across her shoulder and dabbed at it with none too gentle hands.

"It's nice of you to bandage the wound you could have stopped," she said between clenched teeth.

He wrapped the cloth around her shoulder tightly. She almost blacked out when he tied the cloth together. "And what could a lone merchant do against the likes of him? You can't possibly think any of us stupid enough for that. Look, Master, I'm sorry you were injured, but there's nothing any of us could do. That should hold it for now, but I'd see a healer if I were you. You look like one who could afford it."

The man shuffled back toward his store front, his hunched over back unusual for a man of his youth. The rest of the merchants avoided her. She approached one booth and picked up an apple, rolling it around in her hands. "How much is this?" she asked but received no answer.

Adelei rifled through her coin purse for a notch, easily ten times what the apple was worth, and placed the coin on the counter of his booth. The booth's owner bumped the stand with his hip until the coin fell to the dirt below. Puzzled, she picked it up and placed it on the shelf. "You dropped this." This time the tall man looked her straight in the face as he bumped his cart, causing the coin to fall again to the dirt.

"He won't take your money," someone else said, and she snatched her coin from the ground.

"And why not?"

The voice's owner was the same young man who'd bandaged her shoulder. He stood in the doorway to a store selling maps and other odd sketches on scraps of paper. "You're marked now. Damaged."

Adelei frowned. "What do you mean?"

"Even if the Alexandrians didn't have a fear of Amaskans, beggin' your pardon, Master, once you become *his* target, no one will deal with you. You're cursed."

"So you know of the rumors about him."

"The Monster? Aye. And now he's in charge of this kingdom, no one wants to cross him." The merchant held two fingers to his forehead for a moment.

"You seem willing enough to deal with me. Besides, King Leon is still King of this land, is he not?"

"I'll not be here much longer, Master. I plan to peddle my wares today and then head out for better lands, lands not here. Lands far from the Monster's reach if I can manage. I would suggest ye do the same. If what I hear is right, the King isn't long for this world and with him gone, everything that holds this kingdom together will go with him until only *he* remains."

"I can't leave, not yet. I have a job to do," she said. "But I thank you for the warning. And the cleaning of my wound. What do you know about this Prince of Shad? Is it true what they say about his interests?"

"Aye. Though I've no proof of it, it's obvious enough that he's up to no good when he creeps around the city at night. Even the public girls be lockin' themselves up on nights he comes 'round."

One of the other merchants hissed and knelt to kiss the ground in reverence to Sharmus. When he rose, he eyed them both angrily before spitting out a few words of warning. "Sharmus protection on us. You shouldn't be talking to her. You'll bring the Shadian wrath down on us all."

Adelei kicked at a loose pebble on the cobbled road. She didn't like this at all. She'd never seen a merchant turn down a profit, let alone pack up and run.

"If you don't mind my sayin', this job you're referrin' to—if it's to take down the prince, I would think twice on how much they be payin' you. No amount is worth takin' on the Monster and his circle of mystics. I'm not the type to concern myself with the debate of whether mystics be holy or evil, but the kind he has workin' for him, they are dark, Master. Dark as evil gets. You'll never touch him. That whole kingdom be rotten to the core and full of those that'll keep it that way. Soon enough they will overrun us and take over this land as well."

"The Boahim Senate—"

"You think they don't know? You think they don't know what goes on in Shad? Either they be evil right there with him, or they be like me. Afraid and running. Why else would they stay on that tiny island of theirs instead of putting a stop to his reign?"

She couldn't help the goosebumps that brushed across her flesh, but she did suppress the shiver. No need for them to know that even she was afraid. Instead she stood taller, in spite of her wounded shoulder, and raised her chin up. "Maybe they just need the right evidence," she said, smiling at the man with a warmth she didn't feel. "Justice will always prevail; trust in that if nothing else. Thank you for your willingness to talk with me."

The merchant palmed something, then slid it into her pocket before he turned away.

"Bringing death upon us all. Damned assassins," one of the others muttered. They were afraid. They couldn't help it.

The vocal man called out to her as she strode away, his voice trembling as he spoke. "May your Way guide you and Sharmus' protection upon you."

Indeed, friend. I'm going to need it. Adelei walked back toward the castle, and people stepped away from her or avoided looking at her altogether. Maybe she actually bore a mark or maybe it was all the blood. Either way, people shut their doors and locked them as she passed. For a town that was well-populated, the area was crawling with nothing, a fact that left a cold sweat across her skin.

She slid her hand into her pocket and found a piece of parchment. The hastily scrawled letters were badly spelled but the message was clear.

They meet at the baker's. Follow him there.

Finally, something pointing her towards the evidence she needed. Assuming she survived long enough to follow him again. A mystic. Not just a healer, but old magics long forgotten.

Gods help me, what a mess. I'll be lucky to make it out of this alive. Her shoulder throbbed with each step she took, a silent doomsday bell ringing in her head.

CHAPTER TWENTY-FOUR

The report to King Leon left Adelei exhausted. It took everything in her to calm his rage after he saw the blood on her clothing, let alone the shoulder wound. It was a father's rage that threatened to undo Adelei's plans and his own. His physician treated her shoulder as she divulged the details.

"Do nothing—not yet. I need more time to find evidence of his collusion with the Tribor. Time to follow him to whatever bakery for a meeting," Adelei said. King Leon listened, jaw clenched. "Or better yet, let me search his rooms. If you want justice, I need proof. I need those journals."

In the end, he granted her request, though only because he was too angry to do more than listen to her plans for the evening. An hour later, Adelei stared at Margaret, who donned the sepier's clothes.

"He wasn't fooled last time." Margaret tugged at the clothing as she stared at herself in the mirror.

"You said he was until he saw the bruise on your cheek. Just think of the garden and you'll be fine. His Majesty will tell everyone you aren't feeling well. You'll only need to duck in once to 'inform Michael' and that should do it."

"What if he comes over to me? He does seem fairly obsessed with you."

Adelei tucked a stray hair back under the head scarf. "If he does, you'll have to be me."

Margaret caught Adelei's hand in her grasp. "I don't know if I can do this again. I'm not strong like you. It was one thing to pretend from afar when you were ill, but this—"

"You were strong enough to follow him into the gardens that evening. You have more strength than you know. Trust your instincts." Margaret gave Adelei one last glance before she strode from her bedchamber. The look spoke of her terror, but the façade fell over her gentle features and changed them to stone.

Instead of the sepier's outfit or even her courtly disguise, Adelei wore the Amaskan clothing that had laid unused since she set out for Alexander. Head to toe black hugged her body like a second skin. Exposed flesh was covered in blackened grease.

The last time she had worn these clothes, she had killed a man. He had been an evil man, that she had no doubt, but were the ones before him as evil? As deserving of death?

The window at the end of the hall near the stairwell was open, and she slipped through it to the rooftops in a smooth motion. This portion of roof she could walk across until reaching the proper wing.

Then it would get tricky. She crouched on the tiled roof. If the guards across in the towers saw her, they gave no indication, and she breathed a sigh of relief. The courtyard below was empty except a stablehand or two lingering as they played some game. Adelei cursed the full moon overhead but moved one foot in front of the other.

The movement was achingly slow, the half-walk, half-crawl required along the tiles, but she held her patience until she reached the state suites' wing. Even slower than before, she inched across the roof until she sat near the edge. The guard tower rose less than forty feet from her, and she both cursed and thanked the Gods for their inattentiveness as she swung over the side, fingers gripping the roof's edge. Sweat broke out across her forehead as she glanced down at the window ledge beneath her.

When she'd told the King that she'd be dropping into the prince's rooms, she was pretty sure this wasn't what he'd had in mind. Adelei allowed her body to still as she hung limply from the roof. Arms extended, she took a deep breath and let go.

She kept her sights on the window ledge below her during the six foot drop and like a court acrobat, she caught the metal bar of the garden planter that surrounded the window. Her feet hit the stone side, and she bounced once to slow the momentum. As much as she itched to climb up to the window ledge itself, which was infinitely safer, she held firm to the planter.

No sounds within the room. It would have been easier to traverse the halls, but the number of guards and servants guaranteed that everyone would know of her room search before the night was over. She hung a moment longer to ensure no one was present. Fresh blood trickled down her shoulder as the wound reopened, and it screamed in agony.

Adelei pulled herself up to the ledge and crawled in through the opened window. Two nights of watching warranted the information she'd needed. In the evening's heat, Gamun's windows would be wide open to allow for a breeze. The moonlight cast the only light in the room, and Adelei allowed a moment for her eyes to adjust to the semidarkness.

She retrieved a small candle from her pocket, which she lit with a lightstone. No trace of her visit would remain. A sitting room, similar to the one she and Margaret shared, was lit by her candle.

Two doors lay before her. The one to the right led back to the castle halls. *Guards on the other side of that door, so slow movements. The door ahead of me must lead to the study or bedchamber.* When she pulled it open a crack, the hinge gave no squeaks. *Someone's kept this well-greased.*

It was the study. Papers lay in stacks strewn across a smaller desk and shoved haphazardly along bookshelves. Even the books' pages held more papers. *It must have taken a great many pack animals to bring all of these books from Shad.* A bed-sized desk was the cleanest and the place where she started her search. She moved her fingers along the dark wood. At first she found nothing out of the ordinary. She was resolved to look through a stack of papers neatly placed in the top drawer, but when she got to the last page, it wouldn't move.

"What in all hells?" The corner was affixed to the drawer's bottom. She tapped on it lightly. While it made the thud of wood, there was a hollow *thwap* to the sound. At the end of the drawer was another piece of paper—this one stiffer. A false back perhaps? Adelei curled her fingers over the back. Behind it, a hook dangled.

Something clicked when she wiggled the hook, and Adelei slid the false bottom aside. Several inches below was the drawer's true bottom.

And it was empty.

Damn. Double damn.

As she closed up the desk, Adelei noticed the splotch of ink that trailed off the desk's corner. Several splatters marked the floor. All pointing to the left corner nearest the desk. Three of the four walls were lined with bookcases, and the left corner was no exception. Most of the books were bound copies of treatises and histories, though a few were personal accounts of the Shadian royal family.

One book with a spine as old and decrepit as Boahim itself didn't belong. It was a copy of *The Book of Ja'ahr*. How had it escaped from the Order? Her hand rested on the book. If she took it, she might tip her hand that she'd been in Gamun's rooms. But to leave it there would have been at great cost to the Order.

Adelei tucked the book into the cloth belt at her waist. Toward the bottom shelf, tucked between *A History of Alexandrian Rule* and *The Power of Purposeful Influence* was a black journal. The only reason she noticed it was that it knocked into her ankle as she passed. It was half the other book's height but long enough to stick out from the shelf.

The spine held no title, and when she picked it up, one of the pages fell out. She swore and as she moved to stuff it back into place, she spotted it.

Amaskan code. By the Gods, what was it?

A decade old if the dates were to be believed and handwritten in cursive, Adelei squinted to read it. At first look, they were meeting notes. Various dignitaries passing through Shadian court. Gamun's impressions of each meeting and how his father handled the treaties offered. She flipped to the book's front and found more boring princely prattle, but ten pages in she found what she'd been looking for.

A single diagram detailed the bones of the human body. Out to the side, notes were scribbled on the best ways to break bones without instantly killing a victim. Gamun had drawn pictures of animals paired with notes about how he'd practiced the techniques. While unpleasant, nothing in the first journal gave evidence to his mutilation of girls.

But the code bothered Adelei. First he had a book found only within the Order, and now his personal journals were in the Order's private code. Hadn't the ambassador said the code had come from his father's lands?

Her candle had dipped lower than she liked, and she scanned the nearby bookshelves for other journals of a similar look. In the second one, she found what they needed. Pictures and details of how he'd broken some of the village girls he'd encountered at the tender age of fifteen. From there, the journal grew worse. Her stomach churned at some of the images as he possessed an artist's hand, his drawings detailed and accurate. *How nice.* He'd added color to his drawings for authenticity.

Adelei found three more in total, each one adding to the number of dead and broken girls. The prince never mentioned anyone by name, though he had an accomplice who dumped the bodies. The last journal picked up only a few months back, and Adelei flipped to the last few pages. The letters were slanted and the handwriting neater than previous entries, but when she saw the word *sister*, her eyes tumbled across the sentences.

> *I'd hoped to have made her last, my little flower, but her cries were too audible here in the castle. It was a mistake to have brought her. Now I suppose I'll have to get rid of the spawn's mother as well. Still, at least I can enjoy her this evening. Her dead body may prove entertaining as the Alexandrians try and figure out what happened. She was beginning to bore me. Besides, I have someone else in mind. I never thought I'd be one for a fighter, but by Echana, that one will be fun to break. Even more so than her sister.*

Adelei frowned. He had sworn he wasn't responsible for her death, that she was his niece. The handwriting *was* different, but who else would write in his private journals? The first two sentences had been scratched out and written fresh in scrunched up letters above the original lines. Had he been thinking of another target and changed his mind? Adelei skipped ahead a few more pages until she reached the last one, titled this morning.

Why is my father always right? He warned me to move slowly here and allow the Tribor to work, and it seems he was right. The Amaskan has suspected me for a while, which is a complication and a fun one at that. That little mouse may have more fangs than I suspected. I thought it might be interesting to kill them both together though. Do twins scream together as they die? Will they die at the same time, I wonder? Might be an interesting experiment if the Tribor fail in their attempt tonight. Her shoulder still burns with my heat, but there is fire and then there is fire. *She will beg for me before I am done with her. Which sister will outlast the other?*

His plans made Magistrate Meserre appear a saint, and her muscles clenched in response. If Adelei took the books with her, he'd certainly know she'd been there. What she needed was more time to read them. *This whole thing bears more investigation, but I've already been in his suite too long.*

She tucked one of the journals, including the most recent, back into place. The middle one she hid at her waist with *The Book of Ja'ahr.* The door to the sitting room was cracked as she'd left it, and she listened before exiting the study. Adelei climbed on to the window sill. A small stone lip ran horizontally across the castle wall, where it connected with the roof of another portion of the castle. With her shoulder, it would be a painful climb, but it was her only option if she wished to remain unseen. She lowered her body and ignored the screaming protest of her wound as she inched her way along the ledge by her fingertips. Adelei was halfway across the distance when someone said something below and she froze.

Pain pierced her shoulder, nerves screaming for respite. The couple below didn't look up from their conversation, even when her shoulder finally gave out and one arm swung limp before she reached up and grabbed the ledge. The soured dirt taste of blood hit the back of her throat after she bit her tongue. Adelei shuffled along the ledge as quickly as she dared and dropped down to the second floor roof with a thump. Her feet rolled with the impact, and she fell backward on to the tile, lying spread eagle.

Her shoulder burned. Her vision darkened, and she lay there a good ten minutes before she could move her arm without biting back screams, though the shoulder hung limply at her side.

A quick scramble across the roof led to another window, and she popped through it. Her sudden entrance startled a page half to death and he dropped the books he'd been carrying. "Sorry," she muttered and then held a finger to her lips. Wide eyed, he nodded and retrieved his books in a scramble of papers and fingers. The window placed her in one of the more obscure halls of guest rooms. Her breath was labored by the time she returned to His Majesty's sitting room.

He'd be in the great hall still. She scribbled a note for her father and handed it to one of the guards. Adelei hid the journal in one of the pockets of her father's rarely worn overcoats—the place they'd agreed upon earlier in the afternoon. When he returned, he would know to look there for whatever evidence she had found.

Adelei stumbled into Margaret as she left. Her sister's dark pupils were violently obvious against the visible whites of her eyes. The head scarf so carefully worn earlier tilted precariously on Margaret's head, and her limp betrayed an injury to her leg as she hobbled over to a chair.

"What happened?" Adelei called for a healer, then shut and bolted the door.

"The plan mostly worked. At least at first. But the last time I popped into the court to 'have a look around,' Gamun came over to threaten me, or I guess *you*. Said that if you didn't agree to his proposal, he was going to make my death very slow. And then he touched me. This warmth spread through my thigh and—" Margaret flushed, then poured herself a glass of wine from the pitcher beside her.

The way she tossed that back, that must've been some touch. Margaret poured a second glass, while Adelei wet a shred of cloth in the wash bowl and dabbed at her sister's leg. Her sister hissed between clenched teeth but mostly ignored the wound.

"I guess he expected the touch to do something else. It was the oddest sensation. It was...well, I suppose it was the way one's supposed to feel about one's husband. I wanted nothing more than to be with him, but at the same time, I knew better."

She smiled. "He has trouble in that area. If he's not hitting you, he can't... Anyway, I didn't push him away at first—I couldn't—but when he kissed me and touched my shoulder, he knew I wasn't you. Before I could move, he'd burned me. I didn't have time to look for a weapon. I mostly stumbled away from him while he stood there, licking my blood."

Margaret made a choking noise deep in her throat and swallowed more wine. "But I did it." She thrust a fist into the air. "I did what you taught me."

Adelei frowned. "What exactly did you do?"

"I hit him. While he was standing there enjoying my blood— I mean, who does that? How sick does one have to be to—well, I walked up and hit him. Right in the nose, Adelei. I think I might have broken it."

She held out her fist. The skin was split across several knuckles and dried blood caked across her pale fingers. The knock on the door startled them both. Adelei opened the door to Roland, the King's physician. "Gamun's a mystic, but not like I've ever seen." Roland set to work on Margaret's leg first, and Adelei continued, "I know Alexandrians abhor them, but in Sadai, they're used by those that can afford them. As healers though, nothing more." *At least, not that I know of.*

"Unlike the helpful ones in your Sadai, I've read of mystics using blood to control people or using other powers to harm. It's part of the reason they aren't encouraged to settle in Alexander. You'll find that most kingdoms who honor Adlain, don't tend to encourage the followers of the Mystic Turoth."

Margaret clenched her jaw as he cleaned the burn on her leg. "Turoth was said to use blood to do what you suggested—control people. Some say he found a way to live past death by using the blood of others, but no one has seen him in over two hundred years," said Roland as he moved to treat her fist.

"Do you think Gamun is a follower of Turoth then?" asked Margaret.

"I truly hope not." They remained silent as the physician treated Margaret, then cleaned his hands of her blood. "Now, let's get a look at that shoulder, which I do believe I told you to go easy on. What have you done to my work?" His fingers gently brushed Adelei's opened wound. The stitches were torn and in some places nonexistent.

"I had a job that required the use of my shoulder."

It was all she said, but he cocked a brow at her before he resumed cleaning the wound. "If it's normal for Amaskans to ignore medical advice, it's a wonder you made it to your twenties."

Adelei chuckled. "Sadai employs mystics, as does the Order, so normally, we're right back out on the job with a small injury like this."

"Small? That?" Margaret winced as blood flowed anew from Adelei's shoulder.

"I've suffered worse, but you're correct, Master Roland. Many die early and often in this line of work." She clenched her fingers into a fist as he stitched up the wound on her shoulder. Her sister remained by her side, paler than before, but she made no effort to leave. *I'd swear being married to this monster has done her good. She's older. As if the child in her has been silenced.*

"This time, I mean it when I say you need to take it easy on that shoulder. Unless you want early retirement, take it slow. It's a nasty wound, and it needs time to heal." Roland gathered his supplies and gave Adelei a last fleeting look before he bowed and left.

The moment he was gone, Margaret spoke, her words halting. "Your job is dangerous. Why do you do it? If you could die...why bother?"

"The Amaskans are supposed to be the bringers of justice." When her sister's frown deepened, Adelei said, "Think of it this way. Your husband is royal blood. He's a highborn of a foreign land, and yet he's here in our country, committing horrible deeds against the Thirteen. How would someone like Lady Millicent seek justice against him for the death of her daughter?"

Margaret flinched. "He killed her daughter? He's the one who..." She swallowed hard. "The lady could petition the King."

"And what could our father do to his son-in-law? A man who's here to fulfill a treaty?"

"She'd have to take her complaint to the Boahim Senate."

"And if the Senate did nothing?" asked Adelei. "If they didn't have enough evidence to truly find the prince guilty? Then what?"

"Well, she would have to gather more evidence and try again."

Adelei nodded. "And in the meantime, the lady could find herself in danger trying to gather evidence on someone obviously unstable. The Amaskans find the evidence needed. If we're hurt, it's part of the job. We're trained to find the truth, whereas Lady Millicent wouldn't know where to begin. Once we have what we need, we act, serving justice much quicker than the Boahim Senate can, and with this method, the Senate doesn't have to get their hands dirty trying a highborn. They've never been great about doing that."

"But that's their sole purpose," Margaret shouted. She slapped her thigh in frustration and winced. "What's the point of all these laws if they don't work? Instead citizens have to resort to hiring people like you. Roland was surprised you were still alive. I mean, how long have you been doing this? How many people have you killed as the Boahim Senate sat idly by and did nothing?"

Adelei flinched at the last question. It was the same anger that had driven her to apply for membership into the Order. But she wasn't sure anymore that justice was who they served. Sometimes it felt an awful lot like vengeance. They were thoughts at the tip of her tongue, and she ached to share them. "Sometimes I think I've been doing this too long. But it's necessary. As you said, the Boahim Senate has been all too compliant to sit idly by in the last two decades. When there is nowhere to turn, people seek other alternatives. Don't worry about it too much. If all goes well, I'll live long enough to set your concerns at ease and maybe even shake up the Senate some."

Adelei stood and tested her shoulder with a gentle roll. It screamed, the tissue angry and sore, but it would do. "Where are you going?" Margaret asked.

"Was the prince returning to supper when he left you?"

"Yes, but—"

"I have a job tonight. Think you can manage to stay away from him? Get Michael to put more guards on your door if necessary."

Margaret rose from her seat as well. "Yes, but I don't—"

Adelei placed her hands on Margaret's shoulders. "Something I found says another attack may come tonight. I need to know you're safe, and I can't be there to ensure that if I'm going to catch your husband. If he does what I think he will, this will give us the connection we need between him and the Tribor. Can you stay safe for me? Hell, go hide in a room not your own. Go visit Lady Millicent. Just make sure Michael's with you."

Juggling her sister's protection and the pursuit of truth and evidence tore at her, but she resolved to marry the two. When Margaret nodded, Adelei left her alone in the King's sitting room. As luck would have it, Michael trailed behind King Leon as they approached the royal suite. "Captain, a word please," she called, and both men stopped. She leaned closer to Captain Fenton's ear and whispered, "An attack will come tonight. Tribor. And I can't be here for reasons I can't explain. Protect her."

"How do you know—"

She held up her hand. "Ask the King. He has the proof."

When she left them, her father pale and the captain confused, she felt a touch better about abandoning her sister for the evening as she rushed into the flood of people milling around outside the great hall. Chortez waved at her, but she turned away as she sought a particular crown bearing head.

He stood along the back wall, cornered by Lady Millicent. The woman's flushed face and shrill voice brought attention to them, and Gamun edged toward a door. The prince tried in vain to free himself from her clutches. He'd washed the blood from his face, but his swollen nose marred an otherwise perfect face, and Adelei bit off a laugh.

Margaret might have broken it indeed. His nose would be many colors come morning, but it wouldn't begin to make up for the bruises Margaret bore.

"You must pay for your crimes, prince or no. I will see you burn in Thirteen Hells for this if I have to send you there myself," Lady Millicent shouted.

Adelei hated to intervene, but she needed to follow him. He wasn't going to leave the castle if the lady killed him. With a sigh, she pushed past the growing crowd to reach the two highborns. "Lady Millicent. There you are. I've been looking all over the castle for you."

The woman jerked her hands away from Prince Gamun's arm. "You can bear witness—here," she said, reaching for

Adelei's hand. She backed away, and Lady Millicent's smile faltered.

"My lady, you're needed elsewhere. Let's leave Prince Gamun to his business."

"But—"

If she frowns any harder, I think she might rupture something. Adelei guided the woman away and back to the mob of guests.

"I don't know what game you're playing—"

"I must insist, my lady. King's orders," Adelei lied. She peeked over her shoulder at Gamun as he ducked out of the room. Once he was gone, Lady Millicent wrest her arm away from Adelei, her eyes hard. "What is the meaning of this? And don't give me that line about the King's orders. I'll have you brought up on charges of treason for lying in the King's name."

"If you accuse the prince now, with no evidence, then everything I have found will be for naught, my lady. I need more evidence, and for that, I need him to make his meeting tonight, if your little act hasn't blown that."

"Oh. Oh, dear." Lady Millicent rubbed her hands together and took a sudden seat on the bench behind her. "I—my apologies. I hope I haven't ruined things. It's just, well, a year ago today is when we found our daughter, and sometimes I lose my ability to think straight when it comes to Alethea."

"I—" Footfalls approached from behind. Adelei spun to face the assailant—a poor, unarmed page—and she seized him by the shoulders.

"Master Adelei, the King bids you to meet him immediately at the entrance near the stables. Please hurry, Master, there was...there was a body." The boy's voice broke at the end, his eyes wide.

"Take her ladyship to her chambers. She's not feeling well." The page helped Lady Millicent to unsteady feet, but Adelei was the one who wobbled as she took off at a run. *I left her alone, and they got to her. Damn Tribor got to my sister anyway.* She swallowed back the acid that rose to burn the back of her throat.

Both hands threw open the rear doors, and she nearly tumbled into the somber scene that met her. Margaret stood by their father, who knelt beside the body. King Leon appeared unmoving, but the slight twitch of his left shoulder betrayed the tears she couldn't see from behind him. When Adelei wedged her way through the small group, her eyes stared at the gruesome sight without comprehension.

Vacant blue met her brown. Eyes that she'd refused to meet a hundred times on their journey, eyes that she had feared showed the truth, stared back with an emptiness that left Adelei alone with her sorrow. *No, not alone. She brought me back to my family; she brought me home.*

Deeply carved symbols desecrated the flesh of Ida Warhammer's face, leaving very little left to recognize, but the scar across her neck had been left untouched. *They wanted us to know her identity.*

Adelei crouched beside the body. She reached out to pull back the cloak that had been hastily thrown over the captain, but Leon seized her hand. His eyes pled with her. "I'm sorry, Your Majesty, but the body may tell me more about who did this to her. I need to examine her."

"I understand, but—" He glanced upward, and Adelei followed his line of sight to Margaret. Ever pale-faced Margaret, who stood bravely at her father's side.

"I don't like you being this exposed," Adelei said. "Captain Fenton, will you make sure Their Highnesses make it safely to their rooms? And that they remain there until I'm finished?" When her sister protested, Adelei silenced it with a cold look before returning to the healer's side. "I need to examine her, but not in the open like this. We're drawing a crowd," she said to the healer, and he signaled a guard.

"Let's go, Your Majesty," Michael said, tapping the King on the shoulder.

"I want to stay with her."

Adelei's chest tightened, and she touched her father's hand. "I understand this is difficult, but it isn't safe here. I can't protect you here. Please, Your Majesty, go with Michael and the princess." At first, she thought he might fight her, but his eyes sought out the shadows surrounding them before nodding briefly. Michael pulled him away from the woman he'd loved for a decade. At her nod, the healers covered Ida's face.

"Do you have somewhere I can examine her without people gathering?"

"We have several rooms in the castle, Master Adelei," said one of the healers.

Once they'd lifted the body, Adelei got a good look at the blood trail beneath the woman. Good Gods, she had tried to make it back to the castle. She wasn't dumped there; she had crawled there. On hands and knees by the look of the blood pools. A shudder ran through Adelei, and she hurried to catch up to the healers. What had she found that she died trying to tell?

Now that the wedding had passed, fewer people filled the castle with each passing day. The highborns set out for their homes, but a few lingered still. A small audience had grown in the hall as the group escorted the body. Hushed whispers passed as people wondered who had died. "Maybe His Majesty?" someone asked, and Adelei winced.

She paused and cleared her throat loudly. "It's unfortunate, but Captain Warhammer has died. She died in service to the royal family of Alexander, who are safe."

The buzz carried her words through hurried lips as she resumed the escort. She would have preferred to say nothing, but the last thing she needed was the rumor mill churning out that Margaret was dead, or worse, the King.

The healers entered a door to the left, and Adelei found herself in a room of healing. Beds were stuffed into corners and herbs dried on lines strewn wall to wall. The healers lay Ida across an empty bed, and this time, there was no one to stop Adelei from unwrapping the body of Ida Warhammer.

Her hands shook. Gruesome was nothing new to Adelei. She'd been the cause of a good number of grisly scenes, and yet the Tribor assassin who had cut on Ida had done his best to make it as bloody and as painful as possible.

"Good Gods." Her eyes passed over more sigils carved into the bare flesh. "How did she manage to crawl like this?"

"Crawl?"

Adelei jumped.

"Sorry to have startled you, Master. The captain crawled?"

She nodded. "The blood outside. She was crawling toward the castle when she died. Though how, I have no idea. Who found her?"

Neither healer answered. "Who?" Adelei repeated.

The shorter of the two swallowed. "Princess Margaret."

And what was Princess Margaret doing outside the castle? Unescorted no less? Dammit. No clothing remained on the captain at all, her skin nothing more than a smear of bright red blood and hanging bits of flesh.

"How in all hells did she make it through the entire city without someone stopping her? I mean, she's caked in blood and naked. Surely someone would have seen her and tried to stop and help her or something." Adelei rolled the body and found the largest sigil yet carved into the woman's buttocks, a triangle that covered most of a well-muscled cheek. "Everyone she passed saw that mark. Everyone in the city must know."

"Know what, Master?"

"The Tribor are here." Both healers stepped back from the body, as if it held a death sentence. Not that she blamed them—the last body they'd encountered had been a poison bomb that had cost Adelei her horse. *Ida*— she closed her eyes a moment to steady her shaking hands. Adelei unfolded Ida's scraped and bloodied fingers. Dirt caked beneath short fingernails, and in her rush, she almost missed the tiny scrap of paper clutched tightly between her thumb and index finger. She opened it slowly, expecting a trap, but it only bore a message.

It's him. Two simple words, yet meaningless. Adelei ground her teeth in frustration. She died having brought Adelei information she already had. She already knew it was him. *Dammit.* She needed a connection. A link between him and the Tribor. The Boahim Senate wouldn't care about two words from a dead warrior. *Him* could have referred to anyone. *Hell, they'll say it could even be the King.*

"Master?" One of the healers touched her elbow, and she jumped. "Are you done with the examination? We'd like to prepare her for the burning ceremony."

"Almost."

There wasn't an inch of flesh that hadn't been cut—the skin between her toes, her armpits, and even her crotch had been devoured by the blade. Adelei touched the woman's eyes to close them and found that even her eyelids hadn't been spared. The word *Itova* was carved into them. "Itova, Goddess of Death. Patron Goddess of the Tribor," she whispered.

She nodded to the healers and stumbled to a corner chamber pot. The few bites of food she'd had that day came up in a rush, followed by stomach acid. It burned her nostrils and throat. Adelei vomited until she crouched shuddering and sweaty. She rolled back from the crouch to sit on the hard, stone floor, and she leaned her damp skin against the cold, stone wall. Ten minutes passed before she felt solid enough to move.

To be able to mourn Ida—a convenience she didn't have. They were still out there. The night wasn't over. Getting to her feet was a struggle as her body fought her. In the hall, the pages and guards avoided her on the trek to the royal suite. After checking that Captain Fenton stood on guard, she retreated to her father's chambers to find him sitting in the dark.

His mind was far, far away from her, and he didn't notice when she lit several candles and claimed the seat across from him. Wrinkles and tears aged him in the dim lighting.

"Father," she whispered, and when he didn't respond, she took his hand in her own. "Father, I need you to come back to me. We have trouble."

"Ida is dead. Did you see? Did you see what they did to her?" he cried, his voice cracking on the last word. "Leave me, I would be alone with my grief."

"Father." He pulled his hand away from her. "Your Majesty, I must report my findings to you. The kingdom's in danger."

Old fingers pulled the crown from tangled, thinning hair, and he handed it to her. "You can be King today. I'm tired. The woman I loved died thinking I believed her a traitor still. Leave me be."

The knock at the door was quiet. Her dagger was in her hands and her body in front of the King before the door opened. Margaret entered and shut the door behind her. "Before you say anything, Michael escorted me here with five guards."

And when you went outside? Alone?

Her sister must have read the thoughts in Adelei's face. "I saw her, Adelei—I could see Ida from the window. She *crawled*. Alone."

Adelei took her sister's hand and squeezed it. "I know," she whispered. "Father's inconsolable." Adelei held up his crown. "Apparently I've been made King. I guess that means whatever I say goes."

When the slight giggle escaped Margaret's lips, King Leon threw his goblet of wine at the wall. It stopped short and shattered on the stone floor. "There's nothing funny about death. Here you two stand making light of... Can you not leave me in peace?" he shouted.

"Father, you're right. There's nothing funny about Captain Warhammer's death, but right now, we need a King. We don't have time for grief. I think that's what Adelei meant anyway."

"The Tribor are here in the city," said Adelei.

"They've *been* in the city. This isn't new," he said dryly.

"We've only been dealing with one at a time, but the marks on..." She swallowed hard as he paled. "There's more than one. A large group of them. It isn't as simple as the Shadians hiring them. The Tribor are convinced they're on a holy mission, that somehow wiping out the Alexandrian royal line will please Itova. They've always had an obsession with the Goddess of Death, but this? I've never seen them this organized. You're both in great danger. Something the captain died to tell us."

Her father's face hardened, and he returned his crown to his head with trembling fingers. "Good. We'll draw them out and end this, once and for all."

"That won't work. It's what they expect. They knew her death would...would affect you, cause you not to think straight. If you go at them head on, you'll never hook the name of their employer. You'd get more out of an Amaskan."

"So what do you expect of me?" His shout reverberated, and the growing headache boxed between Adelei's ears.

"Clear the castle. Like you did before." He blinked before turning damp eyes on her. "Send home the dignitaries and visitors, or away at least. Clear the castle of anyone not a member of the royal guard or the staff. You both go into hiding. Leave me to catch this fool husband of Margaret's meeting with them. Once I have that connection, we can call for the Boahim Senate."

Margaret cleared her throat. "Wouldn't it be better to flee with the rest?"

"They'll only catch you. You both go into hiding in the castle—somewhere Michael and a large group can absolutely defend you to the death, because they're coming for you. And I can't catch a prince and protect you both. Not from that many Tribor." Adelei poked her head outside and returned with Captain Fenton in tow. The plan repeated, she said, "We need somewhere without windows and only one entrance. Somewhere defendable. Somewhere they wouldn't expect royalty to hide."

"I have a place in mind. I'd recommend they go into hiding immediately."

"Agreed."

"If we go into hiding, I...I won't see her burning," King Leon said.

Adelei pursed her lips together. "I'm sorry, Your Majesty. They'll expect you to be there, which is why you can't." Her father's shoulders slumped forward in his chair, his hands lying idly in front of him, empty. And yet he stared at them as if they held something. Adelei whispered to Michael, "He's not himself. Maybe the healers can give him something to help him sleep for a bit, but keep an eye on him. I suspect he's thinking of revenge, something he can't do. I can't have him in the way."

Captain Fenton nodded. "My apologies for earlier. I worried that you might, well, I can see that you want nothing more than to protect the royal family, and so I apologize for doubting your loyalties earlier."

She waved a hand. "Take them into hiding. Guard them well."

"I'm going to take them—"

"Don't tell me," she interrupted. "Don't tell anyone more than necessary."

"I would expect you to be in the necessary group."

She shook her head. "No, you were right before. I'm damaged goods. No telling what I'll do under duress. I can't know until I need to," Adelei said, meeting his gaze. "Take them where you will. Just protect them."

Heavy steps took Adelei to the entrance where Ida had died. Caked blood dried on the cobble, a mark upon the castle's beauty, and Adelei searched the darkness of the city street. *I know you're out there. And as much as I want to track each of you down and kill you, I have another fish in mind.*

An alleyway in view of the castle served as the perfect spot for her surveillance. Dark and dank, it was deserted on a hot night like this, and she crouched down to wait. Her legs fell asleep, and she rubbed her calves to help her circulation. Just when she was about to give up hope, a shadow crossed the blood-splattered cobble. His faint laugh reached her ears as the prince knelt to touch where Ida's body had been.

Gamun craned his head around, searching for something or someone. When he didn't find them, he passed into the late night shadows.

Adelei followed ten heartbeats behind and smiled.

CHAPTER TWENTY-FIVE

Paranoid much?

Gamun's cloaked figure circled around a building for the third time. Adelei crouched beside a vender's lot and sighed. His maze-like path had taken her nowhere in the past hour. At one point, she thought he had spotted her when he stopped and tossed his head back to stare at her hiding spot, but he ventured on. Another five minutes passed, and the sky opened up, drenching them both.

Yet still he waited.

She both thanked and cursed the rain. Cloud cover draped the moon and left the city of Alesta in darkness. The puddles left her leaping to dodge them, and they soaked her boots when she missed. Not that he could hear her over the downpour. She pressed her back to another wall. This time when he circled, a blonde head poked out of the door and whistled twice, the piercing sound barely audible over the thunder that rumbled across the night sky.

Gamun spotted the whistler and followed the figure inside a building. When the door shut, Adelei waited a minute before she crossed the small clearing. Adelei placed one hesitant foot after another and crossed the wooden porch until she'd inched her way to the lone window on the left.

Waterproof face grease wouldn't protect her from the light inside. Sticking her head up over the window sill was a risk. One she was willing to take. Inside, Prince Gamun stood with four other figures, but the storm kept their conversation silent. Darkened ovens lined the walls, and when one of the men moved, he exposed a rotund figure tied to a chair.

The baker. Great, they had a hostage. She ducked away from the window and retraced her steps until she reached the building's rear. *Should be a back door for water access.* As she came around the side of the building, she spied what she'd hoped for. The back door.

Adelei placed an ear to it and strained to hear over the falling rain. Muffled voices and the shuffling of feet on the other side. The footfalls were decidedly louder than they would be from the front room—the rear guard. Across from the porch sat a barrel, which she took cover behind. Adelei tossed a small pebble at the door. It bounced once before landing on the rear porch.

After another minute, she tossed another, this one harder. A head poked out the door, and she tossed a third pebble. This one landed twelve inches from the man's boots. The burly man crouched down to stare at the whitish pebble before peering out into the darkness. When she tossed the fourth, Adelei shortened its length, and it landed with a plop in a mud puddle.

"What is it?" a voice called out in Shadian.

"Not sure. I'll check it out." The guard left his post and ventured out into the rain.

Whoever was guarding their door was an idiot, a hired hand. No Tribor would fall for so simple a trick. Adelei tossed yet another stone. When he was close enough that she could smell the garlic of his dinner, she shoved her dagger through his heart before he could cry out.

She staggered under his weight when he fell. Dragging his body into a nearby bush was difficult work in the mud, and her grip slipped twice. The action wrenched her shoulder again. If it bled, the rain washed it away. The drag marks filled with water fast enough, covering her work.

Adelei approached the back door, her footfalls partially masked by the thunder overhead. The door stood wide open, inside candlelight mixing with the lightning overhead. She cast shadows in such light, but it couldn't be helped.

Skittering inside the door, she found herself in a back storage room. It was empty of people. Only flour bags, salts, and other cooking ingredients held her company. Water dripped to the wood floor beneath her, and she tiptoed gently to close the door. She left the door unlatched and open a crack. If she needed a way out, she wanted one. The voices up front were audible, and she leaned against the wall to listen.

"That wasn't in the plan," a deep voice growled.

"Neither was killing my wife. At least, not yet."

The deep voiced man cursed. "You failed to recruit the Amaskan. We had to change the plan."

"So did I. Besides, the Amaskan fascinates me. If I want to keep her around as a pet, what concern is it of yours?" said Prince Gamun. The wood floor beneath him creaked. "Besides, you have this nice baker to play with. You can have him instead."

"He is of no use to us. The new deal was for the Amaskan. Her in payment for killing the princess now. It's the deal we made with your King Father."

Between the meeting and the journals, it was enough. She waited in the silence and risked a peek through the arch. The ovens mostly obscured her view of the main room. They protected her from discovery, but the hostage sat tied just inside the arch. The Baker's eyes widened when he spotted her, and she mimed for silence. If she left to fetch the Senate, then the baker would die.

The prince's laughter spread goosebumps across her cold, wet skin. "You haven't successfully killed the princess yet. Your failures have been noted. Be lucky you walk away with any prize at all, my Tribor friend."

An assassin rushed across the floor, and Adelei held her breath a moment as he passed by the archway in front of her. One Tribor grabbed Gamun, but he let go with a yelp. The assassin's hand flapped in the air, and Adelei felt her shoulder grow warm where the prince had touched her. She clenched her teeth, fighting the pain as the burning slowly subsided.

"You mess with the wrong people, princeling. Three against one."

It was an empty threat and the Tribor knew it. "You would go against me? Knowing who pays for the food in your belly and roof over your head?" Three faces paled, but the prince didn't stop. He stepped toward the three wearing his familiar sneer.

"You were nothing. A wiped out few with no home until my father gave you shelter. You do what we say, when we say it. That was the deal. And if I say I want the Amaskan, then she's mine."

Adelei eased back from the archway. Her feet were slick on the wet wood as she crossed to the door. When her hand touched the handle, the wood plank beneath her groaned and filled the sudden silence. Adelei dropped into an instant crouch, her throwing knife in hand. She heard the movement before she saw it, and she yanked open the door in time to roll through it and into the mud outside.

A blade buried itself in the door's wood frame a moment later. Adelei didn't stop moving. She rose in the darkness and ran for the cover of the bushes. Several Tribor stood in the doorway, searching for her in the dark. Despite the instinct to run, she didn't move, allowing the storm and bushes to provide cover. One of the men swore, and Adelei winced as her shoulder erupted in pain.

She needed to get away from him. She tried not to make noise, but her sleeve snagged on a branch. Her helpless arm pained her too much to untangle it. A bolt of lightning struck nearby, blinding her in its brilliance, and she used the resounding thunder that followed to tear away from the brush. Adelei set off at a dead run for the castle.

It was more of a sliding run in the growing mud, at least until she met the cobbled road. Several times she slipped in the rain, once landing on her hip with a particularly loud splash as the puddle cushioned the fall. She stopped to check her trail as often as she dared. At first, they swore somewhere behind her as they poked around, but the closer she got to the castle, the less their footsteps splashed through puddles until finally, her trail remained silent. The burning in her shoulder ceased.

Adelei chose a side door entrance to the castle. They would expect her to head straight for the front. When her bedraggled self approached the four guards stationed at the side door, they stopped her with the drawing of steel. She more resembled some water demon of myth than a human. Her tattered clothes clung to a muddy body and grease covered her skin like that of a thief.

"Identify yourself." The guard's blade blocked her path.

"Master Adelei," she groaned, rubbing her shoulder. He leaned closer, studying her face a moment before he beckoned to another guard. Adelei wiped at her face with a soaked sleeve, but most of the grease remained. Four guards now huddled to discuss her, and she sighed.

"Look, I must see Captain Fenton immediately. If you won't let me find him, at least let me warm up near a fire until you fetch him." The moment her teeth started chattering, her legs took up the chorus, and she swayed on her feet. A guardsman offered her a steadying arm, which she ignored. "Also, someone might want to send a few guards to the baker on the lower east side. There's a corpse there that should be brought to the castle immediately."

One guard frowned before running out into the rain, and a second set off inside the castle. The third, a beefy gourd of a man with a bulbous nose that exploded onto his face motioned for her to follow him inside to a storage room.

No fireplace, just piles of baskets and dried foods. At least it was warmer there and dry. Adelei sat on the floor in the corner. *Poor bastard.* Even if she'd wanted to rescue the baker from his captors, there was no chance of that now. The minute they'd seen her, he had been a dead man. Probably before that.

Warmth radiated through the wall behind her, and a quick mental map placed her on the other side of the kitchens. Between the warm wall against her back, the throbbing of her shoulder, and the fading adrenaline, she relaxed and fell into a light doze.

When the door flung open, cold air spilled across her face. Adelei rose, dagger in hand, before the sleep cleared her eyes. "Come with me," said guardsman big-nose.

Adelei sheathed her dagger and rubbed her eyes. They passed through a series of hallways to one of the servant's halls and stopped before a room she could have sworn was a storage closet. Linens lined the shelves. *Great. Another closet for me?* She walked in with a sigh, only to find her father, sister, and Michael seated at a tiny table in the corner.

"I didn't want to know where they were hiding," she muttered to Michael.

"When one of my guards reports someone in your state is at the castle demanding to see me, I figure it must be a matter of life and death. For all I knew, the Thirteen hell-birds were flying in behind you to kill us all. Besides, from the look on your face, you have information. Information the King may need." Captain Fenton gestured for her to have a seat.

"Do you need a healer?" Margaret pointed at the torn sleeve of her tunic. "You look—"

"Scary, yes, I know. Your Majesty," Adelei interrupted. King Leon looked right through her. She reached out a mud-caked hand and left bits of dried mud flakes behind on the shoulder of his tunic.

He looked up then, brows furrowed. "What happened to you?"

"I went chasing a rat."

"Was it chasing cheese?"

"It was." Adelei drew her knees up under her chin. "Prince Gamun met with three Tribor in a bakery in the lower east side of the city. Apparently, the original deal was that Gamun was to recruit me. When I wouldn't take his offer, his father changed the deal. The Tribor were to get me as payment for killing Her Highness. Gamun's changed his mind though." When her father cocked an eyebrow at her, she added, "It seems I'm fascinating and am to become his new pet."

Michael grimaced. "How do you know the men were Tribor?"

"Gamun called them as such. Apparently their resurgence is due to his father supporting them and giving them refuge in his kingdom, which we'd long suspected but didn't have proof. Prince Gamun had to remind them of that fact when they threatened him for reneging on their deal. They seemed fairly afraid of him when he mentioned his father. He also brought out the mystic stuff again—touched one of them when the Tribor tried to attack him. Oddly enough, when Gamun did this, I felt it in my shoulder, even though he didn't know I was there yet."

Michael shot up from his chair, the legs scraping loudly as it skittered back. "Yet? You mean he found you afterward?"

"The floorboards beneath me squeaked. Probably swelling in the rain. They knew someone was there, and they saw my back as I fled."

"If they're on their way—" Michael's blade inched out of its sheath.

Adelei held up both hands. "I wasn't followed. They may suspect it was me, but they didn't follow on my heels."

"If your back was to them, how do you know they saw you?" Margaret asked.

"They threw a knife at me, but they missed. I took a fairly indirect route here. The storm outside is loud enough to confuse anyone, so I doubt they figured out which direction I took. If they suspect it was me, they know I'll eventually end up here. Just to be safe, I took a side door in—the one by the guard tower. We're not in any more danger than we already were."

She glanced at her father. "I take it you have the journal with you?"

He nodded, and Margaret asked, "What journal?"

King Leon removed the book from the pocket at his side, his eyes fiercely feral in the candlelight. When Margaret reached for it, he slapped her hand away and handed it across to Michael instead. The captain flipped it open to a page at random and blanched at the picture. "How long have you had this?" Michael asked.

"Less than a day," Adelei answered.

"I ask Your Majesty's permission to be frank." King Leon waved an impatient hand, and Michael continued, "Why has this not been brought before the Boahim Senate yet? You're in danger the longer we dally."

She met her father's dull gaze. *If we'd called for them sooner, would Ida still be alive? That's what you're asking me, isn't it, Father? Ida's just one more body to stab me in the darkness.*

"I'm sure they had a reason." Margaret frowned at the captain.

"No need to defend my decision," Adelei said. "We needed to know who called for the Tribor. Otherwise, we'd still be in danger after involving the Senate. I don't think there was any way we could've done anything different."

Adelei didn't look at her father, couldn't look at him. His accusations were a solid form before her, the dead captain's name on his lips.

Margaret took her father's hand. "Papa, she's doing everything she can to keep us safe. Adelei can't save everyone." King Leon flinched. "I'm sorry that Captain Warhammer is...but we need you. We need you to call for the Boahim Senate now. There is no time for grieving."

While her lips trembled, Margaret squared her shoulders and patted her father's fingers. Her words, let alone her strength, must have surprised their father as he looked up from his wrinkled, gnarled knuckles.

"Captain, I need an escort to the council room." King Leon stood slowly, as if the action pained him. "Master Adelei, protect her. That is your only job at this moment. Do not leave this room unless absolutely necessary."

"I can't protect you both if we split up."

"I know. Protect her. Let me do my job, since you both seem determined on ensuring that I do before I am allowed my grief." He left with heavy steps and Michael fast on his heels.

Her sister was silent at first, but soon the silence was too burdensome, and Margaret opened her mouth a few times before speaking. "I've seen him grieve before; losing a captain is never easy, but this feels like more. I haven't seen him grieve like this since Mom died..." Adelei said nothing, and Margaret drew a hand to her mouth. "H-he and Captain Warhammer? When did—how?"

"I don't know when, but it's been quite some time. As to the how...I don't know that either, just that they were."

"A long time?"

Adelei nodded. "That's why it was so hard on him when he found out Ida was behind my kidnapping." Her sister stopped pacing, standing stock still in the middle of the linen closet. Her muscles tensed, and she reached out for a blanket which she stuffed against her mouth before screaming.

She turned accusing eyes on Adelei, stabbing a pointed finger in the air at her. "You. You knew this. How did you know this, and I didn't? I'm sick of everyone keeping me in the dark as if I'm some sort of scatterbrained idiot. Bad enough that my husband feels this way, but my own family? Tell me everything. About Ida. About those journals. Don't leave anything out."

"I don't know that Father would—"

"In case you haven't noticed, our father's dying. He's grieving over his love? A traitor to the crown? None of this makes any sense. Soon the Boahim Senate will come and dissolve my marriage. I'll be ruler all too soon. If you want me to be a wise and just Queen, tell me everything."

There was a logic to her words, but Adelei hesitated. She didn't need to know what was in the journals. That was too much for most people. Still, if war was on its way, she might need every scrap of information she could get.

"I can tell you're thinking—trying to find a way out of telling me or what information to leave out," said Margaret, and she stabbed Adelei with her finger. "Don't. I've been lied to enough as it is. If Amaskans stand for justice, give me mine. Tell me what I need to protect my people."

"All right. Let me start at the beginning then. Might as well get comfortable." She watched her sister return to her seat, amazed at the transformation in the young woman before her.

"What?" Margaret snapped.

"When I first got here, you couldn't stand being in the same room with me. Everything about you breathed selfish highborn." Margaret opened her mouth to retort, but Adelei held up a hand to stop her. "But you've changed. You've grown up. It's refreshing and unexpected."

"Maybe it's only unexpected because you didn't know me. Royalty wears many faces, Adelei. I may not know everything, and I'll admit that Father spoiled me something awful, but I'm not the simpleton people think I am. And... Events can change a person. I don't think I can step aside as this monster kills people in my home. Now, no more delay. Get on with it," Margaret ordered, tapping the floor once with an impatient slippered foot.

Adelei laughed at the impetuousness of the order. *This kingdom is in for a shock with her as Queen. Mouse indeed.*

"Some of this I only know from what Ida or Father told me, so I can't guarantee the accuracy of it, but Ida wasn't always Captain Warhammer. Her real name was Shendra Abner, and she was Amaskan…"

Michael closed the door behind him, leaving King Leon alone in the council room. Without hesitation, Leon approached the bookcase on the back wall. His hands found the thirteen books without searching. Long and wrinkled fingers pressed their spines back until all thirteen clicked.

At first, the bookcase did nothing. He wondered if its disuse had resulted in the mechanism's failure, but the latch clicked and when he pulled on the bookcase, it slid aside to reveal a smaller chamber behind it: a room with no windows and no other doors. Just smooth solid stone on all four sides.

When the room was made, King Leon wasn't privy to. The room was carved from the stone of the land itself, a hollow half-cave that existed long before Alesta Castle was built, long before his ancestors were part of the Little Dozen Kingdoms. The room had existed when all were united under one banner, one king—the Kingdom of Boahim.

King Leon's father told him this as he lay dying, knowledge passed down from one successor to another, from King Alexander himself who sat upon the throne of Boahim. Leon held little stock in the ideas and practices of mystics, magic users since banned from the Kingdom of Alexander, but he admitted the usefulness of such a chamber. He walked inside and slid the bookshelf closed behind him. His candle was the only light in the room, which he extinguished with pinched fingers.

The sudden darkness chilled him. "*Ta'asor Ley,*" he whispered, and the orb in the center of the room glowed white. The light intensified until he was forced to look away. When the light faded, an older woman's face peered out of the orb.

"I take it you have good reason to call upon the Boahim Senate, King Leon of Alexander." The corners of her eyes twitched as she squinted at him.

He bowed his head briefly, and when he raised his gaze, a dozen people huddled in the background. Their faces were ancient, and yet there was a timelessness about them as they watched him from the safety of their mist shrouded island.

All those eyes. He shivered.

"It's like you can see into me." He'd only intended to think it, but something compelled the words be spoken aloud and when he did, he clamped a hand over his mouth like a boy.

The woman's lips tweaked upwards. "Ah, yes, I forget that you've not called on us before. I thought of your father. The orb compels people to speak. No room for misunderstanding or lying. Don't let it overly concern you. State your purpose in asking for our help."

"There's a traitor of the worst kind among us. A family that would destroy the world and break us into war."

"There have always been such families. I assume you speak of the rising conflicts between your kingdom and that of Shad?"

He nodded and opened his mouth to speak further on it, but a man so ancient he held the look of death itself, stepped into view of the orb. "The treaty was to stop this conflict. What has changed in such a short period of time that you would interrupt us?" he asked, his wrinkles gaining wrinkles as he frowned.

King Leon spoke, his words halting at first as he talked of Goefrin and the poison, Ida's role in Iliana's kidnapping, and finally of the return of Iliana. He had had no intention of telling them she was formerly Amaskan, but the orb was unforgiving, and he spilled his secrets like water from the Esohn River. They listened, faces unchanged until he reached the newfound information on the Shadian royal family.

Leon removed the book from his pocket and read, his tongue thick and tasting of bile. Their faces mirrored his as he described in great detail the torture and mutilation of many young girls at the hands of the Monster. "He personally beat Princess Margaret and attempted to corrupt Iliana, offering her deals to help him. He told her that if she denied him, he would harm us all. The man knows no bounds and is a danger to the Little Dozen. He's harbored and sheltered the Tribor and brought them into my kingdom to destroy us. No telling what the Shadians will do to my people, or how many Prince Gamun has already killed in addition to Captain Warhammer and the young girl he brought with him."

The hoarseness of his voice only reminded him of the lack of drink. His feet cramped from standing, and his lungs ached with the need to cough. "I'm tired. Too tired for the war that's coming, war that will probably erupt with or without your intervention, but I beg you to consider. Uphold the Thirteen and strip us of the plague that threatens us."

"You say King Havin Bajit of Shad and his son are harboring and supporting the Tribor, whom they've hired to kill your family. But you openly admit to us that you are harboring an assassin as well," the woman said, and Leon flinched. "Not only are you sheltering an Amaskan, but you openly brought her into your kingdom to protect Princess Margaret. You are guilty of violating the Thirteen yourself, and yet you come before us seeking justice. Do you wish us to be involved?"

Her question surprised him. "I don't understand. I was told that you were the upholders of the Thirteen. If I must be brought forward for my role in this, fine, but you must stop the Shadian family before they destroy us all. These journals—"

"—Are fairly damning. But how do we know you truly found them in his rooms? We must speak to the one who gathered this information, not you."

King Leon ground his teeth. "You have me in a difficult position. I ask for help, but to get it, I will have to turn over my own daughter."

"A daughter you yourself admit is a danger. We require her word against the Shadians. And…we would know more about the Amaskan conditioning wrapped around her mind. If she's truly a danger, she must be dealt with."

"But she's my daughter. She's of royal blood. It is not her fault that she has been played a pawn by the Order of Amaska—"

"No one is above the Thirteen. Not even a princess." The woman paused, her eyes locked on his. "If you wish our help, this is our price."

"Damn you," he whispered. Even with the orb's light, the room felt incredibly dark, and he wobbled on his feet.

"Do not come before us again on this without the Amaskan," she said, and the orb grew dark, leaving him alone in the pitch. When he finally moved, it was with heavy feet and shoulders, his crown's weight upon him like a curse.

King Leon held back tears as he readied himself to betray his own daughter for peace.

"...That's everything," said Adelei. Margaret lost her meal to the corner again and wiped her mouth with a scrap of linen. When she sat up, another heave rippled through her, and she emptied her stomach twice more.

"How has he escaped the Boahim Senate's notice until now?"

"I don't know. I can only assume that they haven't had enough evidence to do much more than watch." *Either that or they didn't care. More and more we see their lack of concern these days.*

Her sister shuddered, wrapping her arms around herself as if she could hug away the memories now written in her head as truth. "I'm glad Captain Warhammer is not the traitor I thought her to be—she died with honor—but Prince Gamun, this monster shared my bed. He's in my castle, my kingdom, hurting my people. He must be stopped."

Sounds outside the door reached Adelei, and she leaned against it; she strained to listen as Margaret scuttled into the corner behind a shelf. When the door opened, it was only their father who walked in, his face haggard.

"What is it?" asked Adelei.

"I reached the Senate."

"Are they going to help us?" Margaret asked. Color had returned to her face, but when their father said nothing, she paled. "Wait, they have to. This man is a monster. How can they sit by and do nothing when people are dying?"

Not even the shrill pitch of her complaint registered with King Leon, who looked on Adelei with unshed tears.

They want me. That's their price. Adelei's lips drew thin lines across her face.

King Leon crumbled. He reached out a hand for hers, and she took it. "It's okay, Father. It will be all right."

"What? What's going on?" Margaret asked. Nothing but Michael's footsteps outside filled the silence. "Oh Gods. No, they can't."

"But they can. There are no laws that apply to only some. In their eyes, I'm a murderer."

"But you're not. I mean, you've killed people, but only bad people, right? How is that wrong?"

Adelei squeezed her father's hand. "What did they say? Did they say you were harboring a murderer? Did they threaten you with your own crime?"

He nodded. "They said I was no better than the Shadians for giving asylum to the Tribor. And just like them, I'd hired a murderer to solve the problem instead of coming to them initially."

"This is ridiculous." Margaret shouted. "You hired Adelei because they left you no other choice. And besides, she's your daughter. She's a princess of royal blood—"

"—And so is Prince Gamun." Adelei's words were a whisper, but they reached her sister's ears, and Margaret dropped into a pile of linens.

"So this is it? You find the monster in our midst, and now they're going to take you away with him?" asked Margaret.

"We—we don't know that yet," King Leon said. "They only asked to speak with your sister."

Adelei sighed. "Maybe, but we know what will come next. They will get the information they need from me, and then, once I'm of no use to them, they'll try me for my crimes."

"Maybe not. I will speak on your behalf," her sister said.

King Leon squeezed Adelei's hand and didn't let go. It wouldn't matter. The Boahim Senate would have their justice, and they both knew it. It was the price for their aid.

CHAPTER TWENTY-SIX

"Just beware the orb."

Adelei scratched her brow. "The orb? Are you turning mystic on me?"

King Leon sighed as he hobbled into the Senate room. "The orb will make you speak the truth, even if you don't want to. You can't lie before the Senate. Just... Just be careful what you think and say."

When the bookcase slid aside to unveil the other room, Adelei's brows shot up, but when her father spoke the old tongue and the orb lit up, she stumbled into the wall behind her. "I would expect to find mystic tech in Sadai, but not here. Not in Alexander," she said, her fingers lightly caressing the orb. Her fingertips tingled as the power coursed through them, and her heartbeat hummed along with the orb's pulse until a woman's face appeared inside of it. Wrinkles coursed her face, yet there was a youth to her eyes as they lit upon Adelei.

"So he decided to bring you before us after all." Her voice crackled like dried bugs on the forest floor.

"Actually, she volunteered to come talk to you—a concession that I hope would weigh in her favor." King Leon leaned closer to the orb, his face a frowning reflection of the woman's. Adelei watched the silent battle between the two spawn before her like an event before her time. She placed a hand gently on her father's shoulder. "You asked for my appearance, and I am here. What do you require of me?" she asked, her throat raspier than she liked. Despite the tautness of her muscles, she didn't wish to appear afraid. Adelei shifted her stance and parted her legs. Tense hands hung loosely at her sides as she stared vacantly at the senator before her. The woman's lips pursed and shoulders hunched before she, too, schooled her physical response.

"Do you know who I am, young woman?"

Adelei nodded. "Adela Whitlen, one of the senators for the Kingdom of Estona."

If the woman was surprised by Adelei's knowledge, she held her face in such a careful mask that not even Adelei could tell. Behind her, several voices grumbled and Adelei peered into the orb's depths at forty bodies around a horseshoe table.

They had called for a full senate. It was everything Adelei could do to keep the shock of that from her face, though a glance at her father told her he hadn't known either as his eyes widened.

Senator Whitlen waved an impatient hand at her colleagues, and they settled into an uneasy silence. "You, my dear, have many names if King Leon is to be believed. Identify yourself to this senate."

Adelei hesitated, her thumb rubbing against the side of her index finger. Who was she, indeed? She inhaled the dusty air through her nose—a good, steadying breath before the answer. "I am Master Adelei of the Order of Amaska. And I am Iliana Poncett of Alexander. Both are identities I would claim."

"You admit to being an assassin?" This from a man in deep crimson, whose youthful face bore a slight resemblance to Prince Gamun.

"With whom am I speaking?"

Several members rocked in their seats, their grumbling loud enough to be audible, though not intelligible. Senator Whitlen cleared her throat. "When you are speaking to the senate, you address us all as one. Who we are is not important."

"And yet you made a point of making sure I knew your identity," Adelei said. "I wonder why that is?"

A flush crossed the Senator's face, and she tugged at the corner of her green tunic. "It was my intention to make sure you understood you were addressing the Boahim Senate, not I in particular."

While Whitlen spoke with a steady voice, she focused on Adelei's forehead rather than meeting her eyes directly. "She's lying," Adelei whispered, then swore. Her thoughts were an exposed cliffside to the senate when speaking through the orb. Voices called out—most irritated by her impudence as those senators rose from their seats, their warped faces ever close to the orb.

"Why is it that we need her testimony?" the young senator asked flatly. "This is a waste of time. There's nothing going on."

"Agreed," another woman said as she took another sip from her goblet. "The Shadian family is not behind any attempt. If anything, these assassins are the problem."

Senators called out their opinions at random, and King Leon reached for the hand that stood limply at her side, squeezing it gently before clearing his throat. When it didn't garner the response he wished, he cleared it again, louder this time. A few heads turned his way, but the majority of the group still bickered amongst themselves until he reached out and tapped his thick fingers on the orb. The resounding ring was piercing, and Adelei clamped her hands over her ears. Most of the senators did the same.

"I was under the impression that the Boahim Senate was made up of leaders: people who sought justice on behalf of the kings and queens of the Little Dozen. If all we get is a bunch of bickering old men and women, we'll handle this on our own," her father said.

Adelei stood taller at the steel in his voice. "I am no Tribor assassin. I am Amaskan, and I was brought here to protect the royal family—*my* family—from the Tribor and Shadians who seek to destroy them and end the line."

"We will address your heritage later. King Leon comes to us with quite the tale of betrayal and murder, but most of his words come from your experiences. We would have you tell us what you know," said Senator Whitlen.

Adelei took her time retelling the story, beginning with the moment she was sent from Sadai and met with Captain Warhammer. The mention of the warrior brought tears to her eyes, but she held her calm, even when discussing her own confusion over where her loyalty lay. It wasn't a topic she'd intended to discuss, but the orb compelled her. When she found her tongue loose and her thoughts guiding her toward Master

Bredych and the conditioning, she bit down hard on her own tongue and thought of snow.

"Snow? You were concerned about the snow?" asked Whitlen, brows furrowed into a chasm on her forehead.

"I'm not sure why I said snow. I was concerned about the Tribor. They might give the Amaskans a bad reputation with their bloodlust," Adelei said. It wasn't the full truth, but was close enough to one of her concerns that the orb allowed it. She continued the tale until finally reaching her flight from the bakery.

Her father stepped forward again, his face ashen as he spoke. "The Captain of the Royal Guard has confirmed the baker's body. It was found in pieces, tossed in a waste heap with bits of old bread. I think they wanted scavengers to pull it apart before we found it. And it would've been if we'd not had the rainstorm we did last night."

"You know for a fact that this baker was killed by Prince Gamun?" The man's dark eyes caught her attention, and when he turned, his side profile gave her a shot of his pointed chin. Her thoughts were audible to the Senate, and the man sighed. "Yes, I'm related to His Highness—what of it?" His pouting lips reminded Adelei of the prince.

"How do we know that you will be an impartial judge to the evidence we bring with such a connection to the accused?" asked Adelei.

King Leon nodded. "And I would ask how a relative of the royal family made his way on to the Boahim Senate. The bylaws established at the settling of the Little Dozen clearly state—"

Senator Whitlen interrupted him. "We will take what Senator Raj says into consideration. You need not worry about our ability to police ourselves. We have heard some from the journal, but wish to examine it. You say there are more?"

"Yes, Senator," said Adelei.

"If they say what you've implied and the other journals are still in his chambers, then this is a great crime indeed. One that requires immediate attention." The woman's eyes swept around the horseshoe table, and when none of them contradicted her, she nodded. "Please step back from the orb." The senator gathered her thick skirts in her hands as she stood and closed her eyes.

Both Adelei and her father remained in place until the orb grew. The size of it drove them into the back of the bookshelf. "What is it—" Adelei tried to ask, but the orb's light touched her outstretched hand and shot a tingle through her palm. King Leon tugged on her shoulder, pulling her back into the main room. His ashen face bore a layer of perspiration as he stared openmouthed at the growing orb, and she wrapped a supporting arm around him as he tumbled back. Adelei settled him into a chair.

"The Boahim Senate is coming."

At first she thought she had misheard him, but the hidden room was completely enveloped in light and hummed with an energy that scared her. "How is this possible?"

"Had you grown up here, you'd have learned more about the council chambers of each kingdom. Each King's council is made up of thirteen advisors—"

"I know this. The holy number and number of deities that created our world. What does that have to do with—"

Her father knocked his knuckles on the table before him. "Look at the table. Really look at it."

Adelei pulled her eyes away from the glowing room. The council table with its thirteen chairs—one spot for each of King Leon's advisors. Some years, seats sat empty, but there would never be more than thirteen. The oak table top was inset with a deep carving of the tree of life, its thirteen deity-laden branches reaching out toward each seat at the table. Adelei stared at it without change until the buzzing in the room behind her changed. She touched the grooves in the wood and heard it whisper.

"What is it saying?"

"No one knows," her father answered.

The tree's branches lit with the same glow as they pulsed twice. Each time the light pulsed, there was a slight pop behind her.

"Each kingdom's table serves as a gate, activated only by the Boahim Senate upon utterance of the old tongue."

"Not just any word, either," another voice added. "The right words must be spoken, words and phrases only taught to royal family and members of the Holy Few." Adelei flinched at the strange man's voice and spun around.

The wrinkled old man walked with a hunch that betrayed his age, but he noted her fingers tucking the throwing knife into her wrist and grinned with a flash of white that was neither threatening nor afraid. Her stance shifted as her father rose to embrace the man.

"It's been a long time," said King Leon. "May I introduce you to my daughter, Iliana? I guess she goes by Adelei now, but my daughter nonetheless. Adelei, this is Senator Adan Montero, representative for Alexander."

Adelei offered her hand and found his grasp firmer than she'd expected. "I take it you weren't aware that the Senate could travel in such a way?"

"I'm not sure whether this is good or bad." When he cocked his head to the side, she continued, "If you're needed, on a day such as today, then I'm sure it's good, but travel like this? By mystical means? You could move about in people's lives without their knowledge. Privacy no longer exists with such power."

"With a mind like that, she's wasted on the Amaskans, Leon. She should have been a candidate for the Boahim Senate," another woman spoke, greeting King Leon with a slightly stiffer embrace but warm eyes.

The other Alexandrian senator, I assume. The tree beside her continued to pulse as more senators stepped through the gate, until the room held more bodies than chairs. The glowing ceased at once and Senator Whitlen stumbled through the doorway. Her skin was gray beneath her makeup.

"Next time, you control the gate," she said to the Shadian representative. "I'm not as young as you." Her entrance into King Leon's council room sent a silent signal to the others, and Adelei watched as the older members claimed seats. The younger senators stood behind them. The woman turned to King Leon with an outstretched hand, and he handed over the journal with a moment's hesitation.

Leon ordered mulled wine, which he brought into the room himself with Adelei's help. "Once it's known you're here, everyone will know. I'd like to hold that secret as long as necessary." He set a pitcher on the table.

Adelei crouched in the corner as Whitlen opened the first journal. When she read the first sentence, Adelei flinched. She could read the Amaskan code. Adelei's body screamed a warning, and she dug her nails into the palms of her hands.

"You have something to add, Adelei?" the senator asked.

"H-how can you read the journal? It's in code."

"Did you think the Order's code known only to the Order, young Amaskan?" Adelei nodded, and Whitlen shot her a slight grin. "Leon, what a waste to have her raised with that group of fools. A pity really." The senator faced Adelei, her eyes boring holes through her. "This language is older than the Amaskans, from a continent many months' sail from our own Boahim. Gaenav, the land of steel. The lands of our ancestors, the Thirteen."

"But Gaenav is a myth, and the Thirteen are—" A chill spread across her as the full Senate stared at her. Adelei sounded as naïve as Margaret, and she swallowed hard.

"Adelei, there are many histories of this world. Knowledge held safe by the Boahim Senate. The Order of Amaska knows only what we allow it to know."

She struggled to make sense of the information as the senators returned to the journal. Adelei blocked out the thoughts that threatened to spill across her tongue. She'd already said too much.

Senator Whitlen read every page aloud with ease, pausing only to sip her wine or when a member of the senate needed a brief recess. One senator passed his seat to King Leon. The cough came upon him, but being off his feet helped, and Adelei mouthed a "thank you" to the senator over her father's head.

Heavy woolen dress robes were shed as the bodies raised the room's ambient temperature, and Adelei's mind drifted. The orb still glowed faintly in the secret room. No telling if the orb was still active. As the senators listened to the journal entries, Adelei leaned her head against the wall and thought of snow.

"Adelei?"

The words were gentle as they reached her ears, and she opened slightly gummy eyes to see many more staring at her. Adelei nodded her thanks when someone handed her a glass of water. After a few swallows, she stretched stiff muscles that complained from the oddity of her sleeping position. Most of the faces around her bore a sallow look, but Senator Raj dampened his chair with the waves of perspiration that trickled from him, his eyes darting around at his fellow senators. Nothing in the journal pointed a finger at the senator himself. Why he perspired so…

"Adelei, I would like for you to show me the other journals," Senator Whitlen said and rose from her chair with the pop of old joints.

It was then that Adelei noticed the guards in the orb room itself, a dozen fighters who were as battle scarred as she and certainly more alert. Father would be safe with them there. She nodded to the senator and led her outside the Alexandrian council chamber.

A dozen of the King's guards stood on duty. At the sight of the senator's silver, woven cloak, its tree of life flecked with glittering thread, they turned as one and saluted. Whitlen nodded briefly as they passed. Adelei minced her steps to maintain the senator's pace.

"You wish we were moving faster," the senator said, her green eyes snapping in the light that shone through the hall window. "The prince should be occupied for the moment, so our speed will not change whether he has moved or destroyed the others."

Adelei flushed at the scold. Servants whispered and scurried about with a sudden reason to dust a clean table nearby. Their eyes kept to the floor while they listened, and Adelei said nothing. Whitlen, too, remained silent as she followed the former Amaskan to the Shadian state suite.

The guards stepped aside, again saluting Whitlen. "Where did he hide them?" asked the senator as they stepped into Gamun's study. Adelei pointed out each journal and waited as the senator retrieved them. A quick flip through them and she nodded to herself before tucking them away into a pocket. "Any others?"

"Not that I know of."

"It seems that we owe you a great deal of thanks for uncovering such a heinous creature in our midst. We must return to the Senate immediately to determine our next course of action."

This time as they walked, Adelei doubled her steps to keep up. How she had the energy to move that fast was amazing. Magic maybe? Either way, Adelei didn't trust them. There had been a monster right under their noses. The senator swore the Order knew only so much, yet they had known more than the Senate. Either that or the Senate knew and had done nothing. What else had they been ignoring?

"Share your thoughts with me," the senator said, and when Adelei flinched, the woman chuckled. "That deep frown betrays more than you know, youngling. You haven't decided if you can trust the Senate or not, and it's eating at you."

"I mean no offense," said Adelei, "It's just that in my line of work, you learn quickly that no one is a friend, and no one can be trusted. Especially if they are so blind to the monster in their backyard."

The senator halted and placed a hand on Adelei's shoulder. This time, an icy burn chilled her and spread goosebumps across her skin. Adelei tried to pull away, but found her feet unable to move. The woman's green eyes bored holes into her own. "He left his mark on you." Whitlen pressed harder on Adelei's shoulder, and Adelei squirmed. "You have sacrificed much to bring this man before us."

The burning ceased and when Adelei flexed her shoulder, it moved with ease, no stiffness or pain remaining. "You healed my shoulder. I don't know whether I should be grateful or angry at the intrusion."

"I'm surprised that you bear the familial prejudice toward mystics considering you grew up in Sadai. Why is that, I wonder?" The woman moved her hand to Adelei's head. "Ah—you've had your mind messed with enough. No wonder you distrust so."

Adelei found her feet and jerked herself away from the woman's touch. "I am thankful for the healed shoulder, but let's get on with this. I don't need anything else from the Senate, thank you." Whitlen frowned, but moved on without another word. Adelei rubbed her temples, her head buzzing.

What did you do to me? Adelei shook her head, and the buzzing faded. *Did you damage me so much that even the mystics can see it? Damn you, Master. Damn you to Thirteen Hells for what you've done.*

When they reached the council room, Whitlen held up the other journals. "Our presence here is no longer a secret. I suggest we retire to more comfortable a room to finish reading these diaries. King Leon, could we make use of your drawing room perhaps?"

"If I may be so bold, the audience chamber would do better. There is ample seating and refreshment. I'll have the servants bring more wine and something light to eat."

"Very light," she said. "The details of these journals will do a number on the stomach. Nothing heavy."

Senator Whitlen faced Adelei before speaking further. "Take your father somewhere safe. Guard him and your sister. When we are ready, we will call for you again. And don't leave the castle. We have need of you yet."

A page was ordered to fetch a meal, and members of the royal guard escorted the Boahim Senate to the audience chamber. Leon followed Adelei, his steps even slower than the senator's as they set off for the servant's wing. Michael whisked them behind a door with a fluttering hand.

Margaret rushed to her father and threw her arms around him. "You were gone for so long, I thought for sure something had happened."

"The Boahim Senate is here."

Margaret's fingers crumpled her embroidery as she faced Adelei. "Are they going to...?"

"I don't know. They warned me not to leave the castle. Whether it was for my safety or the safety of others, I don't know." Adelei claimed a seat on a stool across from her sister. This room, like the previous, resembled a linen closet more than an actual room. At least this time they had warning. Captain Fenton had arranged for some furniture to be brought in, though the worn fabric's shoddiness and splintered wood made Adelei believe it pilfered from a servant's room.

Her father claimed the largest chair, whose stuffing leaked out the sides and left small piles of straw around it. He eased himself into its frame as a cough took him, and Adelei winced as the chair shook. Margaret offered him a warm mug that smelled strongly of herbs.

Once the cough subsided, he gripped Adelei's shoulder and released it quickly. "Your shoulder isn't bothering you?"

She rotated the joint, its movement easy and pain free. "Senator Whitlen did it. Said Prince Gamun marked me there. She seemed pretty intent on healing it."

"Be careful," he whispered. "She served the Senate's purpose in healing it, and only their purpose. The Senate is tricky. They'll use people in their pursuit of justice, no matter who gets hurt in the crossfire."

"Much like the Amaskans."

Her father flinched. "I was thinking that, yes, but I'm surprised to hear you say it."

Adelei glanced at her sister, who stared at her embroidery with an intense concentration though her needle didn't move. "I used to believe that what we were doing was right, that we delivered justice when and where the law could not. But—" she paused, seeking out her father's face. His crown rested on his thinning hair, a weight she didn't want, and yet she already understood its burden. "Have you ever felt torn between what you know is right and what you know you must do?"

"Every ruler does. I felt that way the moment you returned here."

"They messed with my head, planted ideas there about what's right, but are they right? Is our justice any better, or just our own brand of delusional thinking? What makes our justice any better than the decisions of the Boahim Senate? Why should any of us have a say in the actions of others?" The questions tumbled out of Adelei, and she clenched her teeth together to stop them.

"All we can do is our best to help others in this world and leave it up to the Gods to guide us in our actions."

"That senator, she implied the Gods were people."

"I know," he answered. "Some believe that as truth. Others find solace where they can and in the Gods of their choosing."

Adelei studied the lines on his face. Lines that spoke of decisions, some correct while others not, but decisions that had led both of them here. She touched his hand, feeling the warmth beneath her fingertips. "I used to think Master Bredych hung th stars in the heavens. He had such knowledge and wisdom, and for a while, I worshipped him for what he could teach me. But since coming here, I'm not sure of those teachings anymore. He seems as zealous as the Tribor, or the Boahim Senate. Brandishing his own brand of 'right' across the world. I look back at my own actions, and I doubt whether they have always been the correct ones. Maybe if I'd never been kidnapped, I'd have had a chance to learn your way of thinking, Father. Even if it wasn't always right, surely it was a better path than the one I've led."

Moisture gathered at the corner of his eyelids. One side of his mouth smiled while the other frowned. "Everyone doubts themselves, Adelei, but you can't allow those doubts to rule over you. You're the only one who knows whether your past decisions were the right ones or not. And if they weren't, all you can do is make amends for them now. Either way, I'm proud of the daughter before me—a strong woman who wants to do right."

He patted her knee, and she felt the dampness on her own cheeks. *I wish we had more time, Father.* She couldn't trust herself to meet his gaze and focused on the plain wall behind him, its grey tone echoing her feelings. "Do you believe we can truly make up for the sins of our past?"

"I'm not a priest, but I truly hope so, Adelei. While the Boahim Senate has their own agenda, at least it attempts to fall in line with the brand of justice I've always believed. I confess that I don't know much about Amaskans, but I know the Senate doesn't kill before hearing both sides of a story."

"I thought the Amaskans looked at both sides, too?" asked Margaret, her embroidery resting in her lap as her fingers ceased tracing over the thread.

"They do, but how do I know they came down on the right side? What if we're wrong? What if I killed innocent people?"

"You didn't. You wouldn't do that," her sister said. "You're a good person. Trust in yourself if nothing else."

Her sister picked up her needle and pushed thread through the soft fabric. Her smile was one of contentment, but Adelei found no joy in the words. But was she a good person? The faces of those she killed spread out before her like Prince Gamun's journals. *I've killed more people than he has. And all because I was told it was the right thing to do.*

"I'm a monster," she whispered too low for Margaret to hear, but her father heard and frowned.

"Don't worry on it too long. My hands aren't clean of blood either. Rulers' hands rarely are," he spoke in a murmur. "We often do things we wish we didn't have to, in order to make things better or safer for others. Who is to say that the Senate is any more just than your Order? I could be wrong. Only the Gods know what is right and true."

Adelei stood. "I...I need something from my room."

Before either could react, she ducked out the door and brushed past Michael in her rush until her pounding feet brought her to the sanctuary of her room. Hands searched through her bag—a saddle bag she kept packed at all times "just in case." Adelei found the small book within. Its well-worn cover was a familiar childhood friend. While she held it, her eyes turned away to rest on the bag itself.

She could do it. She could run. She could have been halfway to the border before the Senate was done reading the journals. Her fingers ran the length of the bag's strap, its leather still rough and dirty from her trek across the Sadain desert. She stepped forward, and in her abrupt movement, she dropped the book. Its pages bent as it lay on its side, and she cried out to see the text of her Order mishandled.

Adelei stooped to retrieve it and bent back the damaged pages. Her thumb caressed the gilded text within, and she smiled.

> *No man knows for sure what Justice may be, only that it must be just. It cannot be served alone to one side, but to both equally: Justice for the rich and the poor, the great and the small. No one is above Justice, which Amaska serves.*
>
> *Service to Justice is a path of thorns, tearing the feet and soul alike. May you live through the suffering and sacrifice required to passionately defend those that cannot defend themselves, for you worship at the higher court of conscience. It supersedes all else.*
>
> *While every man is innocent to his own reflection, every man seeks Justice when it is his turn upon the court. Seek only to serve that which is right, knowing all to be equal in the eyes of the Thirteen.*

She stared at the words. After a time, she closed the book as she shut her eyes in a moment of thanks.

She knew better. To doubt herself was to doubt Anur. She had thought herself innocent, but she wasn't wholly clean in this. If she truly served justice, she couldn't flee. Her other hand dropped her packed bag to the floor. *I doubted myself, because I knew I was wrong. I must go before the Senate and tell them what I know, even if it means my death.* If that was what it would take to find justice for all those slain by Shadian hands, then it was what she must do.

Her eyes teared up as she swallowed the lump in her throat. Part of her cried out to flee, to run, but the rest calmly whispered the words of the Order over and over like a litany.

The Senate will never protect my family with me in the way. She tucked the book neatly into a pocket, smoothing out the bump it made as she left her room behind. Her feet carried her toward the audience chamber where she would wait.

If Adelei sat in the closet with her family any longer, she wouldn't have the strength to do what she must. Not with them looking on her like a wounded hound. As it was, her feet felt heavy as she trudged toward her future and whatever the Gods would bring.

The Senate was deep in discussion as she ducked her head into the room. Adelei seated herself on an unobtrusive stool in the back, which was where they found her several hours later, deep in meditation as she waited.

"Is it time?" she asked, her voice ever so small to her ears.

Their faces mirrored her conflict. Senator Whitlen led her over to the dais as one would lead a small child. "It's time," the woman said. "Do you require anything before we question you?"

"I do not."

The woman nodded once, returning to her seat. "Then let us begin…"

CHAPTER TWENTY-SEVEN

Her throat ached. The muscles in her back burned from a long time standing and not enough sleep, yet Adelei managed to find her voice as the Senate's questions fired her way.

"What is your mission?"

"Why are you here?"

"Who are you?"

"Did you take Prince Gamun's offer?"

The pace left her shaking and sweaty as she fought the resistance in her mind. When they were finally convinced of her truthfulness, the Senate ordered Prince Gamun brought before the council. "While we're glad you've brought such a criminal before us, do you think it fair that this council try him for his crimes while turning a blind eye to your own?" This question from the Shadian senator. It was expected, and Adelei ignored his sneer.

"I don't. I come before you willing to answer the questions necessary for justice to be found."

"Even if it means your death?" This one from Senator Whitlen, and Adelei nodded her assent. A clatter at the back of the hall interrupted whatever Whitlen was about to ask. Five senate guards hauled Prince Gamun into the room by his elbows, his heels doing their best impression of a backpedaling roadrunner.

"You," he shouted, and he jabbed a finger in Adelei' direction. "You did this. Whatever she's told you is a lie. This woman is nothing more than a murdering whore. She tried to seduce me and—"

Whitlen wrapped her knuckles on the wood table. "We didn't need her testimony as we have the details of your crimes by your own hand." She held up one of the journals where he could see it. He paled, his hair whipping around his face as he struggled to free himself from the guards. When they tightened their grasp, he flung a desperate look at Senator Raj of Shad, who shook his head before hiding his face behind his hands.

"I don't know what those are. I've never seen them before." His voice cracked on the last word. "Who are you going to believe? The words of an assassin or those of a prince?"

"This council doesn't recognize royal titles. We deal in facts, in evidence. You will, of course, have the opportunity to explain yourself."

"I have nothing to defend against."

When Senator Whitlen read a page out of the journal, he paled. "What say you to this?" she asked.

"How can you read that?"

The corners of her mouth hinted at a smile, but the steel behind her eyes stabbed Gamun as readily as a sword, and he struggled with his captors. "We have read all three. I ask you again, explain yourself."

Gamun ceased his struggle, spittle around his mouth as he spoke. "If the royal line of Alexander continues, the Little Dozen will fall. This kingdom seeks to possess land until they are again the leader of all peoples. My father has proof of this," said Gamun. "I was seeking only to right this wrong, to give *justice*—" He glanced at Adelei. "—to those who no longer wish to be ruled by His Highness, King Leon Poncett. He schemes to seize what's rightfully not his. I'm no different from this Amaskan, seeking justice where this council has refused to dispense it. You cannot try me for this, and yet not try her for her crimes as well."

"The Senate is aware of this. Iliana Poncett has volunteered to stand trial for her crimes. But I did not ask you about Iliana Poncett. I asked you to explain yourself and these crimes," the Senator shouted and flung the journal to the floor. "Not the ones against the Poncett family, but those against the children and young women of the Little Dozen Kingdoms."

"I'm being framed."

Adelei laughed. "You killed a child the day before your wedding. And you had Ida murdered."

Again the senator knocked her knuckles on the table. Gamun's smile twisted his face into something terrible. "The captain was entertaining. The things she said before the end. Oh how she cried for King Leon, even for her brother. How sick is that?"

The senator hit the table with her hand, but Gamun continued, "Her own brother slits her throat and in the end, she begged for him. Pleaded even." Adelei clenched her fists until the sting of blood called her away from her rage. "But my niece, that wasn't me. I'm being set up."

"In your own hand you admit to it—details and drawings—" said Whitlen.

Prince Gamun held out his hand. "May I?"

The guards tightened their grip on him as she approached. Gamun took the journal from her and scanned the page. "This isn't my handwriting. Look at the way the letters slant. I don't slant. Compare it to the rest."

"So you admit the rest is your handwriting?"

He was trapped, but he didn't struggle. Gamun grinned as he returned the journal to her waiting hands. Whitlen handed it to another member, who studied it with a magnifying glass held to his only eye. "Hmm, it appears that Prince Gamun is correct."

"See? I'm being framed."

"For your niece maybe, but the other girls? Captain Warhammer?" Senator Whitlen stood a table length from him, her shoulders shaking with unvoiced laughter. "You're not being framed, you're being tried."

Nothing moved. Not at first. Then everything shifted into motion at once. Gamun surged forward and pulled free from the grasp of his captors. He made a mad dash for Senator Whitlen, his fingers grasping something between them as he leapt forward. Guards rushed after him. The Senate remained still.

Adelei spotted the small blade on the inside of his wrist before the guards did. She pulled a knife and threw it where it stuck between Gamun's shoulder blades. His eyes bulged. It didn't kill him, but he staggered toward the guards in a panic. Th prince lashed out, the green tip of his blade drawing a thin line in the fleshy underside of a guard's arm. The guard dropped to his knees and clutched at the wound.

"It burns. Oh Gods, it burns." The guard's screams filled the room and mixed with Gamun's mad laughter.

"It's poisoned," Adelei called out. "Don't let it touch you."

She risked a glance at the guardsman. He huddled on the floor, his arm clenched at his side. A sickly ooze dribbled out of his mouth and spattered on the stone floor. One last shudder and the man ceased breathing. The guards stepped over one another, trying to put space between them and the prince. Adelei stepped forward, dirk in hand.

Gamun's footing was chaotic. His eyes darted in too many places at once as he tried to maintain eye contact with the guards, the senators, and herself. She feinted and stepped forward inside his reach. When he advanced, she sidestepped his blade and shuffled into his blind spot. He saw her dirk peripherally and followed her motion until his back was to the Senate.

You may be skilled in mystical means, but a fighter you are not. She made another false jab to keep his attention on her.

"I've been hoping for this for a while." Gamun's eyes glowed faintly blue, as did the pendant around his neck. "Do you think you can take me? How's the shoulder?"

This time it was her turn to grin as she rolled it around casually. "Just fine, thanks."

He frowned, brows furrowed in concentration, but his magic didn't touch her. "By the way, nice nose," said Adelei, and he snarled.

Behind him, Senator Whitlen advanced a step at a time. Her hands glowed in response to his, a bright white that made Adelei's eyes water. The light left Gamun a silhouette. Whitlen misjudged his wavering movement, and he laughed as she stumbled against a chair.

"You're toying with me. Why not strike?" Gamun lowered the tip of his blade and relaxed his shoulders.

When Senator Whitlen's hands touched his back, the force tossed his body forward in a spastic leap, and he landed in a sloppy crouch. The senator's hands grew brighter, and a sharp ·hriek erupted from his lips as the light enveloped him from head to toe. His eyes bulged, and the muscles of his body clenched tight enough to pop. The stench of his waste touched Adelei's nose before the shrieking ceased abruptly. Blood ran down his chin where he'd bitten off the tip of his own tongue. His body gave one last twitch before it caved in on itself, and he curled into a fetal position on the floor. Now vacant eyes stared at nothing as his mouth moved soundlessly.

"What did you do to him?" Adelei couldn't wrest her sight away from the garish scene.

"Trapped him within his own mind and the night-mares within."

"The Senate is comprised of mystics?"

If she'd had anything in her stomach worth losing, Adelei would have decorated the audience chamber's floor. Prince Gamun mumbled beside the senator, who handled the poisoned blade with great care. "Without mysticism, we wouldn't have the power to hold together the Little Dozen Kingdoms. It's not common knowledge for a good reason."

The look the senator gave made Adelei shiver and warned her of sharing the information. "What will you do with him now?" Adelei asked.

"He will return with us, to be imprisoned until his death. How long is entirely up to him." When Adelei raised an eyebrow at the woman, she clarified, "The sooner he accepts his crimes and seeks redemption, the sooner he can die. And the less painful it will be. The more he resists, the more harrowing his prison will become. When his body finally does shut down, it will be agonizing indeed."

The torches in the room flickered. Several guttered out, leaving only the dais lit. Beside the senator, Prince Gamun laughed—a high, slow titter that twisted knots into Adelei's gut and left her searching for an escape route. The senator reached out to touch the prince when his body seized up with a great jerking motion as if a puppeteer held him. The mad laughter stopped and when the prince's eyes found Adelei's, he reached for her. "Help me," he cried, and she stumbled over the chair behind her.

"What madness is this?" said Adelei. "Senator, what—"

"It isn't me. Someone else is here."

His body rose two inches from the ground. "Please, help me, Father," whispered Gamun. A gust of wind swept through the room, and every torch and candle died. The one lone window cast too little light to see as senators on the dais shouted orders to the guards. Many sets of glowing hands gave some illumination, but none so much as Gamun's eyes. "My father comes."

His father. The King. Oh Gods, the puppeteer.

Senator Whitlen must have come to the same conclusion as she ducked beneath the table where Adelei crouched. "Kill him," the woman ordered.

"What? I don't—"

"Throw one of your knives. Hit him in the heart. You must kill him before the gate is completed."

Adelei held the knife in a pinch grip and sent it straight at Gamun. The blade buried itself in his chest before he saw it, and the glow around him disappeared. The prince's body tumbled to the ground where it lay in a lifeless heap. Whitlen gestured to a guard, who approached the body cautiously. The man nudged it with his boot and when it didn't move, he knelt down close to Gamun's face.

"He's not breathing. He's dead, Senator Whitlen."

The senator's arm shook as she pointed. "Clean this up. Get it out of my sight."

Up on the dais, the rest of the Senate waited, though all of their masks bled fear around the edges. *This was something else, something they weren't expecting.* Adelei opened her mouth to ask, but Senator Whitlen wagged a finger at her.

"There are some things not for your knowledge, Amaskan."

The body was removed, and Adelei returned to her seat on the stool before the Senate. A servant set about relighting the torches in the room, but the audience chamber felt dark with the day's events. Behind her, the doors opened, and Whitlen sighed.

carrying whisper announced Margaret's arrival, and inevitably, ng Leon's.

"Prince Gamun has been found guilty of many violations 1st the Thirteen. His crimes will be written in the histories and 'aims released. Let it also be of note that King Bajit requires r investigation."

"Investigation?" asked Adelei. "He told you his father was coming. The gate—"

"Unlike the Order, we don't have the luxury of killing indiscriminately, Master Adelei. We don't know who was on the other side of that gate," said Senator Whitlen.

The Alexandrian senator cleared his throat. "There are also the rumors about Gamun's birth. Some say he isn't Bajit's son at all. Who 'Father' is demands further examination."

"Agreed. For now, we will dissolve the treaty between the Kingdoms of Alexander and Shad, as well as the marriage between Prince Gamun Bajit and Princess Margaret Poncett." Whitlen handed a jeweled cup to a woman on her right. "Another criminal matter is before us."

"They can't." Margaret cried out, and King Leon hushed her as the Senate stirred.

"Adelei of the Order of Amaska, this council can't ignore the crimes you have committed, many of which are violations against the Thirteen. While we understand that many of these crimes were committed against those we would have sought out ourselves, you are not a senator, nor do you speak for us. Do you deny your crimes?"

"I do not."

Senator Whitlen's eyes tilted at the corners to match her frown. "We would then have the names of those whose lives you've taken, and who hired you to commit such atrocities."

Adelei's shoulders inched upward. "It will cleanse my soul to tell you the names of the dead, but I can't tell you who my clients were. I'm sorry."

A man she didn't recognize stomped his foot upon the floor. "If you confess fully, leniency and mercy may be bestowed upon you. If you can't tell us what we require, it may make things much worse for you."

"I understand."

"Do you?" Senator Whitlen asked. "This may be the difference between a swift end and something much longer." Her eyes trailed to where the prince's body lay minutes before, the floor still damp with small pools of his bodily fluids.

"I understand fully. If I truly am an emissary of Justice, then I must trust in the justice I seek and dispense. Justice must be equal for all, and no special favor should be shown to me." Several council members nodded at her words, and she continued, her insides quaking even as she spoke with a strength she didn't feel. "Isn't the belief of the Boahim Senate: *fiatlech judäk gamur, ruphillo celäm stavo?*"

"Let justice be done, though the heavens may fall," whispered Margaret. From the sound, she stood maybe two feet behind Adelei. Her sister's footsteps were shouts in the silent audience chamber. Margaret rested a hand on Adelei's shoulder.

It broke her heart. *She thinks I'm asking for mercy. Gods abound, give her strength enough for what I'm to do.* Adelei patted her sister's hand. "Senators, I don't want to die," her voice trembled at last, and she swallowed the lump in her throat, "—but if you're truly the court of justice, then you know what must be done as well as I do."

"Give us the names of the dead then," another voice asked.

"Prince Gamun Bajit—" Her sister gasped, but Adelei ignored it. "—several Tribor assassins whose names I don't know. Magistrate William Meserre, Deirdre Bennson, the King of Naribor's Grand Advisor...." Her father cleared his throat. No matter how much a disappointment to her family, Adelei continued the litany until it was done.

Every man and woman she'd ever killed. It had been so easy to list their names. Too easy.

"Give your family some solace in the knowledge that despite these crimes, you will find death quickly—forgiven through your confession. Give us the names of those who sought to hire you. Or give us the true names of the members of the Order."

She shook her head. "The Order makes a point of not sharing true names. I couldn't give you more than one or two. Still, I can no more betray one family than betray the other. For all that they are not my blood and kidnapped me, they raised me. Sheltered and fed me. Taught me what justice is. I can't do what you ask."

Margaret's hand clutched Adelei's collar bone painfully.

Senator Whitlen stepped forward, her trembling hand glowing. "We could force this information from you."

"You could. You could become everything you hate about the Amaskans and mess with my brain. You could compel me to tell you what I won't volunteer. But I don't think you will. For all that you want this information, you aren't bad people. You won't stoop to that level to get it."

If they did, then the Boahim Senate was no better than the Order. And everyone would know it. *They must stand by their beliefs. If not, all is lost.*

The glowing hand returned to its pocket. "We accept your testimony as is. You will be taken to a cell until your fate is decided."

When the guards took her arms, she allowed them to search her. Their hands moved carefully as they searched for weapons. "I have one tucked in my wrist, one in the lip of my boot, and two at my waist," she offered. The two men dug fingers into her clothing to withdraw the blades before leading her out of the room. Margaret cried out, but Adelei turned her face away.

If she looked, she would give the Senate anything they asked. *I'm sorry, Mae-Mae, but I can't.*

Her father's heavy steps followed behind. Many twists and turns led down to the dungeon, its dank stone slightly damp and covered in places with a thick moss that added to the foul smell tickling her nose. The guard avoided Adelei's eyes as his thick fingers bumbled with the keys before unlocking the cell. Her two escorts didn't bother locking her to the chains along the wall.

"Wait," she called as the guards turned to leave. Her left hand dug into a pocket at her wrist. When she pulled out her lockpick, their eyebrows twitched, but they took it from her with a shrug and shut the door behind them. A tiny slit midway down the door would allow them to feed her, but otherwise, moist stone surrounded her on all four sides—her new prison for however long she would remain in Alexander.

King Leon's voice called out, and then wood scraped the stone before his hand reached through the slit "Adelei?" he called, and she moved to the door and took his hand in her own.

"I'm here."

"Why didn't you tell them what they wanted?" His voice cracked, and she swallowed at its thickness. "Do you owe them that much, that your life would be worth giving?"

"Father, even if I'd told them, I would still be a dead woman walking. There's no way for the Boahim Senate to exist as the seekers and enforcers of justice if they allow me to get away with my crimes."

"But you had reasons for them. Not even my hands are clean of blood. There are decisions I've made—anyway, the Senate overlooks these. They know, as do I, that they are necessary decisions a ruler must make to ensure peace and tranquility in the kingdom. Surely they could grant you the same mercy—"

"Mercy for an assassin? Either no one is above the law or everyone is, Father. I know you think they're cutting royalty some slack, but they're not. Someday soon, there will be a reckoning. They'll hold this knowledge in their pocket until they need something from you, Father, and then they will get it from you in exchange for your life. Didn't you tell me earlier that they never do something for nothing? That they healed my shoulder for a reason?"

He was silent then. Her elbow leaned on her knees, and her head on the cool, damp door. "If what you say is true, the royal families won't stand for it. The Boahim Senate would be in great danger," he whispered.

"They already are, and I don't think they care. In the past few days, I've seen powerful magics that I never knew existed. Father, you didn't see what Senator Whitlen did to Prince Gamun." Adelei swallowed hard. "She locked him inside his own mind. Even worse was the darkness that came. Something was using the prince as a gate. Gamun said it was his father, but—"

"I heard the Senate explain away that bit. The rest...? That's knowledge I don't want."

"If civil war breaks out across the Little Dozen," said Adelei, "I'm not sure we would stand a chance against a force like that."

"I could get you out."

Adelei released his hand and twisted to the slit in the door. She sought his eyes. "I could," he repeated. "Your sister will need you when I'm gone. If war is coming, she'll need someone to help her. Margaret knows nothing of the harshness of battle or war. I fear I've ill prepared her for the future." He sat hunched over on a stool, the deep blue of his cloak soaking up moisture from the floor. Her father's eyes begged her and tempted though she was, Adelei could not do what he asked.

"No." The word caught in her throat, more a croak than a vocalization. "If I escape, there will be no way to stay here, and they would know it was you. They would come after you and—"

"I'm already a dead man," King Leon said. "I don't fear the Senate. Besides, if I knew you and your sister were safe, I would gladly give my life."

"Then you understand why I can't leave."

He frowned, pulling his cloak around him tighter in the dungeon's chill and unbidden tears blurred her vision. "Father, I know I'm not the daughter you would have wanted—" When he opened his mouth to interject, she shook her head. "Wait, let me finish. I don't begin to understand what the Amaskans did to me or why, but I know that in his own way, Master Bredych loved me, as you do now. He saw through the flaws and loved me. It broke him to send me here, away from him, knowing that it would probably end in my death. Even if I didn't know you until now, I grew up with a father's love. I cannot betray that, not even to save myself. I can no more betray him than you could betray Margaret."

"He sent you here as a weapon."

"He sent me *home*. To you. Does it matter why?"

King Leon sighed. A droplet bounced off her hand and her vision blurred again. "Adelei, no matter what you think, you're my daughter. Both of my daughters give my life purpose and meaning. I don't care how many people you killed for him, or how confused you may be about who you are, but know this: you're my daughter. And I love you."

"I'm sorry that it took me so long to remember that," she whispered.

"We could have longer, you and me. To get to know one another," he said, his eyes hopeful for a moment. When she shook her head, it sent a sprinkle of tears across her knees.

"My pride kept me from the realization that one can have two families, two loyalties. You are no more at fault for what happened to me than I am, and while I wish Master Bredych hadn't messed with my mind, I can only assume it was for my protection and that of the Order. I love him as you love me. As I love you. You are both my fathers. For the both of you, I will see justice done. There must be meaning to the Senate's existence if the Little Dozen is to survive."

He surprised her when he nodded. King Leon kissed the top of her hand, the whiskers of his mustache tickling her skin. The sensation reminded her of a time so long ago, when another father's whiskers had done the same, and she smiled brightly. "Oh Adelei, I would move armies to see more of that smile, but in the end, this is your choice. I will respect your decision, but I can't help but wish—"

"I know, Father. Thank you for this gift. Allowing me my choice, my life. And thank you for bringing me home. If I'm to die, I want it to be here." Adelei released his hand after one last squeeze. "Now go. This chill isn't good for you, and Margaret will need as many days as you can give her to prepare her for the coming storm."

When he stood, his joints popping from the strain, she watched the blue blur move from view and like a child of five again, she wrapped her arms around her knees and cried.

CHAPTER TWENTY-EIGHT

The cot they'd left her wasn't warm or even remotely comfortable. When her stomach growled, she assumed it to be morning. Her hips hurt from lying on a hard surface, and she couldn't keep her teeth from chattering as the frost seeped into her bones. Old injuries she hadn't thought of in years ached with a fierceness that rivaled her determination to hold out and betray no one.

Justice would be done. Adelei rubbed her hands together to generate some warmth. A noise outside the door caught her attention, and she sighed in relief. *They've come for me. At least I won't be cold anymore if I'm dead.* She rose with a wince as her knee popped.

It wasn't the Boahim Senate whose mass of dark hair popped around the door. Margaret stepped inside, and the guard locked the door behind her.

"What are you doing here?" Adelei stretched toward the ceiling and twisted at the hips to work the pain. When she returned to the cot, Adelei sat cross legged on its hard surface.

"I came to talk you out of this."

The lace hem of Margaret's delicate dress dragged along the filthy floor. "Did Father talk to you?" asked Adelei.

"Yes."

"Then you know why I must do this."

"No. No, I don't. Why would you give your life to protect the people who wanted to *kill* you? People who kidnapped you, took you away from us? From me." Her shrill voice bounced as she paced all five steps the tiny cell allowed. "I've just found you again. Why does everyone leave me?"

It was the plea of a child. The cry caught Adelei off guard, and her eyes misted over again, gummy and sore from the previous day's tears. "I know this is difficult for you to understand—"

"They're going to kill you," her sister whispered, continuing as if she'd never heard Adelei speak. "Like a common criminal. I heard the Senate talking. They want to use you to send a message to Sadai and the Amaskans they protect. They said it's for justice, but this isn't justice at all."

"If the Senate means anything, they have to abide by their laws."

"Why are you defending them? And what did the Order ever do for you?" Margaret's voice rose to its petulant shriek. "I don't see them here, now, saving you from this."

An image of Min drifted to the forefront of Adelei's mind, then on to Master Bredych. *Master. Father.* He'd rescued her once from the bullies, before setting her loose to find her own way. She rubbed her cheek absently. She and Min had settled their differences, though it had taken a few tries and a few punches before they'd figured it out. And once again he'd left her to find her own path. The knowledge didn't sadden her like she thought it would, but it didn't make the explanation any easier.

"Mae-Mae, listen." Her sister's verbal assault stopped with her pacing. "When I was younger, my father—my other father, he taught me—"

"Don't," Margaret interrupted. "I don't care what some criminal taught you. He stole you. He ordered you killed, and when that didn't work, he stole you. So don't defend him. Not now."

"Yes, he stole me. He wasn't thinking and made some poor choices, which I won't defend, but when he saw me, afraid and alone, he made the choice to raise me as his own. While I could wish that things would have been different, they aren't. All I know is that this man loved me. Loved me enough to teach me everything he knew. Loved me enough to let me find my own way through life, to learn and love as best I could. I wouldn't trade that for anything, knowing two fathers' love. This is my choice,

Mae-Mae. If I'm more than a common criminal, if I'm one who serves Anur, then I must stand trial for my crimes and face whatever comes. '*Honor in everything, especially the kill*.'"

Margaret stumbled over to the cot, wrapping her arms around Adelei. "But I need you, too. When Father dies, it'll be just me. I never thought I would rule alone. You told me I had so much to learn, and I understand it now. I know what you mean."

Min's smile decorated Adelei's memories, and like a contagion, she smiled in spite of the grim future before her. No matter how much she'd tried at first, Adelei had never listened to Min when she'd spoken of her family outside the Amaskans. *I kept telling her families were a liability, but I wish I'd known the truth sooner, had more time.* Adelei stared at the wall.

"Are you even listening?"

"I am, but you remind me of myself," Adelei said, leaning her forehead against her sister's crown of ebony hair. "When I was younger, I had this friend. She kept trying to tell me that family was important—that it's more than just blood, more than just fluid in the body. It's loyalty. It's friendship. It took until recently for me to understand what she meant. When I first got here, I didn't much like you, but I've learned so much from you, sister of mine."

Margaret's hand jerked upward as she moved, smacking Adelei in the chin. "Oops. What in the world could I ever teach you?"

"You taught me much about who I am, about what a family is, and how important it is to defend them. Which is why I must defend the Amaskans, the same way I have defended you and our father. One day you will understand this better. You'll understand about family and sacrifice."

"You're the strong one, though. You should live, not me. I could...I could switch places with you. Let me die so that you can protect our kingdom. Sacrifice me." She tried to sound brave, to sound strong, but her voice trembled as she said it, and Adelei took her sister's face between both hands. She looked upon a face so like her own.

"That's the first time you've called it *our* kingdom," Adelei said, shaking her head. "But no, I can't let you do that. This is my death to choose. Besides, I wouldn't even begin to know how to be a princess. What in the hell would I do with so many layers of skirt between me and a horse's back, hmmm?" She kissed her sister's forehead as they shared a laugh. "That's sacrifice, but not the one you'll need to make. You're going to be a great ruler if you let yourself, if you believe in yourself. There's more of me in you than you know."

"War's coming, isn't it?" The whisper was so faint that at first, Adelei felt she'd imagined it, but when her sister repeated it and leaned her head into the crook of Adelei's shoulder, Adelei shuddered as the memory swept through her.

Both girls had sat, exactly as they did now, the younger curled up against the elder's body as they hid in a linen closet, their mother's voice calling for them. It was a muffled voice that felt distant, yet near as Margaret stifled a giggle. "Shhhh…" Iliana hissed and clamped a damp sticky hand over her sister's mouth.

Margaret bit it and another giggle resounded through the closet. "If you keep giggling, she'll find us for sure. And you know what that means."

"We'll have to clean our room," Margaret whispered, her voice louder than she'd anticipated, and again she giggled until Iliana pushed her aside to peer through the keyhole.

"What do you see?"

The brown eye that peered back at her shone with humor, and Adelei turned the knob, bounding into her father's arms. "There are my two little scoundrels." King Leon laughed as he hoisted Iliana to his shoulder. At his side, Margaret danced in place as she tugged at his arm until he pulled her up to his other shoulder. The two girls peering down from the grandiose height of his six-foot frame, neither frightened as he bounded through the hall.

"How could we be…we were in his arms," Adelei murmured.

"What did you say?"

"Nothing. I was just remembering when father found us in the linen closet. We were hiding from cleaning our room. Things were simpler then. I don't know why it just came to me."

"You said they messed with your mind. Is it possible they made you forget us?" Margaret clutched her skirt between tense hands.

"I'm sure it's possible." Though sometimes, she'd wondered if it was easier to forget. The fear of being kidnapped, the strange people who'd talked about her and handed her off to more strangers. Maybe it was better she had forgotten.

"Something about your expression tells me you aren't so sure. You're tapping your foot again." Margaret pointed a finger at Adelei's foot. "You tap it when you're lying. But you didn't answer my question. Will there be civil war now that the treaty is dissolved?"

"Yes." Adelei stilled her foot. "The Boahim Senate executed the second son of the King of Shad. Even if they don't investigate King Bajit for the Tribor attacks, *which they will*—" she added, seeing her sister tense, "—just the death of the prince will bring the Shadians to our border. Too many agree with them though— that Alexander is taking land from others to take back power."

"But that's ridiculous. Land disputes happen, even with the borders settled after Boahim. We can't help it if the people keep giving us their land."

Adelei shook her head. "Make Father tell you the whole of it. It's not as simple as that."

"You mean he's lying?"

"Not so much lying as trying to protect you. And you were right, if you're to rule well, you need all the information you can get." Adelei rubbed her temples. Her head ached in the cold. "Even in Sadai people talk of the might of Alexander."

Margaret huddled closer. "People will choose sides. War will come, despite what the Senate believes. Alexander will need a strong leader, so you must find the strength to do what's right for our people," said Adelei.

The door before them opened, and both women flinched. "It's time," said the guard, and Adelei nodded.

"I'm sorry that we didn't get more time, Mae-Mae, but be strong for me. Don't let my death be for nothing. Take care of Father for me, but make him tell you the truth. About everything," Adelei said, wiping the dampness from Margaret's cheek. She turned to the guard and stepped through the doorway where several senate guards waited. Adelei closed her ears to the sounds behind her, her face a mask of strength while her insides quaked.

I knew I would die someday. Every Amaskan does. We know our end will come, at the end of someone's sword or king's noose, but I always thought I'd go quickly, serving Anur.

Adelei followed the guards up the steps and down the maze of corridors to the audience chamber. For a moment, her eyes roamed, hopeful that maybe an Amaskan would be there. Someone with a message for her, perhaps. Master Bredych telling her he loved her. No rescue, of course—but at least something to help her keep her peace in the moment.

But the room was empty save the Senate. Not even King Leon was present and once she stood before them, her legs quivered. The blazing fire upon the hearth reminded her of the one at the Order. *A warm fire to keep the family alive. And food to nourish the body, for the body without is without strength. Justice cannot be sought without a strong body and mind and a whole heart.*

She stumbled once as she stepped forward at Senator Whitlen's gesture. "I'm sorry, Iliana Poncett. I asked for mercy, but you were correct in the need for justice. And since you were prompt to remind us that justice must be equal for all, an example will be made of you so that all will know that the Boahim Senate has wide an eye and heavy a hand." The woman pointed at Adelei. "For your crimes against the Thirteen and the people of the Little Dozen Kingdoms, you will be hanged at noon in the fields outside Alesta for all to see."

Adelei's strength gave out and she fell, her knees crashing into the hard, stone floor. Two guards lifted her to her feet. She tried to stand, but exhaustion overwhelmed her; she swallowed back bile and looked out across the Senate.

"Thank you for the slight mercy," she said, "though I would ask a boon of this senate." Senator Whitlen whispered to another before nodding. "The Tribor are still coming for my family, at King Bajit's orders. If the eye truly is wide, lock your sights on the King of Shad and the evil he harbors. Otherwise, it won't matter if you execute every Amaskan in all the Little Dozen. It will have been for nothing, and he will come for you next."

The silence snaked around them, and while they grimaced, the truth burned their faces. Adela Whitlen inclined her head. It would be done.

Guards prodded Adelei forward, turning her at the last minute as she stumbled from the room. All she wanted to do was crawl, tired and scared and hungry, but she stood upright as if she invited death.

Adelei winced when the glaring sun touched her face and hesitated at the gates to the castle. She blinked a few times to adjust her vision. Behind her, the Senate waited, filing in line as they followed. The further the group ventured from the castle, the larger a crowd Adelei drew. At the middle level of the city, the streets were lined with people. When the rotten potato hit her back, she started. Her eyes darted across the crowd, but she couldn't locate its owner.

She managed another fifteen steps before something else hit her, this time in the back of the head, and she stumbled, seeing stars. Senate guards grouped around her and the senators. They held up shields half a man's height, which they used to shove the crowds out of the way. Someone took up the chant in front and by the time it reached the traveling group, many hundreds shouted.

"Justice. Justice."

While the mob continued to pelt the group with rotten food, a burly man ahead pointed a finger at the senators. "Look upon Justice, for it is a lie." he shouted and pulled up a small boy by his tunic. The child's face was a swirl of burn scars and half of his jaw was missing. "Is this justice, senators? Do you remember doing this to my boy?"

Several guards lifted their shields overhead as a rain of bread fell upon the group. Civil war wasn't coming—civil war was here. Adelei tried to keep her eyes on her feet, but as more people shouted angry curses at the Senate, she couldn't help but meet their gazes. Her eyes teared up, but they didn't thank her for her sympathy. A woman missing a leg spit at her, and saliva rolled down the guard's metal shield.

"Murderer," someone shouted, and she winced. It would have been so easy to run. The voice in her head whispered lies, and she sucked in a quick rush of air between gritted teeth. *Inhale. Exhale. Don't listen. Don't run. Inhale. Exhale. Justice be done.*

By the time her feet had carried her to the lower district of Alesta, the senate guards drew their swords as the mob shouted for blood. "I'd forgotten how blood-thirsty a crowd can be," she whispered, but no one heard her over the shouts and boos.

When the procession stopped at the city walls, she risked a glance over her shoulder and felt the heat drain from her face. People stared back at her. Hundreds of people. Maybe even a thousand. She'd underestimated the hatred for Amaskans in this country.

Two pairs of brown eyes stood among the guarded group far up on a platform—her father and sister—and she closed her eyes. She couldn't look at them, their pain held before them for the world to see.

A constructed platform some six feet off the ground greeted her, along with the noose, and she stumbled again. One of the guards pushed her and sent her to her knees. She was little more than bruised meat before the butcher, and she ached as more objects rained down on her.

Her family and the Boahim Senate took their seats to the left, seats hastily thrown together out of reach of the swelling crowd. A senator raised his hand and silence spread across the crowd. Everyone enjoyed a good hanging. Adelei tried to find the end of the crowd and failed. Bodies reached all the way back to the city gates and beyond. It didn't matter that this was justice. The people didn't even know what justice was—they were here for the show.

Mutterings rumbled closer to her, and the Senate member opened his mouth to speak before the silence got away from him. "Iliana Poncett of Alexander, also known as Master Adelei of Order of Amaska," he stated and the murmurs swelled. The crowd grasped hold of her name and ran with it until the din was loud. He raised his hand again, waiting for quiet before continuing. "You have confessed to the murders of forty-five people. *The temple is a gift from Adlain. To kill another is to kill yourself.* Murder is an affront to the Thirteen, and as such, your punishment is death by hanging. Do you have any words for the people of Alexander?"

Adelei stood at the top of the platform, the noose above her, and swallowed what little saliva remained in her mouth. At first, she didn't think she'd be able to speak, but she cleared her throat and blinked in the bright sun as she stared out across the throng of bodies. Then she sought the faces of her father and her sister.

"If justice is to prevail, then there is no room in this world for Tribor and Amaskans. Civil war is coming to Boahim, and if good is to triumph, then you must find the strength to make the decisions that others cannot. Let my death have meaning. Be brave," said Adelei, and she steadied her gaze on Margaret. She didn't know how far her voice carried among the crowd, and she didn't care. Her sister nodded ever so slightly. It had carried enough. Adelei stepped upon the stool as a man looped the noose around her neck.

Her vision filled with tears. In her stomach, knots twisted and sent spasms of fear across muscles that cried out for her to run, to flee, but she ground her teeth and closed her eyes. They didn't understand. They saw only a bully, an assassin, but she was more. *Gods be with me and mine, I am more.* The noose tightened around her neck. Adelei clenched her eyes shut.

"Home is where I die. Delorcini has blessed me twice," she whispered, and the stool beneath her fell away. She opened her eyes a brief moment and her five year old sister stood before her, smiling.

"They won't find us if we hide in here," Margaret said and tugged on Iliana's sleeve as they stepped into the darkness of the linen closet. There was silence. Then a last childish giggle before nothing at all.

EPILOGUE

Two Years Later

257 Atlinas 5ᵗʰ,

When my father died this past spring, he gripped my hands tightly as the spasm shook his gaunt frame. He whispered, "Don't let them take our home."

He made me promise, made me swear to it before he would allow the healers to work. They gave him the drink that would ease his suffering and settle his mind before the poison seeped into his brain. I swore they would never take Alesta, but then, I would have sworn whatever he wished to give him comfort in the end.

In his last breath, he said her name.

A shadow on us both since her execution, as we moved through the motions of life. Both of us wondered if every decision we made was one that she would have wanted, one that gave meaning to her meaningless death. But a scant few days before my father's death, civil war broke out across Boahim. Today it has arrived at Alesta.

The guards' cries send a shiver up my neck. Troops are on the move outside the castle walls. It wasn't unexpected.

Reports alerted me to movement at the border weeks before. I had been content to allow Captain Fenton to direct our army as I sat beside my ailing father, too caught up in my grief to do much more than wave an irritated hand in his direction. But now that my father is gone and I am all that remains of the Poncett line, I must step forward and take this heavy crown upon my brow and lead my people into war.

The Little Dozen Kingdoms are divided. Some believe in the unity brought by the Boahim Senate and their declarations of peace. Others still know them for the bullies and tyrants they are, a plague that should be wiped from the land. King Bajit of Shad screams for their blood for murdering his son. He calls for my death as well, the traitorous "whore" who corrupted Gamun and brought about his murder.

The walls of my childhood home shake once again with the pounding of troops' feet as battle wages outside. No matter how much I try to hide away from the sounds of death, I cannot run from my responsibilities. The sounds permeate my sleep and bring me ill-willed dreams. If these are the visions Adelei faced daily in her duty to serving justice and the people of Boahim, then I can only hope to be half as strong as she was in my attempt to face them.

Burning wood tickles my nose. Fighting has breached the city—the city I swore I'd never allow to fall. Captain Fenton has my servants packing. He thinks I will leave my home, listen to reason, and flee while I still can.

But I cannot. We all must make sacrifices in war. This is my home. A home my sister and now my father have died to protect, and if family means anything, then it means this. This is my battle. This is my war. My kingdom. And whether I wanted the job or not, it's mine and mine to protect.

The people of Alexander bleed for me on this day and for many to come. I should hope that I can find it in me to be worthy of such an act, but as I write this, I tremble still. This façade will only carry me so far, as I have not the strength my sister saw in me. But I will pretend for the world. That is one promise I will keep.

My pen will notate the history of Alexander. I will tell the story of my sister's bravery, a warrior and princess who gave her life for her kingdom and family; and the story of my father, a man who lost everything and still gave more. If I should fall, as I most likely will, I would want the Poncett name remembered. Not for prosperity, but as an example of strength. Of courage. And of love.

The battle is upon us, and I must take up arms. There are battles to be fought and children to be saved, so that no one else shall have to know the pain of losing a father, a mother, a sister, or a child this way again.

The Gods be with us all.

Penned by the hand of
Queen Margaret I of Alexander.

The story of the Poncett family will continue in Book II, Amaskan's War.

ACKNOWLEDGEMENTS

No matter what I type here, there will always be more people whom I've forgotten—not by choice but merely by accident since I'm not great at these things. Sometimes I wonder if publishers stick acknowledgement pages in the back (or front) of books simply to torture a poor author into thanking them *(the publishers)*. And as usual, I've digressed from the main purpose of such a page.

I will not go so far as to say that this book wouldn't have been possible without a long list of people. This book *would* have been possible all by myself, though it would not have been nearly as thorough, as good, or as polished. It probably would have remained on my hard drive until a sector was corrupted and thus died a miserable death.

So many, many, many thanks to Maia & Gayle, members of my critique group who have poured through multiple false starts, outlines, and eventually, the final draft. This book is infinitely better because of your efforts. Thanks to my editor, Mimi, who found mistakes long after the tenth draft. *(She is more than just a "Grammar Chick"!)* More thanks to my beta readers for pointing out countless plot holes back in the early revisions.

Lots of thanks and love to my father, who always encouraged me to keep writing. Also, for continually driving my childhood self to the bookstore for "more books." Special thanks to my friends who have encouraged me to write and read and write some more. Your support is a fount of inspiration on days when my plot tangles threaten to murder me in my sleep. Thanks to my kitties who insist that the keyboard is the most comfortable of beds and no, I *don't* need to write today because kitties.

Thanks also is due to my readers—you are precious to me, and I thank you. May you be fruitful and continue to multiply.

And once again, more thanks than all the world to my husband. It wouldn't have been nearly as much fun without you.

ABOUT THE AUTHOR

Bestselling science fiction & fantasy author Raven Oak is best known for *Amaskan's Blood* (Epic Awards 2016 Finalist), *Class-M Exile,* and the collection *Joy to the Worlds: Mysterious Speculative Fiction for the Holidays* (Foreword Reviews 2016 Book of the Year Finalist). She spent most of her K-12 education doodling stories and 500 page monstrosities that are forever locked away in a filing cabinet.

When she's not writing, she's getting her game on with tabletop games, indulging in cartography, or staring at the ocean. She lives in the Seattle area with her husband, and their three kitties who enjoy lounging across the keyboard when writing deadlines approach.

When she's not writing, she can be found online at:

Website: http://www.ravenoak.net
Twitter: http://twitter.com/raven_oak
Facebook: http://facebook.com/authorroak
Goodreads: http://www.goodreads.com/raven_oak

GREY SUN
—— PRESS ——

Please enjoy this sneak peek at
Amaskan's War from Raven Oak.

Forthcoming from Grey Sun Press.

The rumors crept their way across Sadai's border the way a water droplet rolls across stone—it finds a crevice, a weakness if one will, then trickles inside without warning, forever changing the stone's surface.

Chatter had reached the Order of Amaska, but Bredych had paid it no mind. What did he care of King Leon's struggles? But the whispers had created chasms that echoed inside his old mind. He had tried lying to himself, but news had traveled fast that day.

When a trader had mentioned travelers fleeing the Kingdom of Alexander, fear had forced his fingers into fists. The next caravan to pass the Order had painted a darker picture—some poor soul had been hung in the square at high noon for murdering a prince. The word *assassin* had leapt from their tongues like cinders. When a single Amaskan approached the Alexandrian border on Bredych's orders, the rumors painted the council room black, and Bredych seethed.

An Amaskan had seduced the Prince. No, she had seduced the King. Never mind that, she had tried to kill them all! The king had strung her up for treason and eaten her entrails in celebration.

A dozen different tales, each one grimmer than the one before.

Yet Bredych had refused to believe. His daughter was stronger than that. She was the best Amaskan he had ever trained.

Inquiries for information dried up, and when his sources fled, his knees had trembled like a first year trainee.

Walls painted blue and green left him somber as the sun set

on another day. The powdered gold mixed into the paint glittered as the Thirteen mocked him with knowing looks.

Alone in the council room, Bredych traced the carved figures of the Thirteen with his fingers before depressing the eye of Anur, God of Justice. At first, the wall merely trembled in response. After three breaths, a click sounded within the wall to his right.

He pushed, and the built-in bookcase swung open to expose a room with several lifetimes of dust. At its center, a single orb glowed. Bredych pulled his hood closer about his face. Could the Boahim Senate see him through the sleeping orb?

No other Amaskans knew of the room's existence. The orb was an artifact survived from a different time—something his dear *sister* had discovered shortly after he'd been named Grand Master. But the words needed to bring it to life had been *his* discovery.

"*Ta'asor Ley*," he whispered, and the orb's glow dimmed.

While many seasons had played across his body, the woman in the orb appeared unchanged from the last time he'd seen her. "You dare call upon us! I should curse you where you stand!" she said as she glared.

"You could, but then we would be forced to build boats."

"What do you want, assassin?"

"Knowledge."

"About?"

He paused for a moment, and then answered. "Alexander."

The sudden paleness of her face washed out any beauty she'd held. "War trembles at their border. Beyond that, I won't disclose."

"War with whom?"

"An old enemy with poison in its veins."

She spoke in nothingness as well as Bredych, but the twitch of her eye muscles gave her away. "There is more to this warning of war, Senator. We've heard rumors of death—"

The woman in the orb nodded. "Indeed. But then, you already knew this." The foggy shroud cleared as she leaned forward and whispered, "*Itovestah.*" The crystalline pendant around her neck twinkled once, then the image faded until only darkness remained.

Bredych touched the orb, but it was as cold as her stare had been. He repeated, "*Ta'asor Ley.*"

Nothing. The orb was dead.

Loud footfalls in the hall outside warned of someone's quick approach. He left the orb room and slid the bookshelf back into place. Someone knocked upon the council room door, and when he opened it, a trainee stood outside, face down and waiting.

Like his daughter had once stood.

Bredych blinked back the moisture that threatened to ruin his composure. "You have a message for me?"

The blonde haired boy nodded. "Delmon's returned—with news—should I summon the council?" The words tumbled out of his mouth and at Bredych's nod, he was off down the corridor again.

Instead of the bed his exhausted body craved, Bredych claimed a seat at the long table's end. He waited fifteen minutes in silence. Fifteen minutes to convince himself that hope remained. When the Amaskan council members shuffled into the room, he said nothing.

Dark circles made a raccoon of Delmon, and a jagged wound stretched across his forehead—a twin to match the one across his left cheek. The Amaskan fell into the offered chair, and after a moment's rest, he bowed his head before the council members. One poured a glass of water, which Delmon accepted with a grateful nod.

"Master Bredych—" Delmon swallowed a large gulp of water before continuing. "Troops gather within Alexander and word has it that to the south, the Shadian army approaches."

"War between Shad and Alexander? Would they dare with the Senate watching?" Bredych asked, but Delmon ignored the question.

"I wish that was the worst of the news, Grand Master. No matter where I traveled, people spoke of Amaskans. None of it was new information. That is, until I gained passage into Alexander."

No wonder Delmon bore a scar. He had been lucky that was the worst of it. Bredych said, "You were ordered not to cross the border."

"I—I had no choice, Grand Master."

"Explain."

Delmon ran a trembling hand over his bald head. "When I reached the border, word came that…that one of our own had been killed. I sent messages to the others, and we met in a barn. It was a trap, Grand Master. The man who'd given me this information reported us to the border guards. We were hooded, tied up, and tossed into the back of a wagon. We crossed the border unwillingly. One of the guards interrogated us. Thought we came to kill Queen Margaret."

One of the council members asked, "Queen? So the rumors of Leon's death are true?"

Bredych dismissed her question with a hand wave. "How did you escape?"

Like water over stone, the cold wrapped itself around Bredych's shoulders as Delmon spoke.

"I didn't. They released me, Grand Master, so that I could pass along a message from the Queen herself." Delmon took another sip of his water. "Any Amaskan caught inside the borders will be killed without question or trial."

"And my daughter?"

Delmon stared at his glass. "When the wagon reached the capital city, they killed everyone but me. Queen Margaret herself witnessed it from her balcony. They took me to where they would dispose of the bodies, and…and that's when I saw your daughter."

The man's hands trembled, and water sloshed over the side of his glass. Bredych's muscles quivered with inaction.

"Master Bredych, I'm sorry. Her—her body still hung for all to see. Queen Margaret said nothing of it, but the rumors are that your daughter was hung for treason. The Prince of Shad is dead—"

Ah. So that was why the Shadian army marched on Alexander.

"—And the Senate had encased her body with some spell or another. The guards couldn't take the body down. The Senate meant to use her as an example, Grand Master."

The old woman in the orb had known all along.

Bredych's jaw ached from clenching his teeth too long, and he stood. "Thank you, Delmon. You may leave." To the others, he said, "Arrange a memorial for the dead. And someone fetch a healer to treat Delmon's wounds."

His feet carried him out of the building and down well-worn paths, though he had little memory of the trip. Bredych fled to the coast where he'd walked with his daughter.

She had cursed him for sending her away, for sending her

into the hands of her birth father. She had thrown questions at him, and he had answered by removing the tattoo that marked her Amaskan.

Bredych's fingers buried themselves in the rocky soil as the waves crashed in the distance like footfalls too loud in his ears. Something about the scenario didn't make sense. If Leon had loved her even half as much as Bredych did, Leon wouldn't...he couldn't have allowed this to happen. He couldn't put his own daughter to death.

But then, Margaret stood as queen. Maybe it hadn't been Leon's decision at all.

Tears mixed in the dirt below, which he allowed in the moment before rage bubbled up and burst from his mouth with a shriek.

Whether it was Leon, Margaret, or the Senate that had hung the noose around his daughter's neck mattered little. Bredych wiped the remnants of tears on his sleeve and straightened his shoulders.

The blade slid easily from its hiding place at his waist. Bredych's practiced hands swept the knife across his jaw before his brain could register the sting. When it arrived, it was both less and worse than the ache in his heart.

The tattoo he had worn for fifty-four years landed in a bloody heap of skin on the soil below.

In the morning, he would ride for Alexander.

He would ride for answers...and for vengeance.

JOIN THE
CONSPIRACY

Stay up to date on future releases from the author by **Joining the Conspiracy**, the official mailing list of author Raven Oak.

Get sneak peeks, exclusives, freebies, & more.

Visit **http://www.ravenoak.net** to sign up!

Word of mouth is the number one best way to ensure that your   favorite authors have continued success—better than any paid advertisement.

If you enjoyed this book *(and others)*, please consider leaving a review on Amazon, Barnes & Noble, and/or Goodreads.

Your review is greatly appreciated.